Clouds U

David Flin

Book 2 in the Building Jerusalem series

First published by Sergeant Frosty Publications 2020
Copyright © 2020 David Flin
All rights reserved.

Cover artwork by Anastasia Nikolova

For further Books from
Sergeant Frosty Publications, please visit:

www.sergeantfrosty.com

Dedicated to the hardworking staff at the Royal Marsden Hospital.

Clouds Unfold

Windy was puzzled. He felt fine. The ship rocked easily, and the motion of to-and-fro and side-to-side was quite fun. He didn't really see what the problem was, but Peter was busy emptying his stomach over the side.

"You'd probably have been better off going to the other side," Windy said, standing clear. "The wind's blowing towards us here. On the other side, the wind's blowing away. I know this side was closer, but this wind is, well, it makes things difficult."

Peter didn't answer, and Windy carried on. "Wouldn't it be easier if you didn't eat dinner but just threw it over the side?"

"I'll throw you over the side," Peter managed to get out.

"Just at the moment, you'd not be able to throw anything heavier than your last meal over the side."

"I didn't make fun of you when you were hungover."

Windy thought about this. "I guess you didn't," he said finally. "I've been thinking. You're good with machines and things. How hard are these screw guns to put together? It can't be that hard."

"I'd need to see," said Peter, who had stopped being sick, but looked white. "But not now."

"No time like the present. Might take your mind off things." Windy paused and looked up the ladder to the deck above. "What's Frank up to?"

*****

Frank stared at a flock of seagulls perched on the railing, waiting for food to be thrown overboard. They squabbled and screeched. Frank drew himself straight.

"Eyes right," he practised. The seagulls ignored him.

*****

Thomas lay in his hammock, thinking. The ship regularly went to Persia and back. That meant that there was a good chance that one of the crew would be Persian. If they were going to be training Persians, maybe knowing a bit of Persian would be helpful.

The sailors seemed to be busy most of the time, and none of them wanted to talk to him. Maybe that was because he was a Rifleman. It took him sometime to find someone who'd answer the simple question about whether there were any Persians in the crew. Finally, he learned that there were two Persian stokers. It was progress.

*****

It was morning roll call on the main deck for the platoon. The platoon had difficulty standing in position on the rolling deck and several Riflemen were suffering the effects of sea-sickness, receiving very little sympathy from those who weren't. Peter had more or less recovered.

Lieutenant Hawkins swayed easily in balance with the movement of the deck, and addressed the platoon. "Gentlemen, we have a number of nurses travelling with the Regiment, and they will be looking after our health in Persia. Colonel Dalkeith has stated that while they are not in the chain of command, they will be regarded as officers. Furthermore, now that the ship is underway, and we are on our way to an active zone, disciplinary regulations will revert to overseas operational conditions.

"What that means, gentlemen, is that anyone offering physical insult to the nurses is liable to be court-martialled for striking an officer on the battlefield. The penalty for that can be a firing squad. And, if you consider the matter, you will realise that you do not want to upset the person who will be trying to save your life should you get wounded. I trust I have made myself clear. If I haven't, Sergeant Taylor will explain in his inimitable manner.

"The nurses will be looking after our health out there. To do this, they need to know what our health is now. Nurse Charrington will be conducting an examination of each of you over the next 24 hours. You will all have had your examination by roll call tomorrow. Report to her in her medical office.

"In summary, don't fool around with the nurses, and get your medical examination seen to promptly. One more thing. When we arrive in Persia, the platoon will be growing to company strength with Persian volunteers. A lot of the time, we will be operating independently of the Regiment, possibly far from support, with a lot of barely trained Riflemen. We are likely to be facing many different situations, and we could be dependent on our own resources. I expect each and every one of you to make use of this voyage to learn some useful skill. I will be asking each of you tomorrow at roll call what skill or skills you are learning. All clear? Good. Dismiss."

*****

Windy led Peter to a quiet spot, looking worried. "I can't do this medical. I just can't."

"The nurse will be expecting you. If you don't have the medical, Hawk will be annoyed. He might get sarcastic."

"Yes, but I just can't do the medical. I can't. I can't explain why, but I can't do it."

Peter thought for a moment, thinking things through. "Windy, are you scared that she'll find out something that will have you thrown out? I know you need the pay for your family, but they'd need to find something that would be pretty serious. I mean, you've shown that you can do the job, because you've done the job."

Windy just nodded.

"OK. First thing we need to do is find out what happens in the examination," said Peter. "I'll do the medical. Then we'll know if it is a problem. And we'll need to get Lieutenant Campbell to help us sort out the screw gun. While I'm doing that, you get hold of four seagulls. I've got an idea."

"Seagulls?"

"Yes, four dead seagulls. Not damaged, mind."

"Why?"

"I'll tell you what, I won't ask why you're worried about the medical examination, and you won't ask why I want four seagulls."

*****

He needed to learn a skill. He needed to learn how to be a better corporal. He needed to learn how to write better. He needed to keep an eye on the platoon. Being a corporal wasn't easy.

First of all, he'd have his medical, and get that out of the way. He would make sure Nurse Charrington understood that she was to report any insult offered by any of the men. It would be bad if that happened, and he needed to make sure it didn't. He was sure Lieutenant Hawkins would be cross with if the men misbehaved and would ask him why he let them misbehave.

Cooking. That was it. If they were to operate away from the rest of the Regiment, then having someone who could see that everyone got fed would be a good skill. The ship had a kitchen, only they didn't call it a kitchen.

Someone had got to the medical office before him. While he was waiting, he took the time to prepare a sign to remind people about behaving.

*****

Strike while the iron was hot, thought Thomas. If he was the first to have the examination, he'd be able to continue their conversation from the hospital. Lieutenant Hawkins had been clear about offering insult to the nurses, but he'd said nothing about a mutual agreement.

Thomas smiled when he went in. "Nurse Charrington, I suspect that when last we met, you knew that we would meet again. It may have been Fate, but I rather think you had advance knowledge."

"If you bothered to use your brain, you could have guessed it. Do you really think Lady Dalkeith or Sister Luckes picked four nurses at random to show you what wounds looked like? Of course not.

They wanted to see how we dealt with Riflemen. Take your shirt off. I'll take your pulse, listen to your lungs, take your temperature, and check you for imperfections. When we're out in Persia, you're to report straight away if you suspect you've contracted a social disease."

She took his wrist and started taking his pulse.

"It's probably racing at your touch."

Nurse Charrington frowned. "Rifleman O'Grady, when I'm working, I do not abide being treated with anything other than professional courtesy. This is my job. I'm good at it. I will thank you to remember that."

"Thomas, please."

She started tapping his chest. As soon as he started to speak again, she put a thermometer in his mouth. "Don't speak, Rifleman O'Grady."

She certainly wasn't a dalliance sort of person, Thomas thought. But she had a lovely smile although she very rarely seemed to smile. Just once or twice. There, he caught a brief flicker of a smile. She took the thermometer out, read it, and made a note.

"Nurse Charrington, the last time we met, you declined my invitation to dine because of the separation, but that Fate might have other ideas. When you're off-duty, perhaps we might promenade on the deck?"

"Rifleman O'Grady, you invited me to dine. Very well. When I am off-duty, you may take me to a restaurant where we can dine in elegant surroundings. That was what your original invitation was, and I expect no less."

"But we're on a troop ship in the middle of nowhere," Thomas wailed.

"Fine words butter no parsnips. I have told you my expectations."

*****

Thomas emerged from the medical office, where Frank was waiting. When he emerged, Frank hung a sign up on the door to the medical office and then went inside. Thomas read the notice:

"Nurse not free. Leave alone."

Thomas thought about removing the sign but suspected he'd get into trouble if he did, and he did have a lot to do. Where was he going to find a restaurant on a troopship? And he had to start learning Persian.

Where would he find a restaurant? The officers wouldn't dine in a Mess. They would eat somewhere nice, even if the food wasn't up to much. Hawk said that the nurses were to be regarded as officers, which meant that they should be able to eat with the officers.

The only trouble was that he wouldn't be allowed to eat with the officers. That was going to be difficult to overcome. He would worry about that later. He first had to get Nurse Charrington invited to where the officers ate. He couldn't get one of the officers to invite her. They'd regard her as fair game. He certainly would have done so, and Lieutenant Furley-Smith had shown that he was a hunter.

Thomas briefly thought about Millicent. She'd pursued him; she had been quite persistent. Flattering, really, but then she switched targets as soon as Lieutenant Furley-Smith had appeared on the scene. She'd had a busy day.

He needed to have a word with Lady Dalkeith to get permission. He couldn't speak to any of the officers, but Lady Dalkeith did seem to enjoy arranging people's lives for them.

Joy was busy writing something at a desk, concentrating hard on getting each letter correct. She looked up, and smiled on seeing Thomas, although it was just a friendly smile rather than the big smile she gave Frank.

He explained to Lady Dalkeith about inviting the nurses to dine with the officers.

"You'll not be able to dine with them," she said. "Explain your interest in this. And before you spin me a tale about how you want to see them treated appropriately, I want the honest answer."

"I like Nurse Charrington. I'd like to do something nice for her."

"You do know you'll not be there."

Thomas drew himself upright. "That's not the point, Ma'am. I just want to do something nice for her."

"I will be happier when I know what your angle is, Rifleman O'Grady. I know that you have got an angle."

"Angle, Ma'am?"

"Yes, angle. Don't play the innocent fool with me."

"No, Ma'am. I really don't have an angle or a plan. I just want to do something for her and hope for the best. She's not like any girl I've ever known."

"Explain." Lady Dalkeith glanced towards Joy, who was listening avidly.

"She's, well, determined," said Thomas, carefully. "Strong. She doesn't dissolve into giggles or hysterics at the slightest thing. She's, well, practical. She's pretty, but there are a lot of pretty girls, but she's somehow, well, solid."

"She's not an intended dalliance, a distraction for the voyage?"

"Dalliance? Ma'am?"

"You know exactly what I mean. I'll not tell you again to stop playing the fool."

"Ma'am, I can't imagine she would tolerate just a dalliance."

Lady Dalkeith thought for a long time. Finally, she nodded. "Very well. I shall see to that side of it. A word of advice. Think about who attends these dinners other than officers. And a word of warning. A nurse is of much greater value to the Regiment than a Rifleman. If you err, you will find yourself in my bad books."

*****

Peter went to the medical office. The nurse wasn't free. Obviously, a lot of people were getting their medical done early rather than leaving it. He'd come back later. His next task was to collect some long cleaning rods, carefully choosing the longest and stiffest that he could find. Then he headed back to find Windy.

"Have you got the seagulls?"

"Yes. About the medical,"

"Don't worry, Windy. I've got a plan. The nurse doesn't know you. She's just got your name. She doesn't know what you look like. That means we can ask one of the sailors who's about your size and build to act as a kind of substitute for the medical. It may cost, but it should sort things out. Meanwhile, let's get these seagulls mounted."

"What are we going to do with them?"

Peter explained.

*****

The trouble was, Thomas thought, it wasn't actually a lie. Nurse Charrington *was* different. She was, well, just different. He couldn't imagine a dalliance with her. It wouldn't be a conquest, or anything like that. That troubled him. It had always been so simple before. Maybe it was just seeing Frank and Joy that was confusing him.

Still, he had a plan. Another plan. The sign was still up outside the medical office, so he knew she would be free. He entered the tiny cabin, where Nurse Charrington sat at a desk carefully writing up notes.

"Rifleman O'Grady. Back for another medical?"

"Nurse Charrington. I have a favour to ask of you. My Lieutenant has instructed us to learn a skill. I believe that it would be beneficial to have knowledge of how to tend wounds in the field. While you'd do it better than I could, you'd not be on the front line."

"That seems to be a fair request. Why have you asked me and not any of the other nurses?"

"I've seen you working. I know that you're good at your job."

"Rifleman O'Grady, that's inappropriate flattery."

Thomas started to answer, then paused. He was getting a bit annoyed, and he wasn't sure why. Flattery and charm weren't making much impression. "With respect, Nurse Charrington, it is very appropriate. It is not flattery. You are good at your job. I've seen you deal with wounds. I was impressed. I am sure that you would teach me well."

She remained sitting, put her pen down and looked directly at Thomas, wariness in her eyes. "And you have no ulterior motive?"

Thomas relaxed a little. He thought he understood. He remembered how the doctor had spoken to her. She was probably so used to people questioning her ability that she didn't know how to handle simple praise. "It's true I do have a secondary objective. I would like to spend time in your company. You're honest. But first and foremost, I want to learn how to deal with wounds. That might help my comrades."

"If I teach you, I will not abide distractions. It will be the teaching of those skills, not a social function. Is that understood? No flattery, no personal discussions or questions, just teaching."

"I wish to learn, so I desire the teaching."

"Very well. Be here after dinner. Unless you have managed to locate a restaurant."

"Nurse Charrington, I know that you are good at your job. Trust me to be good at mine."

*****

"Up a bit. Up a bit. There, that's the length." Peter was on the upper deck, watching the railing, as Windy was on the lower deck, holding a cleaning rod vertical.

"Shouldn't we be doing the stuff we're supposed to do?" Windy asked.

"Stop being an old woman," Peter replied, coming back down. "We've got over a month."

"We should be setting an example."

"And that's what we're doing. We're setting an example."

"No, I mean we should be setting a *good* example."

"And that's what we're doing. We're giving Frank a chance to excel. I'll get these fitted. You keep an eye out for him."

*****

There were so many things Thomas had to do in a hurry. He stopped to think how he was going to do everything in time. He needed to speak to the Persian sailors, and he needed to speak with the Wardroom stewards, and he needed to be convincing and charming. That shouldn't be too hard.

Finding the Chief Steward was easy. Explaining that he wanted to help serve at the Army Officers' dinner was easy enough, although the Chief Steward was quick to ask why. Thomas vaguely wondered about telling the truth but decided against it. Instead, he explained that he'd been instructed to learn a useful skill. Since that a lot of what they'd be doing in Persia was officers hob-nobbing with big-wigs, knowing how to do stewarding properly would be useful.

The Chief Steward drove a hard bargain, and it cost Thomas two railway novels to get the opportunity to help them with their work.

*****

Frank and Joy sat as a little table in Lady Dalkeith's cabin. Although it was cramped here, there was more space and privacy here than there was in the bedlam of the troop-deck. It wasn't exactly comfortable here, but it was quiet. Joy was helping Frank with his reading, but he felt very uncomfortable.

"I am Lord and Master here," read Frank slowly. "When I took possession of this castle, I took possession of everything within it, and that, my proud beauty, includes you. With that, he drew the terrified Lady Agatha to him, silencing her protestations with kisses that stirred longing and desire within him, desire that would not be denied."

"Why have you stopped?" Joy asked, placing her hand on his. "You were doing so well."

"This book, it not for lady."

"When you are a sergeant, you will need to be able to read and write well. Shh, Lady Dalkeith's coming back."

"Indeed I am. I am unable to see a chaperone, Joy."

"I was helping Frank with his letters, Ma'am."

"I can see what you were doing. You have shown that you can be responsible, but you will not read railway novels together. Is that understood?"

"Yes, Ma'am. May I ask why, Ma'am?"

"Inappropriate ideas and desires. When you are married. Not before."

"Yes, Ma'am," said Joy with some reluctance.

Lady Dalkeith snorted. "Allow me to demonstrate." She picked the book up and continued reading from it. "With an animalistic growl, the renegade knight tore the bodice off of Lady Agatha, exposing her. He continued to kiss her, his mouth moving across her body, her lips, her mouth, and do I need to continue? Tell me, do you think it appropriate for an unchaperoned, unmarried couple to be reading this together? Corporal Barry, I believe you have duties to attend to. The better you attend to your duties, the sooner you will make sergeant."

*****

It was just as well Lady Dalkeith arrived when she did, Frank thought. If she hadn't, well, he wasn't sure what might have happened, but it might have led to a loss of control.

"Always be in control, lad." That's what Sergeant Taylor had told him. The best thing he could do right now was to practise his voice of command. His quiet spot on the upper deck was clear and empty.

*****

"Shh. He's coming," said Peter on the deck below.

*****

The two Persian stokers had finished their watch. They were surprised when Thomas asked them if they could teach him Persian.

"Turn it up, mate," said the taller in a thick London accent. "We speak English, don't we."

"Yes, but I want to learn to speak Persian."

"Why?" asked the shorter. "What's in it for us?"

"I want to learn Persian because we're going to Persia."

"What are you offering?"

Thomas thought. He had to keep the railway novels intact as best he could. "I'll see what I can snag in the way of food from the Officers' Mess." From what he knew of servants, they always had access to excess food. A lot got wasted.

*****

Notice everything. That's what Sergeant Taylor had told him. A good Sergeant notices everything. Maybe it was just his emotional turmoil, but something felt odd here. He looked around carefully. Sergeant Taylor would have seen everything in a glance.

No-one was on this stretch of the deck. It was right next to the funnel and was uncomfortably hot. The heat was such that paint on the metal walls by the funnel peeled off quickly. That wasn't the source of concern. He would have to ask Peter how you could stop paint peeling from a hot surface.

That was the problem. He hadn't seen Peter for some time. Nor Windy. They were either working hard, or they were finding ways of getting into trouble. They were sensible enough to limit their getting into trouble against people who wouldn't give them too much grief.

Then there was Thomas. He would be getting into trouble, and he didn't have the sense to pick his targets carefully.

A sailor came out, carrying a pot of grease to lubricate some piece of machinery. They ignored each other.

He needed to stay one step ahead of them. Thomas would head straight for a pretty girl. That meant Nurse Charrington. Frank could see that Thomas was smitten. Even though Lieutenant Hawkins had specifically told them not to mess around with the nurses. Frank sighed. Thomas would regard that as a challenge. He might have a lot of knowledge and education, but he could be pretty stupid.

He'd collected the sign, as no-one would be going to see Nurse Charrington now. Now it was time for him to practise giving commands. Four seagulls on the railing. He called them to attention and was astonished when they did so.

When something looks wrong, it probably is. "Eyes right," he called, watching them carefully. Two of the seagulls dutifully turned to the right, two to the left.

"Front." They returned to their original position.

Attention to detail. That was what Sergeant Taylor had told him. Seagulls don't behave like that. Getting left and right was the sort of thing that happens if you're facing the wrong way. He needed to look closely at the seagulls. Their feet weren't on the railing.

Frank walked across to where the sailor was working. The grease in the pot was a thick liquid, and the sailor held the pot carefully. Frank put a finger to his lips.

"Right face," he called out. The seagulls followed the instruction, apart from the fact that they turned left. He looked carefully at the seagulls. There were metal rods stuck into them. He could just see them.

This was just high spirits that needed dealing with by making sure they came off worst in the exchange, rather than being dealt with officially.

He brought the seagulls to the end of the rail so that they were close to the sailor. He gave the necessary instructions. Then he pointed first to the sailor to attract his attention, then at his pot of grease. The sailor looked puzzled, so Frank gestured for him to pick the pot up, then put a finger to his lips.

This distracted him from giving orders to the seagulls and he had to hastily bring them to a halt. That was a trick he had to learn, to be able to think about one thing while giving orders about something else. Sergeant Taylor made it look so easy.

"Front. Right dress." This bought him a bit of time. He pointed to the sailor, then moved his pointing finger to the edge of the railing by the seagulls. The sailor looked confused. Frank repeated the motion. "Mark time," he ordered the seagulls, while repeating the mime. The sailor walked to the railing. Frank pointed to his eyes, shaded his eyes as if searching, then pointed his finger downwards.

The sailor frowned, shrugged, and looked down over the railing. Frank held up two fingers and looked questioning.

"Halt. About face. About face."

Frank motioned tipping the pot and pointed with his finger downwards. The sailor paused, and then smiled. He pointed to the pot of grease, then over the railing, a question in his eyes. Frank nodded.

*****

The other stewards were not happy with Thomas being there. The Chief Steward had said that he could be there, so they couldn't argue, but they didn't like it. They weren't going to make him feel welcome and they certainly weren't going to explain what to do. The cramped steward's space was directly above the galley. Every time food was sent up through the dumb waiter, a blast of hot air emerged.

It was the first time Thomas had been on the serving side of a meal, but he knew the form.

The officers started to come into the Wardroom, and Colonel Dalkeith noticed Thomas. "O'Grady? I lose track of what rank you are. It changes so quickly. Stewarding?"

"Yes, Sir. Lieutenant Hawkins instructed me to learn a skill on the trip. I thought the Regiment might be entertaining some important people when we're in Persia, so I thought knowing how to steward would be useful."

"I'll bear that in mind. It's good to see you putting your mind to work. I look forward to when you've got your mouth under control. That reminds me, John," he said, turning to Lieutenant Hawkins. "You're going to need to think about your company cadre. I intend to keep you in reserve while you train up your Persians and I don't want to disrupt the other companies."

"Yes, Sir. Do we know anything about our Persian recruits?"

Colonel Dalkeith snorted. "We can guess. Officially, they're volunteers. My guess is that we'll get the soldiers that the Persian Army doesn't want but can't get rid of."

"That might be a good thing, Sir. It's not like the Persian army is a fighting army. Their misfits might be useful in a scrap."

"John, you're an incorrigible optimist."

Just then, Lady Dalkeith arrived with the four nurses. The nurses looked a little uncomfortable, mixing above their station. Nurse Charrington did her best to seem at ease, but the display of Mess silver was a bit awe-inspiring. She saw Thomas and shook her head slightly. A smile briefly appeared on her face, gone almost before it had arrived. If Thomas hadn't been watching, he would have missed it.

"I must admit, Rifleman O'Grady, that you are indeed good at your job, if your job is being an incorrigible rascal," she said, slightly awkwardly. She didn't seem to be at ease here.

Think like a servant, Thomas told himself. Don't answer back unless asked a direct question, even when you have a clever response.

Of course, Lieutenant Furley-Smith had to ask the obvious question of Nurse Charrington.

"Rifleman O'Grady promised to take me to a dinner in elegant surroundings. I have to admit that he has delivered, despite my scepticism," she explained.

"Still aiming high, O'Grady," said Lieutenant Furley-Smith.

Lieutenant Hawkins fixed Thomas with a steady gaze. "O'Grady, just remember that the nurses are a lot more important to the Regiment than you are."

"Yes, Sir. That was exactly my thinking, Sir. They're part of the Regiment. We look after our own, Sir. They're family."

*****

Joy was worried. Frank was learning how to cook and the others were learning things. The nurses knew things and were useful, while she didn't really know anything much beyond sewing. Frank was so busy and Lady Dalkeith had said that a soldier's wife had to be useful and practical.

She was scared Frank might lose interest in her. It would be worse when they got to Persia, where there would be a lot of girls who would want to marry an English soldier. The other wives hadn't accepted her, because she wasn't a wife.

There had to be something that she could do. What was she good at? She could read and write well; she knew her numbers well and she'd often taught the young ones when the teachers weren't able to explain properly to them.

Maybe that was it. Maybe, if she was going to be useful, she had to learn to be sort of like a teacher. She'd have to ask Lady Dalkeith if she could ask Lieutenant Hawkins. Thomas always seemed to know a lot of big words and knew how to use them, like the host in a music hall. Maybe he could teach her how to use words.

She didn't want Frank to lose interest in her; she was worried that was what was happening.

*****

Never discuss religion or politics at dinner. That's what his father had always said. Thomas had never had much interest in either. He couldn't see what the problem was. He gathered that the rule applied here as well, but that they couldn't be discussed "as such."

Thomas wasn't sure how one could talk about politics without talking about it as such. The officers were talking about Home Rule for Ireland, and Thomas was inclined to agree with his father. This was possibly the first time he had done that.

He tried to look on the positive side. It was good practise for him biting his tongue in the face of some idiotic comments being made. He concentrated his attention on making sure that Lady Dalkeith, Nurse Charrington, and the other nurses were well looked after.

Thomas saw Lady Dalkeith give a wry smile. He was puzzled. "Ma'am?" he asked, curious.

"Our presence means they can't talk about women. They're struggling. You'd better get your clever replies ready, because sooner or later, one of them will think of the obvious."

"Ma'am?"

"I'm disappointed, O'Grady."

This puzzled Thomas.

"We're missing the obvious," said a slightly paunchy Captain. "O'Grady, isn't it? Good Irish name. What do the Irish think about Home Rule?"

Thomas felt several sets of eyes watching him closely; Colonel Dalkeith, Lady Dalkeith, Lieutenant Hawkins, and Nurse Charrington were paying close attention to him.

"I'm just a Rifleman, Sir. Don't really pay much attention to that sort of stuff." Thomas noticed Colonel Dalkeith nod in approval.

"I've a couple of Irish in my company," the Captain continued. "They're forever talking about it."

"Can't say I've got an opinion, Sir. I leave that to people that understand these things."

"An Irishman without an opinion?"

"I don't get drunk either, Sir."

"Well done, O'Grady," said Colonel Dalkeith. "Captain Castle, I've had occasion to admonish O'Grady for talking out of turn before. I'm glad to see that he has appears to have learned. O'Grady, you've been asked specifically three times. You may answer."

"Sorry, Sir. Forgotten the question," Thomas said desperately, hoping against hope that they'd move on.

"What do the Irish think of Home Rule?"

Thomas sighed. "I'm not Irish, Sir. My name is, but I was born in England." It was his last card to avoid answering.

"Now you're being evasive," said the Captain. "That's usually a bad sign."

"Mostly people don't think about it. They're too busy worrying about finding the rent and where the next meal's coming from, and about the things people worry about. Not got time to think about things they can't do anything about."

"See. I told you they don't want Home Rule."

Leave it at that, Thomas told himself. Unfortunately, his mouth took control. "Beg pardon, Sir, I didn't quite say that. Said they didn't think much about it." Shut up, Thomas told himself, but his mouth ignored the instruction. "It's a bit like votes for women."

There were blank looks from the officers around the table. This told him that they couldn't see the connection.

"It's not about Home Rule, or votes, as such. It's about being taken seriously. It's hard to explain, Sir, but it hurts when people think you can't be trusted with something like that, even though you're trusted with other stuff. I mean, people trust me enough to give me a gun and tell me to fight for King and Country, but not to give me a vote so I can say how I want it run? I can die for it, but I can't vote for it? That don't seem quite fair, somehow. Not that I know much about it, Sir."

"Don't quite follow about votes for women."

His tongue was fully in control now. "Take nurses. They look after sick people. Sometimes they have to make a decision that if they get it wrong, the patient could die. They're trusted be make sensible decisions about that but not trusted to make a sensible decision about who to vote for? Sorry, Sir, I got duties in the meal to attend to."

He saved himself from digging a deeper hole by running away. As he left for the stewards' space, he caught a glimpse of Lady Dalkeith nodding and Nurse Charrington looked as though she approved, although it was difficult to tell. He'd gone too far, he knew it, but he *had* tried to control his tongue.

He tried to calm himself down in the stewards' space by taking deep breaths. He suspected Colonel Dalkeith would ask him to leave soon. He still needed something for the Persian stokers. He had noticed the stewards sending notes down the dumb waiter to the galley beneath. He grabbed one before it went down and found that it was an order for a meal. That was his solution.

He scribbled a note. A meal wouldn't keep, but a bottle of wine was always acceptable. He'd provided six bottles to the Officers' Mess, so they could easily spare one. "Bottle wine, to be delivered to Medical Office C, Troop Deck, Midnight. Compliments Lieutenant Hawkins." He would be able to intercept that, and all would be well.

Reassured, he returned to the Wardroom.

*****

Peter and Windy struggled to get grease out of their uniforms.

"We are going to be in so much trouble," said Windy. "I've still not found a way out of the medical. These uniforms, everything's going wrong."

"Calm down, lad. We work on the screw guns. We make sure people see us working on them. That gives us a reason for having got grease on our uniforms. We get shouted at for being stupid but nothing worse than that."

"And the medical?"

"Substitute. We get one of the sailors to stand in for you. We discussed this. It's all under control."

*****

Frank was confused by the bedlam in the galley. Cooking was not as easy as it looked. He watched them cooking, but they didn't trust him with actual cooking. Cutting things up, however, that was something that he could do and do well.

That put him next to the dumb waiter and took the time to read the instructions. It was practise at reading and it didn't involve ravishing maideins.

He picked up the next note. He read it. It didn't make any sense. Then he recognised the handwriting. It was Thomas' handwriting. He read it again. He understood and he wasn't pleased. Despite instructions to the contrary, Thomas had designs on Nurse Charrington.

Frank pocketed the note. He knew how to deal with this. He knew the recipe for Sicilian whisky. Let's see Thomas talk his way out of that one.

*****

Thomas stiffened on his return to the wardroom. Lieutenant Furley-Smith was flirting with Nurse Charrington. He was being quite blatant about it as well. She was being cool and aloof about it, but he'd seen that many times from maid servants before and they always came around. Nurse Charrington was much more sensible than any maid servant, but this was, well, it was wrong.

"Terribly sorry, Rifleman O'Grady. I seem to be stealing your girl again."

Silence descended on the table and Thomas wondered if it was wrong of him to be relieved that he wasn't the only person to have a tongue that had a mind of its own.

"Lieutenant," said Nurse Charrington coldly. "I'm not a possession of anyone. I'm not something to be stolen. I don't care for being referred to as a girl. Colonel Dalkeith, I have a number of medical reports that need writing up. My apologies for departing so early. I would be grateful if Rifleman O'Grady could escort me to my office, in case someone tries to steal off with me." She rose and walked to the door.

Colonel Dalkeith indicated that Thomas should go with her. "Lieutenant Furley-Smith, I'll speak with you at 7 in my cabin." The Colonel's voice was cold.

*****

Windy and Frank found Lieutenant Campbell and persuaded him to let them work on assembling and disassembling one of the screw guns. Windy and Lieutenant Campbell were both keen to start work on putting the parts together straight away. It was only with some difficulty that Peter persuaded them to clear a space first of all and make a note of all the parts, then work out what tools they'd need before starting.

"You're like an old woman about this," said Windy.

"We've got no assembly instructions. None of us is artillery trained. Let's take it carefully."

"I read that Indian troops could put one together in less than a minute," said Lieutenant Campbell. "How hard can it be?"

*****

Nurse Charrington said nothing the entire way back to the medical office. She walked stiffly and upright, lips tight, and glanced to neither left nor right.

Thomas decided that she didn't want conversation, so they walked in silence to the office. He was puzzled why she had taken Lieutenant Furley-Smith's comment so badly. He decided that it would be best to let her explain, if she decided to do so.

He was also puzzled by how annoyed he was with Lieutenant Furley-Smith's comment. He'd stolen other chap's girls, and they'd stolen his, and no-one worried much about it. He was worried he was in danger of being ensnared. What was worse, that idea didn't fill him with dread.

He stole a glance towards her. She was too stocky to be called beautiful. That was probably because of the hard work a nurse had to do. Good posture. Again, probably be because of her job. Her face was a kind one, but she didn't seem to show much expression. She looked tense.

"I'm sorry for disrupting your evening," she said as they neared the medical office. "You did exactly what you promised, and it was a sterling effort. It's not every day one is literally waited on by a gentleman."

"I am sorry it wasn't as pleasurable as it should have been."

"Not your fault. Treatment of wounds. Shall we make a start?" She held the door to the medical office open for him, which felt wrong to Thomas. The gentleman opens the door for the lady.

She noticed his uncertainty. "I've got the key. You haven't. How were you going to open the door? Tear it off its hinges?"

"I think I might get into trouble if I did that. But isn't it rather late to start teaching?"

"You made a promise and kept it. I made a promise, and I intend to keep it."

"What will people say?"

"That I'm dedicated, which will be no bad thing."

"But might it not lead to gossip about us?"

She thought carefully before answering. "I said I would teach you how to treat wounds. If people choose to gossip about that, then there's nothing to be done about it. Come in and shut the door behind you."

It was a small office, barely more than a cupboard. It was just a temporary structure on the lower deck, one of four. The sturdiest thing in the office was the filing cabinet.

"I'm sorry that I've been bad company for you, Rifleman O'Grady. It's been a hard day. First, no-one comes for their medical except you and Corporal Barry. Then I get interrogated by that dragon, who tries to tell me that she needs to know the results of the medicals. It was hard work making her realise that confidential records are confidential. Then that Lieutenant. I'm sorry, apart from your efforts, it's been a bad day and I've been bad company for you, Rifleman O'Grady."

"Thomas, please."

Nurse Charrington stiffened. "If you're thinking of trying to make advances towards me, please don't. If you're thinking of a serious affection, remember that I am a nurse. I am a good nurse, and I intend to remain a nurse."

"I don't understand. You're a nurse, not a nun."

"If a nurse gets married, she has to leave the hospital and stop working as a nurse. All hospitals are very strict about this. That's why the other nurses have come here, to snag an officer as a husband."

This didn't make much sense to Thomas. "That's not why you came."

"No. I came to do a job. My reasons are my own."

Thomas got the impression that she wanted to talk about it, but that it wasn't something that she felt she could talk about. He stuck to what he could say. "I think it's wrong that you have to choose between nursing and marriage."

"That's the way it is. What would you do? Change the way that the world works?"

"I'm a Rifleman. We get the job done, whatever it takes."

"I admire your determination, Rifleman O'Grady," Nurse Charrington said with an almost indulgent air. "Treating wounds."

"Thomas, please."

"When it is work, it will be Rifleman O'Grady. Likewise, I require to be called Nurse Charrington. These formalities are important in creating the appropriate atmosphere and attitude of mind."

"And when it is not work?"

Nurse Charrington was silent for a long time, thinking before answering, considering things carefully. She seemed almost nervous and hesitant. Twice she started to speak, before pausing and stopping and thinking again. It was as though she was thinking about a step into the unknown. Finally, she came to a decision. "When it is not work, when there is no-one else around who may misunderstand, you may call me Emily."

*****

"How long did that take?" Peter asked.

"Thirty-one minutes," Lieutenant Campbell said. "These have a range of about two miles. Rifleman marching pace is just over five miles an hour. That means that, well, it might be an idea to improve on that time."

"Where does this screw go?" Windy asked, holding up a piece that had been left over.

"Don't tempt me," muttered Peter. "It's a matter of knowing exactly where everything is so that we don't need to look for each piece. Indian soldiers put this together in less than a minute?"

Lieutenant Campbell nodded.

"In the field, with bullets whizzing and in rough ground?"

Lieutenant Campbell nodded.

"From packed on a mule?"

Lieutenant Campbell nodded.

"Thank God the buggers are on our side."

*****

Frank wondered about labelling the bottle as Sicilian whisky, to let Thomas know that his scheming had been spotted and that he was under close observation. He eventually decided against that. That was partly because he didn't have a suitable bottle for whisky. However, there were several empty wine bottles he could use. And it was partly because Joy wasn't around to make sure he got the spelling right.

He placed the bottle outside the medical office. Then he went to the shadows to wait and watch.

*****

She couldn't ask Frank if he was losing interest in her. Lady Dalkeith was at dinner, so she couldn't ask her. Besides, Lady Dalkeith wouldn't be that understanding.

Thomas was Frank's best friend and he was keen on the nurse, so he'd understand. Thomas was easy to talk to as well and he'd know what Frank thought. She could talk to Thomas and see what he thought.

*****

His father would be furious, Thomas thought wryly. He rather thought he was falling for Emily. Not in a 'want to have a roll in the hay' way, but simply enjoying her company and wanting to just be with her.

She was only a nurse, but then, he was now only a Rifleman and that was a long way beneath a nurse. She wasn't like the society women he'd known. They were frivolous and self-obsessed. She wasn't like the servants he'd known either. They were timid little mice.

She'd also made it clear that she valued being a nurse and that was a part of her. It was stupid that hospitals didn't allow nurses to be married. He guessed they didn't want nurses suddenly stopping work to have babies, but it seemed silly.

He also suspected that there were a few doctors who would regard a nurse as some sort of perk of the job.

A bottle of wine by the door. Good. That meant that he could pay the Persian sailors. But he needed to think first and looking out across the sea helped.

*****

Joy smiled. She'd been right that Thomas would be at the medical office. He had just left her office and he was now watching the water go past. He'd be able to help her. She went and stood beside him at the railing.

"Thomas, you're Frank's best friend," she said. Now it came to it, she was nervous and stuttering over her words. He seemed distracted as well, although he didn't have as much to think about as Frank. "Does he really like me? I mean, really like me. I mean, I'm nobody special."

Thomas made a strange snorting sound. "He likes you. He keeps talking about how brave you were in that basement."

"Yes, but that was in the past, and he'll forget." She was worried now, really worried. "What do men like in a wife?"

"No idea. I've never been married."

"Oh. What do you look for? What is Frank interested in?"

"That's two different things," Thomas said. "Frank needs someone he can trust. He's very big on being able to depend on somebody. If I'm honest, prettiness without substance, well, it gets boring. I've found that affection for brainless, chattering society women doesn't last. And as for servants, well, if they can't hold their own, I get bored with them quickly." He was thoughtful as he said that and he sounded, well, a bit sad.

"Frank's doing really well." Joy realised that she was getting worried. "He's doing really well. And I'm, well, I'm just a servant and he's going to find someone better."

"I don't think so. He's very fond of you. He's doing well because he doesn't want to let you down."

"But I'm letting him down. All I'm doing is sewing and cleaning and there's nothing much to that."

"What can you do? I've seen your writing. You write really neatly and quickly. And you said you taught children to read and write. You can teach soldiers to read and write. You've spoken about it. Ask Lieutenant Hawkins if you can do some classes."

"Couldn't you ask for me? You're so much better with words than I am."

Thomas was about to say yes. Then he thought. "It'll be better if you ask. It'll impress him so much more."

"But what if he laughs at me?"

"Lieutenant Hawkins is a proper gentleman. He won't laugh at you. And you write with a very good hand. I think that some officers would like to have you writing their reports for them. Ask Colonel Dalkeith."

"Ask the Colonel?" Joy's voice was very small.

"Why not? You work for his wife. And another thing, Nurse Charrington might need some help in things. Ask her if you could help out. That way you'll learn a bit of nursing."

"Do you really think I could do all that?"

"It doesn't matter what I think. It's what you think and whether you want to."

"There's something else," Joy asked. "It's about, well, when a man and a woman are together. What's it like?"

"Ah. Er. Um. That is, what I mean. Urm."

"You're lost for words! I've made Thomas lost for words!" She smiled, a beam of joy. "But thank you. I'll try and speak with Lieutenant Hawkins. Frank will be so pleased with me." She hugged him.

*****

Frank's blood ran cold. He knew that Thomas was a womaniser. He'd been worried that he would take advantage of Nurse Charrington. But to go straight from spending time with Nurse Charrington to a meeting with Joy, that was too much.

*****

"A bottle of wine," said one of the stokers. It was gone midnight, but they'd only just got off shift. "You're giving us a bottle of wine in payment."

"It's good wine," Thomas said.

The two Persians looked at each other and shook their heads. The taller of them tried to explain. "We're Muslim. We don't drink alcohol."

Thomas thought quickly. "That makes it perfect for trading. One of the hardest things when trading goods is when you want to keep it for yourself."

"Wine. That's drink for officers, isn't it?"

"Exactly. And officers have more money than sense, so you'll get a good deal."

"OK. Deal."

*****

Nurse Charrington had spoken with Lieutenant Hawkins. As a result, Lieutenant Hawkins was not happy. The platoon was ready for morning roll call. Precisely two of them had gone for their medical, Barry and O'Grady. Barry was proving to be an asset as a Corporal.

Corporal Barry had the men awaiting the Lieutenant's arrival. Once the roll call was over, he would have a word with Thomas. Thomas was a friend, so he'd allow him to explain. When Thomas started lying, he'd explain to him what honour meant.

Frank brought the men to attention as Lieutenant Hawkins approached. Hawk looked like he was in a bad mood.

"You were told to get a medical done yesterday. Most of you failed to do so. I gather it was because of a sign. As soon as roll call is over, you will muster outside the medical office. You will wait in the sun until you are called in for your medical. You will not leave that line for any reason save that of nature. Is that understood? Who put that sign up?"

Thomas thought quickly. He knew it was Frank, but given the mood Hawk was in, if he found out it was Frank, he'd take the stripes away and all Frank's hard work would be thrown away. Frank was his buddy. Thomas took a step forward. "Sir."

"O'Grady. I might have guessed. And you did so well last night as well. Why?"

"Seemed like a good idea at the time, Sir."

"And was it?"

"In retrospect, no, Sir."

"Corporal Barry. One task of an NCO is finding a suitable punishment for Riflemen who err. Deal with this and report back. I am very displeased with O'Grady. I want him taught a lesson. Is that understood?"

*****

Joy was scared. She'd decided that she would talk to Lieutenant Hawkins about teaching letters to some of the soldiers, because Colonel Dalkeith was too important to bother and Nurse Charrington was, well, intense. She was scared because Frank hadn't called to say good morning and he'd always done that.

She was scared that she was too late, that Frank had already lost interest.

What was more, she was scared that she was a bad person. When she'd hugged Thomas last night, she'd felt, disloyal feelings. When she'd asked him about what it was like, a man and a woman together, part of her had hoped he'd show her. It had passed quickly, but she didn't know what she would have done had he kissed her.

Then she had an idea. It would have to be secret. Lady Dalkeith couldn't know. But if Frank was to be with her, properly, then they'd be together and that would give her the time to become strong and a good wife for him.

"How can I help you, Miss?" Lieutenant Hawkins asked.

Joy had to stop herself from grinning at her plan and concentrate on this part. She explained to Lieutenant Hawkins about her teaching soldiers to read and write, how she'd taught young ones at the State School and wanting to be useful.

"You're Corporal Barry's young lady. He's a sound man. Very well. I'll get Sergeant Taylor to make the necessary arrangements. Let him know what you need, when is convenient for your lessons. He'll get everything arranged. Lessons will probably be on the deck. That all right? Good. We'll start with a couple of riflemen, see how it goes." Lieutenant Hawkins gave a slight smile. "Try not to distract Corporal Barry, Miss."

When he smiled, Joy felt that she must be a bad person because she found she was thinking of being with Frank. Nurse Charrington had a little office to herself and if she helped her, then when Nurse Charrington wasn't there, it would be empty and she could be alone with Frank.

*****

"Sir," said Corporal Barry. "I've thought about punishment for Rifleman O'Grady."

"Yes?" Lieutenant Hawkins was concerned that it was being brought to him. Barry was conscientious and new, so was probably just making sure. He hoped that was the case.

"We've tried simple administrative field punishments, Sir. Carrying packs, so on. It didn't learn him. There's one thing we haven't tried, Sir. I spoke with Sergeant Taylor, he said to check with you."

Lieutenant Hawkins sighed. "I thought he was learning. He tried hard to keep his tongue under control last night. But you spoke with Sergeant Taylor, and he said that you were to come to me for approval?"

"Yes, Sir. We haven't tried pain. Sergeant Taylor said we could do five lashes without having to go higher to get permission."

"I don't like flogging. Colonel Dalkeith doesn't approve of it. Why do you think it is necessary?"

"I must prove I don't have favourites, Sir. O'Grady needs his mouth brought under control."

"That is punishing O'Grady because you doubt your authority. That's a punishment to cement your position, not because the punishment is deserved. Why does O'Grady cause trouble, Corporal Barry?"

"Because he's from a good family, not used to following orders. Always been used to talking back, no-one ever taught him how to keep his mouth shut."

"And he's a bright boy. He's easily bored and he's looking for things to do. A bored Rifleman is dangerous, Corporal. What's he learning? Battle medicine. That shows he's thinking. Flogging a bored soldier makes them resentful. The crime is disrupting the smooth running of the medical examinations. What's the appropriate punishment for that crime?"

Frank didn't want to admit it, but he had no choice. "Don't know, Sir."

"What's the solution to boredom?"

"Keeping them busy, Sir."

"Good. In this case?"

"Put him to doing work, Sir. Work with the sailors, Sir. They know the dirty jobs on a ship better than I do, Sir."

"That's better. We'll keep flogging in reserve. Get O'Grady in here, then make the arrangements with the Chief Stoker. I rather fancy working in the engine room will be a punishment worthy of the name. And Corporal, your job is to make sure the men don't get bored. Pick two men who are steady and who could do with practise in reading and writing. Your young lady has offered to teach them."

*****

Lieutenant Furley-Smith stood at attention in the Colonel's office. Colonel Dalkeith hadn't raised his voice, but it was abundantly clear that he was not happy.

"I've given some thought to this, Lieutenant Furley-Smith. I'm not sure you realise just how close you came to being the cause of a major problem. I've considered whether or not there is a place for you in the Regiment."

He hadn't realised that the Colonel regarded it so seriously. "Sir," he started.

"Not yet, Lieutenant. What was it that you did that was such a problem?"

"Embarrassed Nurse Charrington, Sir. I've written a letter of apology."

"That was a problem. However, if we got rid of every junior officer who couldn't conduct themselves around a young lady, we'd have a damned small army. What was your big mistake?"

Lieutenant Furley-Smith bristled. When all was said and done, it was only a nurse. "Letting down the Regiment?"

"Same answer. Let me put it this way. What would you have done if, say, Lieutenant Hawkins had boasted to you about having already stolen one of your young ladies and that he was about to steal a second?"

"Honestly, Sir? I would have asked him to step outside and probably punched him."

"Good. What do you think was going through O'Grady's mind?"

"That he would like to pop me one. But he's just a Rifleman."

"He is indeed. It would have been quite possible for him to hit you. If he had done that, we would have had a problem. We're on deployment, on active service. By regulations we are in the field. If he had done it, it would have been in front of witnesses, officer, civilian, and Navy. I would have had no way to have turned a blind eye. I would have had to deal with it. Remind me, what's the punishment for a Rifleman striking an officer in the field while on deployment? I think you'll find it is a Court Martial and the outcome could easily have been O'Grady being shot. Your men are not your servants. You have a responsibility to them. You demonstrated that you haven't yet grasped that."

"Sorry, Sir."

"You owe O'Grady an apology. Unfortunately, you can't give him that apology because that would make matters worse. You should be grateful he showed more sense than you did. As for your future with the Regiment, I've decided that you have until we arrive in Persia to convince me that you are worth keeping. Fail to do so and you'll be on this boat back. Understood?"

Lieutenant Furley-Smith kept his face expressionless, but he thought that this was all a storm in a teacup. It was only a nurse. It was only a rifleman.

*****

The Riflemen waited in a queue outside the medical office. Windy was panicking and Peter was trying to keep him calm.

"The substitute scheme is out," Peter said. "We'd never work it with Sergeant Taylor right there. Right, what you need to do is when she starts the medical, you blow pepper into her eyes. She'll have to stop the medical and that will give us time to get a substitute in place."

"I don't have any pepper. Do you?"

"No. OK, we need to get Sergeant Taylor out of the way. We need to get a message to him to report to the Colonel. So, I go in first. While I'm having my medical, I pick up some of the medical forms and take them to Sergeant Taylor and tell him that Nurse Charrington asked if they could be taken by a responsible NCO to the Colonel."

"Take this seriously, Peter. This is a problem. They make you take your clothes off in a medical. Where are you going to hide medical folders? And even if you got them out, Sergeant Taylor would just tell you to take them. You're a responsible NCO."

"OK. I'll pretend to get badly sick, and that'll get me in. I'll make sure it takes a long time to resolve the problem, and"

Windy snorted and interrupted, his voice desperate. "And everyone will stand in line until you're done."

"Are we disturbing you two?" Sergeant Taylor asked, looming over them. "You're gossiping like old fish wives. Lance-Corporal Miller, it's your turn. If it's not too much trouble."

"It's not my turn. There are people ahead of me."

"True, but Lieutenant Campbell has found a manual for the screw guns and wants to try again with you and Lance-Corporal Grant. In you go."

"I can't, Sergeant. I just can't."

"Why not?"

"He caught a social disease down in London, Sergeant," said Peter. "Not one, but two actresses. *And* he didn't share them."

"Seems you were lucky not to catch a social disease yourself, Grant. Miller, when you catch a social disease, you want to see a nurse, not avoid them. Go in and make a clean breast of it."

*****

Frank took Thomas to one side. He glanced around to make sure no-one could overhear.

"I should gut you," he said. "You cause dishonour."

"Wait, what? You put that sign up. I'm taking the punishment to protect your stripes."

"That why I not gut you. What you did was bad."

Thomas frowned and glowered. "What I did? Take the blame to protect you?"

"You know what you did. Lieutenant Hawkins take pity on you, your punishment just hard work. You should be flogged. You do it again, is bad. Is no good pretend you not know what you do. You work with stokers, understood?"

Frank turned on his heel and left before he did something he'd regret.

*****

"Ma'am, I've asked Lieutenant Hawkins if I can teach some of the soldiers their letters. It will be useful. Can I have time off to do this?"

"Teaching. Yes, that's worthwhile."

"And I think Nurse Charrington could use some help and I could learn about nursing, a bit, which might be useful."

"Now here I suspect an ulterior motive. What is it?"

"Ma'am?"

"Don't try and play the fool. Why do you want to help Nurse Charrington?"

"Sorry, Ma'am. I thought that as she was a Nurse, she'd know about medical stuff, and things. I thought that she'd know about when a man and woman …" Joy's voice faded away.

"You thought to ask a *nurse* about that?"

Joy wondered why that might be wrong.

"I'll consider that," Lady Dalkeith said. "I'll speak with Nurse Charrington."

*****

Lieutenant Furley-Smith chatted with Lieutenant Hawkins in the Officers' Mess. He wanted to find out how he should deal with Riflemen. Hawkins had come up through the ranks and should know how the rank-and-file thought.

"First off," Lieutenant Hawkins said, "they aren't all alike. There are types. You'll come to recognise them. Most important thing is, they're not polite. They'll grumble about every blessed thing. They'll try every trick in the book to get out of something. They'll get into trouble as a matter of course, even when it would be easier to stay out of trouble. The most important thing is that there's a set of rules they accept. Most of the rules vary; most of them aren't written down, but they're there. If they start muttering that it ain't fair, you've got a problem. Talk to your sergeants if you've doubts. That's what your sergeants are for.

"Take last night. You made fun of O'Grady. Worse, you made fun of O'Grady in front of his girl. Worse still, there was absolutely nothing he could do about it. You could have punched him, and he would have had to just take it. Word of advice, watch yourself next time you're playing any sort of sport, like football, with him or his buddies. You're fair game for him. What can I say? Treat them with respect. They're the ones doing the work on the firing line, so treat them right. Oh, and never, ever bluff. If you say you'll do something, do it."

There was a knock at the door. Lieutenant Hawkins opened it, to see two sailors with a bag in hand.

"With compliments of stokers' messdeck for soldier officers, we have available strong wine."

"With compliments? Does that mean it's a gift?"

Obviously, it didn't. Lieutenant Hawkins smelt the cork in the bottle. It seemed familiar. "Are you sure this is wine?" he asked. "Smells like Sicilian whisky to me."

*****

Peter took a deep breath. He was running out of ways of stopping Windy's medical. Things were starting to get desperate. Shouting fire seemed like the next best step.

"And what do you think you're doing?" Sergeant Taylor asked, looming over him.

"I think I can smell burning, Sergeant. I think there's a fire somewhere."

"Somehow, Lance-Corporal Grant, I rather doubt that. You see, the sailors don't appear bothered and they're the ones who know about these things. You're standing next to the funnel. That's where all the burning and stuff takes place. That's why you can smell burning, you dozy Lance-Corporal."

"But Sergeant, better safe than sorry, surely."

"Lance-Corporal Grant, if you say one more word, I'm going to assume you're trying to get out of your medical and that will be a problem. Is that clear?"

"Yes, Sergeant. Should I go in for my medical straight away?"

"Don't be silly. Lance-Corporal Miller is having his medical. When he's done, you go in. Not before but going in as soon as he comes out."

*****

"I can't listen to your chest if you don't take your shirt off," said Nurse Charrington.

"Can't you just listen with one of those devices?"

"I really don't have time to deal with shyness." Nurse Charrington was getting irritated, and her voice was sharp. "Either take that shirt off or I'll have Sergeant Taylor take it off for you. I suspect that will make him unhappy. Remember, I'm a nurse. It's not as though I'm going to be shocked."

"Please, Nurse. It will be the end of my being a Rifleman. My family need my pay."

"Honestly, you soldiers are like children. Either take that shirt off, or there will be trouble."

*****

"Sir, you want see me?" Frank stood at the door of the Officers' Mess wondering why Lieutenant Hawkins had summoned him.

Lieutenant Hawkins held up a glass containing a pale amber liquid. "Sicilian whisky. This has turned up. You're the only person I know who knows the recipe. I need an explanation."

"I not make any, Sir. It not me."

"Then please explain this?" He held out the glass for Frank.

Frank sniffed at it. "It like Sicilian whisky, but it different. Maybe made same way, different recipe?"

"Corporal, are you directly telling me you do not have a still on this ship?"

Frank relaxed a little but did his best to keep a scowl on his face. "I make no still, Sir. Stripes too important to me. Even if I set one up, there not enough time for it to make bottle."

"How did you know there was a bottle?" Lieutenant Hawkins' voice was sharp.

Frank paused. This must be what it was like in Thomas' brain all the time. "It obvious, Sir. It come to you. Someone make it. There no point making less than bottle. No-one bring you glass, they bring a bottle. Is bad business any other way, Sir."

Lieutenant Hawkins considered things for a moment. "Colonel Dalkeith knows more about Sicilian whisky than I do. We'll get his judgement on this vintage."

*****

Lieutenant Furley-Smith was on his own in the Officers' Mess. Colonel Dalkeith had said that he had to prove himself and that he needed to show greater responsibility towards his men. That was a nonsense, obviously. There were always more men. However, he had to show willing, to get back into the Colonel's good books.

Lieutenant Hawkins said that he mustn't bluff and that when he said he'd do something, he had to make sure it was done. That made sense.

The trouble was that he'd said that he would steal O'Grady's girl. If he followed Lieutenant Hawkins' advice, that would be contrary to what Colonel Dalkeith said. On the other hand, if he didn't follow through on what he said, O'Grady would know that he'd made a hollow threat and he'd lose the respect of the men.

This really was a problem, he thought, pouring himself a drink.

*****

"It appears that I owe you an apology, Rifleman Miller. I had thought that I wouldn't be surprised. I was mistaken. You may put your strapping and shirt back on." She examined the medical form closely. "Why?"

"It was like I said, Nurse. The family needs the money. This was something I could walk into, no questions asked. The only other choice was going on the game."

"It's dangerous."

"My Dad worked in a factory. A belt snapped and killed him. My elder brother was an Angel until he slipped. Life's dangerous." Windy started to plead. "Nurse, you can't tell anyone. My family will starve if you do."

"Charities can help."

"Only if they decide you're deserving. We're not."

"Why not?" Nurse Charrington was puzzled.

"Mum's got another kid on the way. Dad died a year ago. Charity Boards can count. We're an immoral family. They said so. Please, Nurse."

"I can get you a position assisting at the base in Persia."

"No, Nurse. The thing is, I like it as a Rifleman, being a soldier. I'm good at it. It's, well, exciting. I get to do things I couldn't do if I wasn't a soldier."

"I can't write a false medical report. They're confidential, but Colonel Dalkeith and Lieutenant Hawkins will have access to them. I must fill in the form accurately. This is your form. Read it."

She held out a piece of paper to Windy, who took it with great reluctance, shoulders slumped in defeat. "Name: George "Windy" Miller."

"That is the name you go by in official Army records. Any other names you might have had in the past are irrelevant. Rifleman

O'Grady is recorded as such, even though he's about as Irish as I am. That is your official name."

"Age: 16. Height: 5'4". Weight: 9 stone 12 lbs. Distinguishing marks: None visible on cursory examination." Windy continued to read on, looking confused.

"I agree," said Nurse Charrington. "There are a number of things it could ask to be recorded but doesn't. Gender, for example. I expect the Army believes that to be a superfluous question to ask about soldiers. I have filled in this form fully and accurately to the best of my ability. I have answered every question that it asks. I have no requirement to volunteer the information to anyone and I don't have the time to go about adding to my workload. I'll not divulge any information to anyone who doesn't have the right to know. Is that understood? If you want my advice, which you almost certainly don't, I suggest you find a way out, because this is not going to end well. For one thing, Nurse Ward thinks very well of you and was quite put out that I was examining you. However, if you insist on continuing with this foolishness, you might want to let a trusted friend in on the secret, to cover your back when questions get asked."

"Thank you, Nurse."

*****

It was hot in the engine room. Hotter than anything he'd ever known. There had to be a knack to shovelling coal as well, because he was bigger than the other stokers and yet they were moving the coal far quicker and easier than he was.

It was noisy as well. Thomas had hoped to practise Persian with the stokers here but shouting: "It's noisy" over the din, in either English or Persian, seemed like a waste of time. Not that it was possible to work for long. A fifteen-minute stint and then replaced by someone else.

He was sweating like a pig at the end of his stint. There was coal dust everywhere. His throat was dry and he itched.

Naturally, this was when the Persian stokers started to teach him how to speak their language.

*****

Lieutenant Hawkins found Colonel Dalkeith in his cabin, writing out something with Lady Dalkeith's assistance. Joy was working on some sewing, looked up and saw Frank with Lieutenant Hawkins and she smiled on seeing him. He simply scowled. She put her head down to concentrate on her sewing so that he couldn't see her eyes filling with tears.

"Sir," said Lieutenant Hawkins. "This was brought to my attention. Corporal Barry said that it isn't Sicilian whisky, but I wanted your opinion."

"And you're bringing this to my attention? Officially?"

"No, Sir. I just want a second opinion on the source of the drink. For information."

"Very well. It's much better when a situation is resolved before it becomes an official problem. The ship's Captain is conducting his inspection of the ship's crew tomorrow. Pass the word to the company commanders that I shall be conducting an inspection at the same time, of the men and their spaces. I don't expect to find anything untoward. Now, boredom is the biggest single problem on trips such as this. I will expect company commanders to come up with ideas to keep the men busy." Colonel Dalkeith glanced towards Frank. "Corporal, you seem to have had an idea, to judge by your expression. Out with it."

"Bridge tournament, Colonel, Sir."

"Bridge? That's an officer's game, really. Didn't think that you would play it."

"We're Riflemen. We get the job done, Sir."

"What do you think, Maeve?" Colonel Dalkeith asked Lady Dalkeith.

"I rather think Corporal Barry and his friends will put up a creditable performance. Joy, it's about time you took on some responsibility. Organise a bridge tournament for tomorrow evening. You shall need to find out how many people will be taking part, make arrangements for scratch teams, and ensure that all the appropriate material is in place. I shall be partnering Colonel Dalkeith."

"Yes, Ma'am. It will be duplicate bridge, Ma'am. Teams of four."

"And that will have nothing to do with the fact that Corporal Barry and his three friends play together constantly and know each other's game inside out."

"Evens things out, Ma'am." Joy paused, wondering if she should say anything more. "They've not been married for 35 years, Ma'am."

"Very well. Duplicate bridge. You and Nurse Charrington will join Colonel Dalkeith and myself. That will make for an interesting contest if we're drawn against Corporal Barry's four."

"Now, Lieutenant Hawkins," said Colonel Dalkeith. "I don't know what this drink is, but it's not the drink I had at the Mess Dinner. This is much more bitter. Almost undrinkable."

"It's definitely different, Sir?"

"Absolutely. No question about it."

"Thank you, Sir. Corporal Barry, you heard the Colonel. There will be an inspection tomorrow. I expect you to bring me evidence that the still that made this has been taken out of circulation."

"What if there no still, Sir?"

"Then I will expect you to bring in evidence that there is no still. You're the one who wants to be a sergeant. Think like a sergeant."

*****

Peter and Windy joined Lieutenant Campbell on the deck. The Lieutenant had the pieces of the screw gun laid out.

"Our first task is to learn how the damn thing goes together."

"Very good, Sir," said Peter. "May I suggest we put a rope around the working area to make a barrier. That way no screws will fall overboard."

"And that is why God invented the NCO. Well done, Lance. Let's concentrate on knowing how it goes together. We'll crack it yet."

"Peter, when we've a moment, there's something we need to talk about."

"If it's anything to do with the medical, we don't need to talk about it."

"But Nurse Charrington said …"

"Nurse Charrington may know medical stuff but she don't know Army stuff. We got a screw gun to sort out."

"Quite right, Lance," said Lieutenant Campbell. "If Indian troops can put it together in a minute, so can we. Providing we don't lose any pieces in the sea."

"Peter, this is important."

"Windy, it really isn't. If it's medical and I can't catch it off you, I do not need to know. I may suspect many things, but I keep them to myself. The screw gun's important. What Nurse Charrington said ain't important. If it was important, she'd have told. She didn't, so it ain't, so I don't want to know."

It was easier putting the screw gun together in the open, with space and light and with a flat sea. They got their time down to eight minutes.

"And these Indians do it from mules." Lieutenant Campbell shook his head. "We're improving and we've got the rest of the trip. It'll be quicker with the Persian chaps helping out. Crew of seven."

"Sorry, Sir, did you say a crew of seven? There's two of us, plus you and you're trying to get us to match the time of seven trained artillerymen?"

"Aim high, that's what my father always said," Lieutenant Campbell said cheerfully.

"Sir, I take it your father wasn't an artilleryman or a rifleman. Aiming high isn't great if you're trying to hit the target."

"Lance-Corporal Grant, you've hit the nail on the head. He works in the Government. Some sort of secretary. Dull stuff. Even tried to pull strings to get me into one of the Home Regiments. Imagine wanting to be a soldier who doesn't do any proper soldiering."

Windy and Peter said nothing. There was nothing they could say.

"I'm going to see if I can get assigned to your company with the screw guns. You two have the knack. Good work. Clear this away and then report to me at the Officers' Mess. I'll give you a chit for a drink."

*****

Lieutenant Furley-Smith had another drink. It was normally a bad idea to be drinking alone, but he had a tricky problem to resolve and a drink was helping him.

If he didn't keep his word, the men wouldn't respect him. Not that this mattered in and of itself, but Colonel Dalkeith seemed to expect it and without a good report, he'd not get the advancement he deserved. If he kept it, there would be a major problem. What he had to do was steal O'Grady's girl without stealing her and without upsetting Colonel Dalkeith. He could see a way of doing the first two, but the third was harder. Borrowing isn't strictly stealing.

The Colonel was very hot on getting the job done. He'd made it the unofficial motto of the Regiment. The job was whatever it was that awaited them in Persia.

Of course. The Colonel wouldn't be able to send him back if there were orders in Persia stating that Lieutenant Nicholas Furley-

Smith was to be given a specific job. He'd need to get a radio message back to his father and ask for something suitable.

He poured himself another drink. The satisfying part was that O'Grady would end up being the one in trouble, however it turned out.

*****

Time spent on reconnaissance is never wasted. That was something Colonel Dalkeith had said time after time. Lieutenant Furley-Smith believed it to be true. That meant that he had to scout out the target first.

He had a perfect excuse. He'd written a letter of apology to Nurse Charrington, but by presenting a personal apology as well, he'd get the chance to see the lay of the land. Who knows, maybe he'd even be able to charm his way to success.

She was at her office, talking with a pretty girl, probably one of the wives of the men. A glance around the office told him that it was small, with just one exit. Sturdy walls, if not particularly pretty. No windows. Set against the walls of the superstructure. The dull beat of the engine was surprisingly loud here. That was all very satisfactory.

He made his apology, taking a covert glance towards the pretty girl. Nurse Charrington nodded coldly.

"As you wish. I have far too much work to do to waste time in idleness. Good day, Lieutenant."

And with that, he was dismissed. By a mere nurse. Hadn't she realised that rank has its privilege? Such a cold, unladylike demeanour. Not at all gentle and kind and forgiving. Certainly not respectful of her betters. However, he would concentrate on the objective.

Colonel Dalkeith would be impressed at the attention to detail he was paying here.

*****

Nurse Charrington tried to put aside her private feelings as that oaf tried to apologise to her. She had no reason to be in his company, unless he needed medical attention, when he would just be a slab of meat.

Different nurses coped with different patients differently. She tried to remain emotionally detached from the patient. One was sympathetic but it did no-one any good to lose objectivity. Of course, that was easier in a hospital, where patients came and went. Unless they were in for a long time, you never got to know them beyond the usual pleasantries. She suspected that it would be different while she was with the Regiment. She would know the patients before they were patients.

Like Lance-Corporal Miller. That situation was not going to end well. Sooner or later, truth would out. When that happened, someone would ask her pointed questions about the medical. She could hide behind medical confidentiality and answering the questions asked, but it would cause problems.

It would also be a problem for Miller, although the precise nature of that problem would depend upon how the truth came out.

"A bridge tournament?" she asked, as Miss Eliot finished speaking. "I have neither the time nor the inclination."

"But Lady Dalkeith specifically asked for you."

"My work takes priority over social events."

"But you need a break. Now I'm helping you, you'll have more time. You'll be partnering me."

"I haven't played bridge for a long time. I'm not inclined to spend much time in the company of officers just at the moment. Creatures like Lieutenant Furley-Smith are best avoided. You had best watch yourself if he's in the vicinity. I saw how he looked at you. It rather suggested that you could not consider yourself safe in his company."

"Then that's more reason for you to come. You can chaperone me there. Make sure that Frank doesn't try to take advantage of me, although he's a gentleman." Joy sighed. Part of her wished that

Frank *would* try to take advantage of her, but he was being strange and distant, and she didn't know why. "But we'll likely play against Frank. Frank's partnering Thomas, you know."

Joy tried to keep her face expressionless. Nurse Charrington shook her head at how obvious the ploy was.

However, the prospect of playing against Rifleman O'Grady had attractions. She hardened her heart. "Rifleman O'Grady is a patient. Furthermore, he's from a class that when he gets bored of playing soldiers, he'll have no interest in a mere nurse, save for a dalliance."

"It's obvious that you're sweet on him and he's sweet on you."

"Really? I rather think you've got an over-active imagination."

"So prove it. Please."

"I'll get no peace until I agree, that's clear. Very well, but it has been a long time since I've played."

*****

He had to find a still, although he wasn't entirely sure what it would look like and he didn't think that there was one to find. He wasn't sure what he would do if he couldn't find one. Previously, he would have chatted with Thomas about this, but he couldn't do that now.

Or could he? He still had to work with the platoon. Thomas was part of the platoon. Thomas might be a dishonourable womaniser, but he also had a twisty mind. And he did owe Thomas for taking the blame over the sign. That was a debt. It didn't get close to paying for his dishonouring Joy, but it was a debt, nonetheless.

Thomas was coming out of the engine room when Frank found him. Thomas looked exhausted.

"You filthy," said Frank to him.

"I know," sighed Thomas. "You know, they don't clean the coal before we have to shovel it." He turned to two stokers. "Khodafez," he said.

"What that mean?" Frank asked.

"It's goodbye in Stoker."

Frank hated to admit it, but he needed Thomas' twisty mind. "I need help from dishonourable cheat." He then explained about searching for the still.

"What do you mean dishonourable cheat? What's the problem?"

"You make time with Joy, after you make time with your nurse. It dishonourable."

"Hang on a minute. Making time with Joy? When? She's scared because she thinks you're looking elsewhere. As for Nurse Charrington, that's more hope than anything. I wish I knew."

"Do not lie. I saw you make time with Joy."

"When? The only time was I've been alone with her was a couple of days ago, when she was worrying that she wasn't good enough for you."

"And you make time with her. I see."

Thomas started to get annoyed. "Frank, you're my buddy. That makes you kind of like my brother. That makes Joy kind of like my sister. She's scared and lonely and worried and doing her best. If you don't sort yourself out, you'll lose her. Talk to her."

"How I know you not lie? All the time, you lie."

"Speak to Joy. Because if you leave her hanging like this, by God, I *will* start making time with her because she deserves better than you ignoring her. Now, this still. It's easy. Make one. Then you'll have one that you can say you found. Say that you found it in the hold. Anyone could have access to the hold and it's out of the way. Anyone could be responsible. If you *do* find a still, then you've got two."

Frank had to admit that Thomas had a devious, twisted, crooked mind. What was his angle with Joy? He was up to something. But speaking with Joy might help. Joy wasn't as good a liar as Thomas was. He'd know if she tried lying to him.

Thomas nodded his head towards the upper deck, where Lieutenant Furley-Smith was standing, smoking a cigarette and seemingly watching the sea roll by. "Now him, that's someone I don't trust."

"Why, is he try to steal your girl?"

"Nurse Charrington is not my girl," Thomas said wearily. He paused. If he said what he thought, it would become true and that scared him. But he couldn't not say it. "I'd like her to be, but I can't see a way of it happening. Besides, she's a nurse. Way above a Rifleman. Out here, a nurse could have her pick of the officers. Why would she bother with a mere Rifleman?" Thomas felt that this was somehow unfair, but it was how things were.

"You right. That officer feel like he up to no good."

"Are we good for the bridge tournament? The officers won't expect us to be able to play well."

"I have much to do."

"Look at it this way. If you want to get promotion to Sergeant, you're going to have to do something to make officers notice you."

*****

"Over-eager, impatient, over-confident lieutenants with optimism for brains," Peter said to Windy. He said it under his breath, because Lieutenant Campbell was explaining the demonstration to Colonel Dalkeith and Major Marshall, the second-in-command of the Battalion.

"The screw gun is in its component parts, Colonel. A Rifleman will push an empty crate into the sea. When the crate hits the water, Grant and Miller will start assembling the gun under my direction. When assembled, they will open fire on the crate. The ship is travelling at ten knots, so in one fifth of an hour, 12 minutes, the crate will be out of range."

"And these guns can be transported on mules?" asked the Colonel.

"That's correct, Sir. It's very exciting."

"Why are some of the screws and bolts painted blue, some red, and some green?"

"Lance-Corporal Grant's idea, Sir. Blue for the barrel, red for the firing mechanism, green for the supports. It lets us carry out faster assembly."

"Carry on, Lieutenant. This could be interesting."

Lieutenant Campbell waved to a Rifleman on the lower deck, who dutifully pushed a crate overboard. The crate bobbed in the water, before settling down and drifting slowly behind the ship. Windy and Peter started to assemble the gun.

"Just like a drill," said Lieutenant Campbell to Peter and Windy. Unfortunately, the tone of his voice was excited rather than calming. He turned to Colonel Dalkeith. "Of course, in the field it will be easier because the ground won't be shifting around so much."

"And I'm confident that being under fire, the noise and confusion of battle, the awareness that getting it wrong could lead to calamity, and quite possibly being exhausted after several days of hard marching in rough terrain won't have any detrimental impact."

"This is the start of the training, Sir. By the end of the trip, they'll be doing this after doing 20 laps around the ship. Sorry, did you say something, Lance-Corporal Grant?"

"Trapped my finger in this screw, Sir. Ready to load, Sir."

"Eight minutes 23. You've done better times than that. Clear to fire. Now, we're not trained artillerymen yet, so we're having to take loading carefully. With practise and a full crew, they'll get better."

"How close do you think you'll get?" Colonel Dalkeith asked.

"The first shot will be a ranging shot. Then we can pull in closer. If that crate were a body of approaching troops and we were using air-burst shrapnel, we wouldn't need to be spot on. Major, you might want not to be directly behind the gun. Recoil. Fire when ready."

Windy took a sight and shrugged. "Watch for the splash, Peter. Then we can correct. Ready, Sir."

"Shoot," Lieutenant Campbell snapped. Windy fired the gun. As the noise reverberated, Lieutenant Campbell explained that he'd been told that it's better to use the order "Shoot" rather than "Fire". "Fire and five sound very similar, and you don't want to say up five degrees and have someone just hear fire, rather than five."

"Where's the splash," asked Windy. He suddenly became aware of a silence in the people around. "Peter? Where's the splash?"

"There wasn't a splash."

"Don't be stupid. I'm not an artilleryman, but I can't miss the sea."

"Lance-Corporal Miller," said Lieutenant Campbell sternly. "I know you would rather not be doing this, but did you have to bring the demonstration to a premature end by hitting the target with your very first shot?"

"Sorry, Sir. Won't happen ag, sorry, what, Sir?"

"Miller, you hit the only obstruction in the sea for miles. Just for that display, you're to disassemble the gun, put it away and then report to me in the Officers' Mess, where I will see to it that you get a chit for a drink." Lieutenant Campbell turned to Colonel Dalkeith. "As you see, Sir, it has possibilities."

"So, I see, Lieutenant. You know what they say about the reward for doing something well? The reward is the opportunity to have to work harder at it. It looks like you'll have command of the screw guns. This means a lot of extra work for you."

"Thank you, Sir."

As they were disassembling the gun, a petite blonde nurse came close, and watched. "Excuse me, Lance-Corporal Miller," she said. "When you've finished here, do you think you might assist me with some repackaging of medical supplies."

"I'll detail someone to help you," Windy replied.

"If you don't mind, I'd prefer an NCO. Only riflemen, well, I would be scared they'd take advantage of. I feel I can trust you. I'm Alice. Nurse Alice Ward."

"I'll make sure they knew better that to bother you, Miss."

"He's spoken for, Miss," Peter added.

"Oh." Her face fell and then brightened. "But not married and she's not here."

"They, Miss. Beryl from London, and Iris from Derby. Plus others I probably don't know about. He'd just take cruel advantage of you."

"Nonsense. I trust him to behave like a gentleman."

"That's what I mean, Miss."

*****

She had to arrange the bridge tournament, help Nurse Charrington, teach riflemen to read and write, look after Colonel and Lady Dalkeith's cabin, and try to keep track of all the railway novels and the money she was making from loaning them out. She was rushed off her feet, with barely a moment to spare.

Lady Dalkeith expected her to play in the bridge tournament, but she also had to make sure the duplicate hands were arranged. She needed someone reliable to do that. Frank always spoke well of one person.

"Sergeant Taylor, I have a favour to ask. It's about this bridge tournament."

"I don't play, Miss."

"I need someone to sort the hands out. Make sure that we've got duplicate hands for each room." Joy explained how it worked.

"Very good, Miss. Do you want me to look after all the card stuff? Leave you free to concentrate on other stuff. And thank you, Miss."

"What for?"

"Setting young Barry straight. Since you come along, he's become a solid and reliable Corporal."

"How long will it be before he makes Sergeant?"

"Normally takes about ten years. The way he's going, I can see him doing it in five."

"Five *years*? Five whole *years*?"

"Lot of responsibility, Miss. Officers decide what the job is. Sergeants make sure the job gets done. I don't think anyone in the Regiment ever made Sergeant in less than four years."

"Four *years*. I'll never be able to wait four years," she said, half to herself.

"Two riflemen, ready for reading instruction, Miss," Sergeant Taylor said, pretending not to hear her comment.

The riflemen came to the area of deck Sergeant Taylor had cordoned off. They sat down at a small trestle table and Joy tried to focus on teaching. *Four years.* "Rifleman Callaghan, I believe you've borrowed Cock O' The North. I take it that it's not about bagpipe songs."

"Er, not exactly, Miss. It's not."

"What's it about? Are you enjoying it?"

"Lot of words I don't understand, Miss." Rifleman Callaghan sounded cautious.

"Ask Thomas, Rifleman O'Grady. He'll explain."

"Aye. That one may not be Irish, but he should be. Not so much kissed the Blarney Stone as swallowed it whole. He's as crazy as a barrel of foxes. Loads of brains and no sense."

Joy stifled a smile. She'd have to tell that one to Frank. *Four whole years*. "Rifleman Wagstaff. You don't have a railway novel?"

"No, Miss. They're immoral and sinful. Reading them is a sure way to burn in Hell, begging your pardon, Miss."

"What do you read?"

"The Bible, Miss. Only book anyone needs."

"We'll read a bit from the Bible. Then we'll practise writing what we've read."

Rifleman Wagstaff read. Joy could tell that he was not really reading, just remembering the words. She'd have to find a way to make sure he read next time. She also noticed that Rifleman Callaghan was trying to draw something in secret. Just like the young ones at school, Joy thought. Strangely, this gave her more confidence. She knew how to play this game.

"Now we'll write out what we've read. But first Rifleman Callaghan, show me what you've drawn."

He blushed deeply. "It's nothing, Miss," he said, trying to hide it. Joy took the paper and laid it on the deck. She rather wished she hadn't, but she had no choice now.

"And what is this?"

Rifleman Callaghan looked desperately around, seemingly hoping that the ground would open up and swallow him. "It's a bit from the book I'm reading, Miss. The hero has surprised a wench in the stables. He's about to, well, not be a gentleman."

Joy tried to keep her voice calm and level. "Some gentlemen do not behave like gentlemen, and some who are not gentlemen do. Why does the wench look like me?"

"I can only draw portraits, Miss. It's nothing personal. Although you are the prettiest girl on the ship, Miss. Corporal Barry's very lucky."

Joy stared at the picture. It was very good. Callaghan had a knack for sketching. She remembered how she met Frank, how close she'd come to being like that wench, only Frank had saved her and had been a gentleman. "I'm the lucky one. I found a true gentleman. Now, both of you write out the Bible verse. No, Rifleman Callaghan. I'll hang on to this picture. If you don't give me your best work in future lessons, I'll let Sergeant Taylor see this."

While they wrote, she thought about Frank. There was something wrong and she had to find out what it was. After a few minutes, she read what they had written.

"Rifleman Callaghan, is this what the Bible verse said? Yea though I walk through the valley of the shadow of death, I shall fear no evil. For I am a Rifleman, and all evil things fear us."

"It's what it *should* say, Miss."

*****

Thomas couldn't sleep. It was the first time he hadn't been able to sleep since becoming a Rifleman. It wasn't the crowded sleeping quarters, with hammocks three deep, touching on all sides. The smell was dreadful and the noise of those who could sleep loud, but he'd slept fine here before.

The trouble was that his mind wouldn't settle down. It wasn't one thing, but many. Joy's smiles to Frank. No-one had ever smiled at him like that. He'd had plenty of different smiles from girls, but none like that.

Sometimes, he thought Emily was smiling like that, but her smiles, when they appeared, were so fleeting that he wasn't sure if it was simply his imagination. And he wasn't sure if he was good enough for her. Six months ago, he would have thought that nonsense. He was from a good family and a nurse would have been just a distraction until he got bored. His father would have insisted he marry someone from a good family, someone like Millicent.

He shivered at the thought of being married to Millicent. She was persistent, but completely brainless.

He'd been tempted by Millicent in London, but he'd got rid of that before she'd settled for Lieutenant Furley-Smith.

"And just how did you get rid of that temptation?" he asked himself, turning over again. "By resisting?"

That troubled him as well. Lieutenant Furley-Smith had just swept in and taken Millicent from him. He wasn't attached to her, but he didn't know that, nor did he seem to care. Things would have been no different if Thomas had been serious about Millicent.

What troubled him was that six months ago, he could easily have been Lieutenant Furley-Smith. A year ago, he had seduced Susan, the parlour maid, who had an understanding with the butcher's son. That was bad enough, but he'd joked about it with his friends afterwards.

Then there were the boards outside the State Schools. There were many names there and the children were proud of them. But apart from the children of the schools, the boards were unnoticed. They were people who weren't allowed in places where decent people go.

He was exhausted but he couldn't sleep. He struggled out of his hammock and pushed his way past cursing sleepers to walk on the deck.

*****

"Ma'am, is it blasphemous?" Joy showed Rifleman Callaghan's writing to Lady Dalkeith. She read it carefully, without any expression.

"I'm not a clergyman or a priest and I'm not theologically trained. I think you should write it out neatly and show it to Colonel Dalkeith."

"Show it to him, Ma'am? Won't he be angry?"

"Write it out neatly and leave it on his desk. Who wrote this?"

"I'd rather not say, Ma'am. If it gets them into trouble, well, I'd rather not say." Joy was nervous.

"Joy, if you are going to be the wife of a sergeant, you must be more confident. When the men go into action, their wives are going to be looking to you for reassurance."

"Yes, Ma'am." Joy straightened slightly. Lady Dalkeith had just told her to be more confident. "Ma'am, about being Frank's wife. I was talking to Sergeant Taylor. He said it might be four years before Frank makes sergeant."

"At least four years. More likely ten years."

"That's a long time, Ma'am." Joy's voice was almost desperate.

"There's a lot for him to learn before he's ready to be a sergeant."

"The thing is, Ma'am, well, I love him to bits. Four years is a really long time to wait."

"Really? I got the impression you were avoiding each other."

"It's a disagreement, Ma'am, but I still love him to bits."

"It doesn't matter, anyway. There's no chaplain with the Regiment and there's unlikely to be one in Persia. You wouldn't be able to get married until we got back to England. That won't be for three years at least.

"But, Ma'am," Joy said in dismay.

"And don't go thinking of a liaison before marriage. That would embarrass the Colonel. That will not happen while you're in my employ."

Be confident, she whispered to herself. "Yes, Ma'am. Ma'am, you've been married 35 years?"

"Yes."

"I sort of read about you in the Army list, Ma'am. You and Colonel Dalkeith."

"That's public information. I don't see why you should waste your time doing that, but there's no harm to it. Clearly I'm not giving you enough work to do."

Joy gritted her teeth. This was going to be awkward, but she had to show confidence. "Ma'am, it says that Colonel Dalkeith is 53, and that you're 51."

"That's incorrect. Out-of-date, at least. He's 54 and I'm 52. What's your point?"

"Well, that means he was 19 and you were 17 when you were married."

"That's correct. Are you suggesting that I don't know what it's like to wait ten years before getting married?"

"No, Ma'am, not at all." Joy paused. "Well, not really. Not as such."

"I can't abide weasels. Say what you mean and don't apologise for it. Yes or no?"

"If I've done my numbers right, well, yes, Ma'am," Joy said in a small voice.

"It was different for me. Garnet was an officer when we married. Ask him what his Colonel said to him when he asked for permission to marry."

"What did he say?"

"Ask Garnet. When you tell me what he said, I'll know that you've taken a step in growing up."

"Ask the Colonel, Ma'am? Something that personal?"

"Young lady, when you are the wife of a sergeant, the wives of the men will come to you with their problems. They will expect you to have the answers and you will need to get the answers."

"But asking the Colonel ..."

"When Corporal Barry is Sergeant Barry, he will need a strong right hand as a wife, not a simpering ninny."

"Yes, Ma'am." Joy needed to think about this. She had to find out why Frank was avoiding her; she had to learn to be strong; and she had to find a way of making four years pass in a flash.

*****

Know your enemy. That was key. He was pleased at how much strategy he was learning strategy. He knew where to go to get the information. Lieutenant Hawkins was O'Grady's platoon commander and would know about him.

"Shouldn't you be spending your time with your own company?" Hawkins had asked. "If Captain Filleul is out of things, you'll have command of the company."

"That's true, but I ruffled O'Grady's feathers. I felt I should put that right."

They talked for a bit. Hawkins didn't seem to be terribly friendly, but that was only to be expected. He wasn't a proper officer. He came up through the ranks.

Despite that, it was time well spent. He learned that O'Grady was good friends with three other soldiers, Barry, Grant, and Miller.

What was interesting was that those four names were entered as a team in the Duplicate Bridge tournament. They would be in one place at one time, under the gaze of other officers, ship's crew and civilians. He must be able to make something of that.

*****

Joy went out onto the deck. She needed to think. She wasn't clever, not clever enough to be able to sort of puzzles like getting promotion for Frank in less than four years, or getting a clergyman to pop into existence, to say nothing about getting things sorted with Frank. She still didn't know why he was avoiding her. It scared her but she couldn't show it.

Thomas was also on the deck. Maybe he could help. He was good with solving problems.

"If we haven't got a clergyman, then we'll have to find one or make one," he said.

"You can be silly. How can we find a clergyman? Look under the beds?"

"You leave finding a clergyman to me. You concentrate on talking to Frank."

"Is he missing me?"

"Talk to him."

*****

Lieutenant Furley-Smith watched as Thomas and Joy spoke. That was the pretty girl who had been working with Nurse Charrington. Lady Dalkeith's maid. He needed to be careful with her. She might only be a servant, but she could be a problem if the Colonel listened to her. He needed to discredit her.

There was one certain way to discredit a maid. Once the suspicion of thievery is raised, it's difficult to ignore. Everyone from the Colonel's cabin would be at the bridge tournament. That would be his opportunity.

*****

Frank gritted his teeth as he saw Thomas and Joy talking on the deck. Thomas had assured him that he saw Joy as a sister. He didn't know whether to believe him or not. He was confused and suspicious.

Thomas had been insistent that he should talk with Joy. It would mean that he'd know the truth, whatever it was.

The trouble was, he was scared it might be a truth he didn't want to hear.

He was a Corporal. He couldn't afford to be scared. Sergeant Taylor said that the men watch NCOs to see how scared they should be; an NCO could never show a little bit of fear. He walked to them. As he did so, Joy looked at him and gave an uncertain half-smile.

"That reminds me, I've got to speak with Nurse Charrington about my medical training," Thomas said. He left them.

Frank didn't know how to start.

"I've missed you," Joy said. "I suppose you've been very busy. I should get used to that, but I've really missed you."

He had to ask the question straight away, before his courage failed him. "I see you making time with Thomas."

"What? When? I haven't."

"I see you. Just along there, two nights ago. You put your arms around him and hold him close. You never hold me like that."

"I'd been worrying that I wasn't, well, I'd been worrying and Thomas helped me. I'd been thinking, well, it doesn't matter what I'd been thinking. That was all."

Frank wanted to believe her. "But Thomas, he prettier than me. Clever, amusing, women like him. I thought you see that he better than me."

"Now you listen to me, Francesco Barrilari. When we first met, I was in that horrid dungeon thing with those dogs. You didn't need to come in and face the danger, but you did. When you saw I was just an orphan girl of no account, you could have left and no-one would have known, but you came anyway. When we were heading out and the dogs attacked, you could have left me, but you didn't, even when they might have killed you. And ever since, you've been really kind and thoughtful, you've worked hard. You're not as pretty as Thomas, your face is scarred and a bit scary, but you've got the biggest heart of anyone I know and I love you to bits."

Frank felt guilty. "I was scared. When we coming out of that basement, and dogs turning on me, you could easily leave me, escape, but you stay and fight and save me. It bravest thing I ever see in girl. You do this for me. But I thought you get tired of me, and Thomas …" His voice trailed away.

"As we're going to be married, we've got to trust each other. Lady Dalkeith and Colonel Dalkeith aren't always worrying about what each other's getting up to. They trust each other. That's how it will be with us. If I worry about something, the first person I'll talk to won't be Thomas, or Lady Dalkeith, or Nurse Charrington, but you. And you'll talk to me before talking to Thomas, or Peter, or Windy, or Sergeant Taylor."

There was something Frank had to know. "You hug Thomas, but you not hug me."

Joy looked away. "Because if I did, you'd hug me back. Then I'd look up at you and then you'd give me a gentle kiss and then, well, things would happen." As soon as she said it, she knew that she'd never be able to wait four years. She'd have to do something.

*****

"What are you going to do about Nurse Ward?" Peter asked Windy. "Honestly, what with Beryl and Iris and now Alice, you're getting a reputation to rival Thomas."

"I don't know. What would you do?"

"Me? I'd take advantage of the opportunity. Nice little blonde, just what the doctor ordered."

"No, seriously. Hang on a minute, I've got an idea. It's one that Thomas might have come up with. I need camouflage and I know just where to get it. Little Alice isn't going to fight another nurse over me. I just need to start stepping out with Nurse Charrington. She's very understanding. It's fool-proof."

"That'll be the nurse Thomas is sweet on. The one who's sweet on Thomas?"

"Exactly. Give Thomas a bit of competition so he'll start things moving. Meanwhile, it gets Alice off my back. Afterwards, you can offer her your comfort. It's perfect."

Peter tried to think how he could explain the flaws he saw in this plan. "Windy, even by your standards, that's a stupid plan."

*****

Lieutenant Furley-Smith rubbed his chin in thought. He'd done his reconnaissance. Now he needed a plan. One thing stuck in his brain. If a Rifleman, even an NCO, struck him in public, they would be in big trouble. Provided he was careful, he could provoke them as much as he liked, and they couldn't do anything about it.

He'd need to be careful about the other officers. He would need to provoke O'Grady without the officers realising that was what he was doing happening. But if he took care, this could be a lot of fun.

******

"Did you write this, Joy?" Colonel Dalkeith asked, looking at the paper on his desk.

"Yes, Sir," said Joy. She couldn't say anything else. It was her handwriting. She watched as the Colonel re-read it. He seemed to be struggling to keep his face expressionless.

"It's very neatly written," he said. He finally gave up trying to keep expression out of his face and laughed. "It's very good. I'd be obliged if you could find the time, amongst your duties for Lady Dalkeith, to arrange to have this framed. It will go well in my office."

"Certainly, Sir. Very kind of you to say so. I just wrote the words. Rifleman Callaghan thought of them, Sir."

"Callaghan. Tall chap, always dancing on the edge of insubordination, sketches."

"Er, yes Sir."

"I'll be interested in seeing his reaction when he sees it on the wall next time he comes before me on Defaulters. You're teaching soldiers to read and write, I hear. Good work. Settling in?"

"Yes, Sir. Everyone's been very kind." She paused. She had to be strong. "Sir, Lady Dalkeith said I should ask you what your CO said to you when you asked for permission to marry her."

"Did she? Let's see. You've been worrying about Corporal Barry. Of course, you'll be the wife of a non-com, so it will be different for you. I was an officer. A very junior one, but an officer."

"Yes, Sir. What did he say, Sir?"

"He said no. He said I was too young. He said Maeve was too young, too American, and not at all suitable to be the wife of an officer."

"Yes, Sir." Something tingled at the back of her mind. "Sir, what did he say, if it's not too impertinent."

"It is, but I rather suspect Maeve is toughening you up for your new role. She does that. Couldn't manage without her."

"Yes, Sir." She paused. "Sir, what did he say?"

"Sorry, I was wool-gathering," he said with a smile. "Thinking about the past. My Colonel glared at me and told us that it was out of the question. He said, and I'll never forget his words: "If the Army wanted you to have a wife, it would have issued you with one." That was the end of the matter, as far as he was concerned."

"But, Sir, well, you did get married. How did you do that, if the Colonel said no?"

"I asked to transfer to another regiment. We got married while I was between regiments. Left the Bucks as a single man and joined the Rifles as a married man."

Joy tried to work out why Lady Dalkeith had insisted she find out this story. It was nothing like what she was telling Joy. In fact, it seemed to be completely the opposite. She'd talk with Frank about it.

*****

Nurse Ward wasn't being a pest. She was, however, showing a surprising interest in the screw gun. She sat with Windy and Peter on the deck, watching the sea, talking about the gun and asking why they joined the army, and talking about nursing.

She told them that all the nurses thought she'd come along to find a nice husband. "It's difficult in a hospital, because there are so many more nurses than doctors. Doctors rarely marry a nurse."

"That's why they think you've come," Windy asked. "Why have you actually come?"

Alice ducked her head shyly. "You're a very unusual Rifleman. Most of the others aren't so sensitive."

"He's one of a kind, Miss," Peter said.

"I'm nothing special. You're the one who had his own business and is a proper Mr Fix-it. Honestly, Miss, you wouldn't believe what Peter can do with a screwdriver."

Alice glanced down at her feet. "Honestly, you two are like brothers. Whenever one of you gets married, the wife will have to have a sister for the other."

"So why have you come, Miss?" Windy asked.

Before she could answer, Lieutenant Campbell came hurrying over. "Terribly sorry, Miss. Call of duty and all that. I rather need Grant and Miller for some work. I know they'd much rather sit here talking with you, but that's the Army for you."

"I also have work that I need to catch up on."

"Might I say, Nurse, it's such a fillip to have you with us. If you ever need anything, just ask. I'm new to the Regiment as well, so we could discover things together."

"Are you flirting, Lieutenant?"

"Absolutely not, Miss. I make it a rule to allow the lady to initiate flirting. Gentlemen lead in a dance; ladies lead in a social conversation. Isn't that so, Miller?"

"Wouldn't know, Sir. I'm a Rifleman, not a gentleman."

"Every Rifleman, whatever their rank, is one of nature's gentlemen. Come on, Grant, Miller. I've been doing some thinking about how we'll put the gun together with more people."

*****

Thomas' head hurt. He didn't know if that was because he'd had very little sleep last night, or because the noise in the engine room had been particularly bad, or because Persian wasn't an easy language to learn, or because of the stress of getting Joy and Frank back on track, or because of Emily.

Nurse Charrington. She was working at the moment.

That was also giving him a headache. How could he find a way for her to marry and still remain a nurse? Hospitals didn't allow married women to be nurses. He couldn't wave a magic wand and change the rules. Why was he thinking about marriage in the first place?

He had a nagging sensation that he was on the verge of seeing the solution, aware that there was a solution lurking just out of sight. It was annoying.

He saw Joy chatting cheerfully to a couple of the ship's officers. He could tell by the way she was moving her hands that she was talking about the bridge tournament. He waited while she dealt with that. Then she saw him and came over.

He could tell by the way that she walked and her smile that she'd sorted out the problem with Frank. That made him smile.

"Thank you for making him see sense. Everything's perfect now. Except," She paused. "Except that we can't get married without a clergyman."

"Priest, I guess. Frank's Catholic, more or less."

"There isn't one in the Regiment or on the ship or in Persia."

Thomas could see where this was leading. "Do you want me to find one out of thin air?"

"Yes, please, It's the sort of puzzle you're good at."

Thomas sighed. He'd acquired this reputation and he didn't want to let Joy down. He'd learned from the stokers that the ship would stop at Cape Town to take on coal. "I'll see what I can do."

*****

If he wanted to hide a still, where would he hide it? It had to be somewhere that didn't move around too much or the motion of the ship could make it fall over. That meant not at the front or the back, and below decks. It had to be somewhere people didn't go into very often. It had to have water or some way of cooling so the alcohol would condense. It would take up some space, so that meant it needed to have concealment to shield it from passing eyes.

He thought harder. There would be a smell, so that had to be hidden, which meant somewhere where there was already a strong smell. Somewhere that sailors could go to and expect not to be disturbed while they filled or emptied the still.

It was obvious, really. If there was a still, he knew where it would be. Now he had to think like Sergeant Taylor. What should he do if he found something? He could tell the officers, which would upset the sailors. He could warn the sailors, which would please them, but would mean the officers didn't realise what he had done, which would mean he wouldn't get any credit for it. He needed to somehow get the credit without upsetting things.

He smiled. The answer was obvious. Ask Sergeant Taylor's advice. That way Sergeant Taylor would know that he knew. He would know what to do about it.

First, though, he had to find out if a still had been constructed in what the sailors kept calling the head, although it didn't deal with heads.

*****

"Sergeant Taylor, Colonel Dalkeith tell me to make sure there no still in ship. I check, I find one. I ask instructions what to do."

Sergeant Taylor put down the decks of cards he was sorting. He was tired of sorting out duplicate hands. Miss Eliot had said there would probably be eight teams, and that meant eight tables, and each table would need three decks; one in use, one prepared for the next hand, and one in preparation. One thing was certain, though. "Barry, give me your cards."

"Sergeant?"

"You've played with that deck so long that you recognise the backs of the cards. No way will you play against officers with two unfair advantages."

"Two unfair advantages, Sergeant?"

"Three, now that I think about it. How many hands of bridge have you four played? That's one. There's nothing we can do about that. These marked cards, that's one we can stop you using. If you do well, I'll let you keep one of the decks. Almost new."

"What's the third advantage?"

"You're an NCO. They're officers. They'll be off-balance. About this still. What do you think you should do? Think like a sergeant."

He was always being tested. He'd have to get used to it. "Colonel Dalkeith say he not expect find one when he inspects. He not say he want still broken up. Is sailor still, not ours. We warn sailors keep it out of sight, make sure we get favour from them for warning. Not take the drink, though."

"Why not?"

"I see where it made. I prefer Sicilian whisky."

Sergeant Taylor took a small notebook out of his top pocket, and wrote briefly in it, before returning it to his pocket. "Another left page for you. Well done."

"Sergeant?"

"People I'm keeping an eye on. I make notes when they does something worth noting. Good on left hand page, bad on right hand page. I can see at a glance how they're doing. A little trick of mine."

"Thank you, Sergeant."

*****

Lieutenant Furley-Smith wasn't enjoying being the second officer of a company. Not enough freedom and Captain Filleul kept insisting he know the names of the men in the company. So tiresome. He would prefer to be in and around Court. Being the link between the Regiment and the local politicians would be just the thing.

*****

Joy was shaking with nerves when she arrived at the wardroom. Everything looked to be ready, but she was scared that something dreadful was going to happen. Sergeant Taylor told her that the first three hands were ready and that he had a volunteer for each table to prepare subsequent hands. "I'll keep an eye on the tables, Miss. You enjoy your evening."

She relaxed a little as the players started to arrive. She nervously said hello to them, then made sure the stewards gave them drinks. As more people arrived, she became more nervous. Everyone knew what these events were like; she didn't. If she got things wrong, that would be bad. Everyone was so much older and more important than she was. It wasn't like this with Lady Dalkeith, but that was when it was just Lady Dalkeith. Everyone here her to know what they were talking about. There were so many people and she felt like she wanted to run away and hide. Everyone knew each other and she was alone.

Then Frank and the others arrived. Frank looked around, nodding slightly, then he caught sight of her and smiled. Everything was now better.

*****

Lieutenant Furley-Smith nodded as his plan developed. Everyone was at the bridge tournament. Colonel and Lady Dalkeith would be there, as well as their maid. O'Grady and his friends would be there, along with O'Grady's girl.

That meant that they would be out of the way. Lieutenant Furley-Smith made his way to the Colonel's cabin. One big advantage of being on a ship was that doors were never locked. Something about not getting trapped in a room if the ship starts to sink.

He knocked on the door, despite knowing there was no-one inside. The knock was for the benefit of anyone passing, who'd not see anything unusual. Entering without knocking would be unusual and he didn't want to attract attention. Camouflage in the field.

The maid was the girl of O'Grady's friend, and she was close to Lady Dalkeith. Separate her from Lady Dalkeith and you separate O'Grady from Colonel Dalkeith. It will also hurt O'Grady's friends, which will hurt him.

"Thank you, Colonel," he said as he entered. "This won't take long, then you'll be able to enjoy your bridge." Again, all for the benefit of any onlookers.

He shut the door behind him. All doors seemed to open inwards. He wondered why that should be before concentrating on the job in hand.

Everyone knew that maids were light-fingered thieves. It would just be a matter of casting suspicion on her and watch the sparks follow. It was just a matter of finding what would be a suitable thing to plant. First, check the dresser. Servants are like magpies, always after bright and shiny little objects.

A couple of nice emerald earrings. They'd actually look nice on the maid. The sort of thing that she might take. Now, where to put them? It had to be somewhere that she'd hide them, somewhere she wouldn't look for, and somewhere that Lady Dalkeith would find them when she started looking.

There was a travelling bag beneath the bed in the separate area. Perfect.

And leave, pause as closing the door. "Good luck in the bridge, Colonel."

Now he just had to wait until he bumped into Lady Dalkeith and mention that he'd seen the maid wearing earrings that looked just like ones he'd seen her wearing. "Astonishing coincidence, don't you think? Emeralds go with so many complexions." That would sew the seed of doubt. Now to take a stroll around the deck and plan his next move.

He couldn't be seen to be loitering around Nurse Charrington's office too often. However, all the medical offices had been made the same and were in similar locations around the ship.

This was all rather fun. A light was on in one of the offices.

*****

Nurse Ward knew that it was important to keep accurate records, but it was the boring part of nursing. She'd got into the habit of thinking of other things while writing up. Everyone was at the bridge tournament, so she'd be able to get some uninterrupted work done.

Lance-Corporal Miller was sweet. He wasn't like the other riflemen. He seemed very understanding and she understood how he was successful with ladies, as Grant implied. Almost shy and making people want to mother him. She'd like to get to know him better.

She'd sidestepped the question about why she'd come. Hopefully, people would get tired of asking. She liked nursing, but she didn't like the expectations of some doctors and the way they tried to exploit nurses.

Then there was Lieutenant Campbell. She'd have to be careful she didn't laugh when she next saw him, but he was very much like the border collie her parents had. Full of energy and enthusiasm and with an excited bounce in his step and interested in everything.

She liked it here. She was nursing. She didn't know what it would be like in Persia, but she knew that she'd be important. People respected her and treated her as a professional. People didn't sneer at her or make fun of her.

The door opened and a Lieutenant stepped inside. She'd thought all the officers were playing or watching at the bridge, but she guessed that some had to be on duty.

"Can I help you, Lieutenant?"

He looked surprised to see her, then glanced outside. No-one around. "Actually, I rather fancy you can," he said, shutting the door firmly behind him.

*****

The first game had been a humiliation for their opponents. Two ship's officers, and Major and Mrs Marshall. Both tables had been totally one-sided. Thomas and the others hadn't even needed to use their edge.

Windy had started off nervously, but once he played his first card, he lost himself in the game. Peter still overbid and he still seemed incapable of defending without saying double, but this was balanced by Windy's natural caution and they knew each other's game thoroughly.

When the tables for the second set of matches were announced, Thomas had his doubts that they had been chosen at random. Sergeant Taylor announced that Thomas' team had been drawn against the Colonel's.

First, Thomas and Frank played against Joy and Nurse Charrington. It felt somehow natural, almost domestic.

"I'll thank you to concentrate on the game," said Nurse Charrington.

"We're still easily ahead," Thomas answered.

"It's the score from both tables. I'll thank you to pay attention to the cards."

"Yes, dear," said Thomas, focusing his attention back on the cards. He was aware of a glance between Frank and Joy and a sharp look from Nurse Charrington, but he needed to concentrate on the cards.

Once they were both concentrating, Thomas and Frank were too strong for their opponents. Then it was time to switch tables and play Colonel and Lady Dalkeith.

"Unusual for rankers to play bridge, O'Grady."

"Learned at school, Sir. Play it in barracks, Sir."

"Not poker or vingt-et-un?"

"No, Sir. Poker has got to be played for money, otherwise there's no risk with running a bluff. Vingt-et-un's a game for when you don't want to think too much. Bridge can be played without money without losing any enjoyment, Sir." He didn't mention that he thought vingt-et-un was a game for half-wits.

Thirty-five years of marriage gave Colonel and Lady Dalkeith an edge. After going one down in six diamonds, Thomas started drumming his fingers on the table as he considered his bidding.

Frank was nervous. He wasn't sure if beating the Colonel would impress or annoy him and what it would mean to his promotion prospects.

Colonel Dalkeith seemed to understand. "Play to win, Corporal. You'll probably lose, but I'm not going to be impressed by an NCO who doesn't always try their utmost."

Thomas and Frank lost the first rubber but took the second. Thomas became aware of several people watching the game, including Nurse Charrington.

He picked up his cards for the next hand and stared at them. This was awkward and he didn't know what to do. Maybe it was coincidence. Frank opened the bidding and his bid confirmed Thomas' suspicions. He was absolutely certain when Lady Dalkeith passed. He stared at the cards, wondering what to do. He was aware of Nurse Charrington watching him. He made a decision and laid his cards face down on the table.

"Sir, I can't play this hand."

"Why on earth not?"

"Because I remember reading a book on duplicate bridge. This was one of the sample hands. I know this hand. I know the conundrums it poses. Despite your having two aces, I can make six spades against any lead you make."

"From what Lieutenant Hawkins says, you're a scheming rogue. Why not just take the win?"

"It would be cheating, Sir. It's wrong to cheat at cards."

Colonel Dalkeith laid his cards face down on the table, steepled his fingers in front of him, and looked squarely at Thomas. "If you explain how you'd make six spades, we'll give you the hand."

Thomas took a deep breath. "You've three choices of lead. If you lead the Ace of Hearts, we'll find that dummy's got King and three of spades and a void in hearts. I trump with the King, not the three, because Lady Dalkeith also has a void in hearts and I don't allow her to overtrump. I lead the three of spades from dummy, which you have to play your singleton ace on. You've no way of giving the lead to Lady Dalkeith, and your length in hearts is useless. If you play the ace of spades, you've no way of getting into Lady Dalkeith's hand. If you lead anything else, I win the trick, play a round of trumps and we're back in the same situation. Sir."

"Well done," said Colonel Dalkeith. "I can see that you're going to give us a problem."

"Beg pardon, Sir?"

"Your brain's too good for a Rifleman and your tongue's too free for an NCO. What shall we do with a problem like O'Grady? Miss Eliot, my thanks for an interesting evening."

*****

Lady Dalkeith walked with the Colonel a few feet behind Joy and Frank. She allowed Frank to escort Joy to the cabin. Joy was bubbling like a teenager, Lady Dalkeith thought. That was understandable and she had earned the moment.

Joy could speak privately with Frank, but she was in public view. She had to be careful what she said. "Frank, Lady Dalkeith keeps saying we have to wait to get married, but she was only a year older than I am when she got married. And Colonel Dalkeith's Colonel, before he was a Colonel, said that he couldn't get married, but they went ahead and did anyway. And I've had an idea. We're on a ship; the captain of a ship can marry people."

"It not proper marriage, I think."

"I think it is."

"I find out. We get married properly, OK?"

*****

"It's late. I'm tired and we've something to discuss before I teach you about treating wounds." Thomas thought Nurse Charrington sounded stern as she shut the door to her office. "I require an explanation."

She sat at the desk and waited. Thomas thought, but remained puzzled. "I don't understand. What do you want me to explain?"

"Do you really not know? I don't know if that's better or worse. Can you not remember what you said when we were playing bridge?"

"I was concentrating on the cards. You said that you wanted me to concentrate on the game." Thomas was puzzled.

"And what did you say to that? In public, mark you, in front of everyone."

"I agreed with you." Thomas was very puzzled.

"What did you say?"

"I said yes."

"That's not what you said. You said 'yes, dear.' Those were your precise words."

"Oh." Thomas thought about the implications. "Oh," he said again. There didn't seem anything else to say.

"What do you think people will think? I thought I made it clear that I expected to be treated with professional courtesy when in a professional situation or in public."

"You're right." He paused. "No, you're not. I do treat you with professional courtesy in a professional situation. Playing bridge isn't a professional setting."

"It was a public setting."

"It was a public declaration of my affection."

"Which I cannot reciprocate. I cannot marry and remain a nurse. I have no intention of undertaking a dalliance outside of marriage. Furthermore, you barely know me."

"I know that you're good at your job, you are dedicated, kind, although you cover it with a brisk, brusque approach, that you rarely smile but it makes you beautiful, that you are the most stubborn woman I've ever met, that you are proud of what you have done, that you stick by your word come what may, that you don't mince words and you'll be honest under every situation imaginable, that you can be infuriating, and that I love you."

"And I repeat. I can't marry and remain a nurse and I won't undertake a liaison outside of marriage."

"Would your answer be different if I find a solution to the conundrum?"

"That will depend on the nature of the solution," Nurse Charrington said, cautiously. She feared she was being drawn into a trap.

"Is that a yes or a no?"

"How can I agree to something without knowing what it is?"

Thomas paused. "If I can find a way for you to marry me and for you to remain a nurse, in a way that's acceptable to you, then you'd consider marrying me?" Thomas was surprised that his mouth, seemingly of its own volition, had spoken of marriage.

Nurse Charrington glanced down at the desk and considered her words carefully before speaking. "How do you propose to solve the puzzle?"

"That will be my secret. Actually, I'll start a poker game, win all the wages of everyone on the ship, found my own hospital with the proceeds, and have it written into the rules of my hospital that you can be a nurse whatever your marital status might be."

Nurse Charrington struggled for a moment to keep a straight face. She failed and a smile started. She shook her head and chuckled. "You are quite impossible. I think if you solved the puzzle, I might be inclined to accept simply to find out what trouble your tongue would get you into next. Until then, please remember I am Nurse Charrington in public or in a professional setting." She paused. "In private, you may call me Emily."

"What about dear, or love, or other terms of endearment?"

"I would prefer not to confuse the issue. Terms of endearment are appropriate when there is a relationship. There is not."

"So not dear or love. How about my little squirrel?"

"Only if you are willing to upset me. I have many ways to take your temperature. I can justify taking your temperature with ease, at considerable embarrassment to yourself."

*****

Nurse Ward stared at the wall of her office. She had to pull herself together. The Lieutenant was right. It would be her word against his, and who would the Regiment believe? An officer and gentleman belonging to the Regiment, or a mere nurse with no connections who everyone thought was just along to snare a husband.

Everyone would think she had tried to trick him into a situation to ensnare him in marriage and he'd evaded the trap. If she said anything, she'd be shunned. People would think she was trying to blackmail an officer and a gentleman. He would make sure the Colonel decided to put her off the ship at Cape Town as being detrimental to good order.

All she could do was dry her tears and pretend that nothing had happened.

*****

Lieutenant Furley-Smith smiled. That had been fun. It was just a rehearsal, a dry run, but it had been fun. It was probably not a good idea to make a habit of it, mind you.

That was how to take advantage of a target of opportunity. He'd learned more about tactics and strategy in these last couple of days than he'd learned in the weeks before. Persia could be a lot of fun. He'd get his own local servants and they'd be even less able to complain. He understood why officers who'd served in India spoke so fondly about the place. They always talked about what they were building, but now he understood what they meant.

He saw the Colonel and Lady Dalkeith on the deck below, returning to their cabin. The maid and that Corporal were just ahead of them. The maid was very pretty. The trouble with her was that the Corporal wasn't English, some sort of Italian. If he provoked him through her, there was a good chance he'd respond with a knife rather than fists. The fact that the Corporal would be hanged would be cold comfort in that case.

Best stick with the plan. Discredit her with Lady Dalkeith and break O'Grady's link with Colonel Dalkeith. Once she had been discredited with Lady Dalkeith, then he could see if that Corporal was interested in her, or in her connections. If the latter, then she'd be alone and vulnerable. That was for the future.

Separate O'Grady from the Colonel, treat his girl as he'd treated the silly nurse and then let O'Grady find him in a very public place. That will be Goodnight, O'Grady.

*****

Joy opened the door. Frank was there. He had started calling to say good morning again. She wanted to hug him, but she knew Lady Dalkeith was writing a letter in the cabin and would see.

"I speak with First Officer about whether captain of ship can marry. He say it a myth."

"But everyone knows that they can."

"It not true. We get married properly. There be no doubt about it."

"Perhaps we can find a priest in Cape Town and get married there."

It was only a quick good morning, but it was enough to make her very happy. Lady Dalkeith looked up from her letter.

"Joy, I want the cabin cleaned thoroughly today. Check all the clothes to make sure there's been no damage. It was choppy last night. Don't forget that you've got to get that writing framed, you've the lessons for the soldiers, and you'll need your lessons from Nurse Charrington. I've got a lot of work to do, so make sure that lunch is brought here. A proper lunch, mark you. Properly brewed tea. Condensation is a problem on the walls and the floor needs cleaning as a result."

Joy's face fell as the list of things she had to do grew. When she made a start, Lady Dalkeith returned to writing her letter. She knew that Joy was in a dangerous frame of mind, ready to dally outside of marriage. It was important to keep her busy.

*****

Thomas was glad he had so much to do. It kept him busy. He'd told Emily he loved her – and she hadn't reacted with disgust. His mouth had taken control again, blurting things out before he was even aware of them. His mouth seemed to know what he was thinking before his brain or his heart did. He was still trying to understand it.

His father would have kittens if he knew. That worried him. He wasn't sure how much he was being influenced by wanting to go against what his father stood for and how much was real.

It worried him that he was thinking like this. Was he getting cold feet?

The trouble was, he had nothing to compare it against. He'd had dalliances, as Millicent had shown, and he knew they didn't mean anything. Was he falling simply because Emily had made it clear she wasn't interested in a dalliance and that made her unobtainable? Was he lured into trying to obtain the unobtainable? Would he lose interest in her if they did become linked?

Would he break her heart if that happened? She was a person who didn't give their heart easily but would give it totally when she did. Would it be safer for her if he walked away now, before hurting her?

Was thinking about what was best for her a sign that this was the real thing?

"If anyone knows her own heart and mind and can make her own decision, it's her."

"That's a long phrase to learn in Farsi," said the Persian stoker.

"Sorry, I was daydreaming. What's the Persian for "Stop doing that"?"

*****

She had to put her bright face on and face the world. Act like everything was normal. Windy and Lance-Corporal Grant and Lieutenant Campbell were busy on their gun, moving four sets of equipment around. She would normally sit and watch them and talk when they were taking a breather, so she sat and watched.

She was still tense, but she trusted Windy and Peter and Lieutenant Campbell. She'd have to find out his first name, because she was certain Windy was a nickname. She'd have to find out Lieutenant Campbell's name, or else she would call him Ross. Then he'd ask her to explain, and she'd have to say that Ross was the name of her parent's border collie and that would be so embarrassing.

She half-smiled to herself. It was possible to get back into the routine, provided she didn't think about things. She had some lemonade ready for them when they took a break. It was part of the routine.

They were finished and coming over. Bright smile on.

They needed their drink. It was getting warmer as the ship continued southwards. She would soon have to start keeping an eye out for sun-caused illnesses. They took their drinks. Windy frowned slightly.

"What's the matter, Nurse Ward?"

"How many times must I ask you to call me Alice?"

Windy took a glass from her, his fingers touching her hand as he did so. She flinched slightly.

He noticed. "I'll call you Alice if you tell me what's wrong."

"There's nothing wrong. It's just the warm weather." She was holding it together.

"Now tell me the truth, Nurse Ward. Please, Alice."

He'd said her name and she dissolved into tears. He put his arms protectively around her while she sobbed onto his shoulder. She sobbed until there were no more tears left. "I'm sorry. It's nothing. I'm just being silly."

Lieutenant Campbell kept his distance, but his voice was firm. "Miss, you're upset. Something has upset you. I'm going to deal with it."

"It's not important."

"Miss, you're one of four nurses. You'll be keeping the men alive. You're important. Even if weren't, you are, but even if you weren't, you're part of the Regiment. That alone makes you important."

"There's nothing that can be done. He'll tell you his story. You'll believe it and that's an end to it."

"Who's he?"

"One of the Lieutenants. I don't know his name." She started crying again. "I don't even know his name."

"Grant, Miller, pack the gun away. Miss, while they're doing that, I'll sit nearby. When they're done, we'll find somewhere quiet, and you can tell me what happened. We'll deal with it."

"You're so like Ross."

Lieutenant Campbell raised an eyebrow, so she had to explain. She told him how when she was upset at home, he'd try and comfort her. "Sometimes he'd put his head in my lap and look up at me and let me stroke him."

"Are you saying I remind you of a border collie? Let me tell you something about border collies. We're sheep dogs. We protect the flock. I've seen them rounding up flocks, protecting the flock with the shepherds on our hills." He glanced at her. "But please, I've got a request. Don't throw a stick overboard. It could be so embarrassing."

*****

Damn the woman. Was she going to stay in her cabin all day? He had to catch her by chance. This was taking all morning. He couldn't lounge around here for much longer, not without finding an excuse to do so.

"Looking for me, Lieutenant Furley-Smith?" The Colonel's voice was cold and formal. Lieutenant Furley-Smith had been paying such close attention to the cabin that he'd neglected to keep an eye on his surroundings and the Colonel had surprised him with his silent approach. That was a mistake he mustn't let happen again.

"Not as such, Sir. I'd been thinking about what you said. Wondering how best to put it into practise."

"I would have thought that getting to know the men in your company would be a good first step."

"Yes, Sir. I intend to discuss each of them with the platoon sergeants. The sergeants have a close vision of the men. However, I was wondering if there might be a benefit in shuffling the Companies up a bit, moving some men to different companies for a short spell. Transfer skills around, get to know men in the other companies."

Colonel Dalkeith stroked his chin in thought. "If we were back in England, that might be a good idea. Going on deployment means that we must concentrate on doing what we know well. We don't have time to learn new things."

"Very good, Sir. In a similar vein, I thought I might be able to learn from Lieutenant Hawkins. He's an officer with a perspective on the men that's different to mine, coming up through the ranks as he did. Perhaps if I were to work with his platoon for a time, I might learn from his different experiences."

"O'Grady's in that platoon. Do you think it wise?"

"We don't get to choose who we work with, Sir. It's conceivable I might need to give orders to O'Grady when we're in Persia. Best to find out if that's going to be a problem here rather than when we're there."

"It's unlikely that situation will arise. First, you need to get to know your own company before you start worrying about others."

"Very good, Sir. Might I say, Sir, Lady Dalkeith's maid looked very handsome with those earrings. Almost looked like real emerald. Amazing what can be done with ingenuity and craft, turning a sow's ear into a silk purse."

"Can't say that I noticed, but I'll pass your compliment on."

*****

Nurse Charrington found it hard to concentrate. Rifleman O'Grady had said that he loved her. She'd answered lightly, without committing herself. Ever since she'd started nursing, she'd turned away both suitors and those who wished for something temporary and without commitment. None had attracted her enough to sacrifice either her career or her self-respect. She accepted that no-one ever would.

That business of his saying that he knew the card hand had surprised her. She was sure there was an angle to why he was so honest about it. Then it came to her. He had talked about the conundrums it posed and then talked about how to play it as the declarer. He'd said nothing about how to defend it. The more she thought about it, the more certain she was that there was a line of defence that could have prevented him from making the contract. By being honest, he'd been able to trick a certain victory out of a possible victory. That would be so like him.

Or maybe he did have a sense of honesty about cards.

She'd made a big thing with Thomas about how she wasn't interested in a dalliance outside marriages. It had been easy to brush off others who said they were interested. She would tell them once, only repeating herself if they raised the subject again. With Thomas, she repeated herself even when he'd not raised the subject. Unfortunately, she knew the reason.

If he asked, she might well agree. That scared her. She'd become so used to being alone that anything else would feel like it was disturbing the routine. Whatever else Thomas might be, he was not one for routine.

She'd told him no dalliances and he'd not tried to change her mind. Part of her was disappointed. She'd set him the task of finding a way to remain a nurse and marrying. She didn't expect him to find a way, but his was the sort of mind that might just. If he didn't and still asked her to marry him, what would she say? He was the first man that there was any doubt about her answer.

She would have to wait and see what happened.

*****

Lieutenant Campbell needed to pace and think. Alice had told him what had happened, and he was furious. He could understand such behaviour from one of the men. They were used to rough work. He had no illusions that they wouldn't misbehave, especially if drink was involved. They knew that they would be punished for it, but they weren't saints.

Such behaviour from an officer was outrageous. They held a privileged position and that came with responsibilities. The nurses were in their care and that trust had been abused. The nurses had chosen to go into a dangerous situation to help the Regiment. They had a right to expect that the Regiment would take care of them.

The Colonel was not going to be pleased. However, he had to be told. Tracking him down wasn't easy. He was on one of his prowls, walking around and watching the men. Talking to their officers and the NCOs, keeping an eye on things.

He finally caught up with the Colonel at the front of the ship. The bows, although he always called it the front when sailors could hear. It amused them.

"Sorry to interrupt you, Sir. Something's cropped up. Can I speak with you in private? It's urgent."

"That sounds like you're about to tell me about some trouble, Alisdair. I assume you've decided that you can't deal with it without involving me."

"It concerns an officer, Sir."

"Very well. We'll borrow one of the medical offices."

Nurse Charrington had just left her office, giving them some privacy. Lieutenant Campbell explained what had happened.

"You're certain this is accurate?"

"Absolutely, Sir. No doubt about it whatsoever."

"Why hasn't she come to me about it?"

"She's scared, Sir. This Lieutenant convinced her that no action would be taken. His word against hers. She thought that all that would happen is that everyone would believe his story and regard her, well, regard her badly, Sir."

"Do we know who this Lieutenant is?"

"She doesn't know his name, Sir. I intend to find out, Sir."

"This shall be handled properly, Alasdair. No private retribution, do you understand?"

"I understand, Sir. Sir, she's scared."

"All the more reason to show her that she has the support of the Regiment and not just individuals in the Regiment. I'll speak with her as soon as possible."

*****

She could mop up the floor and walls and clear away the condensation, but it just kept coming back. It wasn't so bad during the warmth of the day, but it was a pain at night when the metal walls were cold.

There had to be a way to stop the water condensing in the first place. She'd have to ask Peter. He knew about things like that. Meanwhile, she had to make sure there was cotton taped around the walls in a long line near the bottom so that the condensation was soaked up before it went onto the ground.

Next was checking all the clothes. Lay them out on the beds to air them and make sure they didn't crease. Lady Dalkeith would check for thoroughness. That meant checking every piece of clothing.

That was when she found the earrings in her bag. They weren't hers. She'd not put them in the bag. That meant that someone had put them there.

This must be some sort of test by Lady Dalkeith, to see whether she could be trusted. That was the sort of thing she'd heard that some servants got caught out by. Some mistresses planted evidence which they could then later find and use to bully maids. She'd heard some gentlemen did that and used it to blackmail a maid, but Colonel Dalkeith would never do that. Mind you, while Lady Dalkeith bullied, she never looked for an excuse to bully.

But if it wasn't Colonel or Lady Dalkeith, who could it be? Still, it was obvious what she had to do. Trying to sneak the earrings back would make her look guilty of something.

"Ma'am," she started.

"Now, Joy. You need to start thinking how you will run a household of servants. When we get to Persia, you will be the head servant of the Colonel's household. That's a big responsibility, especially for someone of your age."

"Until I'm married, Ma'am. Then I'll have my own house to run."

"We shall see. Once we've left Cape Town, I'll be giving lessons on how to treat Indian and Persian servants."

"Yes, Ma'am. Ma'am, I found these earrings of yours in my bag. I didn't put them there."

"That's very odd. Early on in your employment, if I wasn't sure about your character, I might have tested you. The Colonel wouldn't do such a thing. Have you been entertaining Corporal Barry in here, Joy?"

"Certainly not, Ma'am. I hadn't thought, that is, I don't think that would be appropriate. I'm certain you wouldn't have approved."

"That's curious. It's a strange thief who would sneak in and rearrange rather than remove. Do you have any enemies?"

"No, Ma'am. The wives don't talk to me much. I don't think they like me much, but I don't think they're enemies."

"It's understandable. You're not a wife of one of the men. They think you're taking a place that could have been filled by one of those who failed to win a place. That will end when you get married."

There it was again. Lady Dalkeith usually seemed like she was wanting the marriage to be delayed, putting obstacles and objections in the way. But occasionally she spoke as though the marriage wasn't that far away. "All the more reason for Frank to be promoted to Sergeant."

"When he is ready and able to do the job, and when there is a vacancy. But that's a digression. Why on earth would anyone do this? We may not be able to work out why straight away, but we can determine the who. I want you to start wearing these earrings, Joy. We'll see who reacts to your wearing them."

*****

He hated to inflict this on Alice, but he needed a Lieutenant he could trust. That meant he needed to find out quickly whether the one he had in mind was responsible for the attack. Lieutenant Hawkins was the platoon commander of Grant and Miller. They spoke well of him, and he couldn't imagine John being responsible for this, so he asked him to join them in the medical office.

Alice flinched a little when John first appeared, but relaxed when she saw who it was, or more specifically, who it wasn't.

"Grant, Miller, escort Nurse Ward to see the Colonel in the aft port medical office. I'll join you when I've had a quick word with Lieutenant Hawkins. Is that all right with you, John? Sorry for usurping your position. You'll be safe with Grant and Miller, Nurse Ward."

"Why do I have to see the Colonel?" Nurse Ward asked.

"It's going to be hard, I know, but we have to make sure this doesn't happen again to anyone else. I'll be with you."

"Promise me you'll be with me."

"I promise." When Alice had gone with the two lance-corporals, Lieutenant Campbell shut the door. "We've got a problem, John." He explained what had happened.

"You seem to have everything in hand. What's the problem?"

"Other targets. Until he's dealt with, he's a threat to the other nurses. Possibly the other women as well, although they're less on their own and would be harder targets."

"And?"

"I was hoping your platoon could provide round-the-clock guard. A couple of riflemen nearby. They're constantly buzzing around, so it could be done with discretion."

"Why my platoon? I've 32 riflemen. Four nurses, that's 8 per nurse. Two riflemen at a time is one in four. That's a heavy workload. Why not spread it around?"

"What would a rifleman do if his officer told him to stand aside? You can be trusted, and your people will keep them safe if someone else tells them to stand aside. Something my former Colonel told me. The men in a troop, or a platoon, take after their officer."

"Consider it done. This has unsettled you Alasdair, I gather."

"Naturally. We're supposed to protect people, not take advantage. It's a pretty grim example to set the men."

*****

Lieutenant Furley-Smith had dutifully talked to his sergeant about the men in the platoon, announcing that he intended to hold a kit inspection. It would impress the Colonel and show that he was trying. Good cover.

As he checked the kit, he felt uncomfortable, as though he had forgotten something. The more he went on, the more he was sure that things were not quite right.

"Sometimes you'll get an uneasy feeling in the field. That's when you need to keep a careful eye out." That's what he'd been told. He was certainly getting that feeling. That meant that he needed to think about creating a smoke screen.

"Sergeant, I rather think the men need some activity. Easy to get out of condition on a luxury cruise."

The sergeant agreed, cautiously.

"Good. You will gather equipment to make a gym. Eight squads, so each squad will make a piece of gymnastic equipment, giving us a reasonable size gym. Obviously, you will acquire the equipment honestly and without disrupting the smooth running of the ship. Tomorrow, each squad will create their gymnastic equipment. There will be a prize for the best piece of equipment created. Then you'll use the equipment to keep fit. When you're used to it, we'll challenge other platoons to a contest. I expect you to win."

The sergeant kept a blank face, but he seemed almost approving.

Lieutenant Furley-Smith carried on. "Sergeant Harris will be keeping an eye on you. He will advise you, in his inimitable style, should you transgress the bounds of behaviour. You shall operate honestly and without disrupting the running of the ship."

Furley-Smith turned to the Sergeant. "It will keep them busy, Sergeant. Just make sure they don't get out of hand."

More importantly, Lieutenant Furley-Smith thought, it meant that there would be a lot of men rushing around and causing a distraction. He had arranged his smokescreen.

*****

She had been scared when she spoke to the Colonel. Windy and Peter and Lieutenant Campbell had been there, which made her feel a bit safer, but it was difficult to tell the Colonel what had happened. She broke down when she had to say she didn't know which Lieutenant it was, that she didn't know his name, and that she'd be terrified of having to point him out.

"Lance-Corporal Grant, find Rifleman Callaghan and bring him here straight away."

While Peter went on his mission, Alice looked down at her feet. "I suppose you'll be sending me back to England when we reach Cape Town."

"Why would we do that?" Colonel Dalkeith was puzzled.

"He said that it would be my word against his, that he was an officer and a gentleman of the Regiment and that I was an outsider and no-one would believe me when he told his story. He said that if I told anyone, he'd make sure I was thrown off the ship for disrupting the Regiment."

"Did he? I think he's forgotten who commands this Regiment. Let me put your mind at rest on that matter, Nurse Ward. You're with the Regiment. You are part of the Regiment. You will be a part of the Regiment for as long as you want to be. We'd no more throw you out because of this than we'd throw out a rifleman who'd been wounded in action. Lieutenant Campbell will have the task of personally making sure that you're safe and have everything you need. Any concerns, any troubles, go to him. Understood, Lieutenant Campbell?"

Lieutenant Campbell agreed. "Very much, Sir. I'll make it my personal responsibility to see Nurse Ward is looked after."

Rifleman Callaghan arrived, looking worried.

"You're not in trouble, Callaghan. I gather you sketch portraits."

"Yes, Sir," he said warily.

"I want you to sketch a few now. Some of the Lieutenants. Can you do them from memory?"

"I guess, Sir."

"No guessing. Yes, or no?"

"Yes, Sir, but they won't be much good."

"Sketch Lieutenants Baker, Furley-Smith, Lewis, and Sale. Were any other Lieutenants not at the bridge, Lieutenant Campbell?"

"Just Lieutenant Hawkins and myself, Sir. Sir, it's possible someone might have left during the play."

"I know. Process of elimination. Those four sketches, Callaghan. Quick as you can."

*****

It was an unusual time for a roll call. They'd already had one today. They knew better than to discuss this oddity in the ranks, especially while Sergeant Taylor was standing right there. Thomas watched as Frank started drumming his fingers along the side of his trousers. Index finger for dot, second finger for dash.

Dash dot. Dash dash dash. Dot dot. Dash dot dot. Dot. Dot dash.

"*No idea*". Very helpful. Certainly not as helpful as it was when they had been playing bridge.

Lieutenant Hawkins was coming, so they'd find out soon. He looked annoyed and grim.

"When we're training our Persian volunteers, we'll be in reserve. We'll be doing a lot of guard duty while the other companies are off playing. Luckily, we can practise guarding here. The nurses have agreed that we can guard them in their medical offices. Two riflemen will be on duty just outside each office at all times. The nurses have work to do. Some of it will be private, so you will remain outside, unless you are called in. The objective of this exercise is to see how good you are at protecting the nurses from anyone who might wish them harm. In Persia, assassination and murder of important people is a fact of life, so we must be prepared. Sergeant Taylor will give you a roster of duty times. Questions? O'Grady?"

"Will there be an attack?"

"It's possible. There wouldn't be much point in the exercise if I told you. A lot of guard duty is standing around with nothing to do. You still have to remain alert just in case. Your job is to protect the nurses while letting them do their job."

"Who's likely to be the attacker, Sir?"

"Not a lot of point to the exercise if I told you, now is there? It might be a rifleman, an NCO, a crewman or officer from the ship, or one of our officers. Should someone attack a nurse, you are to restrain them and send for me. Now, assassins in Persia can be clever. I've heard that on one occasion, they dressed up as officers, told the guards that they were relived and could go. We follow the duty roster. Either myself or Sergeant Taylor will tell you when you have been relieved. If someone else tries to tell you that you are relieved, or to absent your post, you will not obey that because these orders take precedence."

"What if it's the Colonel, Sir?"

"One of you will detain *anyone* trying to order you from your post, or who attacks your charge, while the other fetches me or Sergeant Taylor."

"How long will the exercise last for, Sir?"

"Until I tell you it's over."

*****

The Colonel had sent for him. Since the Colonel seemed to value how useful one was to the Regiment, he would be prepared to use his snippet. He'd rather wanted to keep it for when they got nearer Persia but, if need be, he could use it now.

He saw the nurse leaving the office, with Alasdair and those two lance-corporals he'd been working with. She had clearly got upset and complained. Silly girl. Still, probably best if he kept his head down after he'd sorted out this misunderstanding.

The Colonel looked grim. The girl had got her story in first. Not a big problem, but next time he'll have to remember to make sure the true story got told first. If he'd boasted about it in the Officers' Mess, then people would know what had actually happened.

Colonel Dalkeith frowned. "I expect you know why I want to speak with you."

"Actually, Sir, I don't. I've been getting to know my men. I've set them a task I think you might approve of, building a gymnasium to allow everyone to keep fit."

"One of the nurses has made a serious allegation against you."

"If I'm honest, Sir, I haven't had much in the way of dealings with the nurses. Not much time. What sort of allegation?"

"That you violated her. I take this seriously."

"That's nonsense, Sir, with all due respect. I did spend time with one of the nurses, the fair-haired one. But violated her? Permission to speak frankly, Sir."

"I expect my officers to always speak frankly."

"The nurse in question has made it clear that she hopes to ensnare an officer in marriage. She tried to ensnare me. While I allowed her to seduce me, I made it clear that my duty wouldn't permit me to marry."

"That's your story, is it?"

"Absolutely, Sir. Quite frankly, I'm hurt that my word is being questioned. I am an officer and a gentleman. This nurse is clearly a little gold-digger who's not above histrionics to get what she wants."

"I'm not familiar with the term gold-digger, but I have my doubts as to its applicability here. I think I understand the situation. I'll be discussing the matter with Major Marshall and Captain Filleul. You'll be informed as to the outcome of that discussion."

"Sir, if it involves a punishment for me, I can advise you that I shall request a court martial. This is my reputation and my career we're talking about."

"A court martial?"

"Yes, Sir. With officiating officers not of this Regiment, Sir. Which can't happen until we reach Cape Town, more likely Persia."

"You're sounding like a lawyer. I'll inform you of my decision in due course. In the meantime, stay away from the nurses. That's an order. Dismissed."

Time to play his card. "Sir, with regard to the situation in Persia, I've been doing a bit of studying. My godfather works in the FO. Some of the political reports are disturbing. I can present a summary in due course, but the gist is that there is talk that elements of the Persian Army are unhappy with Qajar and may well move to replace him. There's talk of a German-sponsored alternative as well."

Colonel Dalkeith pulled himself together, to consider this. "Why didn't you mention this earlier?"

"Because I'm uncertain about the details and how reliable the information is, Sir. Politicals are notoriously unreliable."

"Get a summary to me by tomorrow. Stay away from the nurses. I'll inform you of my decision regarding your future tomorrow."

Lieutenant Furley-Smith left and when he had done so, Colonel Dalkeith swore. Dealing with this properly was going to be messy.

*****

Windy and Peter told Frank and Thomas. Frank told Sergeant Taylor, while Thomas told Reginald Wagstaff and Jimmy Callaghan. Jimmy told Thomas about the sketches he'd done for the Colonel. Thomas told Frank and Windy and Peter.

Soon, the whole platoon knew. Frank and Thomas went to each pair in the platoon to explain things.

"It something Nurse Ward wish keep secret, so it kept secret. We keep nurses safe, like sisters."

"Frank and I have a scheme to help with forward protection," said Thomas. "We'll clear it with Sergeant Taylor and Lieutenant Hawkins."

Windy and Peter took control of the guarding of Nurse Ward, mainly because they were going to do it anyway. Thomas wanted to guard Emily and he took great pains to make sure Frank instructed the guards thoroughly.

They went to see Sergeant Taylor, who took them to Lieutenant Hawkins.

"This not practice, Sir. Is real problem," said Frank.

"Corporal, I expect everyone to act as though it's the real thing. An exercise that everyone treats as just an exercise is no use."

"Rifleman O'Grady have idea, Sir."

"Go ahead, O'Grady."

"We know that Lieutenant Furley-Smith was responsible for the attack on Nurse Ward, Sir."

"What logic have you used to come up with that? I know he upset you over his comment about Nurse Charrington, but that's a serious allegation you're making about an event that no-one has said took place."

"Lance-Corporals Grant and Miller have been with Nurse Ward. An attack took place. Lieutenant Campbell took them off of working on the screw guns to look after Nurse Ward. He wouldn't do that for no reason, Sir. If it was a rifleman or NCO responsible, punishment would have been meted out by now. Rifleman Callaghan was asked to do sketches of four Lieutenants. Of those four, we know that three were with their men at the time in question, Sir. Only Lieutenant Furley-Smith was unaccounted for. Lieutenant Furley-Smith was called to see the Colonel, Sir, urgently. His comments about Nurse Charrington were, well, it didn't suggest he gives a great deal of consideration to what a Nurse thinks. If she'd been Lady Charrington, he'd have never spoken like that."

"There's not an ounce of evidence in that."

"Frank, that is Corporal Barry and I were thinking about guard duty. It's all very well having a guard close in, but that means you only get to act at the last minute. If you can start the guard from further out, you've more time to act. If you identify the threat, you can keep an eye on it rather than on the target. Well, as well as the target. You can't leave the target uncovered just in case there's another threat. We thought if we kept an eye on Lieutenant Furley-Smith, he'd have less chance of doing damage."

"Haven't you forgotten something, O'Grady?"

"I don't think so. I mean, maybe, but I think I got everything important."

"Three letter word, begins with S. Said by Riflemen when talking to an officer."

"Sorry, Sir."

"As for your idea, Corporal Barry, what do you think?"

"If we wrong, we waste our time, but no harm done, Sir. If we right, we cover threat early on. Riflemen scout out enemy positions, take up forward positions, Sir."

"I know Lieutenant Furley-Smith will appreciate your keenness. It's an interesting idea. While your observations are conjecture and speculation without any evidence, I feel it's a worthwhile test of your theory. Obviously, the test won't work if he knows you're watching him, so I can hardly ask him beforehand. He'll understand. I'll explain afterwards. Furthermore, for the purposes of this test, he is to be regarded as a potential enemy agent. You are to ignore any orders he might give you. If he insists, refer him to me. However, you will treat him with the respect that is due to an officer. Carry on."

When Thomas and Frank left, Lieutenant Hawkins turned to Sergeant Taylor. "What are we going to do with O'Grady? Brilliant idea, but he's not NCO material."

"Yes, Sir. If we made him Corporal, he'd need his own sergeant to keep him in line."

*****

It was a pity that she didn't have much work to do. It would keep her busy and help take her mind off things. She made tea and took some to Windy and Peter, who were outside. They pretended they just happened to be there, but they weren't very good liars. She could tell that they were keeping an eye on her.

It was sweet, and she did feel safer with them around. Windy was sensitive and seemed to understand her. She liked him and she wished they'd met differently. He was always so polite, and he had kind eyes.

If it had been him rather than the Lieutenant, well, he'd have not needed to use force. Maybe Windy could learn to accept what had been done to her.

*****

Lieutenant Furley-Smith made his observations. Two riflemen standing by the medical office, obviously on guard duty. The Colonel warning him to stay clear of the nurses. It rather looked like he'd sidestepped a problem.

Let them protect the nurses. The greater the protection and attention, the better. "The benefit the attacking force has is that they get to choose the time and precise point of attack." That was one of the lessons he had learned.

If one target was heavily protected, he could shift to a less well protected target. All he needed to do was stay out of trouble until Cape Town, when Colonel Dalkeith would get his orders.

It was a pity O'Grady's nurse was not accessible as a target for the time being. He watched as Lady Dalkeith's maid went on an errand.

*****

"Damn and blast the man," said Colonel Dalkeith. "He's as guilty as sin. If he pushes it to a court martial, it will take forever, and it'll sound different. Anyone trying the case will know he's got influence. Any officer stuck out in Cape Town will be desperate to get posted back home and will want to curry favour with him, and they're not going to believe a nurse."

"It's unfortunate," said Lady Dalkeith. "I presume he doesn't intend to resign his commission."

"I doubt it. I can and will make his life hell while he's in the Regiment, but I can't kick him out without a court martial. If he doesn't resign, I'm stuck with him. What's more, I'm fairly sure he's got some unpleasantness cooking. This is no way to prepare for a deployment, the Regiment fighting amongst itself. Mistrust, suspicion, it's a recipe for trouble."

"It is inconvenient. It would be a relief if the problem simply went away."

"I'm not having that poor girl leant on to agree to his lies for convenience. She's put herself into danger to help us. She deserves better."

Lady Dalkeith put her writing down. "Joy, it's time for you to teach writing and reading to your soldiers. You can teach them wherever they happen to be." Once Joy had left, Lady Dalkeith looked steadily at her husband. "How long have we been married? I would have thought you would have understood me better by now. Even if the girl was, as you put it, leant on, that would not remove the problem that has arisen. You've got to consider the impact on the other officers. There could easily be a split."

"A split?"

"There's not a mark on the girl. How many will assume she didn't put up much of a struggle. How many will believe the word of a brother officer over that of a silly little girl? How many will wonder what all the fuss is over? Perhaps you should have been thinking about dealing with the problems that are going to arise. Is Lieutenant Furley-Smith a good officer?"

"Not especially. Bags of self-confidence, good with other officers, but he doesn't like the men. He's here to get his two years in a regiment before moving on to staff work. About the nurse?"

"Can you imagine Joy simply submitting? She'd struggle, there would be marks and that would be evidence that it wasn't simply remorse after the event. I think she's telling the truth, but she's done herself no favours by such spineless behaviour."

"Spineless? She's chosen to come into danger to do her job. That's not spineless."

The argument continued.

*****

Alice moved her chair so that it was a bit closer to Windy. He seemed to understand her. He had nice eyes and he was so kind and gentle. She held on to the cup when she handed him a cup of tea for a fraction, so that his hand touched hers. She didn't flinch because he was gentle and kind.

Maybe Windy wouldn't mind too much about what had happened. He'd be gentle with her. He'd understand her nerves and being with him might wipe out the bad memories.

He was too much of a gentleman to take advantage of her while she was weak. Maybe he would if she appeared strong.

Maybe she could persuade him to take advantage of her.

"Lemonade while we're working, tea while we're talking," Windy said to her. "You're spoiling us."

"It's the least I can do for you."

*****

Something that Rifleman Wagstaff said bothered Joy. He'd said that sinners never stop at just one sin. She'd heard what had happened to Nurse Ward.

If she was going to be the wife of a sergeant, she had to be worthy. Ever since that day in the basement, she'd carried Frank's knife.

When she got back to the cabin, Lady Dalkeith and the Colonel seemed to have resolved their argument. She breathed a sigh of relief. It would have been so awkward if they hadn't.

Then she shook her head in dismay. She was sure she'd made the beds. It was part of the routine. Make the beds while Lady Dalkeith was having breakfast. She was certain she had, but she hadn't. If Lady Dalkeith noticed that she'd been slacking, she would speak sharply to her.

How could she correct that without Lady Dalkeith noticing? Maybe if she put something on the bed, she'd hide the fact that it was unmade. She could deal with it when Lady Dalkeith went out.

"Joy, the bed needs making."

"Yes, Ma'am. Sorry, Ma'am."

"Don't apologise. Just make the bed."

*****

Colonel Dalkeith spent an hour looking through regulations. He finally found what he was looking for. Hopefully it would prevent future misunderstandings about the status of the nurses. He was fairly sure that Furley-Smith wouldn't have taken advantage of a girl from a higher station.

Dallied, maybe, but not forced.

Something niggled away at the back of his mind. In the Officers' Mess, Furley-Smith had said something about stealing O'Grady's girl again. It was that word again.

When had he stolen his girl before? O'Grady hadn't had time to get a girl since he joined the Regiment, not until Nurse Charrington. That meant that it had to have been from before O'Grady joined.

O'Grady and Nurse Charrington. His decision about the nurses would complicate that. He'd have to keep an eye on things. The first hint of disrespect from O'Grady and he'd discover just how unpleasant field punishments are.

It's a bit of a shame he couldn't administer a field punishment on Furley-Smith. It was well-deserved, but officers and gentlemen were above that.

So where had Furley-Smith stolen O'Grady's girl? If not in the Regiment, then before. If before, they had to have been moving in similar circles. That suggested that O'Grady was a gentleman ranker. Not only that, a gentleman of good breeding. That would explain a lot about O'Grady's tongue and a lot about O'Grady himself. For an untrained ranker, he knew a lot about how to steward, at the Officers' Mess. If he were a gentleman, he'd be familiar from the other side.

That begged the question as to why he joined as a ranker. Money or trouble were the usual reasons. There were no indications of money issues. Although, come to think of it, he was firm about playing bridge and not poker. He'd said that poker was only worth playing if money was at stake. Some sort of gambling trouble, either getting into debt or getting caught cheating. If it had been cheating, he wouldn't have been able to resist taking the win in that last hand. He was honest about that. So, it was gambling debts.

Not that it made any difference. O'Grady was a ranker in the Regiment. That was how he would be treated.

Stealing a girl and gambling debts. Wasn't there a scandal some time ago? How an officer had run up gambling debts he couldn't pay and had to come to an arrangement over that. Wasn't there a girl involved in that incident? It would have been a while ago, long before O'Grady and Furley-Smith were around.

Honestly, his mind went off in digressions these days. It was a good job that this would be his last stint with the Regiment. Time to let someone else take over the Regiment.

*****

The nurses were being guarded. It was time to keep his head down. It was astonishing that the Colonel had taken that nurse's word above his. It was even more astonishing that the Colonel cared about the sensibility of a mere nurse.

The nurses were too hard a target at the moment. Guard duty would get tiresome after a while, so best leave that for a while. The Colonel's maid was the girl of that Italian Corporal, who would take revenge. That made a direct approach against the maid too risky. However, that strange little man at Wimbledon had spoken about the indirect approach. Don't go against the strong points, but strike at the weaker supports and isolate the strong points to weaken them.

He had to remember what the objective was. That man had been clear about that. The indirect approach was all about drawing the enemy away from the point of interest. You always had to remember what the point of interest was. In this case, he wanted to do his time in a regiment so that he could move on to the staff and start to put his ideas into practise. ADC to Major-General Younghusband would be a good first step.

He'd rather blotted his copybook with the Colonel, but that could be recovered.

Damage O'Grady. That was a secondary objective. O'Grady had caused him embarrassment. Without his interference, he would have been able to seduce Nurse Charrington. If he'd done that, he probably wouldn't have been tempted into seducing that other nurse.

And a regular tumble, of course. It's unhealthy for a man to go without a tumble for long. It relieves the stress. Too long without a tumble gave him a headache.

The Colonel worried about the men. That was his Achille's Heel. The way to get back into his good books was to be good with the men. He didn't need to be with them for long; once they were in Persia, he'd have detached duties, which would be perfect. Then it struck him, the perfect course of action. The Colonel worried about the men, and the men worried about their wives. Take care of the wives, and you win the hearts of the men. None of the wives were worth a roll in the hay; broad shoulders, arms like a navvy, hips like a battleship. Probably just as well. Avoiding temptation there was probably a good thing just at the moment. But looking after them would demonstrate that he cared about the men. He'd be able to charm the wives into telling him secrets about the girls who were worth his attention. What's more, by behaving himself with the wives, he'd muddy the waters about that misunderstanding with the nurse and gain the respect of the Colonel.

*****

Lieutenant Campbell joined them for tea. "Alice, Colonel Dalkeith has asked the officers and nurses to meet in the Officers' Mess. He's got some sort of announcement."

Nurse Ward looked down at the deck. "One of the other nurses will tell me what it was about later. I'd prefer to stay here and just do my job. *He* would be there."

"That's why you have to go. If you let him drive you away from places, then he's won. If you recover from these wounds, then you've won."

"I'm scared."

"That's only to be expected. I'll be with you."

"It doesn't matter about me."

"Alice, are you going to make me put my head in your lap, look up at you with devoted, big brown eyes and let you tickle me beneath my chin until you agree to go?"

"You wouldn't," she said, uncertainly, a trace of a smile threatening to appear. "Your eyes are blue, for a start."

He knelt beside her chair.

"Alasdair. People are *watching*. They'll think you're mad. All right, but you've got to stay with me."

As the two left, Windy and Peter looked at each other. "Put my head in your lap, look up with devoted, big brown eyes, and let you tickle me beneath my chin?" said Windy in disbelief.

Peter scowled. "Officers," he said. "If it was one of us who'd done what that Lieutenant did, there would be hell to pay. But because he's an officer, different rules apply. It's what I mean about things not being fair. Don't tell me him getting away with it is justice."

*****

It was crowded with all the officers and the nurses in the Officers' Mess. Lieutenant Furley-Smith saw the nurse come in with Lieutenant Campbell. He considered making a comment about leftovers but decided against it. That didn't fit in with his objectives.

Colonel Dalkeith and Major Marshall were the last to arrive, the Major holding a clipboard and looking attentive.

"My apologies for disturbing your work, ladies," the Colonel said. He was using his Important Briefing voice and the officers paid closer attention. "Ladies, gentlemen, I've been looking through Army Regulations. It appears I owe the nurses an apology. According to regulations, civilian medical staff attached to a regiment on extended detached duty shall be regarded as having an honorary rank commensurate with their medical status. The purpose of that is to give them the necessary authority in issuing orders specifically relating to medical matters. Because it is an honorary rank, it is not in the chain of command in anything save medical matters, but they do have the rights, responsibilities, and privileges associated with that rank. It enables everyone to know exactly what the lines of authority are regarding medical treatment.

"I looked through Regulations to determine what the appropriate rank should be. It's quite complicated and I'm not qualified to determine levels of medical skill and competence. I have decided that the nurse with the longest period of service is the senior nurse. I'll discuss details with the nurses at their convenience. For the time being and until further notice, Nurse Charrington is the senior nurse, Nurse Ward the deputy senior nurse, and Nurses Stewart and Plummer on the staff.

"Determining the appropriate rank was not easy. Regulations are not consistent. I shall be urgently requesting clarification as soon as we reach Persia. It appears, as best Major Marshall and I have been able to determine, that the most senior Medical Officer serving with a Brigade or Regional Command would be a Captain of greater than three years seniority. Since the Regiment is self-contained and will be the only unit of the British Army for several hundred miles, it would seem to qualify as a regional command. Their deputy would have an honorary rank of Captain of less than three years seniority, and senior medical staff would be Lieutenants."

"A question, Colonel," asked Major Marshall. "Aren't these regulations intended for doctors and not nurses?"

"That might be the intention. That's something that requires clarification. However, Regulations state Medical Personnel. I'm not going to presume to overturn Regulations without clear authority. Congratulations, Captains and Lieutenants."

"I assume, therefore," Major Marshall asked, "that these ladies are, to all intents and purposes, Officers and Gentlemen, with all the rights, duties, and privileges that apply."

"Thank you, Major. I couldn't have put it better myself."

Major Marshall checked his clipboard. "Colonel, when does this date from?"

"Good question, Major. Very good question. Obviously, the rank starts from the moment they took up their duties, which will be the moment they stepped aboard this ship. My apologies, ladies, for not realising this earlier. And thank you, Major, for some very perceptive questions."

Colonel Dalkeith rose and left the Officers' Mess. Lieutenant Furley-Smith nodded. That had been close. If that change had been made earlier, the silly nurse would have been complaining about what might be called an assault on a superior officer. Any court martial would have taken a serious view of that. The nurses were now off-limits on board the ship.

*****

The four managed to meet while the nurses and officers were having their meeting. Windy asked about the railway novels.

"A lot of them are about someone getting ravished, usually against their will. That doesn't seem, well, just at the moment, I don't think they're a good idea to have around. Nurse Ward was well, she's very upset."

"They're making money," said Thomas. "You're the one who needs the money for your family. I guess it's your call."

"Let's not take the chance."

"If a Rifleman did it, they'd be hanged for it," said Peter. "Let's not give the officers chance to do that."

"Need find priest in Cape Town. It important."

"Gentlemen, I'm glad I've found you together." Lady Dalkeith had managed to approach without them noticing. "I understand you've heard about the issue relating to Nurse Ward. I do not think that the cause of that issue has gone away. Ideally, that would be dealt with through regular channels, but there is a possibility that the regular channels may be slow-moving. The Regiment will need to be operating smoothly when it arrives in Persia. Strange things can happen in ports such as Cape Town."

"Ma'am," said Peter. He paused, considering his words carefully. "Strange things can sometimes lead to big trouble. Big trouble for officers is different to big trouble for us. They get told off. We get hanged."

"There's a long way to go before Cape Town."

*****

Nurse Charrington had fallen into a routine. She was uncomfortable being regarded as the senior nurse, although the other nurses were happy to leave the bureaucracy to her.

The sun was getting hotter, much hotter, so she had to make sure everyone was checked for heat illnesses regularly and ensure that the men wore headgear during the heat of the day. The experienced men needed no telling, but those who hadn't left England before had to be constantly reminded.

She checked supplies and made a list of things that would need purchasing in Cape Town. Perhaps it was just as well that Colonel Dalkeith had appointed her as Senior Nurse. There was a shortage in at least one item.

There was little free time, but she made sure that she put aside an hour to teach Thomas about treating wounds. She developed a habit of going to each of the other medical offices after the lesson to check on the other nurses and how their day had been. Thomas accompanied her as she walked around the ship, waiting outside the office until she had finished talking with the other nurses.

She always visited Nurse Ward last. Afterwards, she would walk with Thomas to the back of the ship and talk for a bit. They would look at the stars, which seemed brighter and shone with sparkling clarity as they went further south. She learned that he didn't get on with his father and that he'd been bored beyond measure at his home. He didn't talk about his mother.

"It was all so meaningless, pointless, and predictable," he said. "I just wanted to do something, to feel alive."

"You wanted to feel alive, so you joined the Army, where you are quite likely to be killed?"

"Well, yes. Didn't someone once say that you never feel alive until you've come close to death?"

"If they did, they're wrong," Emily said. "Death's not a game. It's an enemy, to be fought." Her jaw was clenched as she said it.

"It's different for you. You've got a calling. I've not had one. No-one would have missed me if I had never existed. Outside the State Schools are these boards with the names of students who have died somewhere. The schools honour them. If I had died, I would have been buried, there would be a big monument, and no-one would have stopped to look at it. Why did you want to become a nurse?"

"It's what I've always wanted to do, ever since I can remember. That or a doctor, but a doctor was out of the question."

"Why? Women can be doctors, can't they?"

Emily snorted. "If they can afford the education, the examination fees, if they can find a hospital willing to take a woman doctor, if the associations decide they are suitably moral, and any number of other things. I love nursing. But no-one would trust a woman doctor. The only way to become one is with a lot of money."

"We're going on campaign. I'm sure there'll be a vast treasure room I can find which will pay for you to become a doctor, if that's what you want."

Emily snorted. "I'm too old to start the training to be a doctor. Besides, I like being a nurse. I'm sure you'll find something else to spend your ill-gotten gains on. Perhaps there will be some Society beauty you'll sweep off her feet. Possibly a Persian princess or two."

Thomas looked at the stars for a long time. Finally, he said: "I don't think so. I've rather lost interest in mere dalliances. I've got a puzzle to solve."

*****

They'd gone back to exercising with putting the screw gun together, working on the deck near her office. She worried about Windy, who wasn't as big as Peter or Alasdair, but he flung himself into the work with enthusiasm. When they took a break, she made sure they drank and tried to have lemonade for them.

Nothing had changed, yet things were somehow different since the Colonel had said she was an officer. She couldn't explain how it had changed. The three of them still treated her much the same, but it felt somehow a little bit different.

"You can keep your gin and beer," said Lieutenant Campbell, drinking his lemonade.

"If you say so, Sir," Peter said, sounding very unconvinced.

"Not a good thing to drink alcohol during the heat of the day, is it Captain Nurse Ward."

"Now you're making fun of me."

"Not at all. Well, maybe just a little. That's what junior officers do. How do you think they're getting on with the gun?"

She felt comfortable when they were around. She didn't flinch when she touched them when handing them a cup. She was sleeping better; she didn't feel like screaming whenever anyone opened the door of the office.

She pretended that she didn't hear what some officers were saying about her, that it was just buyer's remorse. "Not a mark on her." "It's not as though it was anything they're not built to take." "Wonder what she did to egg him on." It was only a couple of officers, just a couple of voices. She wasn't even sure who it was because it was never said where she could see. No-one ever said anything when she was with Alasdair. She didn't like going without Alasdair. He always seemed to know how to make her smile.

"They'll forget about it," he said. "They're annoyed that you're more important to the Regiment than they are."

One evening, she made a decision. She asked Windy to step into her office.

"Thank you for all that you've done. It's been really kind of you. I, I think I'm a lot better. The thing is, I'm scared about how I'll be when I'm with a man. You've been kind and gentle and I know you'll be gentle with me, then I'll remember what it's like with you rather than with him."

Windy was silent for a long time, looking anxious. "I can't," he whispered.

Alice felt her heart sink. "I'm damaged goods. I understand."

"No, it's not that," Windy said. "Look, don't tell anyone, but it's, well, it's that I don't like women, not like that. Confirmed bachelor."

"Oh. I suppose Peter's a confirmed bachelor as well. I thought you two were very close." Alice understood now.

"Oh, Peter likes women. No, nothing like that. I'm just, well, not interested in women or that sort of thing."

*****

After roll call, Sergeant Taylor motioned the four to speak with him.

"I've spoken with the Navigating Officer of the ship. It's going to be an interesting day tomorrow. You four will be inducted first. Once that has happened, your duty will be to ensure that the ladies on the ship to whom it is applicable have respectable inductions."

"Induction, Sergeant?"

"Induction, Rifleman O'Grady. Tomorrow is going to be an unusual day."

"Why's that, Sergeant?"

"Because I've spoken with the Navigating Officer of the ship. Respectable induction of the ladies. Make sure of that. Find out who's a pollywog and who isn't. Especially the officers."

"What's a pollywog, Sergeant?"

"Anyone who doesn't know what a pollywog is."

*****

The wives' quarters weren't exactly luxurious. They weren't much better than the men's quarters. In some ways, they were worse.

They were right at the front of the ship, getting the worst of the movement. The noise of the bows coming crashing back down into the water during heavy weather made conversation almost impossible.

Luckily, the sea was calm right now. Lieutenant Furley-Smith couldn't understand why the wives chose to live like this for two months just so they could be with their husbands. It was astonishing, really.

He spoke to the wives of the men in his company, asking how they were and assuring them that he was taking a keen interest in their welfare. "Self-interest," he joked. "If I look after the men, they'll look after me in the field and everyone's happy. What they're most interested in is making sure that you're all fine, so I've come to make sure that you are. It's what an officer does."

Maybe it was the situation of the ship, with so many men and so few women, but some of the wives were surprisingly handsome, much more so than he had expected. Too sturdy to be called beautiful or pretty, but definitely handsome.

He chatted with them. It was quite interesting, really. Like talking with clever monkeys. He carefully turned the talk to Lady Dalkeith's maid and was gratified to find that some of the wives resented her. "She's not married to the Regiment, yet she's here and one of us had to stay at home."

Time to twist the knife. "It's a bit of a bad show, especially the way her man was made Corporal so quickly. Still, that's the way of the world."

That caused them to be curious. He allowed them to quiz him, and he made a show of being reluctant to explain, but eventually speaking on condition of it being confidential. He explained how Lady Dalkeith had hired her in London, not to be a maid, but to satisfy the carnal desires of the Colonel. "Men retain virility for longer than women. Then her man got promoted to Corporal in double-quick time while more experienced men remain in the ranks. Still, that's the benefit of being a Colonel. I'm just a lowly Lieutenant. I can only promote men in my company."

He continued to chat and charm, eventually taking his leave.

That night one of the wives called on him in his tiny cabin. "My John can't know about it. He'd knock me about something rotten if he did. But you can promote him?"

He looked her up and down. Not exactly a Gaiety Girl, but good-looking in a solid sort of way. "I can see to it that there's an opening and recommend him for it. I can get him a promotion, but it will be up to him if he keeps it."

*****

Thomas was puzzled. The stokers were excited about tomorrow. He asked them. He even asked the Persian stokers in Persian, but no-one would explain. He worried about this, but he had so many things to sort out, he couldn't worry too much.

He had to find a priest for Frank and Joy, which would be a pretty useful wedding present; find a way of dealing with Lieutenant Furley-Smith in Cape Town without running serious risks; learn Persian; find a way for a nurse to marry and remain a nurse; find a way to get Frank promoted to Sergeant; learn how to treat wounds; deal with this whatever it was tomorrow; try to get his head around the fact that there was a huge social gulf between Emily and himself, just like there would have been had they met before he joined, only the other way round; keep an eye on Lieutenant Furley-Smith; try to keep his uniform clean while working with the stokers; work out how to dispose of the railway novels profitably; and try to persuade the officers to organise another bridge tournament.

"We'll try and make sure you don't get bored on the voyage." That's what Lieutenant Hawkins had said on their first roll call.

*****

"Relax, O'Grady, you're not in trouble, for a change," said Lieutenant Hawkins. "You are, I understand, the most devious, scheming, acquisitive rogue in the platoon, possibly in the Regiment. At the moment, that's a good thing."

"Sir," Thomas said. He wasn't sure if yes or no was correct, but you can't go far wrong by restricting yourself to Sir.

"I've got an important task for you. You will need to acquire four bear costumes by the end of today. One for each of you and your buddies."

"Bear costumes, Sir?"

"Yes, bear costumes. Big brown creatures, sleep during the winter, much like riflemen do on parade. Growl, eat honey, scare little blonde girls. Bears."

"Yes, Sir. Why bears?"

"To shave pollywogs, O'Grady. That's obvious."

"Yes, Sir. Sir, Sergeant Taylor asked me to ask people, even officers, if they were a pollywog."

"Do I look like a pollywog?"

"Don't know, Sir. Don't know what a pollywog is."

"Enjoy your ignorance while you can, O'Grady."

Thomas sighed. Now he also had to find four bear costumes today. Still, on the bright side, life wasn't boring.

*****

The ship had slowed to a crawl and Lieutenant Hawkins took roll call. Sergeant Taylor was nowhere to be seen. Neither was Windy. The platoon could just see a boat being raised out of the water and onto the ship, but they couldn't see much more than that.

"Corporal Barry, Lance-Corporal Grant, Rifleman O'Grady, front and centre," said Lieutenant Hawkins in an easy voice. "On this special day, can you say whether you are a pollywog or a shellback?"

"Are Riflemen, Sir," said Frank, cautiously. It seemed like the safest reply.

"That's the answer of a Pollywog. As a Shellback, I charge the three of you with the crime of being Pollywogs. You shall answer before the court. As will all dirty pollywogs in this platoon of criminally competent miscreants."

Thomas was about to ask a question when a blanket was thrown over his head. Thus blinded, two sailors grabbed him by the arms and frogmarched him and the others to the front of the ship. He couldn't see anything, but he could hear an excited buzz of anticipation around him. The platoon was nearby. From the sounds of complaints, all were covered with blankets.

"Lieutenant Hawkins," said the Chief Steward. "Are you a Slimy Pollywog or a Shellback."

"A Shellback, my Lord Neptune. Duly attested on the first day of August three years ago."

"A Shellback, you say. But are you a Diamond Shellback?"

Even from here, Thomas could hear Lieutenant Hawkins sigh. "No, my Lord Neptune," he said heavily.

"Then step on to the plank of judgement, to be questioned by this court." There was the sound of jeers, which eventually subsided. "Three crimes are you charged with. My assistant Davy Jones will bring forth the first charge."

Thomas could hear a rifleman speak. "Lieutenant Hawkins, the first charge against you is that you insist on wearing clothes that are green, and not the colour of the sea. Look, even now you offend with this wearing of the green. I find you guilty. How do you plead? See condemned from his own mouth. Guilty as charged. Queen Amphitrite, bring you the second charge."

Nurse Ward spoke. "I speak for the Nurses and Ladies passing through Neptune's domain. Lieutenant Hawkins. You are charged with the crime of being dry. We shall absolve you of this crime. How plead you?"

"I'll be not guilty in a few moments."

"He pleads guilty, my Lord Neptune."

"And for the third charge," said the Chief Steward, "you have been found guilty of making your men march in step and not allow them to swim like honest fish. For these and other heinous crimes, we find you guilty. You are sentenced to wear your clothes back to front for the duration of Neptune's presence on this vessel, be shaved by my trusty bears and cleansed of all cleanliness. Turn the plank and throw him to the bears."

There was a splash, followed by the sounds of a struggle.

Then the blanket was pulled from Thomas, and he blinked in the sunlight. He stood at one end of a plank, stretching half-way across a newly constructed pool of water. Many of the older members of the Regiment and some of the ship's crew, were gathered around the pool. Three men dressed in bear costumes, made gestures at him from the pool beneath the plank. On the other side of the pool were the Chief Steward, dressed in a kilt, holding a trident and wearing a crown of what looked like seaweed. On his left sat a Rifleman that Thomas didn't recognise, wearing a sodden nurse's uniform, and on his right sat Nurse Ward, wearing the uniform of the RSM, which was much too large for her. She held an oversized sceptre of wood.

The bears pulled him forward on the plank, while sailors and riflemen jeered and threw potato peel at him.

"Rifleman Flaptongue," said the Chief Steward. "Are you a Pollywog or a Shellback?"

"You're not going to believe me if I say Diamond Shellback, are you?"

"Correct. The first charge against you is that you are too tall. How do you plead?"

"My Lord Neptune, if I was any shorter, my feet wouldn't reach the ground."

"Guilty. Davy Jones?"

"Rifleman Too-Tall, you are charged with the crime of dishonesty. Answer dishonestly, guilty or not guilty?"

"Hang on, if I answer dishonestly, I'll be saying I'm guilty of dishonesty, and you'll convict me. If I answer honestly … I can't win."

"Correct and guilty. Queen Amphitrite?"

"Rifleman Dryskin. You are charged with the crime of talking. How do you plead?" Nurse Ward giggled a little as she spoke.

"N" began Thomas.

"Guilty," everyone roared.

Lord Neptune glowered. "Rifleman O'Ctopus. You are guilty of the crime of talking, and we sentence you to silence for the rest of the day. No word shall pass your lips and you shall be thrown to the bears. May Cod have mercy on your carp."

The plank twisted beneath his feet; he fell into the pool, where the bears pounced on him, pushing his head under the water for a moment. One held him, while a second smothered his head in some sort of soapy foam, while the third took a large stick and scraped the foam off. Windy was the Barber Bear, looking both apologetic and relieved.

"Nurse Ward wanted someone she trusted nearby, so Sergeant Taylor told me to be here," he said with a shrug. "When we're done, get into the costume. You're a bear for the day, which means you get to growl and throw potato peel at anyone breaking the rules, which means whenever you feel like it."

Frank was subjected to a truth drink, which was a hot sauce mixed in with Sicilian whisky, which seemed to displease him. He was accused of the crime of being Sicilian and sentenced to be French for the day, and of the crime of being a Corporal, for which the punishment was changing ranks every hour.

Peter was found guilty of the crime of having a moustache and was punished with having to shave it off. Lord Neptune graciously showed some leniency and allowed him to keep half of it. "And the

Diamond Shellback can decide whether to keep the left or the right side."

After the platoon, the ladies were brought before the Court. Lieutenant Hawkins, his uniform on back to front, was close at hand. "Remember, make sure it's respectful," he hissed.

"Nurse Charrington, you are charged with being in charge and you shall be punished for this crime."

"Excuse me, don't I get to speak in my defence?"

"Certainly not. A defence is admission of guilt. It proves you've something to defend. You are sentenced to swap places with Colonel Dalkeith. While Lord Neptune rules, you shall be the Colonel and the Colonel will be the Senior Nurse. Colonel, you are improperly dressed. Throw the new Colonel to the bears."

The plank was twisted, causing Emily to fall into the pool. Thomas tried to hurry to help her up but hurrying in a pool while wearing a bear costume is not easy. Emily must have misinterpreted his intention to help, because she struggled and hit him a blow that dazed him for a moment. He realised once more that nursing develops physical strength.

He was dazed for a moment and didn't notice Joy taking the plank, but he became aware of Frank stiffening and getting angry. Then he heard that among the jocular jeers were a group of the wives jeering "Whore", sounding as though they meant it. Joy looked white and uncertain at this, shocked and not really understanding the vehemence.

Lord Neptune seemed shocked but carried on. He charged Joy with the crime of being young and pretty and condemned her to dress and look like an ancient hag for the day. When she tumbled into the pool, she was nearly in tears.

"Frank, I'll find out what this is about," said Peter. "You're too angry, Thomas is too tricksy, and Windy's got to look after his latest lady-love."

Emily raised an eyebrow at this. "His latest lady-love?"

"Beryl and Iris in London, now Alice. He's being a perfect gentleman, but she's fallen for him."

The Court of Lord Neptune continued, with Lieutenant Campbell being tried towards the end. Alice saw him and whispered something to the Lord Neptune, who ordered the bears to lower a boat and have it manned. "Sorry, beared. Queen Amphitrite will pass judgement on this Pollywog."

"Lieutenant Screw-Gun, you are charged with being keen and enthusiastic, like an overgrown puppy. A Sea Dog, in fact. This shall be your punishment." She stood up, walked to the side of the ship, held up her sceptre, and threw it overboard. "Fetch!"

*****

Take advantage of openings. Everyone was at the ceremony, giving him time and opportunity to act unobserved. He'd started to separate the maid from her Corporal. He was the sort to react violently if there was talk about his girl and another man. Convince him that the Colonel was involved, and he'd attack the Colonel. There would be no way the Colonel could side-step that.

Right now, it was just gossip. He had to provide evidence that the Corporal would believe. With everyone at the ceremony, he had been able to slip away unnoticed and make his way to the Colonel's cabin. Those railway novels that had been circulating had given him the idea. All he needed to do was write an amorous love letter from the Colonel to the maid and make sure that it got into the Corporal's hands in a way that he would believe it.

Writing it with the Colonel's pen on the Colonel's paper would be a start. He didn't know the maid's name, but that wasn't important.

"My dearest one. Though the world sees you as the servant, when I am in the embrace of your young arms, I am your devoted servant. I am beside myself when I look upon your naked body and touch your soft skin. My passion grows to meet yours, until we meet that sweet moment of unified bliss. In your arms I feel young and virile. The pleasures we have known fill me constantly with desire and I am unable to contain my passions when I am with you."

He wondered briefly if he was overdoing it, but then realised that subtlety would be wasted on the Corporal. He blotted the letter and put it in his pocket. All that remained was delivering it.

He rose and left.

*****

"Ma'am," Nurse Charrington said to Lady Dalkeith. "If I am to be Colonel, I need to dress the part. May I borrow one of the Colonel's uniforms?"

"I shall accompany you to the cabin. First I need to speak with Joy and Corporal Barry." She summoned them with her finger. "I will mention it to you two, because you will doubtless think of it during the day. I don't want any misunderstandings. It is true that I said that you, Joy, were too young to marry, and that you, Corporal, needed to be a Sergeant. Today, it appears that Joy will be old, and Corporal Barry will be, at times, a Sergeant. You might have considered that, for today, you were married, with all that entailed, as the conditions had been fulfilled. I will not argue with the logic and for today, that holds. It is a pretend old age, and a pretend Sergeant, so it will be a pretend marriage, with pretend kisses and pretend marital relations. Pretend, not reality. I trust you both understand."

"Yes, Ma'am. Even just pretending will be wonderful."

Lady Dalkeith and Nurse Charrington left for the cabin.

Joy waited until they were out of earshot. "Frank, we can pretend we misunderstood."

They started to kiss, then Frank reluctantly drew back. "It make rest of voyage impossible. We wait, do this properly."

*****

Lieutenant Campbell scrambled out of the boat, dripping wet, and headed towards Alice. She put her hands to her mouth, trying not to laugh.

"Of course," he said, "wet dogs usually shake themselves dry next to their owner. My hair's a bit short, but we'll just have to make do." He leant his head forward and shook it from side to side. As he did so, he whispered: "I'm so proud of you, Alice."

She smiled, then she felt sad. If only she'd known Alasdair before, before …

*****

"Bear O'Grady," said Colonel Dalkeith, "it appears I am Senior Nurse for the day. You'll have to instruct me in my duties. Without speaking, which will be a torment for you."

*****

Nurse Charrington looked through the Colonel's uniforms. Lady Dalkeith checked behind the door, bent down and picked up a small piece of paper. "Curious."

"Ma'am?"

"Earlier in the trip, we had an uninvited visitor. Since then, I've been placing a slip of paper on the top of the door when the cabin is left empty. Someone's been in the cabin recently, probably while everyone was at the induction ceremony." Lady Dalkeith looked at the new Colonel. "Tsk. Lady impersonators never look the part. The jacket has to be tight. Loose like that just looks sloppy. Pull it tight, and the chest is clearly defined, telling the world of the attempted deception."

"Stop fussing, Madam," Emily said, trying to get the Colonel's growl.

"The tone's right, but you don't stand like a man. It never works, which is probably just as well."

*****

Peter spoke with the wives. It took a while and he did digress into talking about social injustice, but they eventually they told him of the talk about Joy and the Colonel, which was how Frank got his promotion.

"Who said this?"

"Everyone knows."

"Then everyone's wrong. Firstly, the Colonel loves this Regiment. Whatever he got up to, he'd not do anything that might harm it. Promoting someone who wasn't ready would harm the Regiment. Secondly, I know Lady Dalkeith. Trust me, she wouldn't stand for it. She'd geld anyone who cheated on her. Can you *really* see her letting anyone take her place?"

"Why's the maid here?"

"Because she and Frank fought back-to-back to stop a white slave ring. She'd been kidnapped, he went to rescue her, and they had to fight their way out. Lady Dalkeith's got a soft spot for those who fight for the Regiment."

"Gammon," said one of the women disbelievingly.

"Believe me or not. Can you tell me why a pretty girl like her only has eyes for an ugly bleeder like Frank? Who started this story? Another thing. Officers confirm promotions to Corporal with the Sergeant. You know that. A Colonel getting involved a Corporal? That's daft. Company commander and sergeant do that."

"Lieutenants don't have a say?" one of the wives asked, glowering.

"Only if they're a company commander. Lieutenant Hawkins, for example. Not if they're not. Might advise, but they don't make the decision."

*****

The different departments of the ship upheld the honour of the Court of Lord Neptune by requiring forfeits from outsiders to their little realms. The Bears patrolled the passageways ensuring that disorder was maintained. There was a moment of concern when the rum ration for the sailors went missing. Lord Neptune decreed that it be returned. It was, along with a tin of jam.

Thomas didn't understand the significance of the jam and wanted to ask. He wrote a note and the Colonel looked at it. The Colonel wrote a reply, rather than telling him. Thomas noticed that the Colonel had difficulty writing neatly, with his hand shaking slightly as he wrote. The writing was legible, but not easy to read.

"Putting jam in rum is a serious punishment."

*****

Chaos. That was the only word Thomas could think of. The experienced hands seemed to be policing behaviour to prevent overstepping lines that only they understood, but it was still chaos.

"Rifleman Bear, I need to ask you about your intentions with regard to Nurse Charrington. In the absence of her father, I am, as the Colonel of the Regiment, *in loco parentis*." Colonel Dalkeith watched Thomas carefully.

Thomas pointed to his mouth.

"That won't fly, Rifleman. We're not under observation. We're in the medical office, and I require an answer."

"I don't know, Sir. It's more to the point what her intentions are towards me. The problem is that a nurse can't marry and continue working as a nurse. Hospital regulations don't allow it."

"Humph. Is that the problem? I'm surprised you haven't solved it, devious fellow like you." One thing Colonel Dalkeith noticed was that Thomas hadn't blinked at the casual use of a Latin phrase.

*****

As the sun sank below the horizon, Lord Neptune announced that he would return to his realm at the end of the day and that "misrule and chaos would return when the mortal leaders returned to their positions."

Thomas and Emily watched the stars and talked about the day. Their hands touched on the railing. Thomas didn't know when he'd been this happy before.

"It's been a day where the rules don't apply," Emily said.

"Sore heads in the morning. I saw the bottles at the Officers' Mess."

"Thomas," Emily said, taking a strangely nervous gulp. "My rule about no dalliance outside of marriage. The rules don't apply today."

Thomas stared at the stars. His heart skipped a beat, and he looked at Emily's slightly nervous expression, freckles just visible. He sighed. "They'll apply tomorrow. I want you forever, not just for a day."

Silence hung in the air, then the moment passed. "You're right. It would change everything between us and there would be no way to go back." Emily withdrew her hand.

Thomas wondered if he'd just made the biggest mistake of his life.

*****

It was time to take stock. He'd become obsessed with O'Grady and his little group. To be fair, O'Grady had been the cause of embarrassment and needed to be taken down a peg or two. And O'Grady seemed to think he was somehow entitled to make time with girls above his station.

That was the problem. The man was a damn Socialist, or at least a seducer of women above his station. Seducing down was perfectly acceptable, the natural order of things. Seducing upwards, no. O'Grady had to be taught to know his place.

His father always said that he had a grasshopper mind. Always flitting from one thing to another. Fine when you had to juggle many things, but not so useful with just one task. It was, however, fine for staff work; you organise a plan and get someone to carry it out. That way you can juggle many plans. It's just like running a household. The people decide what needs to be done, the senior servants organise the doing of it, and the lower servants do the physical labour.

There he was again, playing the grasshopper. He had to get onto the staff. His talents were wasted in a regiment. The trouble was, he'd got those two girls on his mind, the nurse and the maid. He'd not settle down until he'd got them out of his system.

The nurse was going to be a tough target. The maid should be easy once he could isolate her.

He sighed and wished that this weren't so complicated. It would be much easier if he had servants to do the leg work. Once they reached Cape Town, he'd be under the authority of the British Envoy, as he would have been seconded to him. That meant the Colonel wouldn't have direct authority over him. That meant that provided he was reasonably discreet, he could take his fun as he found it. He just needed to be patient until Cape Town.

There was a knock at the door, which opened before he had done more than stand up. An angry woman came in, shouting at him, about how he had lied to her.

"Naturally I lied. I lied to you so that I could lie with you." He was rather pleased with that. "What can do about it? Say you had relations with me so that your John would get a promotion? Your John would knock you about something rotten and the Colonel would put you off the ship at Cape Town."

"You're evil," she hissed, taking a step forward, eyes flashing and fist clenched.

"Don't be silly. It would only be evil if you were a lady." He had a thought. "If you don't want me to tell John, you'll shut the door and come here. He can knock you about, but if he lays a finger on me, I'll make sure he's hanged. And that's something that I can do. If you want to keep him alive, you'll do what I say."

*****

Alice jerked herself awake. The sun had risen and she was feeling stiff and cold. She'd been talking with Alasdair on the deck, looking at the moon and stars. She must have fallen asleep. She was in a chair, a green jacket covering her, a slight crust of salt around her eyes. She looked to her left and Alasdair was sitting in the seat next to her, just where he had been while they were talking. He was looking at her and smiling.

"What must you be thinking of me?" she asked.

"That you were tired, that you needed to sleep, and you slept."

"What will people think?"

"After the way some people were drinking last night, they'll mainly be wondering if they're alive or not."

Alice paused and looked at the sea flowing past the ship. "You've been very kind to me."

"Sheep dogs are very loyal."

"But why? I don't understand. I'm just a nurse."

Alasdair shrugged. "I'm just a fourth son, not important. Alan's the first. He gets the estate. Alexander is the second. He's in Society, making contacts, looking after the interests of the estate in London, and is around in case anything happens to Alan. Albert is the third and went into the Church to look after the family in the hereafter. I'm the fourth son and just a confounded nuisance, which is good because it means I can do what I like."

"But you're spending all your time with me. Wouldn't they mind?"

"Mind? Why should they mind? They wouldn't care. I could take an actress home and provided she didn't start interfering with any of the important sons, she'd be welcome. You're sensible, you've got a responsible job, and your name starts properly. They'd love you. Not suitable for the others, but the fourth son's not important."

"You're bitter."

"Not at all. It's just the way things are. I'm always welcome home and they want me to do well. And you'll love the place. Miles and miles of undiscovered thickets and moors and hills, history built into the bones of the land. Our people are happy because that's what the land does. People walk on the hills, they take their troubles, find a secret place, and tell their troubles to the land. The land takes these troubles and covers them with a decent layer of green. It nurtures them and changes them. Years later, you go to the spot and find that your troubles have been turned into a thicket of bushes, or a stone circle, or a new tree, or a badger's sett. The land takes the troubles and turns them into a mystery, a secret place. And you see this, and you remember the trouble, but it's no longer a trouble, but a secret that you've learned from, and it makes you a wiser person."

Alice listened, wondering how much of that he actually believed. "Do you have any secret places there?"

"Of course. When we return, I'll show you them. If you want to see them."

"Aren't they personal? Won't your family mind?"

"Mind? Why should they mind?"

"Won't they think I'm just after money or status?"

Alasdair snorted. "My family's rich. I'm not. The family has status. I'm just a fourth son." He leaned across and ruffled her hair with his hand. "Come on, you've work to do. Your hair's a mess."

"It is now, you villain."

*****

Thomas and the others met before roll call and sat around, eating apples that Peter had found. They'd given up trying to work out why they had roll call, because where else would they be than on the ship?

"The thing is, we've got lots of things piling up," said Thomas. "Dealing with Lieutenant Furley-Smith, we need a priest from Cape Town, Frank needs to make it to Sergeant, we need to find a way to lose the railway novels, and other stuff." He wondered if he should tell the others about the married nurse problem but decided that this was something he had to solve himself.

"Regiment not have priest. Maybe Colonel think it good idea get one." Frank thought. "It long time since I have Confession."

"We'll need two priests, then. One to hear your Confession, and one for the Regiment. Yours will be busy from Cape Town to Persia," said Peter, ducking as Frank threw an apple core at him.

"I'll talk to Hawk about it," said Thomas. "He'll believe I've got a lot to confess. Furley-Smith. We've got to somehow get rid of him without getting into trouble."

"Not good on ship. Everyone knows someone did it. In Cape Town, he just go missing, could be anyone in Cape Town."

"I've got an idea," said Windy. "It depends on what's in Cape Town. If I'm right, we'll be able to talk our way out of things if we get caught. I'll ask about what ships are in Cape Town."

"If we can't sell the novels in Cape Town, well, we'll be able to sell them there. I'll start getting them back from people and hang on to them." Then Thomas chuckled.

"What so funny?" Frank asked.

"Us. We're generalising."

The others didn't get the joke.

*****

After roll call, Sergeant Taylor took Frank to one side. "Platoon 2 of A Company has gathered the bits of a gym, but they've had no instructions what to do with them now that they've gathered them. I've spoken with Captain Filleul. He's agreed that you can organise them into turning the stuff into a gym."

"Yes, Sergeant. Why me, Sergeant?"

"NCO rumour. Grapevine. Learn to use it."

"Not understand, Sergeant."

Sergeant Taylor sighed. "You've a long way to go yet, lad. Sergeant Erskine suspects that there may be a Lieutenant's slot opening up in A Company. If that happens, Sergeant Major Quinn will probably take on that role, because they've been thinking he's officer material for a while. If *that* happens, Sergeant Erskine will do the job of Sergeant Major of A Company, so there'll be an opening for someone to do the job as Sergeant of his platoon, only Corporal Bailey ain't ever going to be more than a Corporal. I suggested you to organise them, give you the chance to make yourself known to Captain Filleul and Quinn. If you do a good job, they might ask for you to do the job when it comes free. It would be as a Corporal, because we ain't going to give stripes until we're sure, but it would be a big step for you. And I ain't going to charge you a penny."

"But that mean being Sergeant of platoon in A Company, not here."

"Lad, even if that slot don't work out, it'll be good experience come what may. Do the job in front of you; and do it good."

"Thank you, Sergeant."

*****

Stress release always gave him ideas. He was losing interest in this girl, but he'd thought of a way to use her to his advantage.

"You're caught in a trap, aren't you, girl. All your own fault for trying to get something for nothing. Still, I'm not cruel. I've got a deal for you. I've a hankering for younger meat. You'll do, but if I get younger meat, I'll not be interested in you anymore. Here's your choice. Bring the Colonel's maid here tonight to take your place and I'll be done with you. Or you can be noble and protect her. If you do that, you'll come here to relieve my stresses, or I'll tell your John I've what I've done. He won't be able to touch me, because if he does, he'll swing for it, but he will be able to knock you about something bad. Then the Colonel will ask why, and you'll end up being put off the ship at Cape Town."

"You're evil."

"So I've been told. Your choice. Either you're here tonight, or she is. Now, get out and do whatever you have to do."

Once she'd gone, he wondered whether he would actually release her. Something to ponder.

*****

"Sir," said Thomas. "Does the Regiment have a priest? It's been a long time since I've given Confession."

"I thought you always claimed you weren't Irish, O'Grady," said Lieutenant Hawkins.

"I'm not Irish. No-one ever asked me if I was Catholic, Sir."

"I see. We'd need two priests. One for the Regiment and one just for you, because you'll need a full-time priest. I'm fairly confident you could sin during Confession."

Thomas dutifully smiled at the Lieutenant's joke.

"But no, O'Grady, we don't have a priest. There's a seminary in Cape Town where you'll be able to give Confession. I doubt there are many Catholics in South Africa."

"And a priest for the Regiment, Sir?"

"I'll ask the Colonel. It could be tight. Funds for support are already stretched with the nurses."

*****

Joy couldn't think of any alternative. She was getting desperate, but hopefully Nurse Charrington could help her.

"Umm, could you give me something?" she asked, waiting for Nurse Charrington to answer. She got worried when Nurse Charrington didn't answer. "Please?"

"Something for what?"

Joy took a deep breath. "Well, you know Frank and I have been seeing each other."

"Really? I can't say I'd noticed."

"We haven't been keeping it secret. I thought you knew."

"I was being sarcastic. You've been seeing Frank. You're worried about getting pregnant?"

"No. Yes. Well, no. Not like that. Not pregnant, but kind of like that, only not like that, if you see what I mean."

"I haven't got a clue what you're talking about."

"Well, it's that I've been seeing Frank." Joy stopped again. This was awkward and Nurse Charrington wasn't making it any easier. "I've been seeing Frank, you see, only I haven't, although I have, but not properly. I wondered if you had something." There. She'd said it.

"You've been seeing Frank, only you haven't been, and you want something that will help with that. I've got some eye drops."

"No, not seeing. *Seeing.*"

"What do you want this something to do, apart from making you coherent?"

"OK. Frank and I have been seeing each other only we've not been doing anything not even kissing and I *really* want to only he says that we have to wait until it's the proper time only that's going to be *ages* away and I won't be able to wait that long and I really want to do more than just think and imagine about things and I want him to take me in his arms and kiss me and caress me and draw me to him and increasing my passion until we lose ourselves in each other. He won't until Lady Dalkeith says it's OK and that won't be for ages, and I really want to and I'm *so* ready and want him so very much. I thought that maybe you had something that would kind of make Frank lose control because I know he wants to and if he loses a bit of control then we'll kiss and caress and transport each other and then everything would be better, you see." Joy panted a little at the end.

"No. Quite aside from the medical ethics, or whether it would even be possible, it would be a bad thing. Afterwards, he'd feel that he had been tricked, he would resent it, he'd feel that he'd been wronged; he would be right."

"But I love him. I want him."

"If you love him, you'll think about what he wants, not what you want. Look, he loves you. Honour is very important to him and he's not going to do anything that he thinks would dishonour you. When he's ready, well, you'll know when he's ready."

*****

"Damn fingers," muttered Colonel Dalkeith. The joints ached as he finished writing his daily log. In a way it was a good thing. It forced him to be brief, succinct, and to the point. His log entries and reports had improved markedly since the signs of arthritis had grown to the point where he couldn't pretend it was nothing.

"You're trying to sort out a problem," said Lady Dalkeith.

"You know me too well, Maeve. Care to guess what?"

"Lieutenant Furley-Smith. You've been snarling about him ever since he threatened you. The Regiment is going on deployment. As far as I can tell, it's not going to be a simple one. What the Regiment can't afford is internal squabbling. Either he changes his attitude, or the Regiment goes along with his schemes, or you take him to Persia and face a disaster, or he leaves the Regiment."

"That's the problem. What's the solution?"

"The Regiment is not going to change. We're not going along with his schemes. He either shapes up or he leaves the Regiment. He's got five, maybe six weeks. Once we reach Persia, the ship will be turning around and heading back, so we can lose him if he hasn't shaped up by then."

"You've got some scheme going. Something that you don't want me to know about. Usual rules apply. If I find out about it, I have to take the appropriate actions. I've no reason to keep a special eye on your four disreputables, but I can't turn a blind eye if I do see anything untoward. Actions have consequences. O'Grady. He's serious about Nurse Charrington. She's serious about him. He's a Rifleman. She the equivalent of an officer. What happened to Nurse Ward means that I have to keep a special eye on the nurses. That means that if those two go one inch further, they are going to have to be very discreet. Very discreet indeed. I'm sure that message will get passed on."

"You're not worried about the difference in social status? She's a nurse and an officer. He's just a Rifleman. Not even an NCO."

"Not in the slightest. Provided he stays clear of gambling and learns to control his damned tongue, they're not a bad match. He gets wherever he's going in a twisty, devious corkscrew. She takes the shortest route between two points. I can see them having some spectacular rows, but his heart is in the right place."

"Joy and Corporal Barry," Lady Dalkeith asked.

"Nothing to do with me. He's got potential and she's a godsend. Just remember, she's what, 16? I remember what you were like at that age. I've seen the look in her eye. They'll not last until Persia."

"I've seen his determination for both of them to stay honourable. They'll be tempted, but they'll hold out till then."

"Ten pounds says you're wrong. No cheating."

*****

Joy listened to the woman, without really understanding what she was saying. It was one of the wives, but she wasn't really making any sense.

"Why were the wives so horrid about me?" Joy asked.

"What? Because you're not a wife. There's a wife back home who couldn't come because you're here."

"I'm going to be a wife just as soon as Lady Dalkeith lets me."

"One of the officers needs to speak to you about your Frank."

Joy started to worry. That sounded like trouble. The woman seemed unhappy, which made Joy even more worried.

*****

Frank looked at the large pile of equipment the platoon had gathered to build gym equipment with. The riflemen in the platoon were sullen and uncooperative.

"Why the hell are you taking over? Why isn't the Lieutenant dealing with it? It was his idea," was the gist of their grumbles.

"I told to get you to finish what started. It simple. We stay here until it finished. You work slow, we here long time. You work hard, you finish early. We stay until you finished. If you here till Cape Town, that fine by me."

"What we going to make, Corporal?"

Frank stared at the pile of equipment. None of it made much sense, just whatever could be found and acquired, mainly rope and wood. He wasn't entirely sure what equipment would be in a gym. There wasn't a huge amount of space, just an area of the upper and lower deck.

"We make obstacle course. Ropes and slides to get between decks."

"Kind of like snakes and ladders, Corporal?"

Why not, thought Frank. "That exactly right. Use spare ropes as entanglements in crawl-ways, they the snakes."

The men started work. Frank split them into three groups, one working on the upper deck obstacles, one on the lower deck, and one making the routes between the two. "We see whether upper or lower deck get best obstacles."

*****

Lady Dalkeith came to see Nurse Charrington. "I don't have any medical issues. I've come to discuss Rifleman O'Grady. He is a Rifleman. You are a Nurse, and the Colonel has decreed that you have the honorary rank of Captain. That is a considerable gulf. I trust that you will bear that in mind."

"There is no problem. I'm responsible for the medical well-being of around 900 people. That keeps me rather busy."

"True, but you don't have a relationship with them. That makes Rifleman O'Grady different."

Nurse Charrington stood up and glared. "What my relationships are or aren't is none of your business, Lady Dalkeith."

"The smooth running of the Regiment very much is my business. It's going to be hard enough when we get to Persia. The men will be in the field, going into danger. The women will be worried. The Regiment takes care of the wives and that means ensuring clear lines."

"Then I can put your mind at rest, although it really is none of your business. I am not a wife, nor a close approximation of one, nor am I going to be. I am a nurse. That rules out marriage and I have no intention of having relations outside of marriage. Your concern is unnecessary, as well as being an intrusion." She didn't mention how close she'd come to breaking her rule when they crossed into the Southern Hemisphere.

"Are you telling me that there is no relationship, because I understand he is smitten with you."

"What he believes is a matter for him and his conscience. I have been crystal clear that I will not give up nursing and that I will not dally. Therefore, there can be nothing between us. Now, if you will excuse me, I do have 900 people to look after and no time to waste on such meaningless and insulting conversations."

After Lady Dalkeith left, Nurse Charrington fumed. That infernal, interfering busybody. Her private dealings were private and of no concern to outsiders.

*****

The wife led Joy towards the officers' cabins. Joy thought that the wife seemed nervous, or unhappy.

"If you marry Corporal Barry, who will look after you if he gets killed in action?"

Joy stopped in her tracks. "If he gets killed?"

"It happens. It's an active deployment. They'll go into action. Some will die. Who's his buddy?"

"Thomas. I don't understand."

"It's quite simple. The Regiment looks after its own. It does not throw widows out onto the scrapheap. If a husband gets killed, someone, usually the buddy, marries the widow. If my John gets killed, I'll marry Andrew, his buddy. We do not cast widows out of the Regiment. So, if your Frank gets killed?"

"Well, Thomas is his buddy, but he's sweet on Nurse Charrington."

"Doesn't matter. If Frank gets killed, he'll marry you. That's the way it's done. If Frank will still marry you, that is."

"What do you mean?" Something was wrong here. She put her hand on the hilt of the knife for reassurance. The door to the cabin opened and the wife pushed her inside.

"I'm sorry," the woman said.

*****

"Alasdair, you seem to be spending a lot of time in the company of Nurse Ward. You may think I'm an interfering old busybody, but I would like to know what your intentions are."

"Intentions, Lady Dalkeith? I wasn't aware I thought things through enough to have intentions."

"Don't play the jackass, Lieutenant Campbell. It's all very well to fool around in the Officers' Mess, but in six weeks, the lives of your men will depend on your decisions. You know precisely what

I mean. Nurse Ward has been through a traumatic event. I will not have her taken advantage of."

"We're friends, Ma'am. Trust me when I say that no-one will take advantage of her while I draw breath. She's sweet on Lance-Corporal Miller, but I don't know if that's reciprocated."

"Lance-Corporal Miller? What is it with nurses and the rank and file of the Regiment? Keep an eye on them. Since she seems to trust you, I'm placing her well-being on this ship in your care."

*****

"What's going on?" Joy asked. "If you touch me, you'll be sorry," she said, seeing who the Lieutenant in the room was. She was shaking and suddenly very scared, but Frank would expect her to be strong.

"That's really up to you." The Lieutenant glanced at the woman. "You can wait outside. I don't want an audience and I'm sure the girl doesn't." The woman stepped outside and shut the door. Joy edged against the wall.

"Don't you touch me," she said. She wanted her voice to be strong and threatening, but it sounded weak to her.

"Or what? Your precious Corporal will protect you? Believe it or not, I'm giving you the chance to protect him." He put a piece of paper on the table. "It's a copy of a letter in my possession. I'm giving you a choice. You can walk out of here, unmolested. If you do that, I'll show your Corporal this letter at Roll Call tomorrow. He'll go insane and storm off to deal with the man in question, who happens to be the Colonel. Not even the Colonel can overlook a Corporal attacking him in public. Your Corporal will be hanged by the neck until he is dead, dead, dead. Or you can spend time with me, and no-one will see this letter."

Joy glanced at the letter. "This is all lies. What are you doing?"

"It's just blackmail. Save your Corporal or save your honour, such as it is. It's your choice."

She couldn't think. It was lies, but would Frank believe her or the words? If she told Frank, he'd go berserk and kill this Lieutenant and he'd be killed for it. If she went along with this and Frank found out, he'd go berserk. If, there were just so many ifs.

"I'm not evil," he said. "I'll even let you think about your options. You've got until Roll Call. Of course, the longer I wait, the more anxious I'll be and that means the less gentle with you I'll be. If you tell him, he'll end up getting dead. If you tell any of his friends, O'Grady and the others, they'll do something stupid that'll put them on the end of a rope. It's rather brilliant if I say so myself."

"I can't think."

"It's not your mind I'm interested in. It's not as though servants think. But I'm in a good mood. Take a walk, clear your head. You'll see you've got no option if you care for that ugly Corporal. By roll call, you'll realise that it's more fun with me than with that ugly brute."

Joy rushed out. She didn't know what to think.

*****

Nurse Charrington was still fuming when Thomas arrived for his lesson. He held his hands up in surrender and she took a deep breath.

"That woman. How *dare* she question my competence." Emily was still shaking with anger.

Thomas knew that she had to be talking about Lady Dalkeith. "She's …"

"If you try and defend her, Thomas O'Grady, we are going to have words."

"This is one of those situations where I can't win. Whatever I say, I'll be wrong. If I'm honest and try to see her point of view, I'm wrong because I'm taking her side; if I don't, I'm being a twisty rogue. Frank's got a bunch of men building some sort of gym thing. I think you might need to stock up on bandages in Cape Town, because we're going to need them."

"Now you're just trying to change the subject."

"Yes. Of course I am," Thomas said. "What did Lady Dalkeith say?"

"That I should tread carefully with you because of the gulf between our status. As though I would be unprofessional."

"She was just asking you to be gentle with my innocence."

Nurse Charrington stared at Thomas for a moment, then shook her head, trying to hide a smile. "Innocent? Thomas O'Grady, when was the last time you could be called innocent?" She paused. "What are we going to do?"

"You are going to do your job, look after us all, and you'll trust me to sort out the other stuff. Medical training. Chloroform. Does it knock someone out?"

"Only in hospitals or bad fiction. It takes about five minutes to have an effect. You're scheming. What are you scheming?"

"How would you get bad fiction chloroform?"

"You're not answering the question."

"Correct. I'm devious and twisty. It doesn't do my innocence any good if I go blurting out what my scheme is, because then people will know I'm just making it up as I go along."

"Diethyl ether and alcohol. No, you can't have any, because it's a devious scheme you've got."

"You don't know what the scheme is."

"That's how I know that it's devious."

*****

Was it wrong to do something very wrong to protect someone you loved? The Lieutenant was right that Frank would go berserk if he read that letter.

She couldn't tell Frank. She couldn't tell Thomas. They'd attack the Lieutenant and that would be a hanging offence.

She'd looked for Lady Dalkeith, but she wasn't around, she was off doing something somewhere.

She wept. She didn't know what to do. Maybe she could stab him while he was busy with her, but then she'd be in big trouble. She'd say self-defence and everyone would say she was a maid and he was a gentleman, which meant she was guilty.

"Row with your Corporal?" the Colonel asked. How had he crept up so silently?

"No, Sir, just things."

"Let me tell you something about rows. Young people usually don't realise. If you're having a proper row, you're listening to the other person. You're disagreeing with them, but you're listening to them. If you're doing it right, you're showing that you care about their opinion. Much better than silence and ignoring them."

Joy wondered if she should tell the Colonel. He'd always been good and kind. "Sir, I'm in trouble."

"Easiest ten pounds I've ever won," Colonel Dalkeith muttered. Joy didn't understand. He carried on. "What's the trouble?"

"Sir, it's," Joy said, trying to hold back the tears. Trying and failing.

"Corporal Barry?" he asked.

"Yes, Sir. No, Sir. Not really, sort of." She glanced up. "Not that, Sir. Frank's, we've been good."

"What's the trouble?"

"It's a letter, but it's all a lie. No-one will believe it and he said if I don't, then he'll" Her voice trailed away. There was one person who would know for absolute certainty that the letter was a lie.

"You're going to have to explain more clearly."

"Yes, Sir." She was more confident, but the Colonel was going to be upset about what she had to say about an officer. "One of the Lieutenants showed me a letter he said was one you wrote to me, about how you've been, been, making time with me, Sir. He said he'd show it to Frank, Corporal Barry, who'd hit you, and you'd have to hang Frank. He said he'd do that unless I went with him, so I could save my Frank or I could save my honour, but he'd have one or the other, Sir."

"You did the right thing, coming with this news to me straight away."

"But, Sir,"

"Have you spoken with anyone else yet? Was it recent? Am I the first person you've spoken to? You brought me this news as soon as it was possible. That is an end to the matter. I've got the grounds. I just need evidence." He turned and started walking, then paused. "Come on. We're going to put a stop to this."

"How, Sir?"

"Good girl. None of this "I can't" nonsense. This is going to take some pluck from you, but you'll be fine. I just need to hear for myself from his own lips what his scheme is. Can you do that?"

She needed to be strong for Frank. "I'll try."

"Come on, then."

"Sir, don't you need to know which officer?"

"I already know which officer. Time's wasting."

*****

She knew that the Colonel was just outside, but she was still scared and shaking like a leaf. She stepped inside and left the door open just a fraction.

"Get out. I don't want to be disturbed," the Lieutenant snarled at the wife. Then he looked Joy up and down, a smirk on his face. "I knew you'd be back quickly. You'd no other choice."

"Please, Sir, I need to read the letter again, make sure I'm doing the right thing."

"It's quite simple," Lt Furley-Smith snapped impatiently.

"Yes, Sir, if you say so, but it's a big thing you're asking of me."

"Nonsense. You'll enjoy it. I certainly will."

"Please, Sir. I need to be sure."

"The letter is on the table. Hurry up. I've got a lot of stress that I need to relieve."

Joy spoke carefully and clearly, looking at the letter. "You're saying that if I don't let you ravish me, you'll show this letter to my Frank, he'll get angry and hit the Colonel and get hanged for it? That you'll either take my honour or my Frank?"

"Don't be silly. It's not as though your honour is worth anything, but I'm letting you choose what you get to keep. Don't worry. Your kind might protest before, but they never complain after."

"No, Sir. Who would they complain to, Sir?" Joy was starting to panic, because the Lieutenant was getting to his feet and had a very bad smile on his face.

The door was flung open and the Colonel strode in. "I've heard quite enough. Lieutenant Furley-Smith, you are relieved of all duties and may consider yourself confined to quarters. Meals will be brought to you. I'll have an armed guard posted to ensure that you stay put."

For a moment, Lieutenant Furley-Smith looked around him, then glared at Joy. "You stupid little servant. This is my career you're playing with." He took a step forward but stopped when Joy drew her knife.

Joy shook. "A step closer and I'll defend myself." Her voice was unsteady, her hand was shaking, her voice uncertain, but she didn't take a step back.

"It would solve a lot of unpleasantness if you were to take that step forward," snarled the Colonel. "There will be a court martial in Cape Town."

The mention of Cape Town calmed Lieutenant Furley-Smith down. "What would I be court martialled for? I think you'll find I've done nothing against Regulations, and I know how much you believe in Regulations."

"I'm your Colonel. The word you are looking for is Sir."

"Of course," Lieutenant Furley-Smith said. He paused, then added dismissively. "Sir. I rather suspect a lot will be cleared up at Cape Town. But what breach of Regulations am I supposed to have committed? Sir. Seducing a nurse who has regrets after the event? Allowing a woman to think she can influence me with sexual favours? Misleading a maid? Not that it matters. You'll get orders in Cape Town that will render all this unnecessary. I think it a shame that you've been beguiled by this socialist nonsense of equality for all. Sir."

"Until Cape Town, you will not leave you quarters, Lieutenant Furley-Smith. That's an order. You are relieved of all duties."

*****

"He's somehow going to wriggle out from under. I can feel it." Colonel Dalkeith tried to settle down.

"One way or another, that won't happen," Lady Dalkeith replied. "You've got evidence, witnesses, and you caught him practically red-handed. It was rash of you to confront him without support."

"It wasn't rash. It was deliberate. If he'd have taken a swing at me, I'd have had him stone cold. If I'd had people with me, he wouldn't have swung."

"That's a good justification, but I know you. A young girl asked for your help. Like a young subaltern, you rushed off to do the honourable thing."

"Why should young subalterns have all the fun? If you'll excuse me, Maeve, people to see."

"I'll send them in."

First in was a dour-looking Rifleman, ill at ease, puzzled and clearly worried and the dark-haired woman from the Lieutenant's quarters.

"You're not in trouble, Rifleman Dawson. You can relax. There are going to be rumours and gossip circulating. I want you to get the true story before you get some garbled version. Lieutenant Furley-Smith has been confined to quarters, pending an investigation. That's in large part down to your courageous wife. Lieutenant Furley-Smith suggested that if she were to be unfaithful and indulge him, then he would see to it that you made Corporal. Naturally, she was outraged. Despite the threats he made against her, she spoke to me about this. Action is being taken against the Lieutenant, so do not consider doing anything private. Believe me when I say I will see to it that justice is done. You're a lucky man, Dawson. Your wife is brave and exceptionally loyal to you."

"Yes, Sir. Thank you, Sir. She vex me at times, always talking about how I should be corporal, but she's a good girl."

"You've a good record, Dawson. Solid, reliable. A bit of devil in you after too much to drink. If you can control that, maybe your wife's confidence that you have it in you to be a good corporal might be justified. It's probable that a corporal's slot will be coming up in your platoon. I'll speak with Captain Filleul and Sergeant Erskine. No promises but start thinking about it. That's all. Dismiss. Mrs Dawson, a word."

Rifleman Dawson saluted and left. Colonel Dalkeith waited until the door was shut, and then looked at Mrs Dawson. "I didn't lie. You need to make it true. There's a line between supporting and encouraging on one hand and pushing too hard on the other. All he needs is to be confident that he can trust you totally. When he goes into action, he can't afford the distraction of worrying about anything other than the job in front of him. Make it true."

"Yes, Sir. Thank you, Sir."

"Keep him off the drink. Now go away and make little riflemen, or something."

*****

Lady Dalkeith wanted to find Thomas. It was evening, so it wasn't difficult to find him. Lower deck, back of the ship, looking at stars with Nurse Charrington. So very predictable. She wondered if they realised the ship would Cross the Line again. Not a relationship, indeed. Maybe they would sort themselves out if they had a good row. However, there was a lot to do until they had reached Cape Town and left it. Other things could wait.

"My apologies for disturbing your astronavigation studies. Rifleman O'Grady, that matter we discussed for you and your comrades in Cape Town. You are to proceed with it."

Lady Dalkeith left and Nurse Charrington simmered. "She is shameless. Completely shameless. Making use of you four to do her dirty work, things that can't be done officially, because she wants them done. One day, you'll get into trouble, big trouble. You'll take the blame and she'll walk away."

"It's for the Regiment. Sometimes things need to be done that can't be done officially."

"And you love the Regiment. If you had to choose between the Regiment and me, you would choose it over me."

"Is that any different to you choosing nursing over me?"

"That's different."

"Is it?"

Nurse Charrington paused and thought. "You have a point. You have the Regiment and I have nursing. That's an end to it. Let's not argue."

*****

Colonel Dalkeith looked at his next visitor. "At ease, Corporal Barry. I wish to congratulate you. Firstly, you've taken to being a Corporal like a duck to water. You're still inexperienced and rough around the edges, but Lieutenant Hawkins and Sergeant Taylor have been fulsome in their praise of your progress.

"You might have heard rumours that you might be moved to A Company. That is not going to happen. The Persian Company, when it is formed, will need a core of people who understand each other to provide a good example. It's going to be hard enough expanding a platoon to company size without changing the NCOs around. You'll be staying with your current unit.

"That's not why I wish to speak to you. One thing that you need to work on before becoming a sergeant is control. A sergeant must always be in control, whatever the situation. You've got a problem in this area. You need to work on it. It's especially relevant right now. There's been an incident involving Joy. She's fine, and she displayed uncommon bravery and common sense and behaved throughout in an exemplary manner. You will hear things in due course about what happened in the incident. Rumour can get it wrong. This is what happened.

"An officer forged a note and tried to use that note to bring dishonour upon Joy. This is that note. Read it, then tell me truthfully what you would have done had you been given the note by someone."

Frank read it slowly, starting to glower and shake with anger. He didn't trust himself to speak.

"I thought so," said Colonel Dalkeith. "That was the intention of the writer of the note. Had you taken any action against me or another officer, I would have had no alternative and would have had to have taken stern disciplinary action against you. Thanks to the bravery of your Joy, the matter has been dealt with and the miscreant will face justice. You have my word on that.

"In the meantime, I suggest that you learn to control your temper. You might want to show your appreciation to your Joy. She kept her own honour and protected yours. You're a lucky man, Corporal Barry."

*****

Lieutenant Campbell took Windy to one side to have a word with him after training on the screw-gun. "What are your intentions with regard to Nurse Ward? She's smitten with you, but if your intentions are not honourable, we're going to have a problem."

"I don't have intentions, Sir. I've explained to Nurse Ward. No intentions, Sir."

A rifleman approached and saluted Lieutenant Campbell. "Colonel Dalkeith's compliments, Sir. He will see you in his office. Straight away at your convenience, Sir. It's what he said."

"Very well. Lance-Corporals, put the screw-gun away." Lieutenant Campbell wondered what the Colonel wanted. There was only one way to find out.

When Alasdair arrived, the Colonel got quickly to the point. "Alasdair, you seem to have settled in well. You'll hear on the grapevine quickly enough. Lieutenant Furley-Smith has been relieved of all duties and is confined to his quarters. It's all very messy, but we're getting things resolved. That leaves me with a Lieutenant's slot in A Company to fill. Captain Filleul's a steady officer. Do you want the slot? You've not been with us long, and I'm not even sure if you're technically part of us, but the slot's yours if you want it."

Lieutenant Campbell thought for a moment. "It's a handsome offer, Colonel. I'm not sure it's the best for the Regiment. I'm not familiar with A Company and I've been doing a lot of work with the screw-guns. We've pretty much got them cracked. Grant and Miller are familiar with them. If we're to make use of them, I'd need them. The Regiment's not familiar with operating with them, but the Persian Company could learn, Sir, without pre-conceptions. I think that's where I would be most use, Sir."

"Good points. 2-i-c of a company would look better on your record than supernumerary attached to a scratch company, but your logic seems sound. Good to see you thinking about the needs of the Regiment. Very good indeed. Think about it. Let me know your final answer when we leave Cape Town."

*****

They could see land in the distance. South Africa was in sight, and they would arrive at Cape Town tomorrow morning. The four sat on the deck after roll call, watching the land drift closer. The ship rolled more rather than pitched, as it had been, and the change in motion upset Peter. He kept going to the side of the ship, while the others expressed their amusement.

Peter groaned. "It's like a hangover without the fun of getting it."

The others made fun of him.

"Be nice to get some shore food in Cape Town."

"Oysters must be good here."

"They're a bit slithery for my taste. The way they just slither down and create a mess."

"Maybe they have eels."

Peter didn't appreciate their sympathy.

Thomas stretched as they watched the ship slowly get closer to land. "The stokers tell me the ship will take five days to re-coal and do a light boiler clean. Get the worst of the ash from the burners. That gives us five days."

"Hawk tell me there to be roll call every sunrise and sunset. Need permission go ashore, but ship people want us off. They say we get in way."

"I haven't been able to find out what other ships are in, but they'll take the railway novels. Easy enough."

"Do we deal with the Lieutenant early or late?" Thomas asked. "Early means we may get another shot if there's a problem. Late means that there'll be no time for the officers to track him down."

"Early," said Windy. "No-one's going to go looking for him."

"Early," said Frank. "Colonel worried something may crop up let Lieutenant wriggle out. Not give that chance to happen."

"Late," said Peter from the side. "I'm going to be dead for the next couple of days."

"Just think," Windy said cheerfully. "You'll have just enough shore time to make certain you lose your sea legs and you'll be as sick as a dog again when we leave. You'll just have got used to the movement, when we'll turn left around Africa, hit a different wave movement, and you'll start all over again."

Thomas and Frank just looked at each other and shook their heads. Buddies were close, but Windy and Peter were closer than most.

"Early," said Thomas. "We've a lot of other things to do. First thing to do is get some stuff from the medical office. We can get stuff in Cape Town to replace it, but we need it first off."

"Not Nurse Ward," said Windy. "She's been through enough without putting her at risk, because there's going to be a period when the stuff is missing before we've replaced it."

"We're not going to take it from Nurse Charrington. She's responsible for the nurses. She can't risk setting a bad example."

"You're just scared she'll blame you and you'll get into a row," said Windy.

"He scared she hit him again, like when he was bear trying to drown her," laughed Frank.

Thomas rubbed his jaw in memory. He was reasonably sure it had been an accident, but it had caught him just right. Maybe that should be it had caught him just wrong. Whichever, his jaw was still a bit sore.

"Just ask her," said Peter. "She'll be as keen to get rid of the Lieutenant as anyone. You can talk anyone into anything."

"I'm not going to lie to her."

"Don't lie, then. Just charm. Tell her that if she lets you have these things, you'll sweep her up in your arms, carry her off into your hidden castle and transport her to ecstasy."

"We're getting rid of the railway novels, remember? You're the one who wanted rid of them." Thomas was not comfortable at the direction the conversation had taken.

*****

"Lieutenant," Frank asked Lieutenant Hawkins. "Men want know when they able go ashore."

"The sailors will be unloading waste first. Have to get rid of that to make room for the new. When the waste is unloaded, shore leave may be granted. Keen to get ashore?"

"Yes, Sir. Need to give Confession. Been long time."

"Don't go sneaking off to get married. You'll need the Colonel's permission first. Get married without that and there will be trouble."

"I get to be Sergeant before we marry. Is important."

"Active deployment is where you want to be if you want rapid promotion. Just try to survive."

*****

"No," said Nurse Charrington. "Not up for discussion."

"But it's important. We're getting that Lieutenant off the ship and somewhere that he'll not trouble women again."

"I have to account for supplies. Also, using diethyl ether and alcohol has risks. If you don't know what you're doing, you could kill him. You don't know how much to use, what proportions, nothing about the use of it. While that might not be a problem for you, it's against medical ethics to kill people. And what will you say to get into his cabin in the first place?"

"We can replace supplies in Cape Town. Do you want him on the ship all the way to Persia? After what he did to Alice, and nearly did to Joy? Besides, I've just had an idea."

"Thomas O'Grady, I get worried when you use that tone of voice."

"It's quite simple," he said.

"That means that it's a twisty, devious scheme."

"You administer it. You know what you're doing, so it'll be done right. No-one will question a nurse seeing a patient. No-one will question why you've got a bodyguard, given what he's done."

"You want to include me in your devious schemes, getting me in to I don't know what trouble?"

"It's for the good of the Regiment."

"Now that is a lie. It's for Thomas O'Grady. It's because you enjoy these capers. You want to do it for its own sake."

"But it is for the good of the Regiment."

"Thomas O'Grady, I am with the Regiment, not part of the Regiment. You can't wave Regimental honour at me."

"It will protect the nurses."

"And?"

"All right, admit it, there is something exciting about it. Will you do it?" Thomas smiled as winningly as he could.

"Very well. Mind you, it is only to make sure that it is done properly and safely and to keep you out of trouble."

Thomas looked at her. He frowned and looked stern. "Emily Charrington, you were just waiting for me to ask you."

"I really do not know what you're talking about."

Thomas looked steadily at her. "That smile you're trying to keep off your face is a coincidence, then. You're struggling to keep a straight face."

She bent her head down to look at the ground and keep her face hidden as she struggled to keep her face composed. Thomas put a hand under her chin and tilted her head up to stop her hiding her face; he leaned forward and kissed her. She responded, then pulled back from him.

"No. I'm sorry. A future isn't possible. A present without a future isn't enough." She stiffened her back.

Thomas dragged his mind back, clearing the fog around his thinking. "I'll solve the puzzle." He muttered to himself.

*****

Thomas spoke with his two Persian stoker friends and arranged to borrow a coal bag and their overalls.

*****

The ship approached the docks, slowly and cautiously. "Don't want another Birkenhead," said one of the ship's officers. Thomas and Windy waited by Nurse Charrington's office. They looked at the variety of ships in the harbour.

"Hope Windy hurries. There's too many to just look at random ships and hope for the best." Thomas was getting worried.

"Here he come."

Windy walked casually across and joined them looking across the harbour. "Sparky said that there's a bunch of ships there. The one we want is the *Terra Nova*. Due to leave later today. Norwegian, with an American captain. It's perfect."

"Which one is it?"

"No idea. It'll have a harpoon gun on the front. I've got to get back on guard now."

Nurse Charrington came out. "Are you ready, gentlemen?" They headed towards Lieutenant Furley-Smith's cabin, pausing by the guards at the door. Peter acknowledged the nurse with a salute.

"Lieutenant's not to receive visitors, Ma'am. Colonel's orders."

"I'm not a visitor. I'm here to give the Lieutenant a sleeping draught. The Colonel doesn't want him trying to get clear in the confusion of docking. I've got an escort to keep me safe." Nurse Charrington put as much clarity into her voice as possible in case anyone was listening.

"Very good, Ma'am."

Frank entered, followed by Nurse Charrington, and then Thomas, who shut the door behind him.

Lieutenant Furley-Smith stood up. "We must be near Cape Town. Finally. Things will soon be different. You two can take your hands off of me. We'll soon see the colour of your ribs."

Thomas and Frank had each grabbed an arm and held him. He didn't struggle a great deal at first, mainly out of astonishment. When the astonishment had passed, he didn't move much because Frank held a knife to his throat.

"You try hurt my girl. I just Corporal, I happy to slit your throat. Stay still, else my knife slip."

"What's going on?" Lieutenant Furley-Smith was suddenly worried.

Nurse Charrington poured clear liquid onto a cloth, carefully checking the amount. "You'll have three, maybe four hours." She then held the cloth to the Lieutenant's face. He struggled, but Thomas and Frank held him firmly. His struggles weakened. Eventually his head slumped forward as the diethyl ether and alcohol took effect.

"He'll have a bit of a headache when he wakes up," Nurse Charrington said.

"Is that a side effect of the fumes?" Thomas asked.

"Hold him still. Thank you." She tipped the Lieutenant's head upwards, held it steady with her left hand, then very carefully, punched him on the jaw with her right hand. "Yes, it'll probably be the effect of the fumes," she said. "It's not appropriate for people to hurt my nurses."

As soon as the Lieutenant had gone under, Thomas and Windy started to take out the stoker overalls. Then they paused.

"Um, would you mind turning your back?" Thomas asked.

"For goodness' sake, I'm a nurse. Oh, very well. Honestly. I'll sort out the bag."

Thomas and Frank finished getting changed. There was a gentle bump throughout the ship as it pulled up alongside the dock.

"Your uniforms are in the other bag, so be careful what you use for the deal. Don't accidental trade away your uniforms." Nurse Charrington checked Frank and Thomas to see that they looked convincing as stokers.

Thomas put the Lieutenant into the coal sack and slung him across his shoulder. Frank went out first, carrying the other bag. "All clear," he hissed, then the others followed. They needn't have bothered about being careful. Everyone was looking at the docks hoping to be allowed to go ashore. A gangplank had already been erected and sailors were carrying waste off of the ship. Frank and Thomas joined the line.

"What you got?" a sailor asked him.

"Coal ash. Don't tell anyone, but it's good for growing roses. You can flog it to the locals." Thomas shifted his grip slightly on the coal sack and staggered down the gangplank.

Nurse Charrington talked briefly with Windy and Peter, who were still on guard. "He'll probably be quiet for a few hours. Tell your reliefs that, please. If he does make any disturbance, I'm to be called immediately." She made sure that her voice carried.

Thomas and Frank reached the bottom of the gang plank and moved into the crowd of people on the docks.

"*Terra Nova*," muttered Frank. "How we find it?"

"Easy," replied Thomas. "Excuse me," he asked the nearest dock worker. "We've a load for the *Terra Nova*. Where is it?"

"*Drie dokke saam.*" The dock worker hurried off.

"Well, that can't be right. It's about to go to sea, so it won't be in dry dock. Let's try in the direction he pointed and ask someone further along."

They passed a couple of ships, then saw a whaling ship with the name *Terra Nova* on the back. They clambered aboard and found the captain of the ship, a tall, lean man with a weather-beaten face and cold, blue eyes.

"What the hell do you want? We're getting ready to go to sea."

"*Terra Nova*? Off to go whaling?"

"That's right. Eighteen months down in the southern seas, feeding the factory ship. A long, hard eighteen month. Back breaking. You running from the law? You're better off in jail."

"Not us. Him." Thomas dropped the sack on the deck.

"Why should I take him?"

"Take him and we give you these books. If you're away for eighteen months, they'll help pass the time."

The captain picked up one of the books and opened it at random. "Uh-huh," he said as he read, turning the pages. "Not exactly literature, is it."

"You will, however, be eighteen months away from female companionship."

"Not unless any of the crew's got a good disguise on. OK. You got yourself a deal. What's his name?"

"George. George David Lloyd. He cheats at cards. He dishonoured my sister."

*****

Colonel Dalkeith opened the official mail. Always do that as soon as possible.

"Damn." He smashed his fist on the table.

"What is it?" Lady Dalkeith asked.

"Orders. Lieutenant Furley-Smith is to be the aide to the Persian envoy. Promoted to Captain. Appointment to date from time of ship departing London. Ridiculous post-dating. Damn."

"What's the problem?"

"That means he answers to the envoy, not to me, not to the Regiment. Damn. That means that anything he does on the ship, he answers to the envoy, not to the Regiment. Direct orders. Nothing I can do to wriggle out of it."

"You don't need to do anything before the ship leaves Cape Town. Keep him in confinement until then. You've got more urgent matters to deal with while we're in port."

"You're scheming."

"Garnet, I've been in your company ever since we sighted land. Exactly when and what have I been scheming?"

"Is that Maeve talk for: 'You don't want to know'? One of these days, I'll catch you and then I'll have to take action."

"If I recall, when one of the wives steps out of line, you ask the husband to keep her under better control. Perhaps if I am scheming, you ought to keep me under better control."

*****

Sergeant Taylor gave out mail to the platoon. He called out the name, and the soldier stepped forward to take his mail. Thomas had mentally switched off. There was no-one in England who'd write to him. No-one in England knew where he was. Come to that, there was no-one in England who knew he was alive.

"Lance-Corporal Miller. Lots for you. Several in coloured envelopes."

"Who?" He collected the mail. "Oh, Beryl and Iris."

Sergeant Taylor shook his head. "Lad, the point about having a woman in every port is that they're in different ports."

"Sarge, they share a flat," said Peter. "Windy didn't think to share with his buddy. Greedy, I call it. Actresses. To each according to their need, Windy."

"You're a better man than I am, Miller," said Sergeant Taylor. "I hear actresses are insatiable. You must have lured them with your looks. Corporal Barry. One for you, addressed in dago.

"Rifleman Thomas Cavendish O'Grady. One for you. Expensive envelope. Lady's writing. Return address is Illegible Manor. Looks like a servant in trouble and the Lady of the House has tracked you down. Dismissed."

Thomas took the letter, puzzled. The return address was what had once been his home. He turned the envelope over and over in his hand, trying to work this out. He finally decided that one sure way of solving the mystery was to open the envelope.

Several pages in a woman's hand, very flowery. He started to read, and then had to sit down. It was from Millicent. The first words were very disturbing.

"Dear Son."

He could feel the blood draining from his face. The last time he had seen Millicent had been in London, where she had been trying to seduce him and was eventually whisked away by Lieutenant Furley-Smith. He shivered. He didn't want to read on but couldn't draw his eyes away from the letter.

"What a jolly time we had in London. Such an eventful time and filled with such delights. It quite turned a young girl's head. I'm still quite giddy thinking about it.

"But you wouldn't recognise me now, for I have been transformed from a giddy young maid, easily beguiled by handsome Riflemen with broad shoulders and charming smiles, to a respectable Lady of the House. Little did I know what schemes my father and your father had when they came down to London on that fateful Sunday. But your father was concerned about not having an heir

for the estate. Entre nous, the family finances were not all that they should be for such a gorgeous house. Father was concerned that I was in danger of becoming an old maid and of course, he has wanted an heir to look after his businesses. He's not getting any younger and wants to pass the reins on. Imagine my surprise when the result of their discussions was that your father asked me for my hand in marriage. Well, I was not convinced at first; there was the difference in ages to consider, and the suddenness, and your father's stern demeanour. I confess I thought it some sort of jape at my expense, but it turns out that they were in earnest, and beneath that stern exterior, your father is the most passionate and considerate man, wise and kind and, dare I say it, looking like a man half his age now. What a weekend. First, I was pursued by you on Saturday, then on Sunday by Nicholas, who you must call Lieutenant Furley-Smith, I imagine. And then, on Monday, I married James. We spent two weeks in the islands of Greece, and James told me about the many legends of the area. We scrambled over many of the places of legend, and between you and me, some of these Greek legends seem to have been very passionate and disturbingly lustful, but it is not surprising when you see the wonderful private places we chanced upon. We had the most delightful time, and now I am ensconced back in what is now our joint home. But that is not all the news that I have for you. No. Not merely all of this, but your father's wish for an heir is in the process of being granted. I know science says there is no way of predicting whether a boy or girl will be granted by Providence, but a mother knows, deep down, and I am confident that by Easter, you will have a darling little brother. I thought it might be rather jolly to ask Nicholas to be the Godfather.

"I shall write regularly to my darling stepson. Hark at me, people will think I am a veritable wicked stepmother, and it will be odd to think that the playmate of my girlish years is now my little boy. As your stepmother, I must warn you of the dangers that face you in Persia, with all those dusky, wanton maidens who will try to lure you from the path of virtue – how well I know those temptations. As your childhood friend, I must plead with you to write and tell me of every little piece of gossip and scandal.

"Millicent Cavendish. I still get a thrill out of writing that. Mrs James Cavendish."

Thomas stared at the letter, his mind numb. He did some counting. That didn't help matters one little bit.

"Problem?" Peter asked. "Looks like you've had some bad news."

"You remember that time in London? That thing at Sir Sarahun's house?"

"Where Frank met Joy? Hard to forget."

"You remember that suffragette? The one who'd cuffed herself to the railings."

Peter stroked his moustache. "The brainless oppressor of the working class? Pretty thing. Nearly put her over my knee. Which could have been fun if there hadn't been an audience. Didn't she keep following you around?"

"That's the one."

"If she were one of us, she'd be a working girl. An easy tumble. The sort that hasn't a brain, but rattles from chap to chap and can't imagine why they lose interest after a couple of nights."

"That's my mother."

Thomas explained about the situation. Peter thought about this. "Lucky you're here and not there. Might have guessed, though."

"Guessed what?"

"You were one of them. Smooth tongue, inability to keep your mouth shut, knowing all sorts of useless things. Are you studying us for a bet, or what?"

"Believe it or not, I hated it there. It was all, I don't know, nothing mattered. No need to work or do anything. Here, well, I've got friends, for one thing."

"We'll make a comrade of you yet."

*****

"Why does everyone keep asking me what my intentions are towards Alice?" Lieutenant Campbell sounded aggrieved.

"I can't speak for anyone else, but Nurse Ward is a nurse, and I am the Senior Nurse. That means I have a responsibility to her. She's in a fragile state and I will not have her taken advantage of under such circumstances."

"She's clever, she's kind, she's nice, and she's been hurt by a bounder. I hope that she considers me a friend."

"Remember, she's a nurse. She can't marry and continue to work as a nurse."

"Why not?"

"Hospital regulations. All hospitals are the same. Nurses are not to be married."

"Well, it's not a problem. Alice needs a friend and I'm honoured if she considers me that friend."

"I'm going to hold you to that, Lieutenant Campbell."

*****

None of the other officers had wanted to do it, so Sergeant Erskine had to. It was his job, but it wasn't a pleasant one. Word had it that the Lieutenant had tried to seduce one of the wives. Some officers didn't think. If the man had responded, that would be a Danny Deever. If he hadn't, well, they were going on deployment. Young officers get in the thick of it and they really shouldn't want a Rifleman with a grudge just behind them.

"Mail for Lieutenant Furley-Smith," he said to the two guards. They nodded and let him pass. He went in, looked around, and came out.

"You're guarding Lieutenant Furley-Smith?"

"That's right, Sergeant."

"One of you had best get the Officer of the Day here fast and the other one of you had best have a good explanation."

*****

"What do you mean, he's gone?" Colonel Dalkeith asked Captain Filleul. "How can he be gone?"

"Lieutenant Furley-Smith is not in his cabin. The guards say that he hasn't left it. My company has started a search of the ship, although this is hampered by the sailors trying to unload."

"How long were these guards on for?"

"They'd only just gone on duty. Took over from Lieutenant Hawkins' men. Twenty minutes."

"I want to speak with Lieutenant Hawkins. Make sure your two guards are certain Furley-Smith didn't leave his cabin. Check the ship, top to bottom. Send the other company commanders to me. If he's not on the ship, we need to find him. Oh, and no-one to leave the ship until further orders."

"Yes, Sir."

Once Captain Filleul had left, Lady Dalkeith spoke. "Why try and find him?"

"Because he's our responsibility. I will not have him evade justice. Joy, find Rifleman O'Grady and tell him I wish to talk with him. I need someone who can think like Furley-Smith and might be able to guess where he would go."

*****

"Rifleman O'Grady. I've need of someone who can think like a devious, deceiving rogue trying to get out of trouble. Naturally, I thought of you."

"Am I in trouble, Sir?"

"Not yet, O'Grady, not yet. Lieutenant Furley-Smith has made a run to evade justice. I rather suspect that you might have a good idea where he has run to." Colonel Dalkeith paused before continuing. "A court martial is bound to assume that his running is convincing evidence of his guilt in previous matters, that it's demonstrating that he's evading his duty as an officer, making him unfit to be an officer, to say nothing of the fact that running in itself is a serious offence."

"I'm not sure I understand, Sir."

"If we find him and drag him back, I've got him stone cold on desertion. If we do not find him, he can slip away, hide for a year or so, then return to England and smooth things over."

"And you think I know where he's run to, Sir?"

"I think you've got the sort of mind that knows how these knaves think. I need him back. In his position, where would you go?"

"Disguise, Sir. I'd need to stay out of sight while I got clear. People will be looking for an officer and gentleman, Sir. They wouldn't be looking for a black stevedore. Plenty of them about and they all look the same. Overalls, just like the stokers wear and coal ash rubbed into the skin blacks you up a treat, Sir. Lieutenant Hawkins had me helping the stokers, Sir. We've had plenty of stevedores coming and going, Sir. Who'd notice one more? As soon as I was off this ship, I'd want to get well clear. As far away as I could, and outside British jurisdiction. That means getting on another ship, Sir, the first leaving, because I'd want to be clear before the hunt started. Last I saw on deck, Sir, that whaling ship was getting ready for sea. That's where I would have gone if I were a devious rogue, Sir."

"Captain Filleul, check it out."

"Sir," said Thomas, "are you sure that he'll be found guilty, even if he claims he was abducted. That's what I would claim in his position, Sir."

"If he claims to have been abducted, I would want to see the wounds on him and his assailant. That was his defence with regard to Nurse Ward. No wounds means no resistance means no rape. Well, no wounds means no resistance means no abduction."

*****

"Sir, the whaling ship *Terra Nova* left port twenty minutes ago."

"Damn. Get me the captain of HMS *Vector*. Maybe he can help."

*****

Windy and Peter stood at attention in the Colonel's office. Stare at a point above his left shoulder. Don't move a muscle.

"Lance-Corporals Grant and Miller. You were on guard when Lieutenant Furley-Smith ran. How did you come to let him?"

Peter coughed. "Two sailors went in with a meal, Sir. Two sailors came out. I think maybe he swapped clothes with one and came out then, Sir. The other sailor would have come out after the guard had changed, Sir. They'd think nothing of it."

"Not even checking the log of who had entered? It's not very impressive. I expect better from NCOs. You let me down. You're Riflemen until you can learn to do your job. Since you can't keep people on the ship, you're denied any shore leave. Grant, one-week stoppage of pay and spirits. Miller, one-week stoppage of spirit ration. I'd stop your pay, but I'm inclined to believe that this was the result of your youth and inexperience rather than stupidity."

*****

"Sir, message from HMS *Vector*. They caught up with the *Terra Nova*. The *Terra Nova* said that they did have a Rifleman officer on board, but shortly after they'd cleared the port, he woke up, found out where he was bound, jumped overboard and swam."

"Good God. He drowned, then?"

"No, Sir. He reached the *Zohan*. That's a tramp freighter. It's currently flying the Brazilian flag."

"What do you mean, currently flying?"

"It varies, Sir. Changes nationality a lot, Sir. It's a tramp freighter. That's what they do."

"Where's it going?" Colonel Dalkeith snapped.

"It's a tramp freighter, Sir. It's going wherever the captain thinks he can sell his current cargo. It was heading east, Sir. HMS *Vector* can't follow it. Ocean's a big place."

"It could be headed anywhere from East Africa to Australia."

Captain Filleul looked unhappy. "Unless it turned around."

"Damn. Well, at least I can destroy his career." He took out a pen and started to write, grimacing with pain as he did so. "Regret to report Captain Furley-Smith has deserted the Regiment while on active service." He put the pen away and stretched his fingers.

"Shore leave may commence, except for those confined to the ship. To be back by 2359. Let's add to Corporal Barry's experience. He will be Corporal of the Guard from 2200 to 0200. Along with his three comrades."

*****

"Don't wear your best uniform, lad." Sergeant Taylor shook his head as he saw Frank laying out his kit for guard duty.

"It important to present good appearance on guard duty. Officers come and go."

"Lad, you'll be on duty when the men come back. They're coming back from a night out. They've been on the ship for a month, cooped up. They will come back all frisky. Don't wear your best uniform."

*****

"What's the matter?" Alasdair asked.

"Nothing," said Alice, crying. She was trying to tidy up the office and Alasdair wasn't leaving so that she could cry properly.

"Border collies are very sensitive to moods, you know. You can either tell me what's the matter, or you can make me keep asking. I'm not going to go away and leave you upset and in tears."

"You must think I'm weak and useless. I've been miserable all the time."

"I think you've been amazing. You went through something horrid, and you've continued to do your job. You've been bright and cheerful for the patients, you've done your job. It's only when you're away from everyone that you've had a weep." Alasdair put his arms around her and let her cry on his shoulder. "Bottle it."

"Sorry, what?"

"Like what we do at home, sort of. Write out your troubles. Put it in a bottle. We'll find a beach and throw them out to sea. The bottle will take your troubles somewhere and you'll be left with the knowledge, but not the troubles. I'll come with you to make sure they don't come back."

"Alasdair, why doesn't Windy like me? He said he doesn't like women, but he's got girls back home. I think it's me that he doesn't like. I mean, he likes me as a friend, but I thought he'd want me."

"You silly thing. If he's got a girl back home, he's probably staying loyal to her."

"Girls. Three at least."

"Then he probably needs a rest. He doesn't look the sort but looks can be deceiving." He started to smile, a grin spreading across his face. "I've just had a thought. Why don't you write a letter to him? I've got an envelope you could put it in. Write it from, I don't know, Ruth Pendleton."

"What do I write?" Alice was confused.

"Since young Miller seems to be a bit of a sly philanderer, we'll give him a surprise. This Ruth is writing to tell him that he's got her in the family way. That might surprise him."

*****

Colonel Dalkeith looked through the papers and effects in Furley-Smith's cabin. He was disturbed that Furley-Smith could have gone so far off the rails without him noticing. He should have noticed. He'd failed.

His officers weren't saints. They had flaws, like everyone. It was his job to know what these flaws were and make them work for the Regiment. Which of them was rash, which were cautious, which could be trusted to operate without supervision, which of them could be relied upon to come up with ideas. Alasdair pretended to be air-headed, but he thought about how to deal with problems. This screw-gun idea. Not exactly new, but it could, in the right circumstances, be very useful. And it kept the men busy, which was always useful on these trips.

He picked up a sheath of papers and glanced at them. Notes about Persia. According to these, a request for the Persians to provide a live-in maid for the officers' quarters. "To ensure that the officer can devote his time to the things that matter and enable the batman to fulfil Regimental duties."

In principle, it wasn't a bad idea. He knew what was in Furley-Smith's mind, but the officers were going to be busy and there was a lot for the men to get used to. He could read the riot act to the officers about what would happen if they abused this privilege and let the request stand.

Notes on the King. Weak, vacillating, unloved by the Army, means well, very personable and charming. Richer than Croesus but loves getting gifts that are unique. "Things that money can't buy."

Colonel Dalkeith read on. This was exceptionally useful. Furley-Smith might have made a first-rate staff officer if he wasn't such a bad officer.

Notes on the Persian Army. Well-equipped, large. Estimated paper strength over 200,000. Senior officers more interested in Court intrigue than soldiering and spend all their time politicking at Court. Mid-ranking officers give up on leading their troops, preferring to get involved in the games of Court intrigue. Junior officers do the work but are scared of making a mistake because that reflects badly on their superiors. Consequently, they do nothing unless they are directly ordered to. They never step beyond that. The troops are from the lower orders. Pay is an issue. Corruption is endemic and pay is usually diverted to other pockets. Estimated effective strength around 8000. Of these, 3000 are Cossacks with Russian officers, who follow their own agenda.

"In short, we're on our own," Colonel Dalkeith muttered.

Another sheet of paper on potential enemies. First word: Conjecture. That was helpful.

Actually, it was. Rough outlines on how strong each of the groups were likely to be, who was likely to be supplying them and how much support they got, what they wanted to achieve and how they operated. It was grim reading, but if this was in any way accurate, it was like gold-dust.

*****

"We have some things we need to get, Joy."

"Yes, Ma'am. Ma'am, I was hoping to look around the town with Frank today."

"He's Corporal of the Guard for when the troops return."

"Yes, Ma'am, but that's not for hours."

"He'll need time to prepare. He's going to be exceptionally busy."

"I don't understand, Ma'am."

"Joy, how long have the men been cooped up on the ship? How drunk do you think they're going to get tonight? How boisterous do you think they'll be when they come back?"

"Oh. Will Frank be all right?"

"If he's not, he'll never make Sergeant."

*****

I'm scared. Windy isn't interested in me, not in that way. He's kind and gentle and he would have erased the bad memory, but he's not interested in me. I think it's because I'm spoiled goods. Alasdair is sweet, but he sees me as a sister. Peter is strange. He's got a secret and he puts on a blank face when Alasdair is around. He jokes with Windy, though and they seem to understand each other. But Peter's not interested in me. I'm scared that I'm a ruined woman and the only men who will be interested in me will be scoundrels and villains.

I've got to relearn how to be strong if I'm to be of any use to anyone. It would be easier if I had a lot of work to do, but that's wishing pain on my boys. I have to learn how to be strong again, but I don't know how.

Alice read the piece of paper. It was what she felt; she shivered a little as she read it. She folded the paper up tightly, put it into a bottle, then corked the bottle. She prayed that Alasdair was right and that this helped her. She was beginning to hate herself for being weak when everyone needed her to be strong.

*****

Frank examined the shore side of the main gangway. The soldiers would have to come up this when they returned. His guard would wait for them at the top. He checked with the ship's Officer of the Day, who had that it would be high tide when the soldiers returned. That meant, the officer said, that the gangway would be quite steep, because the ship would be high up.

That was good because that meant that soldiers coming up would have had a hard climb. Any trying to fight the guard would be at another disadvantage straight away. The other gangplank would be closed for the night, so returning soldiers had to use this one. He'd made sure that the exit at the top was narrow, so troops could only set off from the gangway onto the ship one at a time.

He'd made sure that the gangway would be a foot above the deck, so that they would be stepping off awkwardly.

He checked that everything was in place. Book to record who went off and who came back, with times of departure and return. Clock at the desk, and a second clock in the drawer. Windy to keep the records, Peter to escort troublemakers to confinement, Thomas to be the muscle, and he would be in control.

He returned to the top of the gangway. Tonight, this would be his domain.

"Corporal," said Lieutenant Campbell. "Alice and I will be looking at the beaches today. I'll be back in good time. I plan to be nearby, to keep an eye on Grant and Miller. I don't have many men to look after, so I need to look after the two I do have."

"No, Sir." Frank was firm. "It bad idea. Men come back, maybe drunk. Maybe they try fighting."

"That's exactly what I mean. I'm pretty useful in a fight. Boxed a fair bit."

"No, Sir. If they try and fight and hit me, I hit them back, then when they wake up, they on defaulters for drunk and resisting the guard. They hit you, when they wake up, they up on serious charges. Your job is stay out of way, Sir. Not protect *you*, to protect *them*. You stay well out of way, Sir."

"But damnit, Corporal, there's just four of you. Will that be enough to cope?"

"Sir, if they not drunk, they know better than to try hit Corporal's Guard. They need to be very drunk to try. If they that drunk, then we able to cope. If they not drunk and try cause trouble, we have equaliser."

"What on earth is an equaliser?"

"One punch, they go down and stay down."

"If you're sure, Corporal."

As Lieutenant Campbell left with Nurse Ward, Sergeant Taylor nodded and left the side of the gangway. Corporal Barry was shaping up well. Still as green as grass but he was learning fast.

*****

Joy stared in fascination at the stalls that had been set up between the ship and the dock gates. It wasn't the stalls, trying to sell anything from fruit to leather. She'd seen these before. It was the people. There were black people and brown people dressed like ordinary people. They weren't waving spears or doing war-dances or anything like that.

Lady Dalkeith bought a newspaper and Joy had an idea.

"Ma'am, when you've finished with the newspaper, could I use it?"

"Why?"

"For my reading classes, Ma'am."

"Very well. Keep up, girl. There's no point buying from dock stalls when we set out. If you must buy from them, buy when we return. That way you don't have to carry whatever you waste your money on."

"Yes, Ma'am. Ma'am, those black men. Are they Zulus, like at Isandlwana and Rock's Drift? We read about that at school."

"No idea. There are a lot of different tribes in Africa. If we've time, you can ask when we return. Although I hear that some Zulus are cannibals and enjoy eating blonde white girls."

"Ma'am, they look just like normal people, only different."

"That's enough, now. There's something we need to get you. Adderley Street, I believe."

"Yes, Ma'am. What is it?"

"Patience. That's what we need to get you"

Cape Town wasn't like London. There weren't many cars. Many of the cabs were horse-drawn. The streets were really wide, but the shops looked normal. They passed a shop selling dress material, a bookshop, and countless other shops.

"Here we are," Lady Dalkeith said. "As we're going to Persia, where the Regiment will be on deployment, we need to get you something for self-protection."

"Ma'am?" But Lady Dalkeith had already started to enter the shop and Joy was speaking to her back. Joy followed her inside. Guns on the wall and in cabinets, solid floors, and two shop assistants who looked like normal people. Joy was half-expecting them to look like desperadoes, or soldiers.

"Ma'am, this is a gun shop."

"Where would you expect to go to get a gun? A flower shop? Gentlemen, the girl needs something portable for *in extremis*. Please don't waste our time with something barely capable of stopping a rat."

"Ma'am, a gun?"

"Joy, we'll be going to Persia. It's not like Sloane Square."

"But the Regiment will be there."

"Not necessarily. It might well be busy. Credit to you for drawing a knife on Furley-Smith, but you'll need something with a bit more stopping power in Persia."

"Ma'am, I don't know how to use a gun."

"We'll just have to find someone to teach you. I wonder where we might find a soldier? Stop being frivolous. Corporal Barry will be easier in his mind if he knows you can look after yourself."

"Yes, Ma'am," Joy said, resignedly. "Ma'am, how come you know so much about guns?"

"I'm from America. The frontier, pioneers."

"Was Boston on the frontier, with cowboys and Indians and outlaws and Deadeye Dick robbing the Deadwood Stage?"

"Joy, if you scratch an American, you get a frontiersman. If you scratch an Englishman, you get a sailor."

"Yes, Ma'am. Ma'am, what you do you get if you scratch a Sicilian?"

"Blood."

*****

They'd taken a cab as far as they could out of town. They walked to the beach and stood as far out on it as they could. Waves came up the beach, first from the left, and then from the right, and washed over their feet. Alasdair carried their shoes, and they walked barefoot on the sand. Alice held the bottle.

"Do you want me to throw it for you?" Alasdair asked. "I can throw it further."

"No. It only counts if I throw it."

"Well, to the right is the Atlantic and Brazil. To the left is the Indian Ocean and Australia."

"I'll let the waves decide," Alice said, throwing the bottle as far as she could. She watched the splash, then watched as it bobbed up and down on the surface. She'd taken her fears and put them in the bottle and thrown them away. The bottle bobbed, slowly getting further and further away, until she wasn't sure where it was. She didn't know if this would make her strong again.

"Thank you, Alasdair."

"What for?"

"For not chasing after the bottle and bringing it back. Ross would have."

*****

It was dark and relatively quiet. Most of the soldiers had gone into the town. So had most of the sailors. The coal ash had been taken off of the ship and been left on the docks. Thomas noticed that one of the stall owners had taken to selling rose fertiliser. Thomas was surprised that a number of the stalls remained, and the stall owners had sticks with a wooden head close to hand.

"Why?" he asked.

"Why what?" Peter replied. "They're open because around 800 people with a month's pay less what they've spent will be coming back soon, most of them drunk. They'll make a fortune. The knobkerries are in case people decide to try and not pay."

"I don't like it. It's quiet," said Windy. Everyone glared at him.

"If you finish that sentence, you can deal with the first brawler."

"First two coming back," said Frank.

It was Lieutenant Campbell and Nurse Ward. Frank saluted them as they stepped on board, pretending not to notice that Lieutenant Campbell's uniform was a mess, rumpled, covered in white stains, misshapen in places, and that he didn't have a cap.

"I slipped and fell in the sea, Corporal. These things happen. I suspect some of the men will come back in a worse state."

Frank tried to ignore Nurse Ward trying to hide her giggling.

"Yes, Sir." He also refrained from telling Lieutenant Campbell that a soldier returning in that state would go on report. "Roll call is at 0700, Sir."

"Which is your way of saying I'd better smarten myself up by then. Not to worry. I'll be helping Nurse Ward write an important letter. I'll be all smart and presentable in time."

They went off, trying not to giggle.

"Officers," said Peter. "If I'd come back like that"

"If you'd come back like that, then I would have got into trouble for letting you," said Windy. "Writing a letter. I doubt it."

Peter thought. "With him, it could be true. Just because you'll sleep with anything in a skirt doesn't mean that everyone's like that. He's got to be more careful."

"Why's that?"

"Name like Campbell? He's from Scotland. Half the men there wear skirts."

*****

"Here come the first," said Thomas, looking across the dock. "Two soldiers and a girl. The girl's trying to come on board."

The three started to walk up the gangway, pausing frequently. Thomas thought there was something odd about the woman.

The first soldier reached the top of the gangway, paused, saluted, reported his name, threw up, tripped and fell over, landing in the vomit, got up looking confused, then sat down.

"Clean it up, then get to your hammock," said Frank.

The rifleman took his cap off and started to wipe the deck. He was wiping nowhere near the area he needed to. Peter tapped him on the shoulder, gave him a mop and pointed to where he should work. The Rifleman smiled, took the mop and started work. After a moment, he was using the mop as a support, until Frank shouted in his ear.

The second rifleman managed to salute, report his name, step off the gangway, and remain upright. "I'm not drunk," he said. He proceeded to march off reasonably smartly. Unfortunately, he headed in the wrong direction, reached the railings around the deck of the ship and started to clamber over. Thomas restrained him, took him back to the gangway.

"Is he drunk and incapable, Corporal?"

"If he can make his own way to his hammock, he fine," said Frank.

The girl reached the top of the gangway and saluted. "Rifleman Marie Dainton returning from shore leave, Corporal."

"Rifleman, you not Marie Dainton. Report properly."

"Rifleman Downton, Corporal."

"Rifleman Downton, why aren't you in uniform?"

"This is my uniform. I swapped it with my actress friend. I'm now a music hall star and she is a rifleman."

"If you not in uniform at roll call, your company commander put you up on charge. Go to your hammock."

After that, things started to get busy.

A woman, middle-aged and wearing a rifleman's uniform sashayed up the gangway, easily fending off the attempted familiarities of the Riflemen in line. "Sergeant Major," she said to Frank. "One of your riflemen attacked me and stole my clothing. I demand compensation."

"Madam, you cannot come on board. Come back 0630, Corporal's Guard see exchange of clothing take place."

She went back down the gangway, loudly demanding compensation.

"Rifleman Callaghan, why have you got a parrot on your shoulder?"

"Won it, Corporal. It talks."

"*Kettie kop*," the parrot squawked.

"Of course," Rifleman Callaghan said, "it's an African parrot, so it speaks African. It'll learn English."

"Not on this ship it won't. Thomas, sell it to one of the stall owners. You've one minute."

The next rifleman reached the top of the gangway, saluted, reported his name, stepped off the end, and swung a punch at Frank. Frank blocked the blow. While the rifleman concentrated on Frank, Peter hit the man in the kidneys. The rifleman fell to the ground in agony.

"You his buddy? Put him in his hammock." Frank looked around to see what the next crisis was going to be.

"Put him on report, Corporal?" asked Windy.

Frank shrugged. "He not land blow. No report. He had reminder. You," he said to the buddy. "Make sure he OK in morning."

And still they came.

"It's a goat, Corporal. Regimental mascot. We call him Billy."

"It dead."

"It's not, Corporal. Farmer say African goats look like this."

"It not have a head. It dead." Frank was almost shouting in frustration.

"It'll get better, Corporal."

"Take it to regiment mascot store. Sailors call that galley. Peter, tell that ship officer to go away."

One of the ship's officers had stepped out onto the deck for some fresh air. A couple of the riflemen saw gold braid and started to move menacingly towards the officer.

"Stand to attention, you fellows," said the young officer. Fortunately, Thomas and Frank reached the riflemen in time. Thomas brought one down with a rugby tackle and Frank tripped the other up.

"Go away, Sir," said Frank.

"I beg your pardon?"

"Corporal said he heard you were wanted in the engine room, make sure all the coal ash had been removed, Sir."

And still the riflemen returned.

"I've come to join the soldiers," said a large black man. "You're leaving city soon?"

"Come back in morning. Speak to Duty Officer."

"I must join now, straight away." The man was insistent.

"Wait here. When Duty Officer have time, he speak with you." Frank turned to look at two riflemen trying to sneak away. "Where you two going?"

"Back to our hammocks, Corporal."

"And what about that sign?"

The two riflemen looked at the ten-foot-long sign they were carrying, which read *Furnicular carriages to Table Top Mountain.*

"Yes, that sign," said Frank.

"Won it in a poker game, Corporal."

"Leave it against the railing."

The night went on. Frank had expected more fights, but the soldiers didn't seem very interested in getting into a fight.

"Have you repented of your sins, Corporal," bellowed Rifleman Wagstaff as he returned to the ship. "Repent, for you have broken the Commandments of God and you shall burn in Hell."

"Commandments not in Army Regulations," said Frank. He was concerned because it had been a long time since he had been to Confession.

"Thou art a Philistine. Like Samson, I shall smite you with the jawbone of an ass." Rifleman Wagstaff rushed forward brandishing a stick with a metal end. Frank ducked just enough, and the knobkerrie caught the edge of his cap, sending it spinning over the side of the ship into the sea. His head rang slightly, the stick had just touched him. Luckily, Thomas and Peter were close at hand. They restrained Rifleman Wagstaff with rather more force than have been strictly required.

Frank put his hand to his head and felt some stickiness. A bit of blood. "Drunk and resisting the guard," he said. "In cells."

"I'm not drunk. I'm punishing sinners."

"I say you drunk. I am Corporal of Guard. If you not drunk, you hit me when in your right mind, so I know you drunk. Take him away before he make things worse. Now you stop that," he shouted over the side. Four riflemen had got into a fight with about half a dozen stall owners.

"We've still got ten more minutes, Corporal. We ain't paying these prices."

"You have one minute by my clock," Frank shouted. He motioned to Windy to switch the clocks. The second had been stopped at 2358. "One minute, or you overstay leave. Colonel not like that."

That caused the remaining Riflemen to rush to get back on board and out of the way. Over the next ten minutes, another dozen riflemen returned, came on board and were recorded as having returned in the nick of time.

"How many not back?" Frank asked Windy.

"Fifteen. Thirteen Riflemen, Corporal Richards, and Captain Filleul."

"Change clocks around."

They waited for twenty minutes with the clock stopped at 2358. Corporal Richards escorted eight riflemen back and led them up the gangway. "Are they in time?" he asked.

"Skin of teeth," Frank said. "They very lucky." Frank nodded to Windy to change the clock back to the original.

Five minutes later, Sergeant Taylor came out on deck. "How many not back?"

"Five riflemen, Sergeant." Frank paused. He didn't want to explain about Captain Filleul.

"Full report, Corporal. Let me guess. Captain Filleul pushing his luck?"

"Yes, Sergeant. How did you know, Sergeant?"

"Sergeants know everything, Corporal. What are you going to do about the missing?"

"In morning, before Roll Call, I check police stations if they not returned by then. Overstay leave not as bad as miss roll call."

"And for Captain Filleul?"

"When I finish guard, 0200, I must report it to Major Marshall."

"And Captain Filleul knows that. He's pulled this stunt once too often. He needs to set an example, not make use of procedure to get an extra two hours leave. I'll take over here while you report his absence to Major Marshall. I'm relieving you for ten minutes."

Frank went to Major Marshall's cabin. The Major was not pleased at being disturbed. He was even less pleased when told why. "Very well. I'll be up and meet him on his return. Return to your post, Corporal. I'll be there in ten minutes."

Half an hour later, Major Marshall stood discretely out of sight as one of the missing riflemen returned. The rifleman had returned with an elderly woman.

"Are you this man's officer?" she asked Frank.

"I am Corporal of Guard, Ma'am."

"The reason this man is late back from leave is that my carriage suffered an accident and two men tried to waylay me. This man came to my rescue, drove the villains off, then helped me to return home with my possessions. Once home, I drove him here so that he wouldn't be too late."

"I must report all lateness and reasons for lateness. Colonel will hear of story."

"Very good. I am inviting Rifleman Charlton to tea tomorrow, assuming his duties permit. I trust that the Colonel will ensure that they do."

The lady left. Rifleman Charlton started to move to go to his hammock.

"Just a moment," said Sergeant Taylor. "Why did you help the lady?"

"Kindness of my heart, Sergeant."

"Corporal Barry, what do you think?"

This one was easy. The lady was similar in some ways to Lady Dalkeith. "Lady have pretty maid, I guess."

The expression on Rifleman Charlton's face told Frank that he'd guessed correctly.

At 0145, Captain Filleul arrived at the bottom of the gangway and bid farewell to a lady who had accompanied him. He came up the gangway, casually saluted at the top.

"Just in time, am I, Corporal?"

Frank looked at the clock. "Not exactly, Sir."

"A word, Phillip," said Major Marshall. "In private, I think."

The next guard came and relieved them. Frank breathed a deep sigh of relief.

"Enjoy it, Corporal?" Sergeant Taylor asked, a big grin on his face.

"It busy, Sergeant."

"Remember, 0530, check with the police stations and get our missing lambs back. It's 0230, so you've three hours to sleep before the next day starts. Not too bad for a first time, Corporal."

*****

Twenty minutes before roll call, Frank called to say good morning to Joy. He was exhausted, tired, his head hurt from where Wagstaff had hit him. Nurse Charrington had put a stitch in the wound. He was hungry, having missed breakfast while collecting the strays.

Joy gave a big smile when she opened the door. He immediately felt better.

"How was Guard duty? Was it hard?" Joy asked.

"It was fine. Easy. Piece of cake."

*****

Alice was asleep in the chair. They'd talked and written the letter, then talked some more. Finally, she'd drifted off into sleep while they'd been talking. Alasdair had thought about whether he should make her comfortable in the chair, or wake her up, or try and move her without disturbing her and putting her on the bed, where she'd be more comfortable. He took the chance, picked her up and laid her carefully on the bed, putting a blanket over her. She didn't even stir.

She probably hadn't slept properly since the incident. Now she was dead to the world, catching up on all that missed sleep. He put a blanket over her and smoothed a strand of hair away from her face. Then he settled down in the chair and tried to sleep.

Of course, he woke up feeling stiff and sore, but a quick run would sort that out. Alice was still asleep. The poor girl must have been exhausted. He tried to stretch out some of his kinks; then she stirred and opened her eyes. She looked confused, in that half-awake, half-asleep phase.

She looked briefly startled, like a frightened fawn. Then she saw him and relaxed. Then she looked worried.

"Have I slept here? What will people say?"

"I rather think they'll very carefully not say anything. I rather think that many people will be too busy nursing sore heads to notice."

"There'll be talk."

Alasdair sat on the edge of the bed and stroked the side of her face with the back of his hand. She flinched very briefly before relaxing.

"It actually might be a good thing," he said. "If they think that, no-one will make advances towards you until you're good and ready for them. You can take as long as you need to recover."

"But what about you? What if …" Her voice trailed away.

"Look, I'm going to sound pompous now. I've a duty to protect people. That's my job. If I can't help a friend, what good am I?"

"How will I know?" Alice sounded anxious.

Alasdair knew what she was talking about. "You've got it the wrong way around. You're worrying about the act, not the person. When you find someone, it'll work out. Find the someone first, because if it's not someone you want, it will turn out bad. That'll be bad."

"Alasdair," she started, then stopped. "If people are going to gossip, maybe we could give them something to gossip about." She held her breath.

"Why not? Mislead and confuse and play all sorts of tricks. That could be fun, seeing how much we can fool them." He ruffled her hair. "Look, I've got to get ready for roll call. If I miss that, not only will there be gossip, but I'll be in trouble. I rather suspect you'll have a lot of people to treat with scrapes from last night."

Alice went back to her office and Alasdair prepared for roll call. The uniform he'd worn yesterday was in a desperate shape. He'd probably be able to recover it, but his batman was going to have to work hard. Mind you, it had been worth it to see Alice smile when she'd pushed him and he'd fallen over while they were standing in the water.

Mislead and confuse. He knew what Alice meant when she'd suggested giving people something to gossip about. She wasn't ready. At the moment, she needed a friend, not a lover.

He could be a friend, but he wasn't good enough to be her lover. He wasn't important, just a fourth son and of no significance.

*****

Peter managed to unfold the newspaper. Finding space to read the paper wasn't easy and it was only a Cape Town paper. It wouldn't have much about important matters. Still, even out here, it must be obvious that the system was untenable. Soon people would soon see that things were inevitable and would embrace the necessary changes.

It wasn't going to come easily, and it wasn't going to come without cost. The capitalists wouldn't just give up power.

Peter turned the pages of the newspaper. The foreign section was pretty thin. A few platitudes about Russia and complaints about German ambitions.

There was a lot on a local labour dispute. This was promising. Not that he could do anything about it. He read the report closely and snorted in disgust. The capitalists were using divide and rule and the South African workers were falling for it. Mine owners promise to only use white miners for key positions in mining operations, at higher pay. Then the owners decide that these positions are no longer key and replace white miners with black miners, at much lower wages.

What did the miners do? Work together to present a united front against the true enemy? Of course not. The white miners start attacking the black miners, who attack them right back. The capitalists rub their hands with glee and continue to cause division between the workers.

A brief mention of the formation of the Party in South Africa. Dismissed in a few words as extremists, black-lovers, and

Socialists. After a moment's thought, he thought this was a good sign. The newspaper was worried and hoping the Party would go away. Historical inevitability meant that they were wrong. Sooner or later, by one path or another, the Party would sweep away the capitalists.

The capitalists would resist the inexorable march of history. If they expected the Army to support them in putting down the workers, they would be in for a shock. It's one thing to shoot on foreigners, but putting down disturbances at home? Not a chance. It would be shooting on their own kind.

In the meanwhile, he'd keep his head down and wait for the inevitable to start.

*****

"No." Frank was firm. "It wrong. Girls do not do this."

"Lady Dalkeith does. She said I had to." Joy was equally firm.

"It wrong. That why Regiment here."

"And when the Regiment's not around? When you're off somewhere, what am I supposed to do? Hope for the best? Submit to outrages? Mr Shaw had the answer to that."

"There no Mr Shaw in Regiment, so he not understand and he wrong, whatever he said. What did he say?"

"Not bloody likely. I'm going to learn. You can teach me, which I'd prefer, or someone else will. Thomas or Peter or Windy."

"Girls can't shoot guns well. They not built same as men. Arms too weak."

Peter and Windy stopped even pretending to work on the screw-gun while they listened to the argument being held on the deck.

"Lady Dalkeith can."

"That different. Is wrong for girls."

"It's a deployment. It could get dangerous. You won't be there to protect me all the time. When you're not around, I'll need to be able to look after myself. Do you think a soldier's wife is helpless when her husband isn't around? Ask some of the wives."

"And if you able to look after yourself, what you need me for?"

"If he doesn't know the answer to that one, there's no hope for him," muttered Peter, loud enough for everyone to hear.

Joy's snort could be heard some distance away. "What do I need you for? Just at the moment, I think not a lot." Joy folded her arms and looked Frank in the face. "Do you want me to give you a clue?"

"What do you mean?"

"For a Sergeant, you can be really slow," she said, stepping forward and kissing him. She had intended it to be just a quick kiss. She felt his arms go around her waist and she put her arms around his neck and held on. It was only supposed to be a quick kiss, but she was losing her sense of time.

"And what, exactly, do you two think you are doing?" said Lady Dalkeith from a million miles away.

"It my fault," said Frank.

Lady Dalkeith snorted. "I see Joy was fighting you off with all the strength at her disposal. Joy, what were you doing?"

"We were having an argument, Ma'am."

"Really. Let us be grateful you weren't having a stand-up row. That might have been in breach of laws on public decency. Corporal Barry, I have told you before. Now I'm warning you. A repetition will be unfortunate."

*****

Thomas held the door to the shop open for Nurse Charrington. She wanted medical supplies, and this was the place she said she needed to go. It was certainly an unusual shop. Lots of strange instruments on shelves around the room and locked cabinets behind the desk. Nurse Charrington took out a notebook and checked her notes.

Thomas took down a strange set of tongs and looked at them. They were huge. "What's this for?" he asked Nurse Charrington.

"Rifleman O'Grady, there are no circumstances whatsoever that I would need to use it on you. You can stop worrying."

"Riflemen can get unusual injuries. I saw several last night."

"If I need to use it on you, I will write the incident up in an article for the BMJ and they will publish it, despite my being just a nurse and a woman."

Thomas was about to argue that she wasn't "just" a nurse and a woman, but some instinct suggested to him that letting her sort out supplies would be better. Waiting patiently would be best.

Discussions took a long time and waiting was boring. He would have thought he would have got used to waiting, but this was somehow different. He liked spending time with Emily, but she was paying him no attention and was concentrating on the shop keeper. What made it worse was that they were talking, and he didn't have a clue what they were saying because it was all technical. He felt excluded.

He heard noises outside and looked out. Two groups seemed to be gathering. Workers of some sort, one group at each end of the street. Blacks in one group, whites in the other. Maybe a dozen in each group. It looked like it would break out into a fight, and people on both sides carried clubs and knives.

The police would be along to break it up soon but, at the moment, it looked ugly. Get Nurse Charrington out and away before trouble started, or wait in here until any trouble was over?

Nurse Charrington didn't seem to be in any hurry, and she frowned when Thomas tried to hurry her. Wait it out, then.

He watched through the window, standing by the doorway. Whatever else happened, he'd make sure that no trouble spilled over to threaten Emily. As he watched, the brawl developed with a speed he couldn't believe. One moment, the two gangs were at either end of the street, the next minute, they were fighting. The heart of the brawl was not far from the door to the shop.

At least it was possible to tell the gangs apart. The sudden violence shocked him, and the brawl was a mess. He leaned against the door to make sure no-one burst in and watched. The fighting was fierce, but something troubled him about it. It wasn't the actual violence. Some of it was sickening, but he realised it was because he could see individuals being isolated.

That surprised him. He realised it wasn't the violence that was troubling him, but that they weren't very good at it. They were fighting as individuals, not covering each other.

Emily heard the disturbance and had looked around. She saw Thomas at the door.

"Is everything in order, Rifleman?"

"Bit of a brawl outside, Nurse. It won't come in here." He tried to sound confident and reassuring. Nurse Charrington nodded and returned to her discussions with the shop owner. Thomas kept an eye on the brawl. When the police arrived, he breathed a sigh of relief. Nurse Charrington had finished making the purchases and was arranging for delivery.

"What?" Thomas exclaimed. The police had formed at one end of the street, ordered those fighting to disperse, then levelled rifles and fired over the heads of the brawlers. The fighting stopped and those involved stood looking bemused. The smell of cordite hung in the air.

"Disperse," came a brief shout from the police, followed by a single shot, then a volley, fired straight into the crowd. The crowd turned and fled, apart from those that lay on the ground.

As the crowd fled, Nurse Charrington started to push past Thomas.

"Stay back," Thomas said, blocking the door.

"I'm a nurse. There are wounded. I'll need protection."

In fact, there wasn't anything left to provide protection from. Everyone who wasn't lying wounded on the ground or who had fled were being taken into custody by the police.

"Thomas, bind the wounds on this one," she said, indicating a man with blood flowing from a wound in the leg. She moved on to another patient.

Thomas looked at the wound. The man was holding his leg, blood flowing through his fingers. Thomas forced the man's hands aside so that he could see. A deep wound in the upper leg, but it had missed the big artery. Or was it a vein? Deep but not long. Pressure on the wound. Strange how you focus on the job. Pressure on the wound. Use the man's cap as a pad. He was saying something, shouting, but Thomas didn't hear it. Hold the cap in place. Take the man's scarf to tie it in place. Metal bar the man had to act as a twist for the scarf. Twist and twist to get the scarf tight. Done.

"There you are. Get it stitched at a hospital."

"Rifleman," called Nurse Charrington. "Stay with this one. Keep him comfortable. Talk to him, until."

"Until?" Then he looked. A stomach wound. A bad one.

"Until." She spoke firmly before she hurried to the next patient.

He took hold of the man's hand, who gripped him.

"It's cold," the man said. A tanned man, looking pale, about Thomas' age, with calloused hands. His body kept twisting and arching, his breath coming in short, laboured gasps.

"It's getting late. The sun's down. That's why it's cold."

"I've got to be OK for work tomorrow. I have to go to work." His voice was a raspy whisper.

"You'll be fine. What's your name?"

"I have to work. I promised." Then his grip tightened on Thomas' hand, fiercely, and his body shuddered. Thomas saw the man's shoulders slump slightly, although the grip didn't slacken. There was a silent sigh and his eyes seemed to lose focus. The eyes blurred slightly, as though a veil had been placed over them.

"What's your name?" Thomas asked, before he realised the man was no longer breathing. He unwrapped the fingers from his wrist and stood up, laying the man on the blood-covered street.

The police took control of the situation. Thomas shook his head to clear it.

"We're done here," said Nurse Charrington, taking his arm and leading him away. "The police have this under control. My supplies will be delivered. The wounded are stable. There's nothing more we can do here."

Thomas was in a bit of a daze as they walked. After a time, they drew close to the docks.

"Was that your first death?" she asked.

"I guess you get used to it," he said. His voice wavered and his legs weren't as steady as he would have liked them to be.

"No. You learn to control it, but it's always a blow when you lose one. You remember those you made a difference for. It didn't matter what you did here, he was going. In those cases, all you can do is make the journey a bit easier. It's hard, though. Still, you seem to have been paying attention during my lessons."

Thomas blurted out: "How can you be so calm and matter-of-fact?"

She stopped in the street and stared at him. "Do you really not understand? Would you be happier if I was having hysterics and being helpless and needing to be protected from the big bad world? When people come to me, they need me to reassure them. If I can't do that, I'll be no use as a nurse."

"But how can you just be so calm about things?"

"Because that is my job. That is the person I am. Since it seems to trouble you, I think it best if we ensure that from now on our relationship is purely professional."

"But Emily,"

"Nurse Charrington, if you please. Obviously, I'll continue with your medical lessons. You've proved you can use the training. It will be useful to you in the field."

"But, Nurse Charrington, I'm trying to understand. Please."

"It doesn't really matter if you understand or not. I am what I am. Fortunately, we discovered this before any commitment was made. Now, if you'll excuse me, I have a great deal of work to do, and you will need to report the incident to your officer. Thank you for escorting me into town, Rifleman O'Grady."

She swept up the gangway ahead of him, walking quickly.

*****

Nurse Charrington checked the level of diethyl ether in the bottle. It was definitely lower than it had been when she left to order medical supplies. She'd made sure that evaporation wasn't an issue. The bottle was tightly stoppered. She'd made sure the other nurses knew that they had to record any usage.

Some had gone. It hadn't been used. It hadn't evaporated. Therefore, it had been taken in her absence. Everything else was fine, just this. Not large quantities, but enough to be noticed. She'd marked the bottle just before she left, so it had happened while she was out.

This had to be stopped. She had to leave the office and whoever it was probably watched and waited until she was out. Why take just that one thing?

The obvious solution was for someone to watch the office when she was out, or to actually be in the office while she was out.

Yesterday, she would have asked Thomas. Rifleman O'Grady. That was no longer advisable. She thought briefly about asking

Frank but decided to go to Lieutenant Hawkins. She was an officer and she needed to act like an officer.

She explained the problem to him.

"The Colonel needs to know." He stood up, looking quizzically at her. "I'm surprised you came to me rather than to O'Grady."

"I'm not sure why you should be surprised. As I understand it, this is a matter which needs to be dealt with officially. That precludes taking unofficial action. Rifleman O'Grady would only be able to take unofficial action."

"I see." It was obvious from his tone that he didn't, but Nurse Charrington decided not to comment on this.

*****

That had come out of the blue. Thomas' mind wasn't working properly. One moment he had been looking for ways to solve the puzzle. The next, everything in his life had fallen apart. He'd been trying to understand, then his hopes had been casually torn apart.

He didn't know what to think. She had something that was important to her, something that mattered to her and that let her make a difference.

Frank had something. He wanted to be a sergeant, and he was doing everything he could to be a good one.

Lady Dalkeith had something. She was the Colonel's hidden hand. He could see it now. The little exercises for the four of them, doing things the Colonel couldn't be seen to do. He didn't know what they were being prepared for, but there had been too much for it to be anything other than a deliberate plan.

He had nothing. A vague sense that things weren't right, but that might be just hearing too much of Peter's grumbles about things. He'd just drifted along, doing things that amused him at the time.

Maybe he needed a purpose. He wouldn't find it here, though. Maybe it was time to cut his losses and leave. It wasn't like there was anything keeping him here now. He looked over the side and saw a ship leaving the port. Plenty of ships in the harbour, coming and going.

Desertion was a serious matter. If he deserted and got caught, they'd hang him for sure. But then, so what? It's not like anyone would miss him if that happened. He'd prefer not to be hanged, but he needed to find his purpose and he couldn't find it surrounded by the Regiment.

*****

Colonel Dalkeith looked angry when the problem was explained. "Not merely do we have to put a stop to this, we've got to find out who's responsible and make an example of them. If we don't, the problem will resurface later on. Stealing Regimental supplies is bad. Stealing Regimental medical supplies is appalling. Ether, you say? If you ran out, you'd need to work on patients who were conscious."

Neither Lieutenant Hawkins nor Nurse Charrington disagreed. The Colonel had put it bluntly, but he wasn't wrong.

"What if it's a sailor?" Lieutenant Hawkins asked.

"I don't care if it's a sailor, a soldier, or a ghostly apparition. This needs to be stopped, and not just put off. Very well. I'll leave the tactical details to you, John. I want this person caught. I'd suggest someone concealed in the office when Nurse Charrington leaves, someone watching on the outside to make sure he doesn't have the opportunity to flee. No-one will question O'Grady being in the office."

"I would prefer Rifleman O'Grady not to be involved in this, Colonel." Nurse Charrington's voice was tense.

"Why on earth not? He's burly enough that whoever tries to get in will have a fight on their hands. However that goes, it will give time for the support to arrive before the thief can escape."

"I think it best if Rifleman O'Grady were not involved, Colonel," Nurse Charrington said, her voice level and without emotion.

"Lieutenant Hawkins will handle the tactical details." The Colonel was puzzled. "Is there anything that I need to know about? I had the impression that you and O'Grady had an understanding."

"You were mistaken, Colonel." She gave a weak, wry smile. "It was more of a misunderstanding."

*****

Lieutenant Hawkins knew that there was something wrong as he saw the men lined up for roll call. The men looked worried, Sergeant Taylor looked stern and grim and expressionless. He approached with Nurse Charrington. He would soon find out.

"Riflemen Grant and Miller. Fall out after roll call. I've something to discuss with you. Roll call report, Sergeant Taylor."

"Rifleman O'Grady absent, Sir." Sergeant Taylor's voice was flat and hard.

"Overstayed his leave?"

"No, Sir. He signed back in last night, Sir. Hasn't signed out."

"Corporal Barry. Where is he?" Lieutenant Hawkins turned his attention on Frank. If anyone knew, it would be him.

Frank could only shrug his shoulders and look straight ahead. "Not know, Sir."

"He might have said something about helping the stokers with a boiler clean, Sir," said Peter.

"Check it out, Sergeant. I doubt that he's there but check it out. Nurse Charrington, a word in private, if you please." He took her to one side. "Do you know anything, Ma'am? This is serious."

"I've no idea. We returned last night, fairly early. I haven't seen him since."

"How was he when you returned? The two of you ..."

"There is no two of us, Lieutenant. Anything beyond that falls into the realms of might-have-been and wishful thinking. He might have been sweet on me. I'm sure he'll recover."

"You silly girl. Can't you tell the difference between being sweet on someone and being in love with them? Women should not be allowed on deployment, they're more trouble than they're worth. This is bad. Seriously bad. At the moment, he's AWOL. If we don't get him back fast, it becomes desertion. That's a hanging offence. Damn."

Nurse Charrington felt a lump of ice form in her stomach. "The Colonel wouldn't go that far, would he?"

"If it's desertion, he'd have no choice. Damn." He returned to the platoon. "Grant and Miller. I've got instructions for you. There have been thefts of medical supplies from Nurse Charrington's office in her absence. Miller, you'll be inside, waiting, hidden. Anyone comes in without cause, detain them. Grant, you're on the outside keeping the entry under surveillance. If anyone goes in without cause, you make sure they don't flee the scene. Whatever it takes to keep them there."

"Sir, what about Rifleman O'Grady?" said Windy. "We're his friends."

"If he's run, I don't want you involved. If you catch him, you could well be putting a noose round his neck. If you don't, people might wonder if you helped him get away. You two and Corporal Barry are to remain on board until this is resolved. Carry on."

*****

It was dark and uncomfortable in this little boat, but at least he had a bit of solitude and could think. Well, he should be able to think, if his mind would settle down and stop churning. He had to be serious for once.

That was part of it. He'd never had anything to be serious about. Nothing had ever mattered. Everything was fine and if it wasn't, nothing too bad happened. His father sneered about the Uniform of Honour. To everyone, it was a joke. Gutter-scum who no-one would miss, of no more account than toy soldiers.

Then there were the State Schools. The Headteacher at Joy's school had been in a tough position, but no-one cared. The memorial boards outside the schools and the way the children of the State Schools treated them. The children had been used and abused and discarded and ignored, yet they took pride in doing the job. They'd nothing else, but they had something to believe in, even if it was a lie.

In some ways, the Regiment was like a State School. If every last one of them were wiped out in some action, the officers might be missed, but no-one would give a second thought about the soldiers. The State Schools had a sort of pride and they looked after each other. The same was true of the Regiment.

What they faced wasn't fair. It certainly wasn't taken seriously by outsiders. But they did it and the cost was recorded on the memorial boards. It mattered to them. Men like Frank and Peter and Windy.

Nursing mattered to Emily. Nurse Charrington. It wasn't just some job; it was what she did. No cynical malice, no Clovis Sangrail, no frivolity or frippery. Just saving people's lives.

If he died, what difference would he have made? There were people who were alive because of what Nurse Charrington had done. Windy was sending money home to keep his family fed. Peter was trying to share his dream of a world that was fairer. Frank was working to become a sergeant to run a platoon. Hawk was working to train them. Grand schemes or little dreams, they all had something.

What did he actually care about?

*****

"Some sort of exercise, Lieutenant?" Major Marshall had stopped Lieutenant Hawkins. "You've got your men searching the ship, I've seen some of them searching the docks, and I've had captains of some of the other ships in the port complaining about your men bothering them. Would you mind telling me what exactly is going on?"

"It's just an exercise. Their uniforms were disgraceful at roll call. Rather than let them go into town, I've set them a task."

"Next time, please clear such exercises with me first. I don't appreciate having complaints coming out of the blue. Can I reassure the Colonel that this will be resolved shortly?"

"I'll report before long. One way or another, it will be over soon."

*****

Joy stood trembling. Lady Dalkeith was not happy.

"What do you mean, you don't know?"

"I don't know, Ma'am. Frank, Corporal Barry was happy before roll call when he said hello. I haven't had chance to see him since, Ma'am."

"The Colonel is in the dark. He does not like being in the dark. Sometimes he needs to be officially in the dark, but it helps to know what's going on when he's pretending to be in the dark. Corporal Barry's platoon is involved up to its grubby neck. I'm asking you again. What is going on?"

"I don't know, Ma'am," Joy wailed.

"Why don't you know?"

"Because nothing was wrong before roll call. Frank's been busy since then and it would be wrong for me to disturb him while he's working on Regimental business."

"Find out what the problem is. I suggest you speak with O'Grady. He's usually at the bottom of any mischief."

"Yes, Ma'am. Ma'am, does that mean I can interrupt Frank while he's working?"

"Certainly not." Lady Dalkeith's voice was abrupt.

After Joy had left, Colonel Dalkeith entered the room. "A problem arose at roll call," he said. "That probably means someone was not at roll call. I'm going to take a stroll round the ship. See who's searching and who's missing. Know who's gone and you can work out how they'll run."

"Then you'll advise me, I'll advise Joy, and she'll advise Corporal Barry." Lady Dalkeith knew the game as well as Colonel Dalkeith.

"And the problem will be solved with my being none the wiser."

*****

"Do you have news, Sergeant Taylor?"

"All the Captains of the other ships deny anyone sign on with them today. He may have stowed away on them. Short of searching them, we won't know. None of them are leaving today. He's not in the engine room. The stokers like him, but they don't like him enough to hide him when that's hiding a deserter. Still checking the docks."

"So, no news yet. Time's running out, Sergeant."

*****

"What's going on?" Windy asked Nurse Charrington. "Yesterday, you and Thomas were close. Now he's gone AWOL, and you say it's nothing to do with you? What's happened?"

"I don't think it's any of your business."

"He's my mate. It's my business."

"But you've got a rather big secret from him."

"If you're threatening me with that, don't. What's happened?" Windy sounded exasperated.

"It's between us. When he's back and if he's happy to tell you, then fine. Until then, I have to assume he wants it kept secret. He didn't tell you, so that's what I have to assume. What's Thomas' secret?"

"If he wanted you to know, he'd have told you."

"That's true," Nurse Charrington said reluctantly. "It looks like he didn't trust me as well as not understanding or respecting me. I know better now. Will you be all right? In case whoever it is comes?"

"I hope they do come. Whoever it is will be restrained within an inch of their life."

Nurse Charrington just stopped herself in time from pressing for more information. That was what Thomas had done to her. "He'll be all right, won't he?"

"If he's lucky, we'll never see him again. If we do see him again, then he's in big trouble," Windy said. He was worried about what would happen.

*****

Colonel Dalkeith sat and thought. It was either Rifleman Miller or O'Grady. He'd seen everyone else. Grant had been watching Nurse Charrington's medical office. He was trying to stay out of sight, but he could do with more training in remaining concealed. Grant outside watching meant Miller was inside waiting. That meant it was O'Grady that was missing. That tied in with what Nurse Charrington had said.

His first assumption had been that O'Grady had gone on a bender and was sleeping it off somewhere, probably in police custody. However, he'd returned last night and hadn't signed out again.

It had been noticed at roll call, which meant he wasn't at roll call. He'd had a conversation with O'Grady about how Furley-Smith would run and he'd been spot on. O'Grady would remember that conversation and make use of it. He'd know the first thing we'd do would be to search all the places he could use to get out of British jurisdiction. We'd search other ships in the harbour. There was no chance of those ships keeping him hidden if it meant upsetting the port authorities here and they knew we could make things difficult for him. O'Grady would want us to think he'd make a fast break for it; get a head start and keep it. That's not what he'd do. He'd go to ground somewhere, wait for us to finish searching the ships, then move on. That's when he'd make his break, while we were stretched elsewhere and after we'd cleared the ships.

He'd go to ground. Where? If his name were O'Grady, he'd seek sanctuary in a church. Assumed name, however. Disguised as a stoker? He'd suggested that about Furley-Smith. No. The stokers wouldn't go the distance for him. Once we started asking, they'd give him up. O'Grady had no-one he could trust, so he'd hide alone and out of sight. Somewhere he could slip off the ship when it was night with no chance of anyone seeing him.

Obvious, really.

*****

Thomas sat and thought. What did he care about? He thought he'd cared about Emily. He did care about her, but she'd made it plain she didn't care about him. She'd ended any hopes he had there. All he could do was accept that and move on. That was what she wanted.

What *did* he want? He kept coming back to the memorial boards outside the State Schools. The people on those boards were remembered and honoured by the children. They had next to nothing. The people who ran things held the State School children in contempt, as expendable and of no account. Despite that, everything that mattered was done by them.

If he'd never left home, what would he have done? Inherited the estate, married, hunted and gone to balls, had an heir to pass the estate onto. He would have gone to his grave without doing a single thing that helped anyone else.

That was why he had left home; because nothing mattered. That was what he had to do. Something that made a difference.

Now all he had to do was work out what.

*****

All she could do was harden her heart. With luck, she'd never see him again. She'd almost given her heart to him. She'd thought he understood her, and she'd been wrong. Never again.

If he didn't understand her, she certainly didn't understand him. What was he thinking off, going AWOL? He had his buddies, and he could certainly have his pick of available women.

Presumably he'd joined up with a false name. That was a common enough thing. He'd kept that hidden from her. It was plain that he didn't trust her enough to reveal this. She'd thought he cared for her, and she'd been wrong.

She had nursing. It would have to be enough.

*****

The door opened slowly and cautiously. A sailor stepped into the office, looking furtive. Windy crouched lower behind the desk. He shouldn't be here. If he was looking for Nurse Charrington, he could see that she wasn't here.

Wait a moment. He needed to catch the crook red-handed. Don't want him to wriggle out with some fast-talking excuse. Windy knew that Peter had seen and was moving into position. He couldn't see that; he just knew that he was.

The sailor carefully laid a shirt on the desk. He smoothed the collar, then looked among the bottles. He took down the bottle of diethyl ether, unstoppered it, used a dropper to take a few drops from the bottle, restoppered the bottle and carefully returned it to its place. He then used the dropper to put a couple of drops of fluid onto the shirt.

Windy stood up and hit his left palm with his right fist. "Resist arrest. Please."

"What you talking about? Just a couple of drops. Cleans up stains a treat."

Peter blocked the doorway. "Is he resisting arrest?"

*****

Emily had to take her mind off things. The best way to do that was to focus on someone else's problems. She had a responsibility for Nurse Ward.

Inevitably, Nurse Ward was talking with Lieutenant Campbell. They stood by a railing and were watching the workers in the docks; standing close to each other, but not quite touching. Talking comfortably.

"I'm surprised you're not taking in the sights of the town," she said. It was weak, but she still wasn't thinking clearly.

"We'll be going in a bit," said Nurse Ward. "We just need to see the Colonel first." She paused and glanced up at Alasdair, conspiratorially. "We need his permission."

Alasdair looked uncomfortable.

"His permission for what?" Nurse Charrington asked.

"Spending the night ashore." Nurse Ward spoke in a rush.

"Lieutenant Campbell. A word in private, please." She took him to one side. "I thought it had been made plain to you. You claimed to be a friend, not a lover."

"That's still the case. Look, Alice wants to make sure she won't get, offers, until she's ready. This is a way of making sure of that. If people think we're lovers, they'll leave her alone. It's just a pretence."

"Do you have the first idea how stupid an idea this is? Do you think it will put off anyone who was seriously interested? Do you think it will help her be ready? Most importantly, what if it stops being a pretence for one of you?"

"I've got to help her. She's a friend. You have my word I'll not let anything hurt her."

"I'm going to hold you to that, Lieutenant Campbell. On your word of honour, if that means anything to a Rifleman."

Lieutenant Campbell stiffened. "Furley-Smith was an aberration. A stain."

"Make sure you talk to her and listen and, above all, *understand* her."

Lieutenant Campbell was surprised at the vehemence in her tone. "Is everything all right?"

"Someone has been stealing medical supplies. Until that's resolved, things are not all right."

"What can I do?"

"Look after Nurse Ward. Be honourable."

*****

Joy had made the suggestion. It made sense but Frank didn't know whether he wanted to look or to cover for Thomas. If Thomas got away, he'd be safe. However, if he was caught, it was better to catch him quickly. The longer things went on, the worse it would be.

It was Joy's suggestion. That meant Lady Dalkeith would find out. That meant the Colonel would find out and would ask why the suggestion wasn't followed up on. He had to do it.

Reluctantly, he started checking the lifeboats. If anyone was going to find Thomas, it had better be him.

*****

Thomas had half an answer. He had to make a difference. People like his father didn't need any help. It was people who had been to State schools who needed help.

The other question was Emily. He thought he understood her now. Sort of. Not really, but better than he did. Was it the end there? Maybe that was the price that he had to pay for wasting his life so far.

Run or stay? That was another question. Actually, the answer was very simple. Whatever else happened, he couldn't leave his friends.

It was time to come out. He started to stand up to get out of the lifeboat when the cover was drawn back.

*****

Colonel Dalkeith sighed in relief. That had been easy enough. The stewards had discovered that the ether removed stains from clothing. They had been using it to keep the ship's officers' shirts spotless. The Captain of the ship could deal with it now. He had been made aware of what the consequences of a shortage of ether to the Regiment when it had been in action might have been.

It hadn't been malicious, but it had been very stupid. It would be dealt with, and no-one seemed to be asking how a steward had suffered injuries from what appeared to look remarkably like a one-sided brawl. Nurse Charrington was treating him. Colonel Dalkeith doubted that she would display a compassionate bedside manner.

Now for the hard one. This was going to need very careful handling. If he wasn't careful, he might run out of options.

Lieutenant Hawkins was present, and Sergeant Taylor brought O'Grady in.

Disturbingly, Rifleman O'Grady seemed calm. Colonel Dalkeith decided to start off with a straightforward question.

"You understand the seriousness of your situation?"

Thomas looked straight ahead. "The charges are serious, Sir."

"They're not yet charges. At the moment, we're looking to see what charges are appropriate, whether it's desertion or going AWOL. Both are very serious indeed."

"Yes, Sir. I did neither, Sir."

Colonel Dalkeith thought he had heard every excuse possible. This was a new one and it worried him. It made the possibility of mishandling this that much greater. "The facts seem clear enough. You were not at Roll Call. You were found in hiding and you had no leave to be absent. That seems to be a clear-cut case of Absent Without Leave." Push the emphasis on to the lesser charge. "Are you claiming that you had Leave?"

"No, Sir. I was not absent. I was not at Roll Call, but I was not absent."

"Should I get a nurse in to see if you're drunk? Not absent?" This was getting dangerous. If this went wrong, O'Grady would talk himself into desertion charges. That would mean a hanging and he had to make sure that this was avoided. Apart from anything else, it would be bad for morale.

"I'm not drunk, Sir. I simply wasn't absent. I was on the ship. I just missed a roll call." Thomas stood straight and stared over the Colonel's shoulder.

"Sergeant Taylor. Can you confirm that O'Grady signed in from shore leave yesterday?" Colonel Dalkeith thought he saw where O'Grady was going with this.

"Signed in, Sir. Corporal of the Guard remembers him returning, Sir. He'd returned."

Colonel Dalkeith cut the explanation short. "We have got proof that he returned from shore leave. That's what I needed to know." Now, how to phrase this question so that O'Grady didn't talk his head into a noose. "You returned from leave. But you were not at Roll Call. Where were you at that time?"

"Where I was found, Sir. On board the ship. The ship is effectively the Regiment's barracks when we are on board. By being on board the ship, it's the same as if I was in barracks. Because I was in barracks, I can't have deserted or gone AWOL, because I did not leave the barracks, Sir."

"You were hiding in one of the lifeboats. Why? Was it to wait until after the other ships in port had been checked, so you could then run?" Colonel Dalkeith wanted to make sure this was all on the record.

"No, Sir."

"Then why? Why hide in that lifeboat?"

"Personal matter, Sir."

"This could be a hanging matter." He had to make sure O'Grady knew the stakes involved. "If you want to keep your neck out of a noose, you're going have to be a lot more specific."

"Nurse Charrington told me there was no possibility of a relationship, Sir. I was upset. Couldn't think straight."

"You seem to be thinking straight enough now."

"Yes, Sir. Had chance to think things through, Sir."

"I see. Sergeant Taylor, Rifleman O'Grady had no belongings with him when Corporal Barry located him?"

"No belongings, Sir."

"Did he resist in any way when Corporal Barry located him?"

"No, Sir."

"Did he try to run in any way when he was located?"

"No, Sir."

Colonel Dalkeith looked to Lieutenant Hawkins. He did not dare ask him if O'Grady was normally reliable. He needed to ask the question in the right way to get a satisfactory answer. "Is Rifleman O'Grady normally punctilious in following orders?"

Lieutenant Hawkins considered his words carefully before answering. He also understood the importance of giving a satisfactory answer. "Up until this incident, he'd always carried out orders to the best of his ability."

There was light at the end of the tunnel. "Rifleman O'Grady. I'm inclined to believe you had no intention of running. I'm therefore ruling out desertion and AWOL. However, you have made a bloody nuisance of yourself, put a lot of people to a lot of trouble and set a bad example to other members of the Regiment. You absented yourself from a formal parade and you've shown no remorse for that. If I allowed that to go unpunished, I would be failing in my duty. Since we are deployment, I feel that dealing with it under field regulations is appropriate. You may either accept the ruling or ask for a court martial. I might add that a court martial may not come to the same conclusion that I have regarding the charge of desertion. Will you accept my ruling?"

He had to ask the question and he had very little leeway in how he asked it. He hoped O'Grady had the sense to accept.

"Yes, Sir. I just want to get on with things."

Colonel Dalkeith breathed a sigh of relief. "Very well. I'm going to make an example of you. You have been a confounded nuisance. Flogging would not be an option were we on Home Service. We aren't. We are on deployment. The cat has been outlawed. The cane hasn't. Ten strokes, with your platoon on parade to witness. Do you have anything to say?"

Just acknowledge and we can close the book on this one, Colonel Dalkeith thought.

"Yes, Sir. Not about the punishment. That's fair. It's just that I had chance to think. The thing is, I had a confusion and no-one I could talk to, Sir."

"What do you mean, you had no-one to talk to?"

"I couldn't speak to the other riflemen. My confusion might have infected them and caused them to have the problems I had. The confusion. I couldn't speak to the NCOs, Sir. They'd be obliged to take official notice. Same goes for officers, Sir."

"What is the point you're making?"

"If there was a chaplain in the Regiment, Sir, I would have had someone to speak to, who could have put my mind at rest, without troubling others, or it becoming official. A proper chaplain, who can hear Confession, Sir."

"Where would we find a chaplain?"

"Several missions and seminaries in Cape Town, Sir."

"O'Grady, was this your plan from the start?"

"No, Sir. I was confused, Sir. I wasn't thinking straight."

"I see. Lieutenant Hawkins. Get the platoon ready to witness punishment. Sergeant Taylor. You will administer punishment."

*****

"It's one thing to patch people up with what the enemy does. It's disappointing to patch people up because of what our side does." Thomas lay face down on the bed in the medical office while Nurse Charrington checked the wounds on his back. And, embarrassingly, those to his bottom as well.

Five strokes to the bottom and five to the back. Spaced so that a blow didn't land on a previous blow, which might have caused extra damage.

"My medical advice for you would be not to sit down too much." Nurse Charrington kept her voice level.

Thomas wanted to talk with Nurse Charrington, but he felt this wasn't the time or the place. Not when he was lying face down without any trousers on. He wasn't sure what to say.

"What do you think you were playing at?" Nurse Charrington sounded a little exasperated.

"I don't know."

"You could have ended up being killed for it."

"I don't want to seem ungracious, but I'd rather not talk about it. I'm a soldier. Sometimes we get killed. That's how it works."

"And my job is to try and stop soldiers getting killed. You behaved in a very silly manner."

"I'd rather not talk about it. When all is said and done, it's not your concern. Didn't you say that you wanted our relationship to be purely professional?"

He couldn't see her eyes fill with tears. "I did. I apologise. I must ask you to avoid actions that could result in unnecessary injuries. I'm sure I will have plenty of necessary wounds and injuries to deal with." She took a deep breath. "I enjoyed our conversations. I would like to continue them."

"I don't think that's a very good idea. It's too easy for friendship to blur into relationship."

"If that's what you feel best." There was a catch in her voice. "I'll miss our conversations."

Thomas wanted to hug her and tell her it would be all right, but he was lying face down and she had been the one to say she didn't want a relationship. He'd miss the conversations, but he knew he would want a relationship if they continued. Pain shot through his back as she covered a wound. She had broken off things because he didn't understand about being a nurse.

"I think it for the best," he said. He wanted to ask her to help him understand, but that was what caused this in the first place. Perhaps it was as well he was confined to the ship for the rest of their time in Cape Town. If he went into town, he would do something stupid.

*****

A corporal was waiting for him when he got out of the medical office. "Colonel wants to see you."

"What, now?"

"At your earliest convenience. In Colonel speak, that means now."

Thomas was puzzled. He'd been punished and gone straight to the medical office. He couldn't have got into trouble in that time. Certainly not serious enough trouble that required him to go before the Colonel again.

"Relax, O'Grady. You're not in trouble. Not as such."

Thomas didn't find that last sentence very relaxing. "Yes, Sir."

"Besides, it's your fault. You were the one who wanted the Regiment to get a chaplain. That's why I'm going into town. I'm going to need an orderly. I chose you as a volunteer."

"Yes, Sir." There wasn't anything else he could say.

*****

Windy read the letter Lieutenant Campbell had given him. He'd said that it had arrived in a later delivery. He knew Lieutenant Campbell was lying.

He had to show it to someone and the only person who would understand was Nurse Charrington. When he arrived at the medical office, Nurse Charrington was wiping her eyes, clearly pulling herself together after crying.

"What's the matter?"

"There is nothing that is the matter. What can I do for you?" Nurse Charrington wiped her eyes and pulled herself together.

Windy knew she was lying but didn't know what to say. He showed Nurse Charrington the letter. "Apparently, I got a girl into trouble. She's asking me to send her the money so she can come out to Persia and marry me, let me do the honourable thing. I thought I should check for a medical opinion."

"And you say Lieutenant Campbell gave you this letter? I think you should be careful. Responding could lead to inconvenience."

"Thomas could come up with something. Maybe you and he could think of something."

"Rifleman Miller, there is no him and myself. Whatever there might have been was just the emotions of the voyage south. We've come to our senses in time, and I can now focus my full attention on my duties without any unwanted distractions."

That explained why she was upset. "Are you sure? Everyone thought …"

"Then everyone was wrong. It was nothing and that's probably for the best. I certainly do not want any well-meaning people interfering and trying to resolve this matter. It would just make things more painful than they already are. It is of no importance. Incidentally, if Lieutenant Campbell asks you if you intend to do the honourable thing, what will you say?"

"That's easy, Ma'am. I'll just tell him that I'm not an honourable man."

*****

Thomas and Colonel Dalkeith were being driven to the Seminary. Thomas had difficulty sitting down and he wasn't sure if Colonel Dalkeith appreciated this or not.

Colonel Dalkeith was obviously feeling garrulous. "While I've got you here, Rifleman O'Grady, there's a few things you can clear up for me. How are you getting on with solving your puzzle?"

"Puzzle, Sir?"

"Don't play stupid, O'Grady. Not with me. The puzzle of how Nurse Charrington can marry and still continue as a nurse."

"Not my problem, Sir. Not my puzzle."

"Why on earth not?"

"It's her puzzle, Sir, not mine. Nurse Charrington has made it plain enough to me that there is no 'us', Sir."

"And you've just accepted that?" Colonel Dalkeith sounded surprised.

"Yes, Sir. If anyone else had tried to keep us apart, I would have fought. She doesn't want me. That's an end to the matter, Sir. May I ask a question, Sir?" Thomas was desperate to change the subject. This was too painful.

"You may ask."

"Why me? Of all the people to have come along with you, why me?"

Colonel Dalkeith steepled his fingers. "Several reasons. Firstly, as an example. I'm showing your platoon that once punishment has been administered, the slate has been wiped clean. Your being here demonstrates that to them, which is an important element of any punishment. Secondly, you're the one who suggested finding a chaplain for the Regiment. It's only fair that you get to see whoever it is first. Thirdly, I suspect that it's not going to be easy to find a chaplain on such short notice. I rather suspect your devious mind might come in useful."

Colonel Dalkeith studied Thomas closely. "The slate's been wiped clean. The incident is over. Tell me, did you intend to desert?"

"Honestly Sir, I don't know. I really wasn't thinking straight. You'd got it all worked out, though, Sir."

"O'Grady, your trouble is that you think you're the only one in the Regiment who is a devious rogue. Fox taking a peacock indeed. Do you know why I keep peacocks?"

"Can't say that I had thought about it, Sir."

Colonel Dalkeith was enjoying himself. "They're such annoying creatures, don't you think? Sooner or later, some devious rogue will try to do something about them. Sometimes the Regiment has need of a devious rogue."

Thomas decided that silence was the wisest course of action.

*****

Windy told Peter and Frank about the break-up between Thomas and Nurse Charrington.

"I've got an idea," Windy said, as they sat in the sea-front bar. "Nurse Ward wants someone nice to help her resolve a problem. If we persuade Thomas to spend time with her, he resolves that problem, Nurse Charrington will get jealous, come and sort things out, Thomas will realise which of them he loves, he'll get back together with her, and Nurse Ward will be able to get together with Lieutenant Campbell without any performance anxiety. What do you think?"

Frank and Peter looked at their drinks while considering this.

"I think it worst idea I ever heard," said Frank, astonished.

Peter agreed. "Mind you, I think it's possible to come up with a worse idea."

"How?" asked Frank. He wasn't convinced.

"Windy, what's your next idea? Whatever it is, that'll be a worse idea. We'll not be able to get them back together until we know what drove them apart."

*****

Colonel Dalkeith and Thomas left the Seminary with nothing to show for the trip.

"One down," Colonel Dalkeith said cheerfully. "Tell me, O'Grady, what drove a wedge between you and Nurse Charrington?"

"I don't understand, Sir."

"It's a simple enough question."

"Yes, Sir. That was the answer. I don't understand. I don't understand what being a nurse involves. I don't understand how it all happened, and I don't understand Nurse Charrington, Sir."

"O'Grady, the day that you do understand women, write a book. You'll make a fortune. We'll see the Bishop next and see who he can suggest."

*****

Alice and Alasdair had walked for what seemed miles along the beach. They had walked and talked, before ending up on a deserted cove. They sat together and watched the waves.

"Alasdair, why have you been so kind?"

"Because if I get wounded, I want a nurse who likes me looking after me, rather than one who'll rub salt into the wound."

"Can't you be serious for once?"

Alasdair smiled ruefully. "Not easily. I'm not used to anyone taking me seriously."

She put her hand on his. "I do. Thank you for everything. I can even sleep properly now, thanks to you. I know that whatever happens, you'll be there for me."

*****

Colonel Dalkeith was running out of patience. Thomas coughed slightly.

"Pardon me for saying, Sir, but we're going about this all wrong."

"We've had no joy for the last six hours, and now you've decided we're going about this wrong? Tell me, Rifleman, exactly how you would go about it?"

"We're trying to find someone ready, willing, and able to leave on 24-hour notice to go to Persia for at least two years. We shouldn't be talking to people who've got a comfortable position here and who are settled. We should be looking for someone anxious to leave, someone without commitments here."

"Haven't you forgotten something?"

Thomas racked his brain. He'd covered most of the essentials. Then he realised. "Sir."

"Good point, O'Grady. Prison next."

"Prison, Sir? They're not going to release someone. Even if they were, the chances of them having a priest who would be any use, well, it's not likely, Sir."

Colonel Dalkeith sighed. Strange for O'Grady to miss the point. "O'Grady, a priest visiting the prison."

*****

Would people never stop calling? Nurse Charrington was annoyed. These weren't professional calls, just busybodies sneaking after gossip. She considered putting a sign up telling everyone to stay away, but that wouldn't be professional.

This was Lady Dalkeith. It was unlikely to be a professional call.

"People are worried," Lady Dalkeith said without any preamble.

"Why should they be worried?"

"They're worried about you. You and Rifleman O'Grady."

"You can advise everybody that there is no cause to be worried. My private life is my own business. I will do my job professionally and with all the skill I have, with no distractions. I don't see that anyone need concern themselves with anything beyond that."

"You're being very stubborn."

"That's part of being a good nurse, Lady Dalkeith. When the time comes, I have no intention of letting Him win."

"It's not a contest between you and Rifleman O'Grady."

"I'm not talking about Thom, about Rifleman O'Grady. You'd understand if you were a nurse. However, you may rest assured that I have nothing distracting me from my work."

*****

Colonel Dalkeith and Thomas had tried the prison and hospital, without success.

"Do they have State Schools here, Sir?"

"We may as well give it a go."

*****

There was a Chaplain at the State School. The Chaplain was happy, with conditions, to go with the Regiment to Persia. He said he was being retired soon, and that his replacement was eager to start. He said that he had no intention of retiring from doing God's work. He was a big man, well over six feet tall, broad-shouldered, and looked more like a heavy-weight boxer than a priest. He claimed to be in his 60s. It was hard to tell, but he looked no older than mid-40s.

"I'm going to do God's work on Earth until I go to be with God in Heaven," was how he put it.

"What's the condition?" Colonel Dalkeith asked.

"I've heard that your regiments take soldiers with few questions asked about their background. People escaping trouble. There are four in this school, old enough, big enough, and fit enough to pass muster. They are in trouble with the law here. They have repented. Their joining and sailing with you to Persia and away from difficulties here is the price of my coming with you."

"What denomination are you?" the Colonel asked.

"Methodist," the chaplain replied.

"Not ideal. We'd prefer Anglican."

"Well, I'm a Wesleyan Methodist. That means I go where God sends me. If some Anglican were to try and part me from my flock, he'd have a fight on his hands."

"O'Grady, is that theologically sound?"

"Sir, I don't think the men will mind about his theology. Catholic would be better, obviously. But, Sir, well, look at him."

"What about these boys? I'll see them before I decide. If they pass muster, they'll go in the Training Platoon. We're due to expand it to company size anyway. It'll be useful to get some recruits with a bit of training before we get Persian volunteers."

"Yes, but Sir, well, *look* at him."

"O'Grady, we'll be accepting Persians. We accept Irish, Sicilians, even Harrovians. They'll be on the receiving end of jokes. I suspect they already know that, and they consider it better than the alternative."

"But, Sir, Zulus?"

Colonel Dalkeith sighed. "O'Grady, not all blacks are Zulus. Chaplain Mhlangana," he said, stumbling over the name. "Exactly which tribe are you from?"

"I'm a Zulu, Colonel Dalkeith." The Chaplain stumbled over the name.

"They're going to call us the Black Watch," Thomas muttered. This was going to cause problems.

*****

Alice and Alasdair walked along the beach and asked her to tell him about her family. Almost unconsciously, they held hands as they walked.

"Nothing special. Dad drives a bus. I'm just a nurse, but they're proud of me."

"You're not *just* a nurse. You're a Regimental nurse. When will you realise that you are an important and very special person?"

"Out here, maybe. Back in the hospital, I'm just a nurse."

"So, stay with the Regiment. That way you'll be important. You know, even when you were a nurse at a hospital, you were special."

"The doctors didn't think so."

"The patients did, and they're what a hospital's all about."

"Alasdair, how do you *always* seem to know exactly what to say to make me feel better?"

"Because I'm not clever enough to lie." Alasdair shrugged. "When I say you're a credit to the Regiment, that's what I mean."

"There you go again. Alasdair, could I stay with the Regiment? After Persia, I mean."

"I don't see why not. Soldiers get hurt in England just as easily as abroad."

"I'd like that."

"Soldiers getting hurt so you can play at being nurse?" Alasdair said with a grin.

"No, silly. You know what I mean."

*****

"March them aboard, O'Grady."

Thomas tried to get the four recruits into line. Each of them wanted to be first and they didn't listen when he told them to line up by height. It was all right for Frank. When he did it, everyone simply did what he told them to do. They didn't mess around like these recruits.

Eventually, by pushing each of them into place, he got them lined up. He tried to ignore the jeers of the soldiers who were on the ship, looking down to the docks.

"What's this, the Black Watch?"

The jokes were crude and obvious, and the recruits stiffened at them.

"Like for like," Thomas said. "They use words, you can respond with words. When you're not on parade, that is. No more, no less. On parade, you move a muscle out of line, and you'll find out what field punishment is. Trust me when I say that you don't want to find out."

He marched them, after a fashion, to Nurse Charrington's medical office. "Stand there. Wait there. The nurse will see you, one at a time for your medical. You will behave yourself or it will go very hard on you." He vaguely remembered hearing that blacks had greater trouble controlling themselves in the presence of ladies than other races and he wouldn't permit any untoward behaviour.

He led the first recruit in and explained to Nurse Charrington what was required. Then he stood by the door.

"On the other side of the door, if you please, Rifleman O'Grady."

"I thought it best."

"Yes, they are that colour all over. Kindly wait outside, Rifleman O'Grady."

Thomas went outside. He'd keep an ear open, just in case. Naturally, a group of curious riflemen had gathered to look at the newcomers.

"Remember," he said to the recruits, "you're on parade, and you will be until you're dismissed. This will be when your officer tells you that you are dismissed."

*****

"John," said Colonel Dalkeith. "Brought you a present from Cape Town."

Lieutenant Hawkins sighed. "That sounds ominous, Sir."

"Four new recruits. It lets you get a head start on getting new recruits ready for action."

"I'd best see them, then."

They went along to the medical office. Lieutenant Hawkins looked at the line of recruits and the other soldiers trying to look as though they hadn't been jeering. He shook his head.

"Is it new Army policy to colour code new recruits? I think now might be a good time to discuss how Sergeant Taylor and I believe we should organise the Recruit Company."

"Soon John. I need to get the new chaplain settled in."

*****

Frank returned to the ship. Windy and Peter had stayed on at the Music Hall, hoping to meet some of the actresses, but Frank thought Joy might prefer him not to be involved in this. He wasn't quite sure how he'd done it, but he seemed to have accidentally bought a shark on the way back to the ship. It was dead and it was difficult to carry it, but he'd been told it was lucky.

As he staggered up the gangway with it, he wondered if it was lucky for the shark. Then he wondered if it was a good present for Joy. Maybe he'd had too much to drink.

The Corporal of the Guard smiled on seeing him. "You're to report to Lieutenant Hawkins straight away, you blackguard."

"What you mean, blackguard?" He wasn't going to get into a fight with the Corporal of the Guard.

"You'll see."

Glowering, Frank dragged the shark along the deck and up the stairs to Lieutenant Hawkins' cabin. He finally got there, knocked, and waited.

"Come in, Corporal. Leave the shark outside, for God's sake. Have you been fishing?"

"No, Sir. Been to music hall."

"Of course. Silly question. Stupid of me. Sit down, Corporal. You're not in trouble. Something has come up and I want to review your progress. I've had Sergeant Taylor's report on you and I've been watching you closely. You've been reliable and hard-working. I was impressed by your obstacle course. That's a good thing for when we're heading to Persia. Well done. You're still as green as grass and your written reports are not good enough. Work on them. Overall, I'm reasonably satisfied."

"Thank you, Sir."

"If you were an experienced NCO, this is the point where you will be asking yourself what the catch is. Here it is. When we get to Persia, we're getting a lot of recruits. We'll be growing from a platoon to a company, four platoons. I'll be breaking the current platoon into two. Platoons one and two will each be half-and-half Riflemen and recruits. Each rifleman buddies with a recruit. That should get them up to speed more quickly. Platoons three and four will be entirely new recruits. We'll have to do the best we can with them. That's the bad news. The good news is thanks to your buddy O'Grady, we've got the first four recruits already and they're on the ship. If they can be trained up before we reach Persia, they'll be an example to the other recruits in platoons three and four. I want you to take responsibility for training them on the ship. Sergeant Taylor will help you, but I want you to do it, not him. He's going to be busy in Persia because he will be both Company Sergeant, and Sergeant of platoons one and two. Do a good job, and you'll go a long way towards convincing me that you can have a crack as NCO of one of the trainee platoons."

"That's Sergeant's job, Sir."

"It is. You would be a Corporal doing a Sergeant's job. I don't promote someone to sergeant if there is the slightest chance they can't do the job. You will not be a Sergeant, but you would have the chance to prove whether or not you've got what it takes to be one. I would suggest you get some sleep. You're going to get precious little of it when we're underway."

"Yes, Sir. Thank you, Sir." Frank's eyes were bright. Another step closer to Sergeant. Joy would be pleased.

*****

"Drink, Chaplain?"

"I am a Methodist, Colonel. How many sins are committed by good people while they are intoxicated?"

Colonel Dalkeith noticed movement outside the Officers' Mess, glanced through the window and saw a corporal dragging a shark along the deck. He decided not to debate the Chaplain's point. "There's the question of rank. Regulations aren't clear."

"That's fine because I can't have a rank. If I have a rank, I can't talk to people on equal terms. A rank would mean I was either senior or junior to them and they couldn't confide in me. And anything told to me is confidential. Sanctity of the Confessional."

Colonel Dalkeith was beginning to regret taking on a chaplain for the Regiment. "But you're not a Catholic."

"Doesn't make any difference. They'll need to confide. That means knowing that whatever they say is between God, them, and me, and no-one else. I'll need an office. I'll hold my first Confessional when the ship's underway."

"But you're not Catholic."

"That doesn't make any difference. Some of the men are, they need Confession, I'm their Chaplain, so it's up to me to provide for their needs. Don't argue theology with me and I won't argue military regulations with you. If you don't agree, I can walk off this ship."

"That's blackmail."

"Of course. What else would you expect from me?"

******

"We had better be getting back," Alice said. "Thank you for being so kind. I can't remember when I was last so content." She leaned up and kissed Alasdair lightly on the cheek.

He cupped her face in his hands, gently, and kissed her lightly on the lips. He kissed her a second time, longer, then he stepped back. "You're right. We must get back."

That had taken all his willpower. A thought crossed his mind. "More like won't power," he muttered to himself.

"What was that?" Alice asked, puzzled.

"You're on the mend."

*****

Roll call was painful. Most of the platoon were nursing hangovers and feeling the worse for wear. No-one quite knew where the new recruits should go, and the recruits didn't understand when Sergeant Taylor shouted at them.

Windy and Peter had come back very late and very drunk. Windy was still wearing a feather boa. He did, however, seemed to have found time to shave.

Frank was still annoyed over the sailors who worked in the kitchen. He'd taken the shark to them, and they'd told him what he could do with it. He wasn't convinced that was physically possible. He wasn't quite sure how he could get back at them, but he had to do so in a way that demonstrated he would be a good Sergeant.

Thomas wasn't drunk but he wished he was. Nurse Charrington's office was just in his eyeline, and it hurt to see it. He also wondered what he would say to the Chaplain. He couldn't avoid it after having made a fuss about his having needed one. It had just seemed like a good way of getting one for Frank and Joy. He'd have to think what sort of problems he could come up with that the Chaplain could help him with. Since he'd nearly deserted, he'd have to be creative in inventing a problem. Then again, would that be wise? What if he actually needed a Chaplain? Then again, discussions with a Chaplain were confidential, so no-one else would know. Then again, if the Chaplain realised that he'd been lied to, well, that wouldn't be good.

It had to be a lie that wasn't a lie.

Sergeant Taylor addressed the platoon, explaining that before the ship would leave, the lifeboats had to be checked for stowaways.

"Or missing riflemen," came a muttered voice from the ranks.

"Rifleman Callaghan, report to Sergeant Taylor after roll call," said Frank. The voice hadn't been sufficiently muttered.

"Who'd want to stow away on this?" Thomas wondered as they started checking.

Naturally, that sent Peter off into one of his explanations about the iniquities of the system. "You're the fisherman, Frank. Do we throw the little stowaways back and recruit the big ones?"

Windy checked in a lifeboat. "Peter, how drunk were we last night?"

"Merry. No more. Why?"

"What did we do after the music hall?"

"I'm not sure. Why?"

"Only there's a pile of women's clothes in here."

By now, a handful of riflemen had gathered round. "What would anyone want with women's clothing?"

"It can be a useful disguise," said Thomas. "If you need to get out of somewhere, having a good disguise helps."

"Windy," asked Peter. "Why is the pile of clothes groaning?"

"Thomas? What's the explanation?" Windy sounded desperate.

"How should I know? I was with the Colonel."

"Yes, but if there's any scheme, you're at the bottom of it."

A woman's head appeared from out of the clothes.

"I think we'd better have a word, Riflemen Grant and Miller," said Sergeant Taylor. Corporal Barry, escort the lady from the ship. Miller, Grant, this is not a good example to set our new recruits."

"I don't know about that," muttered Rifleman Callaghan. "Wish I'd thought of it."

*****

The ship got underway. Naturally, it immediately started to rain. Frank started teaching the five new recruits the basics, much to the amusement of onlookers. "Riflemen Grant, Miller, either end of the line. Show the recruits how it's done. Where's O'Grady?"

Thomas had slipped away as soon as he saw Frank looking around and calling Peter and Windy up. He decided this was a good time to speak with the Chaplain. The Chaplain had been found a cabin that was a little bit bigger than a cupboard. A chair, a bed, a desk, a trunk, and about half a dozen books. Automatically, he tilted his head so that he could read the titles of the books.

"You're the young man who was with Colonel Dalkeith. I understand you had a worry." The Chaplain indicated that Thomas should sit on the chair while he sat on the bed.

"You're not a Catholic?" Thomas asked.

"I assume that you are, O'Grady. I'm Methodist, but I'm bound by the same rules as a Catholic with regards to these discussions. You, me, and God are the only ones to know what passes here. You tell me your concerns, I tell you what God says, and you do it."

"And if I don't?" Thomas was curious, rather than belligerent.

"There's a space by that obstacle course that's about the size of a boxing ring. You've heard of Muscular Christianity? If you don't follow the advice you're given, you'll find out how the Lord helps his servants smite those who stray."

"But you're, well, old."

"And you're young. Tomorrow at noon, duties permitting. I'll ask the Colonel to ensure that they will permit."

"You want me to box with you?"

"Little youth, I want you to *try*. Remember how Dempsey and Carpentier ended? Now, what troubles you?"

Thomas bridled. He wasn't used to being called little. Mind you, the Chaplain was a bit taller than his six feet, and deep-chested, more so than Thomas. Thomas explained about Millicent's letter, his encounter with her in London, then Lieutenant Furley-Smith, her marriage, and everything.

"You've got the letter?" Thomas handed it over and the Chaplain read it, then shook his head. "The traditional penance for sleeping with your mother is plucking your eyes out. That's a joke, O'Grady. I'm not saying you need to do that."

"You know about Oedipus?" Thomas asked.

"Do you think I lived in a mud hut, kept a dozen wives, and drank strong liquor from the skulls of the dead? I'm a Methodist. We don't drink liquor. And we must study. You, an O'Grady, knows about O'Dipus?"

"Wasn't allowed to read about him at school, so we did. That's how the teachers encourage you to read. They tell you that there's some books you can't read."

"What I see is this. You slept with a woman. Neither of you were married to anyone, so that makes it fornication, not adultery. A sin, but not a mortal one. Both of you were willing, so no compulsion is involved. You didn't know that there would be a marriage involved at a later date. What's the complication?"

Thomas explained about the expectation and the mathematics.

"That's a matter between God, husband and wife. What else?"

Thomas wondered if he should mention the situation with Nurse Charrington. He decided that keeping his mouth shut had been a hard-won lesson.

*****

Lieutenant Campbell waited until Corporal Barry had finished instructing the new recruits. Five new recruits made this ideal. Two experienced hands and five new recruits. Normally there would be seven to a screw gun team.

Obviously, the new recruits couldn't be expected to be that good at being artillerymen, but they looked fit and strong. That was also important. They'd probably not be as quick to learn as real soldiers, but they had time on the voyage. Telling them apart was going to be tricky, but necessary. To get the time down, they would each need to have a specific role.

Still, if Indian troops could manage, and manage well by all accounts, there was no reason these blacks couldn't manage.

He'd better warn Alice that there would be eight working on the gun, rather than three.

*****

Frank didn't know what to do about the shark. If he did nothing, he'd have to throw it over the side, and that offended his sense of parsimony. Throwing it overboard would be such a waste.

Still, there didn't seem to be any alternative. He'd get the recruits to carry it up to the side. "Riflemen Recruits Abe and Billy, stand fast. Others dismiss."

The new recruits had been given manageable names: Abe; Billy, Charlie; Davie, and Edward. He wasn't entirely sure which was which yet, but he'd work on that. Davie was the big one. He'd always get picked for heavy lifting.

"Corperaal," Abe said. "Why are you throwing food away."

"Because no-one can cook it."

Abe beamed. "Corperaal Father, I can."

Frank smiled. This was one way to get the attention of the officers. "I'm going to Confession. Then we'll get shark cooked up for officers."

He was going to do this without Thomas.

*****

She wasn't prying, Nurse Charrington told herself. She needed to advise Lieutenant Hawkins on the fitness of his new recruits and to tell him how Rifleman O'Grady was recovering. The recruits were strong and fit. One of them had worked on boats here. The other four were little more than schoolchildren, that age between boy and man.

"Is the situation between you and O'Grady resolved?" he asked, bluntly.

"I don't believe that is any concern of yours."

"One of my men was damn near hanged. That makes it my concern."

"It has been resolved. Not necessarily to my satisfaction, but it has been resolved. In a few days, he will have quite forgotten there was any situation that needed resolving."

"Are you sure? Good. Distractions are the last things the men need out there."

"I can assure you that I will not cause any distractions to your men. If you will excuse me, I have work to do." She left quickly. It was for the best, she told herself. She heard him mutter something about women on a deployment being a confounded nuisance.

She walked in a daze to the railing where she had always used to talk with Thomas. She was here to do a job. If Lieutenant Hawkins thought there would be anything else, she'd have to redouble her efforts. It wasn't as though she would ever have any distractions now.

"Is everything all right, Miss?" Sergeant Taylor stood next to her at the railing. She must have been lost in thought because she never heard him arrive. "I saw you leave the Lieutenant's cabin, Miss. You looked a bit distraught."

"It's nothing, thank you Sergeant."

"I'll hazard that he said something tactless about O'Grady, and something tactless about women distracting the men, Miss."

"What was said was between us, Sergeant. I don't hold with tittle-tattle and gossip."

"Lord love you, Miss. The Regiment runs on tittle-tattle and gossip. Now don't you mind the Lieutenant. He's worried sick and can't show it. It comes out in stupid comments sometimes. He didn't mean no harm."

"Do you know him well?"

"We were buddies together when we first joined. We been through all sorts together, so, yes, I know him well."

"What is he worried about? I gather this platoon will be in reserve in Persia."

"Here's the thing, Miss. When you're in reserve, that means that when you're called on, when you're needed, things are in the, things are serious. You got to get it right. On deployment, the reserve can be needed in the blink of an eye. We've got a platoon worth of newly trained recruits, none of whom have seen action. We've got five black buggers we know little about and how they'll be under fire, and we'll get three platoons of whatever rubbish the Persian Army wants to get rid of. We've no experienced NCOs, no officers what knows these men, and our new recruits ain't never even fired a Lee-Enfield before. We're going to have to teach them every blessed thing, them Persians probably can't speak English, so we're going to have to learn them that as well, and all the while, we might get called into action on a moment's notice when everything's falling apart, and we got to hold it all together. The Lieutenant is responsible for it all, and he's got no-one he can share it with."

"Except you, Sergeant."

"That's true, Miss, except me. But what he really needs, Miss, is a wife. Nothing beats a good wife for settling a man down."

"Are you married, Sergeant?"

"Was, Miss, was. Married twenty years to the best girl in the world. Pretty as a picture and heart as big as a mountain. Died of fever two year back in India. You know what she said to me, her last words? She said: "I'll be watching you, Reggie, so don't you be getting gloomy. And I'll be waiting for you, but don't you be in any hurry, because I can be patient and I'll expect some good yarns from you when it's your time." Then she died. The Lieutenant, he doesn't know the stability a good wife gives a man, but I do, so don't worry about being a distraction, Miss." He smiled. "I ain't going to let them have time to be distracted."

"Thank you, Sergeant. That's been a comfort. You and your wife were very fortunate."

"I was the lucky one, Miss. Doris married a wild boy, and I couldn't let her down."

"It sounds like you were right for each other."

*****

The galley staff had refused point blank to let Frank cook the shark there. They claimed there wasn't enough room and that he'd just get in the way, particularly as Abe would be there as well.

A good NCO can always cope with setbacks. It was hotter than Hell in the boiler room with the stokers, so Frank and Abe went there. The shark was beginning to smell, but that was all right. The English liked game to be on the verge of being rotten. Shark had to be game.

"How it get cooked?" Frank asked Abe.

"Fish sliced, flash cooked on hot surface. Maybe ten minutes. Put salt, pepper, spice on surface, put fish on, pour beer over it as cooks, stop it burn."

It sounded straightforward enough. "You keep smiling, Recruit Abe, or we'll lose you in the coal dust." First thing, find something to cook it on. Hot surface. A shovel held in the furnace would do nicely. "You clean shovel. I find way to keep meat warm between cooking and getting it served in Mess."

Frank thought. He could reheat them in the galley and it wouldn't matter if they got cold in between. What else? He couldn't get over-confident. Salt, pepper, spices, beer. Beer was easy. The stokers got a beer ration while working and the stokers Thomas worked with never touched it. Salt was easy enough. Plenty of salt in the sea and the water would boil off. Pepper was straight forward. The galley had a red pepper thing that no-one knew how to use. No-one would miss that. That left spices to find. He was going to be a Sergeant. Sergeants can find anything anywhere.

That made it obvious. He'd ask Sergeant Taylor. He'd been to India. He'd know about spices. Sergeants knew everything.

"Recruit Abe, I get other bits. You prepare shovel. It must be clean. Spit and polish, like I show you for boots. It must be clean enough to eat off."

Sergeant Taylor was surprised when Frank asked about spices. "You becoming all culinary? Can't your girl cook for you?"

"If on deployment, girl not there. Still need to eat."

"Good thinking. How are the recruits?"

"Keen, but green."

"Keep your eye on them, especially round the nurses. Blacks aren't like Indians. They get urges they find it hard to control, so we have to teach them how to control them. So, our blacks are green, Corporal? Let's hope they aren't yellow as well."

"Spices, Sergeant?"

"Spices is like herbs. Herbs is like grass and flowers, all ground down. Ask Nurse Charrington for a pestle and mortar, then find grass and flowers."

"Grass and flowers? We're on ship."

"Initiative, lad. We've still got vegetables and things. Potato peel, nut shells, lemon pips. They all grind down to make herbs."

"Are nuts vegetables, Sergeant?"

"They grow in the ground, don't they? That means they're vegetables."

Frank had a thought. "Tea. That from leaves. Therefore tea a vegetable."

"Now you're getting the idea."

Nurse Charrington seemed to be distracted but loaned him a pestle and mortar. "Bring it back clean, mind."

Then it was a matter of collecting the vegetable parts and heading back to the boiler room. There was another problem. How was he going to stop coal dust getting everywhere?

"When we cook on camp, we wrap meat in mud. Fire makes mud hard. When cooked, we break hard mud off. But there no mud." Abe's face fell when he thought of this.

"That why I the Corporal and you the Recruit. Look around. Lot of mud. Coal is dirt that burns. Wet coal dust, make mud. Fire dries out coal dust, it will flake off when we cook it."

"We stop coal dust getting on by putting coal dust on?" Abe didn't sound convinced.

"It's the water that makes the difference. We try first, make sure it work."

He cut a small slice, prepared it, and put it on the shovel.

"The shovel's black and shiny. How you get it like that?"

"Boot polish, Corperaal. Then spit and polish. Like for boots."

The shovel blade was certainly shiny. "Ten minutes, you say."

There was no way anyone could hold a shovel for ten minutes in front of the furnace, so he put it on the coals, shut the door as far as he could. Then they waited. Ten minutes later, he withdrew the shovel.

Or at least, what was left of it.

"That lesson for us, Recruit Abe. Furnace hotter than oven." He looked at the twisted remnants of the shovel. "If furnace hotter than oven, we cook for shorter time." It was a good job he had done a trial run.

One minute worked better. They tried a taste and it seemed OK. Next was the task of cooking enough for the officers. It was just as well he only needed to cook each steak for a minute. Ten minutes each would have taken forever.

They got into a routine. Frank prepared a steak, put it on a shovel with the spices. Abe removed the shovel from the furnace with the cooked steak and grabbed the shovel with uncooked steak. Frank took off the prepared steak, removed the coal dust, poured beer over it, stacked it, and got the next shovel ready.

It was hotter than Hell. They were exhausted when they finished.

"Why you join?" Frank asked.

Abe's smile instantly vanished, to be replaced by a scowl. "I worked on a fish boat. We went out and did well. Filled the boat quickly, so we got back sooner than expected. I got home early, found my wife with another man, an Indian. I fought him and he died in the fight. Police said it was murder, so I needed to leave."

Frank considered this. "Understood. Remember, women on ship are wives of other men. We have plenty of enemies to fight without fighting ourselves."

"The nurse who saw me. Is she the wife of a man on the ship?"

Keep it simple. "Yes. She and her man in middle of row, not talking. But it come right."

"Why doesn't he make her obey him? I make him an Afro day sack, that will help him master her. Wives must obey their husbands. That's what God says."

"We let them sort it out themselves. Interfere, they both turn on you." Frank wondered if that might help them but decided this would be a last resort. He sent Abe to carry the steaks to the galley, while he disposed of the shark remains in the furnace, then returned the pestle and mortar to Nurse Charrington. He asked if she would be going to the Officers' Mess. She told him that she was far too busy. "If you could arrange some sandwiches to be sent to me here, please, Corporal."

"Whatever go on between you and Thomas, I am Frank to you. He my friend. You're my friend."

"That's kind of you. I really am busy, though."

She was not too be persuaded. Frank had to get to the galley.

Things were not going well at the galley. The stewards refused to let Abe in with the food and they weren't happy about letting the food in. "What does a black know about cooking?" was the Chief Steward's comment.

"Blacks eat too. They know how to cook."

"And you're covered in coal dust. You can't serve this to the officers. What is it?"

"It African dry sack," Frank said. "You tell officers I make it."

The Chief Steward looked at the steaks. He wrinkled his nose. "What was in the sack?" He tasted a small bit of it. "Well, Army officers are pigs and will eat anything. Don't expect any leftovers, OK?"

"You tell them, OK?"

"Don't worry. We'll tell them what they need to know."

*****

"What's this, Steward?" Colonel Dalkeith asked.

"African tree snake, sir. Very popular South African dish. I thought you might like something from South Africa."

"Can't say I ever heard of it. What's it like?"

"Bit like South Africa. Bit savage, strong, quite rich, lacking in presentation, but good when you're in the field."

"Well, let's see what you've cooked up for us, Steward."

*****

The new recruits were certainly strong, Lieutenant Campbell had to give them that. There were only four of them here; Corporal Barry had commandeered the fifth, the thin one. These four were young, strapping lads. Keen as mustard when they realised they were going to work on a big gun. Not artillerymen, but when it came to moving large lumps of metal into place and holding it there while Grant and Miller did the screws up, they learned quickly.

"One minute 23." Lieutenant Campbell nodded gravely. "Not up to Indian Army standard, yet, but not bad for a first day."

"Sir," said Recruit Davie. "What is Indian Army standard? We going to beat it."

They were definitely keen. "If you make one minute 15 this time, I'll go through the firing procedure, and then we'll fire it."

That gave them a burst of energy and they chattered away as they worked. Lieutenant Campbell looked at his watch. One minute 16. He looked at the men, sweating and standing ready, waiting for him to give the time. "One minute 15," he said.

Alice came out of her office. "Time for dinner," she said.

"Just got a bit to do here. You go ahead. I'll be along shortly."

"Go on my own?" Nurse Ward sounded a bit panicky, looking around anxiously.

"I think you're ready. I'll be along very soon." He came across, placed both hands on her shoulders and looked her in the face. "You can do this. I'll be right behind you."

"I'm scared," she whispered.

"And once you've done it, you won't be."

She straightened. "You'll be close?" She turned and walked towards the Mess. Lieutenant Campbell watched her all the way to the door into interior of the ship.

He turned to the men. "Right. Firing drill. We'll fire one round out to sea. Tomorrow, we'll switch roles and you'll function in a different position. You've got to be able to fill any slot, in case there are casualties. We've got three guns. By the end of this trip, I'll want each of you to be able to take the one and two positions on the guns, then we can train up these Persians."

The men realised they were only getting one shot today, so they took care over it. After they had done it, the blacks cheered and jumped ecstatically after the shot, while Grant and Miller stood solidly, waiting for further orders. Presently, the blacks realised that they should get into line.

"I can appreciate your enthusiasm and excitement. That's a good thing. But if I had decided we needed a second shot, you wouldn't have been ready. Learn from Grant and Miller. They're sound men; you could do worse than take note of them. Now that you're in line and ready, we'll fire a second shot. Recruit Davie, you will act as the firer. Everyone will get their chance in due course."

When the gun had been cleaned and put away, he made sure the men had got to their mess. Then he went to the Officers' Mess. He'd missed the first course, but he felt he'd done well.

"I did it, Alasdair," Alice said when he sat next to her.

*****

The galley staff, as always, finished off the leftovers after the officers had eaten.

*****

Nurse Charrington had expected Thomas, Rifleman O'Grady to come for his lesson. She was disappointed that he didn't. After a while, she went for a walk. He was in their old spot near the rear of the ship. She walked briskly over to join him.

"You didn't come for training today."

"No. I don't think it a good idea. I'll ask Nurse Ward to train me. Or Nurse Stewart."

"Don't be silly. It's just a matter of being professional about it."

"Nurse Charrington, it might be easy for you to be professional about it. I'm finding it harder. There will be occasions when we need to work together, but I see no advantage in seeking them out. If you will excuse me, I've a shift with my stokers."

She watched him leave, frustrated he was being so difficult. If he wanted to be taught by another nurse, so be it.

*****

Next morning, all around the ship, many platoons had difficulty at roll call. The men were there. The NCOs were there. Many officers weren't.

Sergeant Taylor looked around. The other platoons looked like they were in a similar position. "Corporal Barry, take Recruit Abe and go and see if Lieutenant Hawkins has any special instructions for us."

Frank hurried off, then slowed to a quick march. No point looking worried. Elsewhere, he could see men being dispatched from their platoons. He knocked on the Lieutenant's door. He could hear sounds from inside. He opened the door.

The room stank. Lieutenant Hawkins was sitting on the bed, hunched over a bucket into which he was vomiting. He was sweating and looking seriously unwell.

"Recruit Abe, go tell Sergeant Taylor we need nurse."

As Frank glanced out, he could see similar conversations being held at many of the officers' cabins.

*****

While Corporal Barry and Recruit Abe checked on Lieutenant Hawkins, Sergeant Taylor asked the men how their training was getting on. Rifleman Callaghan had a problem.

"I've been learning navigation at night. The ship's navigating officer said that you could tell which way was north by finding the right star. You find it using the Plough, which is a consummation in the stars. Only I've been looking for it and it's gone. It's not there anymore."

"Rifleman O'Grady," said Sergeant Taylor. "If you don't return the Plough to its proper place by the time that we reach Persia, you'll be up on charges of theft of Divine property. Is that understood?"

"But Sergeant, I didn't take it."

"I'll expect it to back before we reach Persia and no more will be said about it."

The RSM went around the companies. RSM Moyle had decided that those with the necessary skills would restore the situation. Everyone else, and he emphasised this was vitally important, was to be kept too busy to think. The situation was grim. Reports suggested all the officers except Lieutenant Campbell were out of action, as were all the nurses except Nurse Charrington and all the stewards for the Officers' Mess.

Sergeant Taylor turned to face the platoon, his face carefully composed into an impassive expression. It was very important not to worry the men. "Corporal Barry. You've been practising your cooking. Now's the time for us to see what you can do with it. The galley staff are all on the sick roster, so you're looking after the officers until the galley staff are back on their feet. Speak with Nurse Charrington about what to cook. Take two of the recruits. O'Grady. You've been studying medical stuff. You're Nurse Charrington's aide. She's the one nurse we got standing and we got 34 officers down. She's going to be busy. Miller, Grant, Callaghan, Wagstaff. Take the remaining recruits. You're on clean-up duty. Clear away dirty buckets, get rid of the dirt, supply clean, empty buckets. You're also making sure everyone has plenty to drink. What is it, O'Grady?"

"Sergeant. Nurse Charrington told me it was important to keep dirty and clean separate. People cleaning up shouldn't bring drink. Drink carriers have to be clean, she said."

Sergeant Taylor didn't like being contradicted by a rifleman in front of the men, but what O'Grady said made sense. "If that's Nurse Charrington's advice, then we'll go along with the trained nurse. Miller, Grant, take one of the recruits. Drinks to all the ill. Check with Nurse Charrington what they can drink. Callaghan, Wagstaff, take the other two recruits. Bucket emptying duty. And take them back clean. Corporal Barry, your girl is to look after the Colonel. Everyone else, I think we need to get on with checking our equipment. This sea air might be good for you, but it ain't good for equipment."

Thomas and Frank met Nurse Charrington at her office. "Corporal Barry. Cooking. First of all, everything in the galley needs to be cleaned, thoroughly. All items to be put in boiling water for at least ten minutes. Knives, cutlery, pans, everything. Every surface cleaned. Nothing gets cooked until you've done that. There will be a need for a lot of drinks. All water is to be boiled before it goes out. When you're done, call me and I'll check that you're good to cook. Only cook things from tins. We don't know what food caused this, so we need to be careful. There'll be a lot of need for drink, not much for food. Keep everything clean, and clean everything after use. Understand. Come on, Rifleman O'Grady, keep up."

Nurse Charrington walked briskly as she started her rounds and Thomas had to hurry to keep up. "Rifleman O'Grady. We'll check on the nurses first. See how long it's likely to be before I can have some assistance. Then the officers, then the galley staff. First check is triage. Do you remember what triage is?"

"Those who'll get better without us doing anything. Those we can't do anything to save. Those where we can make a difference." He paused. "Is anyone likely to die from this?" He hadn't really thought about death. People got ill, then they got better. He had to push that thought from his mind.

"I can't say until I've seen them, can I. Keep up. While we're walking, we're not doing anyone any good, so don't dawdle."

Lieutenant Campbell was with Nurse Ward, looking worried. Nurse Ward sat on the bed, blankets around her shoulders. She looked pale. "She complains of being cold, she's perspiring, I mean, she's glowing a lot. She feels feverish," Lieutenant Campbell said.

Nurse Charrington noted the bucket. "Keep her warm. Lots of blankets. Lots of drink. The sweat, the vomit, that's the bad stuff coming out. Clean water in, lots of it. She'll be weak for a while."

"Would she be better off in my cabin?"

"Yes. Less distance for me to walk. Rifleman O'Grady, have someone help the Lieutenant take Nurse Ward to the cabin."

"That's not necessary," Lieutenant Campbell picked her up in his arms. "She's no weight at all." Thomas held the door open for him. "You get on with your duties," Lieutenant Campbell said. "I'll look after Alice. I'll send someone if there's a problem."

He carried her to his cabin, struggled briefly with the handle, then carried her inside.

"This isn't how I expected to be carried over a threshold," she whispered.

"That's right. Make fun of me," he said with mock severity. "I'm under strict instructions to make sure you get better quickly. Nurse Charrington needs you."

*****

Frank decided that if Nurse Charrington wanted the galley clean, then he would get it clean. That meant washing and scrubbing every surface. Abe washed, then Billie scrubbed, then he wiped.

"Kitchen was clean," Frank said, "but not Rifleman clean."

"But Corperaal, when we …"

"That was different, Recruit Abe. We concentrate on getting this clean. We get it Rifleman clean."

*****

Nurses Stewart and Plummer weren't well, but they were being looked after by the RSM, who had several Riflemen doing the actual work. It would be at least two or three days before the nurses were back on their feet.

The next person that she had to see was Colonel Dalkeith.

And Lady Dalkeith. Nurse Charrington was surprised to see Lady Dalkeith was also struggling and ill as well as Colonel Dalkeith. Joy was struggling to hold things together, trying to keep them warm, trying to keep them clean, trying to keep the room clean.

First things first. That was to check on the patients. Lady Dalkeith was ill, but not badly so and would recover shortly. Colonel Dalkeith was more of a puzzle. He had food poisoning, but there was something else. Arthritis in his fingers, but something more.

"Do you find yourself getting out of breath easily?" she asked.

"I'm not as young as I was. Only to be expected."

Nurse Charrington frowned. She wanted to look into this but that would have to wait until there wasn't an emergency going on. "Joy. Clear away the waste. Make sure they get plenty to drink. Make sure they keep warm. Everything else can wait until things are back to normal."

"Just put buckets outside," said Thomas. "I'll make sure they get picked up and clean ones left for you. I'll also make sure food is sent to you. Leave you free to look after the Colonel and Lady Dalkeith."

Nurse Charrington looked curiously at Thomas but said nothing. They went to see the other officers. Some were not too ill, others more so.

"I've got an idea," said Thomas suddenly. "You can't do it all."

Nurse Charrington stiffened. "It is something that has to be done. I'll thank you not to tell me what I can and cannot do."

"But you could use some help. The wives of the men can help. They're not nurses, but they can keep an eye on the ill and come running when there's a problem. It will save you going around and that will let you spend your time doing nursing stuff rather than trying to find out where you're needed."

She didn't want to admit it, but he had a good point. "Very well. Please arrange it. I'll brief them when I do rounds."

"The thing is, otherwise you'll be spending a lot of time walking to somewhere just to find out you didn't need to go to just to find out you didn't need to go there."

"I agree. Could you arrange it, please?"

"Only it makes more sense to keep the expert for the important parts and get the wives to do what they can to help you."

"Rifleman O'Grady, can't you take yes for an answer? I approve of this. I agree. You might try listening when you're scheming to have your way."

"Of course. I apologise. I'm so used to people discounting what I say because I'm just a Rifleman."

"O'Grady, whatever else you are, you're no ordinary Rifleman. It's time to see the galley staff and then you can get your wives sorted out."

Thomas caught a ghost of a smile on her face, but it must have been his imagination, because when he looked, it was nowhere to be seen.

"Keep up, Rifleman O'Grady. Don't dawdle."

*****

Lieutenant Campbell had to sternly tell Alice to lie down. "You will be no help to Nurse Charrington at the moment. First, you get better. Then you can help. The sooner you get better, the sooner you can help. That means resting now.

"I'll be all right." She tried to stand up, only to wobble and for Alasdair to steady her, pick her up and lay her on the bed again.

"Rest. That's an order," he said.

"I outrank you," Alice said weakly.

"Not when you're lying on my bed in my room." He sat next to her. "Don't fret. You're quite safe here." He had seen a look of panic appear in her eyes. "You outrank me. I'm not going to assault a senior officer and it's my duty and privilege as a friend to look after you."

Nurse Ward relaxed a little. That is, until the vomiting started again. "How can you put up with this?" she asked.

"Because you're my friend, you silly thing. Today, I get to play at being a nurse."

*****

Nurse Charrington looked in at the galley. Frank, Abe, and Billy had worked hard at cleaning it.

"That's looking much better," she said.

"Recruits work hard," Frank replied. "They did well. They worked like blacks."

"Well, they would," Thomas commented from behind Nurse Charrington.

She ignored him. "Pots, pans, cutlery, everything in boiling water for ten minutes. That's after cleaning them. And boiled water ready for people to collect. Is everything under control?"

"Of course. We use only tinned food."

*****

Thomas escorted Nurse Charrington back to her office. He suggested that she wait there and those looking after the invalids would come running if anyone needed help. "Get some sleep while you can," he advised. "You're likely to need it."

"I am well aware of how to pace myself in such matters, Rifleman O'Grady. You go and see to your wives."

Again, there was that ghost of a smile. Things were too busy for him to wonder what this meant. He went to find Sergeant Taylor, to get permission to use the wives. He wasn't with Lieutenant Hawkins. He wasn't in the Sergeants' Mess. Time was getting on and Thomas had to make a decision for himself.

It was better to ask forgiveness than permission. He strode off to the wives' quarters, trying to seem confident.

What he hadn't expected was just how eager the women were to find out what was going on.

"No-one tells us anything. We've heard all sorts. Are all the officers dead? What's going on?" This was the gist of what he gathered from half-a-dozen anxious women crowding around him and shouting.

"Ladies. I'll answer your questions, but you've got to let me speak." He was eventually able to get their attention. When he explained they could help, he found that he had difficulty keeping them still long enough to explain what they had to do.

"Look, I've been out in India before," said one dark-haired woman. "I knows how to deal with fever. They gots to sweat it out, and the sweat needs replacing. Simple enough."

"Well, there's also a lot of mess."

"It's obvious you've never had children underfoot. I'll be happy to help the Colonel out. He's a good man, a real gent."

Thomas tried to remember who the woman was. "Mrs Dawson, isn't it? Look, could you sort out who wants to help? I'll make sure they get allocated an officer to look after."

"So that makes me what, like a Corporal of the Wives?"

"I don't have the authority to say that. I'll talk about it with the Colonel when he's recovered." Thomas paused. He knew his tongue was about to get him into trouble. He just couldn't help himself. "It would be useful if you had a speaker, someone who could pass on concerns to the officers, things you're worried about and who could get information and pass it to the others, officially. Cut down on rumours and uncertainty like we had earlier here."

"So, what, we'd report to you? You're just a Rifleman. A pretty one, but just an ordinary Rifleman."

"I'll get something sorted out. Let's deal with what's in front of us." Thomas wondered what he was talking himself into now.

*****

"It's a metaphor, ain't it." Peter said to Windy and Recruit Davie. "The officers lie around, and we clean up their shit."

Recruit Davie thought about this. "No. Manalesi and Nkosiphendule, and Riflemen Callaghan and Wagstaff are cleaning up the shit. We're taking water to the officers."

"Davie, your names don't fit round our tongues. They're Charlie and Edward. Those are good soldier names. Charles means brave man, and Edward means guard."

"Manalesi means provider and Nkosiphendule means gift from God."

"Hang on," said Windy. "David means gift from God. We've called the wrong one Davie."

"Well, we can't change their names now. Anyway, you're missing the point."

"Well, what is the point?"

"That officers make themselves sick by stuffing themselves and we get to clear up after them. What happens when we get sick?"

"Depends how sick we are. That's what the nurses are for. Get us better when we get sick."

"And what are they doing right now? Helping us? No, they're helping the officers."

"Firstly, they're not. They're sick themselves, apart from Nurse Charrington, so they aren't helping anyone. Secondly, if they weren't sick, they'd be helping the people who are sick, which happens to be the officers."

"You're arguing with each other again," said Davie.

"No, we're not," said Peter. "We're just having a disagreement."

"What's the difference between having a disagreement and having an argument?" Windy replied.

"A disagreement is when you listen to the other person. An argument is when you don't."

"Are you saying that you actually listen to a word I say?" Windy asked.

"No, but you don't listen to me, so that makes it OK."

Davie shook his head. They were now arguing over whether they were arguing. He didn't understand white people.

*****

Chaplain Mhlangana went around to visit the sick. There was little he could do for them physically, but they would get better more quickly if their souls weren't troubled. The most troubled of the sick was Lieutenant Hawkins. He wasn't sicker than anyone else, but he was the most troubled.

He was troubled because he was worried.

The Chaplain sat beside him and asked him why he was worried.

"Because this company has to be ready. There's no way we'll be ready and some of them are going to get killed because I haven't trained them well enough, Nick."

"Nick?"

"It's what the men call you."

"Why Nick?" The Chaplain was curious.

"There you are, an old man, dressed up with a dog-collar, and you're as black as the ace of spades. Old Nick."

"They think I'm the Devil?"

"Of course not. It's a joke. They call me Hawk, but they don't think I'm going to fly away and hunt small birds."

"You're troubled about those under your command."

Lieutenant Hawkins explained what the problems were. The Chaplain was there for some considerable time.

*****

"I think we'd better have a word with the RSM, O'Grady." Sergeant Taylor shook his head. "You're a Rifleman. You're not supposed to think. You've got the wives all worked up."

"Sergeant, the wives were already worked up."

Regimental Sergeant Major Moyles was not happy with Thomas. Thomas stood at attention while the RSM walked around him, tutting like a clock. Finally, he stopped in front of Thomas and looked up at him.

"Do you have the first idea what you've done, Rifleman O'Grady?"

"Tried to help, Sergeant-Major."

"You tried to help. You thought you would try to help. In trying to help, you've been and gone and opened Cassandra's Box, that's what you've done." The RSM drew himself up to his full height of five and a half feet and took a step closer to Thomas, so there was only an inch between them.

"Pandora's Box, Sergeant-Major. Cassandra was the one who made accurate prophecies but was cursed that no-one would believe her."

"Well, O'Grady, I can make an accurate prophecy. You've opened a box and dumped a shit-load of trouble from an aging stable on us."

"Augean Stable, Sergeant-Major." It didn't seem to help. "I just thought that the wives could help."

"Let us assume, Rifleman O'Grady, that you are right and that they can help. Let's just assume that. Do you think it's going to be easy to get them back into their box and not cause trouble from now on? They're going to be interfering, getting in the way, distracting the men, being a right nuisance."

"Sergeant-Major, I've had a thought. Why put them back in the box? They can still help, even when things are back to normal."

"Rifleman O'Grady, if the Army wanted you to think, you would have been issued with a brain. Sergeant Taylor, why does this Rifleman believe he has the equipment to think with?"

"He's an Irishman, and a Gentleman-Ranker to boot, RSM," said Sergeant Taylor.

"Teach him, Sergeant Taylor. Teach him."

Sergeant-Major, about my idea. The more time the men have for training, the better we'll be in action. If the wives do the Regimental laundry and things like that, then the men will be able to spend the time that they would have spent doing these things on training. The women will get to feel useful, so they won't have the time or energy to cause trouble. The men get to see the wives being a help and will feel more like soldiers because they can see what they're protecting. The NCOs can focus on the men, because the wives will be less trouble, the officers will be happy because the troops will be less fractious, and the Regiment will save money because we won't need to pay locals to do laundry."

"Is that it? Sergeant Taylor, is this what you've had to put up with?"

Thomas was still in full flow. "If you make a Rifleman a Corporal, so that the wives have a specific person to go to so that they can tell their troubles and find out what's going on, that means the other NCOs and officers wouldn't be troubled needlessly."

"Now we see the angle." The RSM sounded relieved. "No, I'm not making you a corporal, O'Grady."

"Not me, Sergeant-Major. Rifleman Dawson. He's got a wife with the Regiment, so he wouldn't get, um, distracted. His wife admires the Colonel. He understands how the wives think. It will cut down on wrong gossip."

There was a long silence while Sergeant Taylor and RSM Moyles considered the implications.

Thomas continued. "When Corporal Dawson is on deployment, he'll need an assistant, someone who won't ever be going out on deployment. The nurses will be too busy, and I guess the Chaplain may go out. But Joy, Lady Dalkeith's maid, she can do that. She already knows Mrs Dawson."

"O'Grady, have you ever been a Quarter-Master?"

"No, Sergeant-Major," Thomas said warily.

"I'm surprised. You've got the devious, twisted mind for one."

"Yes, Sergeant-Major. Sergeant-Major, I thought that if the system was up and running before the officers were up and running, we'd be able to report on how it worked. Then they would have solid information on which to base a judgement."

Regimental Sergeant Major Moyles looked at Sergeant Taylor, who looked back. The RSM came to a decision. "If it's wrong, there will be hell to pay. Guess who'll be in the firing line if that happens, Rifleman O'Grady."

*****

RSM Moyles had considered everything. Much as he hated to admit it, O'Grady had made a good case. He felt quite sorry for Reggie. Having to deal with that all the time must be stressful.

"You're not in trouble, Rifleman Dawson. Nor you, Mrs Dawson. We want to try something out." He then explained Thomas' plan, without saying where the idea had come from. "The plan is that the wives have one of them as a spokesman, to communicate with the Regiment. We'll have a Corporal she liaises with. Won't be a Corporal running a section, but it'll be a Corporal. Job needs that authority. No shame if you don't want the job. It's a new job, we're not sure how it'll turn out. Are we going to call you Rifleman Dawson or Corporal Dawson?"

*****

It was going to be a couple of days before things started to get back to normal. Nurse Charrington knew that she'd have to grab what sleep she could whenever she could. She'd done her rounds; everyone was as settled as they could be. Now was a good time to catch a couple of hours.

The trouble was that she couldn't sleep. It should be easy now that she had sorted the situation out with Rifleman O'Grady. She had demonstrated that they could remain professional and not become romantically entangled.

That would be impossible. They'd demonstrated that. He didn't understand what being a nurse involved and, without that, he couldn't understand her. She'd always known that at some stage, she would have to make a choice between nursing and romance. In the end, it had to be nursing that she chose. That was productive and useful. If she gave that up, she would be doing nothing.

But she enjoyed Thomas' company. His wit kept her on her toes. Just so long as he accepted that things were what they were.

She couldn't sleep and it annoyed her. She was tired and she needed to sleep, but she couldn't. Perhaps seeing how Nurse Ward was getting on would help.

Lieutenant Campbell opened the door to his cabin, put a finger to his lips and glanced back into the room.

"She's sleeping. It's right to let her sleep?" he whispered.

"Yes, of course." Nurse Charrington was slightly envious. "How are things between you?"

"I rather think that is not your concern," Lieutenant Campbell snapped. He was instantly contrite. "I'm sorry, that was too blunt. I'm just worried about her."

"As she's one of my nurses, anything that may affect her performance as a nurse is very much my concern."

"I see." Lieutenant Campbell's voice had stiffened. He stepped outside the cabin and shut the door behind him. "Alice is my friend. I will not jeopardise that for anything. It is that simple. It may be hard for people to accept this, but if I'm honest, I frankly don't care whether people accept it or not. Will that be all?"

"If you could arrange to have me informed when she wakes, I'll see how she's progressing. Sleep is a good thing, so I'll not disturb her."

Lieutenant Campbell nodded and went back inside his cabin. The deck was still busy, but Nurse Charrington felt lonely. "Stop feeling sorry for yourself. You've work to do." Another set of rounds would exhaust her so that she would sleep solidly.

*****

Thomas stared at the sea. It had been a busy day and he felt it had been productive. He'd done well and the officers seemed to be recovering. He should be feeling pleased, but he didn't. He didn't really feel anything.

That wasn't true. He felt satisfied that he'd helped with resolving the problem.

Truth be told, he missed spending time with Emily. Ordinarily, he'd say there were plenty more fish in the sea. The trouble was, that wasn't true on the ship. What was more, he wasn't that interested in other fish. Not any longer.

When he thought he saw Nurse Charrington smile, it was hard to be purely professional. He could avoid her as best he could, but there would always be occasions when their paths crossed. He needed to find something else to work at, to fill the time he'd spent learning medicine. It needed to be something unarguably useful. It needed to keep him well away from her. Ideally, he'd be able to do it somewhere that she would never go. It had to be something that would be approved.

Then it struck him. If he was on guard duty, he could avoid her by standing still. The beauty of it was that he could claim to be on guard duty at any time or place. No-one ever asked who put you on guard duty. It was the Rifleman's equivalent to carrying a rag and a tin of polish.

*****

Frank arranged the tins in order in the galley. He'd made sure that everything was clean and ready. The trouble was, all the officers were still ill and there was no-one to serve. Not even Lieutenant Campbell, who wasn't sick, but just sent a message asking for sandwiches.

They'd got the hang of making weak tea, but that was about all they'd had to do. It was disappointing.

All he could do was wait. Abe and Billy were getting impatient.

"Settle down," he said. "You learn that much of soldiering is wait for something to happen. Long wait for battle, then everything happen very quick. Must learn to wait and be ready for when things happen."

"You listen carefully to Father Corperaal," said Abe. "He is wise in the ways of battle."

Frank wasn't quite sure how he felt about being called Father.

*****

Thomas had a thought. There was a problem coming up. All the NCOs were busy with the officers being sick. But the problem was getting closer with every mile the ship sailed north.

"Chaplain, the ship's going to cross the equator. There's a sort of tradition on Crossing the Line. Everyone who hasn't crossed the line before is judged and embarrassed."

"I've heard a bit about it. It might be a good time for our boxing match."

"The thing is that everyone on the ship crossed the line on the way south. Everyone is a shellback, not a pollywog. Well, almost everyone. The new recruits aren't."

"That's true." Chaplain Mhlangana sounded curious.

"I read about the fights between the white and the black miners. I saw one, only they might not have been miners. That got me thinking. How will the new recruits act if all the blacks are attacked by everyone else, even if it's in play? I hoped you could explain to them."

"I could, but it's going to be a short ceremony if there are only six victims. You'll have to think of something to make it longer and better."

"What, just like that?"

"Of course not. You've got almost a week."

"Won't the officers object?"

"O'Grady, what's the whole point of the ceremony? I'd suggest making it a contest between those who have done it and those who haven't."

Thomas smiled. He'd had an idea. Now for the hard part. Keeping it secret.

*****

"Alasdair," said Alice, sleepily. "Was that true?"

"Was what true?" he asked, sitting on the bed as she sat up. He gave her some water and watched as she drunk it.

"You know. What you said about friends." Alice looked carefully at the glass, not trusting herself to look anywhere else.

"Of course, you silly thing. Do you think I'd sit and mop the fevered brow of someone who wasn't a friend?"

"But why? I mean, my parents have a garden that's the size of this cabin. Your parents have a garden that's in four counties. How many horses does your family own? My sister has a rabbit. You can't put a saddle on a rabbit and ride it over the estate."

"Are you sure about that? Have you seen the size of the rabbits we have in Scotland? They're not like your English rabbits, domesticated and tame. These are feral border rabbits, fearsome beasts that can bring down an elephant."

Alice started to giggle. "But there aren't any elephants in Scotland."

"Well, no. Not anymore. The border rabbits drove them to extinction."

They giggled together, then Alice put her cup down carefully. "Seriously, why? I'm no-one special."

"Don't you say that. Ever. You had no advantages, no money or influence easing the way for you, and you are now one of the most important people in the Regiment. Look how far you've come. If you say you're no-one special one more time," he paused.

"What?"

"I'll do what any border collie would do. I'll make a total mess of your hair." He paused and stroked her hair before continuing. "Alice, have you thought what you want to do when we've finished in Persia?"

"Go back to a hospital, I suppose." She sounded less than enthusiastic. Alasdair looked at her and she felt she had to explain. "Here, people treat me as though I'm important. I'm someone special. In a hospital, I'm just a nurse." She paused. If she said the next thing, she couldn't unsay it.

"Go on," Alasdair said gently.

"I wish I could stay with the Regiment forever."

"When everyone's better, we'll ask the Colonel. You're part of the family."

"Alasdair, I ..." She paused. She didn't know how to say this.

"If you're about to say what I think you're about to say, you should not think about romance with anyone until you're better. And I don't mean this sickness. You wait until you want to, not until you think you ought to. Anyone worthwhile will wait for you."

"Alasdair, how can I ever thank you?"

"I'll tell you what, when I get badly wounded in action, you save my life, and we'll say we're equal."

Alice shivered. "Please, don't joke about that."

*****

Joy woke up with a start when there was a knock at the door. She must have fallen asleep in the chair at the desk. Luckily, both Lady Dalkeith and Colonel Dalkeith were asleep.

It was one of the wives, Mrs Dawson. Joy put her finger to her lips to indicate silence. "They're sleeping."

"I just wanted to say thank you. Rifleman O'Grady told me what you done."

Joy rubbed her eyes. She felt like she'd missed part of the conversation. "What I did?"

"Yes. You got the Colonel to sort out that man, you got me out of trouble. You got my John's name known and he's now Corporal. We ain't treated you like one of us, but you is in all but name."

Joy still wasn't any wiser. She'd have to ask Thomas what he'd done. "It was nothing," she said, uncomfortably.

"Maybe to you. It meant a lot to me. I thought I'd return a favour. John and I know of somewhere we can have some privacy. If you and your Corporal want some privacy, I'll show you. That Lieutenant's old cabin isn't used for anything."

"We're not married yet," Joy said, trying to convince herself. This would be wrong.

"But you will be. Looks like your babies are waking up."

"My babies?" Joy looked around and saw Colonel Dalkeith starting to wake up. A moment later, she had to rush across to clean up.

*****

Thomas wanted somewhere private that he could plan for the Crossing the Line event. Somewhere that no-one would interrupt him.

*****

Things were settling into a routine. People were slowly on the mend. Nurse Charrington was tired, but it was easier to handle in a routine. The Riflemen would find it hard to get rid of the smell from the cabins. They would have to use a lot of elbow grease.

She didn't want to tempt fate, but things seem to have gone relatively smoothly. The men and the NCOs had been wonderful. She'd have to write up her report and observations and she'd have to do that fairly quickly.

This must be what it felt like to be a sister on a ward. She'd proved to herself that she could do it and she was certain that Colonel Dalkeith would give her a good reference after this. It was still far too early to think about after Persia, but that would come around all too quickly.

She looked at the wake from the ship. "That's rather like how I feel," she said. "All churned up, splashing around and trying to be calm and level. It takes a while to settle, but I'm still churned up inside." Then she turned before realising that Thomas wasn't there and there was no kind word for her.

"Get used to it," she told herself. "You've got your nursing and nothing else." She squared her shoulders. She could concentrate on nursing without any distractions. It would have to be enough. And she certainly didn't want anyone pitying her.

She gave herself a half-smile. Now she knew why ward sisters were so often sour and bloody-minded. It would probably be for the best to avoid Thomas until she only thought of him as Rifleman O'Grady.

*****

He had people he needed to talk to. Thomas guessed that the sickness had been caused by food the officers had eaten and Frank had served food that day. From the way Frank had described it, Thomas guessed the stewards had not told the officers where the food had come from, that they would have wanted the credit for themselves. Shark steak was unusual enough that they might have received praise for it.

He also guessed that something unusual might have caused the upset. The English stomach wasn't used to the dish. He'd heard that foreign food often did this. He would make sure that suspicion didn't fall on Frank. That would be unfair.

The Chief Steward was recovering. Not better, but he was on the mend. He complained how Frank and the black recruit had caused all of this. "I should have known better than to have let dagos cook for the officers. The officers will hear of this. I'm not taking the blame for what that dago Corporal done."

"Is that wise?" Thomas asked. "I mean, you are responsible for what goes out of your kitchen."

"It's a galley. And it didn't come out of the galley."

"You mean you served food to the officers that wasn't cooked in the galley under your supervision? Won't that get you into trouble?"

There are moments that you want to savour, Thomas thought. The expression on the Chief Steward's face was priceless. Let him stew for a moment, then throw him a lifeline.

"Look, it's obviously just one of those things that happen. New food that people aren't used to. It happens all the time in India. I would guess that's what happened here. The locals are used to the dish, but it takes a while to get accustomed to things. No-one at fault, and you've learned that when serving exotic new dishes, that it's best to start off with small portions."

"But it was that damn Sicilian Corporal."

"Best let sleeping dogs lie. Or sleeping Dons. Sicilians get very touchy when their honour is questioned."

"What would he do?" The Chief Steward sounded concerned.

"No idea. He's much more inventive than I am. In his position, I'd simply dump your body overboard one night. No-one would be any wiser until it was far too late, and it would be assumed you'd not fully recovered from the illness, gone to the railing to vomit, slipped and been caught off balance when the boat lurched suddenly. But Frank's more inventive than I am. On the other hand, unfamiliarity with strange food, and everyone's happy."

The Chief Steward wasn't happy with the deal. "There's no way he's coming back into my galley."

"Guess who's been running it while you've been ill. Guess who hasn't made any recovering officer ill. I hear the food has been dull and boring. "Tasteless mush", someone said. But it's been edible and kept them going. Not bad for a fill-in. Best just to close the book on this one."

*****

There were only four officers for dinner. Lieutenant Campbell was there with Nurse Ward, Major Marshall and Captain Filleul. No-one was talking very much, which meant that they were concentrating on the food.

Billie opened a can of stew. Four people. Stew for ten. No wonder all the stewards looked so well fed. Then there was a loud crash, and the stew was all over the floor. Frank was about to shout at him when he remembered what Sergeant Taylor had told him.

"Save your shouts for when you need them. Shout too much, and they stop listening. If they know what they did wrong, there's no need to shout. Save shouts for when they don't know what they did wrong."

Frank shook his head sadly. "Next time, Recruit Billie, don't open a can on the edge of a table. Make sure all of can is on table, not just part of it."

"Chaplain Mhlangana said that Corporals and Sergeants will shout at us a lot," Billie said, a bit surprised.

"There's no need. If you ever do it again, *then* I will shout at you." He glanced around. "Recruit Abe, what Hell you doing?" he shouted.

Abe stood nonplussed. He had mopped the floor, cleaned it, and was getting back to stirring the soup.

"You cleaned floor. Good. But you didn't wash hands before going back to working on food. Always wash hands before work on food. Every time. Nurse Charrington say so."

Abe looked hurt. "You shouted at me, but not at Billie."

"Billie knew what he had done wrong. Now you know what you did wrong. Keep learning, one day maybe you be Corporal."

The soup took longer than expected to get ready, but eventually it was.

"What soup is it, Corporal?" Lieutenant Campbell asked.

"Malignant Town Owl, Sir." It sounded unlikely, but that's what the label seemed to say.

"Mulligatawny, Corporal," said Major Marshall. "Is that wise? It's strongly flavoured and cleans the system out. Not sure that's quite what we need."

"Nurse Charrington say OK if from tin, Sir."

"Actually, Major," said Captain Filleul, "I rather fancy that the theory is that after a bad system clean, a good system clean helps settle things down. Make sure all the disease is cleaned out. It's like an oil change on a car. Empty the sump, then flush through to clean it, then fill it."

"The body's not like a car, Phil."

Well, thought Frank, at least that started conversation. It wasn't what he'd talk about when eating, but that's officers for you.

*****

Thomas tracked down Peter and took him to one side. "Can you do something for me?"

Peter was suspicious. "No. Whatever it is, it's a bad idea. No." He paused. "What was the idea?"

"You know we'll be Crossing the Line again? Well, that will be a day for people to let their hair down. We've done one. Just repeating that will be boring. So, let's do something different."

"Why us? Why not let the officers and NCOs handle it? That's what they're paid for."

"Peter, I'm disappointed in you. Equality. The rights of the working man. Justice and freedom for the masses."

"What's that got to do with Crossing the Line?"

Got him, thought Thomas. "I want you to arrange a mutiny. Take the officers and NCOs prisoner and bring them for justice at the Court of King Neptune."

"Why me and not you?"

"For some reason, NCOs don't trust me. They watch me. That's why I can't do it. You're the one that understands the Uprising of the Proletariat and how that works. While the NCOs watch me, you can arrange things. Then we run Neptune's Court, everyone has a good time, and you find out why it wouldn't work if you ever did it for real."

"It will work. It's an historical inevitability. The history of the world is the transferal of power from the few to the masses."

"Because State School children are so well-treated these days? Look, let's not argue politics. You understand how to arrange it, I can provide a distraction and afterwards, everyone will have had a good time. Just one thing. King Neptune's Court will be at one end of the obstacle course."

"Why?"

Thomas sighed. "There are not enough Pollywogs, so we're going to spice that up a little. That's in my hands. You just arrange a mutiny for King Neptune. The ship's crew is off limits."

*****

"Joy, I trust you've not been shirking? A considerable amount of laundry seems to have built up."

Lady Dalkeith was obviously feeling better. Joy, however, was worried. She had cleaned up after the Colonel and she thought that something was wrong.

"Ma'am, I just need to speak with Nurse Charrington."

"Not a social call, I trust. Very well. Do not take long. There is a lot of work for you to do here."

*****

Nurse Charrington looked at the cloth Joy gave. "I'll look into it. It's almost certainly nothing to worry about, but I'll make sure. You did the right thing, but it's nothing to worry about."

When Joy had gone, Nurse Charrington looked at the blood-stained cloth, and then started to consult her medical books.

*****

Windy had an idea. He needed to protect his secret. Only one person knew what that secret was. Now that Nurse Charrington was not seeing Thomas anymore, other people would start bothering her. He could prevent that.

He explained his plan to her.

"You want to start walking out with me? You? Rifleman Miller, there's a technical problem here. Several, in fact."

"But none anyone else knows about. Look at the advantages. It will get Nurse Ward off my back. It will provide cover for me. It will provide a shield for you so other people don't bother you. It might make Thomas jealous. And it could be fun fooling people."

"Rifleman Miller. Do you have the first idea how ridiculous this suggestion is?"

Windy grinned. "Oh, yes. That's why it would be such fun."

"Flattered as I am to be regarded as a bit of fun, I have to say no. I'm not here for fun or romance or dalliance. I'm here to do a job. No more, no less. If it doesn't help me do my job to the best of my ability, I'm not interested. I'm certainly not interested in making Rifleman O'Grady jealous. That would imply I care what he thinks. I don't. He has his life. I have mine. We have few, if any, points of overlap. The less interaction there is between us, the better for all concerned. I am extremely busy. If you don't have a medical issue, may I suggest you return to your duties."

*****

Thomas hated to admit it, but he was enjoying this scheming. It would have been nice to have been able to share it with Nurse Charrington, but that was not to be. Perhaps it was for the best. He could now concentrate his efforts into achieving something worthwhile and he was starting to see the bigger picture.

*****

Lieutenant Hawkins stood up unevenly, then sat down. He was still too weak to be back on the strength, but he was getting there.

"I disagree, Sergeant Taylor. From what I've heard, since they've stopped seeing each other, they've both thrown themselves into their work. That's a good thing. They're both working and not wasting time in watching the stars. They're here to do a job, not to play happy families."

"All due respect, Sir, they're going to burn up. There's nothing supporting their workload. Look how good Corporal Barry's done since he got a girl that he was serious about."

It was just the two of them in the Lieutenant's cabin.

"That's a rarity, like you and Doris. Most of the time, women are just a confounded distraction. The men worry about the women and not about their duty. As I understand it, Nurse Charrington wants as little contact with O'Grady as possible, O'Grady want as little contact as possible with Nurse Charrington. I believe this will be beneficial to the Regiment. Arrange for O'Grady's duties to ensure that these wishes are met and do not try creative ways of evading that. Is that clear, Sergeant Taylor? Besides, it would never have worked between them."

*****

Things returned to normality. A small group of wives watched as Frank started giving Joy shooting lessons on the deck. The wives didn't stand too close, as Joy didn't seem that good at it.

"Hold hands steady," Frank said. "Lean forward slightly. No, like this." He stood behind her, put his arms around her to hold the gun with her to show her how it was done.

"No, lean forward, not back," Frank said as Joy leaned back closer to him. He found it distracting as her back pressed up against him. "Concentrate," he said. "Focus on the gun."

He had to take his own advice. With Joy pressed up against him like this, his arms around her and holding her hands, his cheek next to hers, with her hair brushing against him, it wasn't easy to think about the gun. He could sense that she was distracted as well, although she was looking at the gun and looked serious. He could smell her breath and feel her breathing.

"Breath out before you fire. All breath out. Look at target, hold trigger, squeeze gently, not rush, just hold and gently increase pressure, smoothly, is no rush, prepare yourself for the moment of release, and there." There was the bang and the smell of cordite. Joy flinched slightly at the suddenness of it, but she remembered to keep the gun pointing away from anyone when she looked up at him with bright eyes to see what he thought.

"I'm not convinced either of you were fully concentrating on the lesson," said Lady Dalkeith. "Joy, would you have been happy if Corporal Barry was teaching one of the other wives like that? Corporal Barry, would you have been happy if a soldier had been teaching Joy in that manner."

Frank felt awkward, then Joy spoke.

"Ma'am, when you say other wives? Does that mean that I'm?" Her voice trailed away.

"I see what you're thinking," Lady Dalkeith said. She considered the matter. "On balance, I think you've demonstrated that the relationship between the two of you is not a mere fancy. Please ensure that the gun is made safe and put securely away." She waited until Joy had checked the gun and put it away in its case.

"Very well. In due course, I will expect to see that the gun has been cleaned. Ordinarily, it is very poor practise to store a gun without cleaning it. However, I feel safer with it stored. Now, while I am not giving you permission to marry, I am giving Corporal Barry permission to ask you, at his convenience. Please remember, Joy, that if you have any doubts at all, you should decline his request."

The last sentence was spoken to thin air. Joy flung her arms around Frank and looked up at him expectantly. Frank looked around.

"It a private thing. Not a public talk," he said. He felt awkward and embarrassed.

"And you have got a gun to clean, Joy, then laundry to do. You can have your discussion with Corporal Barry later when your work is completed."

Windy and Peter had watched from nearby. "What odds are you offering that she says yes?" Peter asked Windy.

Windy just snorted in derision.

*****

"That's wonderful news, Frank." Thomas was excited for a moment, before seeing Frank's expression. "For crying out loud, what's the problem? You aren't getting cold feet, are you? The two of you go together like ham and eggs. You're not scared she'll turn you down? Why the glum face?"

"There is a problem," Frank said carefully.

"What possible problem can be left? Neither of you are married or engaged. Lady Dalkeith gave her approval. Joy's going to say yes. There's plenty of witnesses. If you ask me to be best man, I'll say yes. The Colonel will approve. What's the problem?"

"There no priest. There won't be priest until we get back to England." Frank sounded glum.

"What do you mean, no priest? What do you think I, we got in Cape Town? He may be big, black, and old, but he's a priest."

"He not a real priest."

"What do you mean, not a real priest?" Thomas shouted. "He's a real priest. We checked. All the documents, references, everything. The Colonel approved him. What more do you want? God almighty to come down and give His blessing?"

"The priest not Catholic."

Thomas counted slowly up to ten. Then he counted again. It didn't help. "He's a priest. Isn't that enough?"

"No. Must be Catholic priest. Otherwise marriage not a Catholic marriage."

"You really are the most infuriating little Corporal in the whole Army. Just live in sin with her and make an honest woman of her when you get back."

"No. Joy deserve honourable marriage."

Thomas drew a deep breath. "OK. It needs to be a Catholic priest. Anything else? Do you need a family estate to move into? An income of five thousand?"

"House would be good."

"Go away. If we don't get things sorted, you'll be too old to get married." Thomas felt like he was getting nowhere.

*****

Frank had to explain the facts of Army life to Abe. "No. They not make you a Lance-Corporal while you still a recruit. You have to wait until you trained."

"But I can speak to the others in their own language. I can be their Lance-Corporal. They form a section, and I'm their Lance."

"No. Not until you trained. Probably not then. Being a Lance-Corporal is hard work."

"But Corporal Father, we won't know until we've tried."

"First, finish training. That mean not hopping from foot to foot all excited when at attention. NCO must be calm and in control. Finish training. Do well. Impress me. *Then* I speak with Sergeant Taylor."

Abe ran off to the others. It was probably just as well Frank couldn't understand what Abe said to them.

*****

Sergeant Taylor wondered what he should do. In essence, there was nothing he could do. Lieutenant Hawkins had given him a clear order. He'd also told him not to abuse the intention of the order. There were dozens of ways to work around the order, but all of these would go against the spirit of it.

If he did anything, it would break the bond of trust between them. It would be different if it were any other officer. It would also be different if he was sure he was right and Lieutenant Hawkins wrong. He was fairly sure the Lieutenant was wrong about O'Grady and Nurse Charrington, but not completely sure. The Lieutenant had listened to his opinion.

All he could do was keep a close eye on O'Grady and Nurse Charrington. Especially O'Grady.

"Sergeant, could I have a word?"

Speak of the Devil. "O'Grady. Let me see. You've got a scheme to loot Persia nine ways from Sunday and you want someone reliable to fence your ill-gotten gains? You've come to confess that you're not an Irishman, but a Zulu in a cunning disguise? The ship's crew have mutinied, and we're now pirates on the high seas?"

"No, Sergeant, but they're excellent ideas. No, I've been thinking about our barracks in Persia. Will they be laid out like the dragoons did on exercise?"

"That's the normal procedure, O'Grady. More space between company quarters, for the reasons you displayed so flammably."

"That's what I thought, Sergeant. It still means that a whole company's barracks are at risk. Maybe we would be more secure if each company had several smaller barracks, maybe squad or section-sized."

"Too much of an experiment, O'Grady. Too much work involved."

"That's what I thought, Sergeant. Isn't that what this platoon is for? Trying out new things. We'll have blacks and we'll have Persians and all sorts, so maybe we should try it out?"

"I suppose you've got a scheme for all this." Sergeant Taylor shook his head. It was hard work keeping up with the reprobates in this platoon.

"Yes, Sergeant. We can build our own accommodation. Small huts. Say 4 riflemen to a hut. NCOs to have their own near their squad or section. It wouldn't be much, but they would get some privacy. Make the company more secure, give the riflemen something to work on, give the NCOs some privacy."

"Very well argued, O'Grady. I'll mention it to Lieutenant Hawkins. Now, what's your real reason?"

"Sergeant? I don't quite follow."

"O'Grady, you've always got a deeper reason. You're too devious and twisted for your own good. My own good, come to that. I want to know what your deeper reason is."

"Well, Sergeant, I thought that until the blacks and the Persians get used to British discipline, there might be disturbances through not understanding. Did you know Persians don't drink alcohol or eat pork and their Sunday is on Friday?"

"Oh, they're Musclemen. Didn't know that. How did you know?"

"Couple of the stokers are Persian. I've been teaching them stuff."

"I'll mention your idea to Lieutenant Hawkins. Is that your deeper reason, or have you got another deeper reason?"

"Sergeant, I've turned over a new leaf."

"That's what I'm afraid of. Carry on, O'Grady."

Perhaps Lieutenant Hawkins was right. This scheme of O'Grady sounded solid.

*****

Billy came to speak with Frank. "Corporal Father Barry. What do I need to do to be a Corporal like you? I'm stronger than Abe, and a better fighter, and a better shot."

This is going to be a long day, thought Frank. "Recruit Billy, first become Rifleman Billy. Then we can talk about being Lance-Corporal. But first step is become good Rifleman. Tell Recruits Charlie, Davie, and Edward the same."

"Recruit Davie said since he's the biggest, he's going to be a Sergeant by the time we get to Persia."

"Recruit Davie is wrong. It takes years to become a Sergeant."

*****

"You want to do what?" Windy squeaked. He had difficulty expressing his views and his views rose to a sharp falsetto.

"Arrange a mutiny," said Peter calmly. "Crossing the Line, you silly. It's what happens. Chaos. Overturning the order. Just for the day." He said the last sadly.

"Peter, that's how the French Revolution started. Just some people mucking around with cake, and it got a bit out of hand."

Peter shrugged. "That's the French for you."

"And the Americans back in their Independence thing. Governor holds a tea party that goes wrong, and then it all starts up."

"Serves them right for being American."

"Peter, we *lost* that one."

"No, we didn't. We burned the White House. It's on our battle honours. They invaded Canada, so we burned the White House, and then they landed at Stoke-on-Trent, and that's when they freed their slaves."

That wasn't how Windy remembered the history of America being taught. "And the Boxer Rebellion. That was about opium."

"Typical Japanese."

"The Boxers were Chinese."

"Japanese."

"Well, whichever. Then there was the Indian Mutiny. That was all about cow fat."

"Windy, what's your point?"

"That mutinies get out of hand. They start off as just a bit of a joke, but they get out of control."

"That's why I want you to be King Neptune," Peter said triumphantly. "You can make sure it doesn't get out of control."

"Me? As King Neptune?"

"I can't think of anyone less qualified than you, which means you're perfect, because it's Crossing the Line."

Windy struggled with the logic.

*****

"Corporal Father Barry," said Recruit Davie.

"First, you need to finish training, become Rifleman, not just Rifleman Recruit. If you make good Rifleman, we think about promotion."

"Corporal Father Barry, how"

"NCOs know everything, lad. That's why we're NCOs."

"I have much to learn. Will you teach me?"

*****

Nurse Charrington closed the books. There were many things that it could be, but she had her suspicions. She also suspected Colonel Dalkeith knew.

She called on him in his cabin. "Might I have a word, Colonel? In private."

"About O'Grady?"

"No, Colonel. There is nothing to have a word about with regard to Rifleman O'Grady. I have neither the time nor the inclination to devote in that direction. I have a job to do that is rather more important. It's about the health of an officer in the Regiment that came to light during the recent incident."

"Your office, then."

A few minutes later, and Nurse Charrington wasn't sure what to say. "I gather you coughed up blood during your illness. There could be many reasons for this. It could be minor or more serious. I'm not a trained diagnostician, so perhaps you could answer a few questions."

"*Anno Domini* comes to us all."

"Colonel, there's nothing I can do about aging. However, some things I can do something about. Weight loss? Loss of appetite? Shortness of breath? Easily tired?"

"No. No. Yes. Maybe. Whatever your suspicions, they are medical, and therefore confidential. They will remain that way."

"Of course. I understand medical ethics. Are my suspicions correct?"

"I'm not medically trained in the least. How would I know?"

"Colonel, that's prevarication. I cannot abide prevarication. Yes, no, or refuse to answer, but don't prevaricate."

"Tell me, Nurse Charrington, if your suspicions are correct, what could you do about them?"

"Thank you, Colonel. I think you've answered my question."

*****

"Rifleman Grant, your gun is made of wood and paper."

"Made strong by the revolutionary power of Comrade Neptune, Lieutenant Campbell. Comrade Neptune has decreed that all officers will answer for their crimes at the Revolutionary Riflemen Council."

Alasdair ran his hand through his hair as he stood by the door of his cabin. He wasn't sure where to start. "Comrade Neptune?"

"Amongst the Gods and the Proletariat, there are no kings or outmoded institutions of privilege. Who better to lead a proletarian uprising for equality and justice for all than a divine entity?" Peter sounded convincing to start with, but he had trouble saying the last part.

"Isn't Zeus King of the Greek Gods?" Alice said, sitting up on the bed.

"And Neptune's overthrowing the regime and instituting a Workers' Revolutionary Council on Olympus, and we're instituting a Rifleman's Revolutionary Council on this ship, Ma'am." Peter pointedly didn't comment on the fact that Nurse Ward had been lying in Lieutenant Campbell's bed. He wasn't fooled by the pillow and blanket on the floor next to the bed. "Terribly sorry, Ma'am, but since you are also officially an officer, we're going to have to ask you to face the Council, where you will be tried, found guilty of crimes against the masses, and sentenced to devilish torment by the merciful Comrade Neptune. If you don't mind, Ma'am."

*****

Joy opened the door. Riflemen Callaghan and Wagstaff stood outside, their uniform jackets on back-to-front.

"Ah-ha, wench. We've come to take Colonel Dalkeith to be tried before the Divine Revolutionary Council," said Rifleman Callaghan.

"Not bloody likely," said Joy, swinging a punch which caught Rifleman Callaghan on the jaw. He was caught by surprise and staggered back a step. His feet got tangled up with Rifleman Wagstaff's, he tripped and fell to the ground.

Rifleman Wagstaff smiled, a rare event.

"Joy, I rather suspect we're being invited to the Court of King Neptune," said Lady Dalkeith. Joy stood in the doorway, blocking the entrance, fists clenched and glaring at the Riflemen.

Rifleman Callaghan stood up. "The Revolutionary Council of the Court of Comrade Neptune," he said, rubbing his jaw. "My congratulations, Miss, although how Corporal Barry will keep you under control is another matter. That's a fair right cross you got, Miss."

"What's going on?" Colonel Dalkeith called from his desk.

"We're being arrested and summoned before the Divine Revolutionary Court of Comrade King Neptune, if I understand correctly."

*****

Peter called at Major Marshall's cabin. Mrs Marshall opened the door.

"I'm afraid the Major is not here. One of your colleagues is already checking the cabin for him." She stood to one side, indicating a man in a bear costume checking under the bed. Peter was suspicious.

"The bears are supposed to be at the Revolutionary Court," he said.

"The Major can be a tricky one," the bear growled. "King Neptune dispatched some bears to seek him out."

"There is no King Neptune. What's his proper name?"

"Not King Neptune? King Poseidon, sorry, forgot we're in Greek waters."

"Wrong, Major Marshall. It's Comrade Neptune."

Major Marshall removed the bear head. "Comrade Neptune? Seriously? How's a chap supposed to guess that? Oh, well. The disguise was worth a try. I believe the expression is: It's a fair cop, Guv, cor strike a light, blow me down."

*****

Frank lined the recruits up. They were puzzled by the pool on the lower deck and the chair on which Rifleman Miller was sitting, dressed in stoker overalls. Half a dozen people in bear costumes were in the pool, waiting beneath a plank. The officers were lined up by the plank. This was all very strange.

"Line up and listen carefully."

"Corporal Father, what is going on?"

"Save your breath, Recruit Pollywog Abe. You'll need it. You find out soon enough."

Rifleman O'Grady stood up next to the chair and addressed the soldiers gathered around the pool.

"The time has come, the Comrades said, to talk of many things.
"Of boots and packs and inspection time, and permanent revolution
"Of riflemen in charge, and officers and damn, I've forgotten the rest.

"Dearly beloved, we are gathered here together to demonstrate the mercy of Comrade King Neptune, who inspired this mutiny. Remember that, for future reference, Colonel Dalkeith, it's all Comrade King Neptune's doing."

Colonel Dalkeith stared steadily at Thomas. "I think I know precisely who to blame, O'Grady."

Thomas took a moment to check everything. "Before we start with the trial of the competent, we have pollywogs in our midst. Comrade Neptune, your decision regarding the pollywogs."

Windy stood up in his disguise as Comrade Neptune. "It has come to my attention that we have both officers and pollywogs. The officers will be subjected to trial by wit and the pollywogs to trial by physical prowess. The pollywogs will be tried first, initiated into the ranks of the Shellbacks. Then they may witness the trial of the officers. The trial of the pollywogs will be thus. Each pollywog will be brought forward and will do the obstacle course. Or will attempt to do so. When they reach the end of the first obstacle, a volunteer Shellback will start the course and pursue. If the Shellback catches the Pollywog, the Pollywog will be thrown to the bears, who will initiate him. If the Pollywog makes it to the end of the course without being caught, the Shellback will be thrown to the bears, and the Pollywog will be initiated by me. I will pass judgement and have them thrown to the bears. I need a volunteer to pursue Recruit Pollywog Abe, and Corporal Barry has been selected."

While Abe was getting ready to start, Thomas looked around. He had a feeling that something wasn't right. Then he realised what it was. Nurse Charrington was nowhere to be seen.

"Be back soon," he told Windy and headed off. Everyone's attention was on the obstacle course, and no-one saw him leave.

*****

"Can I help you, Miss?" The Chief Steward was puzzled to see Joy. He hadn't seen her much. Maid to the Colonel's wife. Rumour had it she was the Colonel's recreation and he had to admire his taste.

"I'm just wanting to get something straight," she said. "I'm engaged to Corporal Barry. Well, I will be when he asks me. There's not been time, but we're engaged to be engaged."

"Corporal Barry. I see, Miss."

"You see, Thomas told me that he'd spoken with you about things and sorted things out. Well, I thought about it. I think you still want to get even, even though you're even, and you're counting on the fact that he won't gut you like a fish because that would get him into trouble with the Colonel."

"I don't know what you're talking about, Miss." Maybe she was going to try and bribe him with her body.

"You think that Frank is an honourable Sicilian and would confront you face to face, like a man, and deal with you. He's got honour. Well, he won't do that. You see, he won't need to."

"I still don't know what you're talking about, Miss." Was this the prelude to a bribe?

Joy took out her knife and fingered the edge. "I've killed with this before, you know. From behind because I'm not a man with honour. What do they say? A woman will do anything to protect her husband and children. I'm not ashamed to stab a man in the back. Low down, in the kidneys. It's a painful way to die, Nurse Charrington said. Here's the deal. You forget about revenge against Frank, and you keep your kidneys. You do anything, and you'll always be looking over your shoulder."

"When you say you've killed before …" The Chief Steward was finding it hard to reconcile this with the pretty girl, but his eyes were drawn to the knife.

"Frank and me, and three of them. Frank killed two and was struggling with the third. I stabbed the third in the back. Again and again and again until, well, until. You do anything against Frank, and I'll stab you like a rabid dog, because I'm always going to protect him, whatever it takes. OK? Oh, and can I have a sandwich?"

*****

"Nurse Charrington, what are you doing?" Thomas looked at her working at her desk.

"Catching up, Rifleman O'Grady. Is there a problem? I'm busy."

"Yes, there is a problem. We're Crossing the Line and you're in here working. You're missing out."

"I've already crossed the line once, Rifleman O'Grady. I've no need to repeat the experience. This is a perfect opportunity to catch up on paperwork. There's rather a lot of it after that illness."

"But you're missing out on the fun."

"Fun? I'm here to do a job of work, not to have fun. I have responsibilities. Don't let me detain you. I'm sure a release is good for morale of soldiers."

"What's got into you, Emily?"

"Nurse Charrington, if you please. I'm working. I have a job to do and I'm doing it. I would appreciate it if you could let me do it."

"But you need a release as well."

"No, I don't. Now please leave me alone."

"I don't understand. On the way down to Cape Town, I fell in love with you, and I believe it was returned. Since Cape Town ... I don't understand. Explain it to me. If I understand, maybe I can accept it, but I can't accept what I don't understand."

"There's nothing to understand. We have nothing in common. You're a gentleman playing at soldiers until you get tired of the game and go back to your world. I'm from a State School, I have no family and nursing is my whole life. Anything you wanted, you got with a snap of your fingers. Anything I wanted, I had to work to get. You're a devious trickster who can charm the birds from the trees. I'm not. You're in the profession of killing people. I'm in the profession of stopping people from getting killed. You're with the Regiment until you get bored of it. I'm with the Regiment until it returns to England. You can marry whoever will have you. I can only marry if I give up the one thing in life that I love. We literally have not a single thing in common. I would ask you again to leave. Please do not bother me again."

"Is that what you really want? What about the trip down?"

"What I want is immaterial. I have a job to do and that is an end to the matter. Please, just leave me alone."

*****

The recruits had taken the contest surprisingly well. It wasn't quite within the letter of the rules for Recruit Davie to stand at the top of a rope climb, wait for Rifleman Harding to come near the top, and push him into the pool. Recruit Davie explained that defeating an enemy in battle was better than running away. Comrade King Neptune ruled that he had a very good point, one that should be explained to the Comrade Bears forthwith.

"Splash", said the water as Recruit Davie found himself pushed to follow Rifleman Harding.

Then it was the turn of the officers. Thomas should have been here to act as the Herald, but he was still missing.

"Sergeant Taylor, introduce our Capitalists."

"Yes, Comrade King Neptune," Sergeant Taylor said in a voice that managed to convey the unspoken warning that Windy had better not step out of line in the near future, because vengeance would be swift.

"They're not Capitalists," said Peter wearily. "They don't own the capital. They're …"

"They're Capitalists in the wider meaning of the term. Throw Comrade Grant to the bears. Sergeant Taylor?"

"First charge is against Colonel Dalkeith. He stands accused," said Sergeant Taylor, in a tone that suggested he'd finished speaking.

"Of what charge does he stand accused?" Windy asked.

"Of standing. Look, he's standing. Heroic worker fish don't stand for anything."

"Very well. Colonel Dalkeith, you will sing a song. If you sing badly, your punishment will be to be thrown to the bears. If you sing well, your reward will be to avoid that fate. Instead, you will be rewarded with instant transport to join the bears in their lair."

… "Major Marshall. You stand accused of being too clever by half."

… "Lieutenant Campbell. You stand accused of not knowing if you're English or Scottish."

… "Lieutenant Hawkins. You stand accused of being sober and decent. Sometimes."

The Court continued.

*****

Thomas stared at the sea. Emily was right about him. He'd pretty much been a parasite until he'd joined the Regiment. Everything had come easily; he'd never had to struggle. If she was right about that, then she was probably right about everything else.

Which meant what, exactly? He had a lot to make amends for. The words of the marching song came back to him. "They'll bury my body in an unmarked grave. Who cares anyway?"

Well, no-one would care about him. His buddies would grieve for a time, but not for long, because they knew the risks of being a soldier. No-one back home. Why should they? It wasn't as though anyone was better for his ever having existed.

He'd just have to try and make amends. If that meant he had to take a few risks, it wasn't as though anyone would miss him. Maybe an unmarked grave was all he deserved.

Besides, it could be exciting.

*****

She had made the decision. She didn't know if it was the right decision, but it was a final one. If nothing else, the Regiment would need her full attention. That was all that mattered.

Maybe she would stay in Persia when the Regiment returned to England. She would have to learn the language, but she would probably have good prospects for advancement.

The more she thought about it, the more attractive the idea became. She wasn't getting paid much, but she wouldn't be able to spend anything for the next two years and the money would build up. She wouldn't be rich, but she would be comfortably well-off when the time came.

The idea had merit. The idea had a lot of merit.

It even solved the conundrum of marrying and still remaining a nurse. Of course, there was only one man she would ever want to marry, and she'd turned him away. Still, at least she'd found the solution to the puzzle, even though there was no longer any puzzle that needed solving.

*****

Windy breathed an almost audible sigh of relief. Thomas had found his way back. A long rope was laid out in a circle and Windy motioned for Chaplain Mhlangana and Thomas to step into it. The Chaplain and Thomas stripped to the waist and put on boxing gloves.

"Now, Shellbacks," Windy said, his voice starting to give out. "Finally, the much-delayed boxing contest between the Godly Chaplain Goodman in the Black Corner, and Devilish Tricky Rifleman O'Grady in the clover-filled Irish Green Corner."

"Comrade King Neptune," said Rifleman Callaghan. "Circles don't have corners."

"They're metaphysical corners. Throw Rifleman Callaghan to the bears. Three-minute rounds. Only hit with the gloves. No hits below the waist. No hitting when they're down. Ten count to decide the winner, or until one of you can fight no more."

Thomas wasn't particularly worried. He'd been a pretty good boxer at school, he'd kept fit, and the Army had added to his strength. He weighed up his opponent. Bigger than he was. Longer reach. Deep-chested, probably able to endure a lot of punishment before tiring.

On the other hand, he was standing solidly, like a sturdy tree. Little foot movement. Loose guard, more prepared for attack than defence. The tactics the Chaplain would take were obvious. Let Thomas come to him, then hit and if he took a couple of blows while landing one of his own, he'd settle for that.

The Chaplain had the longer reach, but little movement. Thomas could extend his reach by drawing the Chaplain's hands out of the line, bouncing in, land a blow before he could react, and dance back out of range. It was how Carpentier fought, and he had been described as the ultimate exponent of boxing, a perfect blend of speed, power, grace, and intelligence. The Frenchman had cut a swathe through the ladies of society with his Gallic charm as well.

Focus and float around, just out of reach. Turn him round and in, strike, and out. The Chaplain's return hit air as Thomas swayed out of the way. Faster fists than he'd been expecting, but the Chaplain was standing solidly.

Aim for the shoulders, weaken the return attempts. When he'd weakened them, he could move in closer and trade blow for blow to advantage. Mind you, hitting the Chaplain was like hitting teak.

"Don't go easy because of my age," the Chaplain said.

He hadn't been. Or had he? Thomas snorted. It was just mind games.

Three minutes passed in a flash. He'd blocked or dodged everything the Chaplain had thrown at him and he ignored the crowd baying for him to stop dancing and start fighting. It was strange how you only noticed the crowd during the one-minute break.

Another three minutes, another round of chipping away. The Chaplain still wasn't breathing deeply, but Thomas had got into the rhythm of moving in and out and knew he controlled this fight.

Another three minutes. The Chaplain was starting to feint and to try and anticipate his moves in. This was a good way to put Nurse Charrington out of his mind. Find things that need constant attention, with risk attached, and control the flow.

During the next break, the thought crossed his mind that maybe Peter had a point, of a sort. So many people from State Schools were good people. Rough, maybe, but good people. Nurse Charrington. The boards outside the schools. Joy, all the others.

Up again for the next three minutes. Not long before he could move in for the kill. Everything kept coming back to the State Schools. Maybe that was where his future lay. In, strike, out.

He'd need to finish his time in the Regiment. In, strike, but blocked, and out.

And then what? He knew nothing about running a State School. In, strike and miss, and out.

Focus. He was starting to get sloppy with his attacks. He'd been a teacher briefly, just to see what it was like. The school had had a nurse. He'd seduced her, back in the days when he hadn't found the woman he loved. What was her name? Mrs Hunter. That was it. Her husband had been a merchant seaman, away for long periods.

In, strike, a good solid blow.

Mrs Hunter. She was a nurse, and she was married. Damn, why hadn't he remembered that when it might have mattered? It was too late now.

Damn, he'd got distracted and hadn't danced out and a left was coming in. Duck to the right to evade.

Double damn, he'd not noticed the Chaplain's right and he'd ducked straight into the blow. The fist could only have moved six inches, catching him on the side of the jaw and rocking his head back. Recover now he's out of range. Shake head to clear it. He tried to take a step to the side, but his feet weren't moving, they weren't doing what he wanted them to do. He tried to force them, but his knees were weak. He wasn't able to take the weight of his body and crumpled.

Then the ground started to shift and rock, then floated up sideways to meet him. He could see people's feet on the floor, only the floor was vertical, like a wall, but they were just standing there on the wall. He'd just rest his eyes so he could make sense of this.

*****

Medical office. He was lying on a bed in the medical office. He wasn't sure how he got here. It was comfortable here and he felt secure. Nurse Charrington would take care of him.

Everything was the wrong way around. The bed was against the wrong wall. What was going on?

"What's going on?" he asked.

"You've just cost me a shilling, Rifleman O'Grady," said the nurse. "I told Nurse Plummer your first words would be 'Where am I?' I'm disappointed that you aren't predictable."

"Nurse Charrington?"

"No. As your quick and ready wit will have noticed, I'm not Nurse Charrington. Nurse Stewart. I was first to you and I've taken care of you since. I suspect you want to know how you are." Nurse Stewart was short and stocky, dark haired and very brisk.

Actually, he didn't. He wanted to know why Nurse Stewart was looking after him, not Emily. Nurse Charrington. "Has she been to see me?" He tried to keep his voice casual. It wasn't important one way or the other.

"She came around soon after you were brought here. She said that you were my patient, that I was to treat you and that she would leave me to it. That I was to have her called if your condition deteriorated."

"I see. Thank you." It really was over. He was just another patient to her. Very well, if that was how things stood, there was no more to be said.

Sergeant Taylor arrived and asked after Thomas. Naturally, he asked Nurse Stewart, not Thomas. Then the two Persian stokers arrived and asked him how he was, then Lieutenant Taylor, then Captain Filleul.

"Everyone out," said Nurse Stewart briskly. "One at a time. I'll put a notice up about visiting hours. I'll thank you, Rifleman O'Grady, if you insist on getting hurt, not to be popular."

They came, they went. Thomas got the impression that Captain Filleul was mainly interested in flirting with Nurse Stewart.

Actually, he was being quite blatant. Thomas remembered Captain Filleul from when he'd been on Guard duty in Cape Town. Returning back late with a young lady. This annoyed him.

"Captain, I hope you got the letters from your wife in Cape Town."

"Your wife?" enquired Nurse Stewart.

Thought so. Thomas continued. "Yes, Ma'am. Lovely little daughter, as well. Mrs Filleul couldn't come though, not in her condition. The men have bets on whether the baby will come before we reaches Persia or not."

"I see."

Two syllables, and so expressive, thought Thomas. Serve Captain Filleul right. You don't do that. Not to family. The Regiment is family, and the nurses are part of the family.

Sergeant Taylor came in last. This was interesting. It was Sergeant Taylor, only it wasn't. He was being, well, courteous and polite. Almost gentle. At least, he was when he was speaking to Nurse Stewart.

"I don't know how you arranged this, O'Grady, but you seem to have wangled a day of rest being looked after by a young lady. Don't worry, your workload hasn't been forgotten. It'll be waiting for you when you get released, so you'll still have the same amount of work to do. Wouldn't want you to feel that you weren't pulling your weight."

Sergeant Taylor and Nurse Stewart? Thomas thought. Maybe. Maybe not. Should he interfere?

It might mellow Sergeant Taylor.

"O'Grady. Whatever you're plotting, don't."

"Plotting, Sergeant?"

"Plotting, O'Grady. I know you're plotting something. There's a giveaway that tells me exactly when you've got a devious scheme brewing."

He couldn't help himself. "Giveaway, Sergeant?"

"Yes, lad. I can always tell. Whenever I can see you breathing, I know you're scheming something."

*****

Frank lined the recruits up. "You do well so far. You not Riflemen yet, but you good recruits. You might work on screw-guns, but you also need to be Riflemen. Recruit Abe, what most important thing a Rifleman need to do?"

"Fire a rifle?"

"Very good. Before he can fire rifle, he must know how to look after rifle. Today we learn how to look after rifle. When we get to Persia, you expert in that. Then we teach you shooting."

Of course, the recruits were excited that they would actually get to handle a rifle. Frank was pleased he had made sure there were no bullets.

*****

"Joy, a word," said Colonel Dalkeith. "I've received a fairly serious complaint about you."

"About me, Sir?"

"Yes, Joy, about you. The Chief Steward said that you threatened him."

"I never did, Sir. I mean, he's a lot bigger than I am. Why would I threaten him anyway?" Joy was aggrieved.

"That's what I thought. He's a lot bigger than you and you seem to have no reason why you would go out of your way to threaten him without cause. I told him that if it was with cause, then it wasn't a threat. This Regiment doesn't make threats. Promises, yes, but not threats."

"I don't quite follow, Sir."

"I rather suspect that you do, Joy. Just keep your instincts under control. Fairly soon, you might find yourself running a household of servants. That needs control, not threats."

"A household of servants, Sir?"

"One way or another, it's likely. If nothing else, the Nurses will have far too much work to do to manage without servants, and they'll have neither the time nor the training to manage the servants. If Lady Dalkeith is agreeable, that will be your job."

"Me, Sir?"

"Yes, you, Joy. Corporal Barry is not the only one who will have to learn a lot very quickly. If you have questions about how to do this, I suggest you speak with Lady Dalkeith."

*****

Chaplain Mhlangana called in on Thomas. "You had been doing so well. What went wrong?"

"How do you mean?"

"Don't play stupid, O'Grady. You had everything under control and I couldn't do a thing about it. Then your mind went somewhere else. Now you're lying here with a sore jaw. If your mind wasn't on someone trying to hit you off the ship, then there's something serious troubling you. What? Because if it's troubling you when you go into action, it might be your buddies that pay the price."

"Not troubling me, Sir. Not as such."

"I'm not Sir. I'm Chaplain. Explain, or we'll do another round and Nurse Stewart will look sternly at me."

"I had half of a revelation. An insight, but I haven't worked out what it means. I think I know what my vocation is, sort of, but I'm not sure how to get from here to there."

"Vocation? You're a rifleman."

"But not forever. Seven years and I've already done six months."

"And what does Nurse Charrington say?"

"Why should she say anything? She's got her life, I've got mine. She's got her vocation and I've now got mine. There's nothing between us. She's made it clear that there is no hope of there ever being anything between us. I might have wished things were different, but they aren't. I'm certainly not going to give up on life simply because I've been spurned in love."

"Have you told her about your vocation?"

"No. I still don't understand it myself yet, so there's nothing to tell. I didn't know before she told me to leave her alone. I'm not going to bother her after she told me to leave her alone. What's more, she's got her own vocation. That's an end to the matter."

"You're being very silly and very stubborn."

"Yes, I'm being stubborn. Whoever achieved their vocation and did something significant without being stubborn?"

"Now you're deliberately misunderstanding. You should talk to her."

"No, I shouldn't. What's more, everything that's been said here is confidential, so if she finds out anything about this conversation, well, it's between you, me, and God. Right? Nurse Charrington is none of those."

"One thing you need to think about. I don't think you should upset people trying to help, or you will end up with no friends."

*****

"They saw that I've been sleeping here," said Alice unhappily.

"So what?" Alasdair stood watching the sea.

"Everyone will know, and they'll think we're, together."

"That's not important. You found it hard to sleep in your office, correct? You sleep better in my cabin. You need your sleep. You look so much better for sleeping well. I don't see the problem. If people want to gossip, let them."

"But they'll think you're, we're, that you're sleeping in the bed as well. You need to sleep as well."

"I need to get used to getting good sleep on the floor. Besides, where else would a border collie sleep?"

She stood next to him at the railing and looked out to sea. She put her hand next to his on the railing, then put it on his. "What if you want to bring someone to your cabin."

"Firstly, who? Nurse Charrington? And risk having O'Grady scheming at me with blood in his eye? Nurse Stewart, who is already like a broody hen over having so many men around? Nurse Plummer, who is nearly 50? Miss Eliot? And upset Corporal Barry? One of the wives, who are married? There are no options."

"Things change. Nurse Charrington and Rifleman O'Grady, well, they're not together now."

"I may be silly, but I'm not silly enough to make a play for Nurse Charrington. If they've really split up, she's grieving. If they've only sort of split up, I'd get it from both sides."

"OK," Alice said. "What about secondly?"

"Secondly, you're my friend. Helping friends is more important than a passing rendezvous. If I had to choose between a good friend and a passing fancy, I'd choose a good friend every time."

"What if it was more than a passing fancy?"

"Never happened yet. Besides, you'd know if it was long before I did."

They watched the sea for some time, their hands still together.

"Alasdair, sometimes collies sleep on the bed, don't they?"

"Sometimes. When their owner is confident enough to let them. You're not. You think you should be and you're trying to run before you're ready to walk."

"What if I'm never able to run?"

"Whatever happens, we'll always be friends. Come on, let's go and ask the Colonel about you staying on in the Regiment forever."

*****

"If I'm honest, I wasn't expecting it to be you two to be asking the question," Colonel Dalkeith said. "Still, it was a question I had been anticipating, so I've done a bit of research." He motioned for Lieutenant Campbell and Nurse Ward to sit down. Since there was only one spare chair, Alasdair held the chair for Alice and stood behind her, hands resting gently on her shoulders.

"It's not exactly urgent, Sir," said Lieutenant Campbell.

"More than two years off. A lot can happen in that time. Still, I expect it will be a very busy two years. I take it this is an inquiry, rather than a formal request? Short answer, yes. In home deployment, the Regiment is entitled to have a medical orderly on strength. A sort of nurse, doctor, and pharmacist combined. It's usually expected that the medical orderly will be male, but there are a few exceptions. Not many regiments have them. Not many people want the job. It's a civilian post. Most nurses aren't able to do the job and no doctor wants to do it. I also looked into it, in case it's relevant. The medical orderly can be single or married. I've no idea if that will be relevant for you two. As it's two years hence, neither do you, so don't even try to answer it. The post is available. Whether you will want it, or whether someone else might also want it, we don't know."

*****

Colonel Dalkeith discussed the request with Lady Dalkeith. "I'm surprised Nurse Charrington and O'Grady weren't the first to ask."

They discussed the matter and Lady Dalkeith raised the obvious question. "Do regulations allow you to have more than one medical orderly? In case Nurse Charrington does apply?"

"Not without getting very creative. I don't think it's going to be an issue. Pity. They seemed well-suited."

"Joy, if you've finished the ironing, I suggest you start your lessons with Callaghan and Wagstaff. If you haven't, I suggest you concentrate more on the ironing and less on listening."

"Yes, Ma'am. Colonel, Sir, could I borrow one of the volumes of Army Regulations?"

"Why on earth would you want to borrow that? Corporal Barry can't leap to RSM with just a knowledge of the words."

"It's the words, Sir. Rifleman Wagstaff knows the Bible, so he doesn't read it, just remembers it, so he isn't learning to read, so I want a book that he'll have to read and that isn't easy to read."

"If they turn into barrack-room lawyers, I'll hold you responsible. Just to be safe, you can borrow the superseded file. Those are the regulations that used to apply, but no longer do so. Just in case Callaghan or Wagstaff get any clever ideas."

*****

First, she would have a word with Frank. She thought she knew what the problem was, but she didn't know how to solve it. Frank would know. She'd arrange to meet him somewhere private and they could talk about it.

She saw Sergeant Taylor, who was watching Frank teaching the recruits. Sergeant Taylor smiled on seeing her.

"Afternoon, Miss. Your intended is undergoing a big test. No regulations covering this. This will be a test of whether he's got what it takes."

"I'll come back later. How's he doing?"

"Oh, no, Miss. You go right in and say your piece to him. It will be the cherry on the top."

"I don't want to disturb him."

"Miss, that's the whole point. How well does he hold it together when there's a lot going on distracting him? Better we find out here than in the field. The harder the test here, the happier I'll be when it comes to reviewing his performance. The more distractions, the better for him." Sergeant Taylor paused. "In the long run."

Joy squared her shoulders. If distracting him helped, she'd distract him. She walked towards the group. Frank had his back to her and was showing the recruits how to clean a rifle. Then she slowed her pace a bit, because some of the wives were also in the line. She hadn't expected that. The recruits were standing still and listening, but it was obvious that the presence of the women was distracting them, because they were grinning and trying to impress with their physique. The women weren't any better. Some of them were pretty and were ogling Frank.

"Corporal Barry," she said, touching his shoulder. She had to make clear to the wives that no-one messed with her Frank. She remembered to call him Corporal Barry and not Frank, to prove she knew how to behave when he was on duty.

"Joy," he said, with relief evident in his voice. "I am teaching people about look after weapons. Some of wives want to learn also. Sergeant Taylor ask me to teach them. I thought I teach them together. Save time and recruits help wives learn."

Joy knew Frank well enough to know that he would not say the next two words he wanted to say, so she leaned up and whispered them in his ear. "Never again?"

"Do you think he'd give me extra lessons if I whispered sweet nothings in his ear?" said one of the wives.

"Extra lessons in what, though, eh Anwyn?"

Frank sighed. "Wives not under military discipline. They distracting recruits."

"The recruits are distracting us," said one of the wives.

"Five recruits, five wives," Joy whispered. "I can see you're very busy at the moment. Can I have a word when you're finished here?" she added, in a louder voice.

"I don't know if he'll say anything, but I'm sure you'll get his message," said one of the women.

"They not under military discipline. It very hard."

There was laughter among the wives. "*That's* the message he's got for her."

The recruits tried not to laugh at that, but they didn't succeed.

Frank turned to face the line. "It important to see when gun being cleaned properly and to know about different weapons. One wife, one recruit. Each watch the other clean the weapon. Make sure it done right. Then swap weapons, clean the weapon you not used to."

"When will we fire them?"

"When you know how to look after them. You ask me to teach you. I teach you. I teach you to Rifleman standard, which is best in world. When I've teached you, you be best women shooters in world. But you must do it how I teach you."

Joy walked back to where Sergeant Taylor was standing.

"Corporal Barry's a very lucky man, Miss. Thank you, Miss."

"What for?"

"Proving me right, and Lieutenant Hawkins wrong."

"I don't understand."

"Lieutenant Hawkins thinks women distract a man. I think the right woman completes a man. No idea how long it will take, but with you behind him, Corporal Barry's got it in him to be a good sergeant. A good part of that is down to you, Miss."

Joy felt like she was walking on air as she went to start the lesson with Callaghan and Wagstaff.

*****

"Come," said Nurse Charrington to the knock at the door. Windy and Peter entered.

She closed the book on Persia she had been reading. "Medical matters are confidential. Whichever of you is not seeing me about a medical matter will need to wait outside."

"See what I mean, Peter?"

"If you've finished discussing my shortcomings, I am very busy. If there is a medical issue, I am at your disposal. If not, kindly leave."

"Look, Emily, we're Thomas' friends."

Nurse Charrington sighed. "Nurse Charrington, if you please. Whatever the situation between myself and Rifleman O'Grady is, it is between us. It is, quite frankly, none of your business."

"You missed the Crossing the Line ceremony," Windy said, accusingly.

"It was an excellent opportunity to catch up on paperwork."

"The Colonel was there. He's got much more paperwork to do than you have. You're just using that as a pretty poor excuse." Windy was getting annoyed.

"I admit the new situation is taking a bit of getting used to. It will settle down in due course."

"You've hurt him badly, you know," said Peter.

"I'm sorry for that, but the pain would have been much greater had the situation continued, because an ending was always inevitable."

"That might be true for you, but it isn't for him."

"Forget it, Windy. We're wasting our time here."

They left, and Nurse Charrington returned to her book. It was hard to read through the tears. It was more important than ever to get on with her plan to stay in Persia. Perhaps she could find a replacement to take on her role here and allow her to resign her position ahead of schedule.

The distressing part was that Thomas would be able to find that replacement.

*****

"Did you come from a State School, nurse?"

"Certainly not, O'Grady. Whatever gave you that idea?" Nurse Stewart didn't sound offended, but she did sound as though she had been slightly insulted.

"It's just that they seem to get a rough deal."

"Nonsense. They get taken in, fed, clothed, and taught. What would be the alternative? They'd starve on the streets. All they're doing is paying back what it's cost to keep them."

"Well, yes, but no-one, that is, everything seems to be so hard for them and no-one seems to care what happens to them."

"Nonsense. It costs a fortune to take them off the street. When you've seen what the ones that don't go into State Schools get up to, you wouldn't be so soft-hearted about them. They're evil little, well, they're evil. Get them off the streets and get them doing something useful. It costs a lot, but it's better than those who avoid it."

"You're probably right," Thomas said. He still remembered the boards outside the schools. In a way, he felt happier. He knew that the children from the State Schools weren't getting a fair crack at life. They were being used and discarded when they got broken. He didn't know what he could do about it. It wasn't about funding a school, or anything like that. Doing things the way they had been done wasn't going to work if that way was wrong.

"Nurse, am I well enough to get up and see the Chaplain before resuming my duties?"

"Will it stop this constant stream of disturbances? If you feel dizzy or sick, you're to come straight back."

*****

Joy had finally managed to get Frank alone. She practically had to drag him to the cabin.

"You've finished your duties. I've got some time. We've both got time."

"True," Frank said. "And this private."

"Well?"

"I'm not very good with words." Frank seemed hesitant.

"You don't need to be very good with words."

"I want to get this right. It important."

"It's just four words, and you already know the answer." Joy was starting to get impatient.

"It still important. And there is problem."

"What's the problem? You'll be a Sergeant soon. Sergeant Taylor said you could become RSM at some time."

"There no Priest."

"There is! The Chaplain. He can marry us."

"He not Catholic."

"He is. He told me he was a Methodist, believed in Jesus and the Bible and never ever sacrificed goats except for the pot. That's Christian, not whatever Zulu religion is."

"He Christian, sort of, but not Catholic. Need Catholic ceremony, which need Catholic Priest."

"It's just one thing after another. Don't you *want* to marry me?"

"Yes, but I want it to be right. It must all be right."

Joy took a deep breath. "It will be all right if it's you and me. Nothing else matters."

"Things need organising. I not want let you down."

"The only way you could let me down would be by not asking me to marry you."

"I not want to ask you when there still so much to do."

"That does it. Francesco Barrilari, will you marry me and if you don't say yes, I'll tell everyone that I had to ask you because you were too scared to ask me and I'm happy to wait until we've got everything in place because I just want to be engaged."

"It wrong. I need to ask you, not you ask me."

"Then ask me. Or say yes. Then kiss me."

*****

Thomas walked gingerly. His jaw still hurt. He'd never been hit that hard before. Eating was going to be a problem. He'd told Sergeant Taylor and Lieutenant Hawkins he was back on the strength. Sergeant Taylor had confined his outpouring of joy at the news to the phrase: "About bloody time."

Thomas spoke with Lieutenant Hawkins. "Sir, I've been thinking."

"That's never a good sign, O'Grady."

"Very amusing, Sir. Sir, we take a lot of State School children into the Regiment."

"Naturally. Why is that important?"

"I wanted to talk to some of them, Sir."

"Why?"

"It's just," Thomas' voice faded.

"Go on. When in doubt, tell the truth. In your case, no-one would believe it, so your secret would still be safe." Lieutenant Hawkins sounded mildly amused.

"As you've probably guessed, I'm not from a State School myself."

"You astound me, O'Grady. Next you'll be telling me it hurts to get punched in the face."

Thomas told himself to ignore the sarcasm. This might be important. "It's just that I don't think State School people get a fair deal."

"So? They're only State School children."

"And yet without them, what happens to the Army?"

"O'Grady. Important three-letter word."

"Sir. Sorry, Sir. I was just thinking that, well, it's not right how they're treated."

"I don't follow, O'Grady. When someone joins the Regiment, no record is kept of whether they've done time, or come from the nobility, or a State School. If someone joins the rank and file, I don't know if their father is Lord Morgan, Daniel Morgan the butcher, or some guy who's long-since filled an unmarked grave. That's as it should be."

"I was thinking, well, beyond the Regiment."

"O'Grady, you're a Rifleman. Unless you plan to lead a mutiny, take control of the Army, lead a revolution against King and Parliament, and impose Utopia by force of arms, I suggest you concentrate on being a Rifleman."

Thomas thought that Lieutenant Hawkins was now abusing sarcasm. Two can play at that game.

"Very good, Sir. Permission to start?"

Lieutenant Hawkins sighed. "O'Grady, since you're on light duties for the day, I want you to put together a layout of your scheme for the dispersed company camp. Use Lieutenant Furley-Smith's cabin. That is empty."

*****

Nurse Charrington tried writing the letter again. Whatever she wrote didn't sound right. Thomas would be able to phrase it correctly, but she could hardly ask him for his help in writing it.

She missed him. He'd find someone else and forget her, but she missed him. Still, no use moping. The decision had been made and it really was for the best. They had nothing in common and there was nothing that she had to offer him.

She had things to do and if she were to die an old maid, then she may as well make the most of her nursing, because that was all she had.

And she must stop feeling sorry for herself. That did no-one any good. She had a job to do, and she had to get the job done, whatever it took.

*****

Thomas mused. The trouble was, he didn't know how much space there would be for everything. He didn't know how much he needed to get into the space that he didn't know the size of. He didn't know what the terrain would be like or which direction the wind came from or where the water supply would be or whether they'd have to store the screw guns and the mules and everything in it, or the kitchens.

He didn't even know how many men would be involved. Emily was good at breaking these things into what was important and what wasn't, but he'd have to manage without her. She would be better off without him; he'd just wasted his life and he had to make serious amends before anyone could take him seriously.

It had been an expensive lesson. It had cost him any chance of being with her, but at least he could make a difference and help other people.

Concentrate on the job in hand. Get the job done, whatever it took. Still, at least he would have a bit of privacy here. He opened the door to the cabin.

It took him a moment to realise that the cabin was already occupied. It took him another moment to realise that the two people hadn't noticed him and seemed rather pre-occupied in each other. He recognised Frank's back, his shirt was half off, and a girl's arms were around his body. Frank and the girl were kissing passionately.

Thomas couldn't help himself. He'd pay for this, but it would be worth it.

"Corporal Barry! Attention!"

Whatever happened after this, it had been worth it. Corporal Barry jerked to attention, struggling to disentangle himself from Joy, whose clothing was as much awry as his was. Joy looked desperately to see who it was, struggling to reassemble her blouse.

"From the looks of it, congratulations are in order," Thomas said. "Think yourself lucky it was me who burst in and think yourself lucky I didn't come in a bit later."

"We're engaged," said Joy, trying to get her breath back.

"I guessed. Unfortunately, I have to work here. You might try Nurse Ward's office after dark."

"I know what happen. That will be the one time she decide to get something from her office."

"Frank, if you think I'm going to play watchdog while you two get acquainted, you've another think coming. Go and talk with the Chaplain, or something. Haven't you got things to arrange?"

"Thomas," said Joy, "can you turn your back please."

"Why?"

"I need to look for an earring."

"I can help you look."

"That not necessary," said Frank firmly.

*****

Alice and Alasdair sat on the bed in his cabin. "Thank you," she said.

"What for?"

"Well, everything, really. You've been so good about everything."

"What else could I do. You're a good friend. Probably the best friend I've ever had. Helping each other is what friends do."

"Alasdair, Colonel Dalkeith talked about us possibly getting married."

"I've no idea whether we will or not. You have only one concern at the moment. Getting better and getting other people better when they get hurt."

"Alasdair, that's two things."

"See what I mean?" he said and ruffled her hair. "Seriously, don't borrow fears from the future. Whatever happens, I'll always be your friend. You've got nothing to be scared of."

*****

Frank and Joy went into the Colonel's cabin. Lady Dalkeith glanced up.

"I take it that you've got something to say, Corporal Barry."

"Yes, Ma'am. Miss Eliot and I have talked, and she agreed to marry me." He'd thought carefully about how to phrase that. It would be so awkward if anyone were to ask who asked whom.

"As I've said, marriage is conditional upon your making sergeant. Now, it seems that young people believe that an agreement allows certain liberties to be taken that should wait until one is properly married. I trust, Corporal Barry, that you will behave with honour in this."

From his desk, Colonel Dalkeith coughed. "Maeve, they've behaved with honour so far."

"More or less."

"They have been tempted, no doubt. I'm sure they will behave with as much honour as we would in their position."

"Sir?" said Joy. She thought that was a strange phrasing.

"Corporal Barry, you just need to be ready for the change that becoming a sergeant and getting married will bring. Congratulations to you both. Word of advice. You'll have arguments. Don't worry about them. Listen to the other person and always make sure you end an argument with a sign of affection."

"A sign of affection, Sir?"

"A kind word. If you're feeling particularly bold, maybe a small kiss on the forehead. The argument isn't the person. If you respect the other person, you'll listen to them. Carry on with your duties, Corporal Barry."

"Ma'am," said Joy, greatly daring. "What about displays of affection?"

"Do you see Colonel Dalkeith and myself engaging in such? I think that should be your first guideline. Remember, Corporal Barry has to set an example, a good example, to those recruits. They are very impressionable."

"Yes, Ma'am."

"Time for dinner, Maeve. Joy, while we're at dinner, would you be so good as to write out in fair copy the notes on my desk."

As they left, Joy had the annoying thought that there was something important that she knew that she couldn't quite place. It was dancing just out of reach. She shook her head and looked at the notes.

"A Fearless Family Affair. Being the Memoirs of Colonel Garnet William Robert Dalkeith."

*****

Frank knew he had to speak with the Chaplain. He wasn't a proper Chaplain. He wasn't entirely sure if non-Catholics were Christian, but he didn't want any doubts about the marriage. He didn't trust a black man as a priest. As soldiers and fighters, but as a man of God? He didn't trust the Chaplain.

He didn't want to admit it, because he was a Corporal, but he was also scared. Joy was simply too good for him. She was pretty and clever and kind, just perfect. She hadn't known anyone else, and she could do so much better than him. He was scared she'd realise that. It wouldn't matter if she discovered that before they were committed. He would be unhappy, but they'd still be honourable.

But what if she found someone better after they were married? Joy was right, but for the wrong reasons. He was scared that if they got married, she'd end up unhappy. He couldn't bear that.

Still, it had to be a proper marriage because Joy deserved that. He wouldn't dishonour her with anything less.

"No Confession, no attendance at service. Barrilari, I'm disappointed. I think you want to ask me about marriage?"

"You not Catholic priest."

"You're not a Zulu warrior, but you're still part of my flock."

"That different. It not same thing." Frank found that English was becoming harder. "It important we married right."

"Well, you can't be married right if you do so when you're not in a state of Grace. Confession first."

"But you not Catholic." Frank was a bit wary of getting into an argument with someone who could beat Thomas in a fist fight, and he was wary of getting into a theological debate with a priest.

"I am God's Servant. I go where He sends me. If He sends me, then that is where I should be. If I should be there, then whoever is there is part of my flock, even if they are the black sheep of the flock."

"You more like black sheep," Frank growled. "I not win argument with you, but Catholic priest needed to make right marriage for Catholic."

"First things come first. You can't get married without having Confession. Marriage while not in a state of Grace? So, Confession."

"You still not Catholic."

"I've been sent here. You've been sent here. If you've a problem with that, take it up with God. If you've a problem with God, speak to me. I have been chosen by God to be your priest. If it helps, think of me as someone you can confide in. You need Confession."

"I have girl I want marry, but not good enough for her."

"Yes, I know. O'Grady told me about you two. I've given the situation some thought and talked with God. It's perfectly clear. You're an idiot. You two have been thrown together. Who by?"

"Things have happened." Frank was uneasy. Priests don't speak like this.

"See. You're an idiot. God has put you two together. Stop arguing with God. If He wants you together, obstacles will get out of the way. If He doesn't, they won't. The obstacles are there to test you."

"There's also, desires," Frank said, hoping the priest would understand.

"I should hope so. If God is putting you together, then you should desire each other. It's part of God's plan."

"We were, that is, we had been, when we were interrupted."

"Did you?"

"No, but I don't know how long we wait. Marriage so far away."

"Get married soon. Turn a sin into something that God intends."

"I not able wait until I sergeant. She deserve someone better than me."

"Is she clever?"

"Yes."

"Is she wise?"

"Yes."

"Is she thoughtful?"

"Well," said Frank. He wasn't so sure about that.

"Does she understand things?"

"Yes."

"Has she chosen you?"

"Yes, but …"

"You're doubting her choice and you're doubting God's choice. If you don't think you're good enough, be better. Now, about my being a Priest. God told me to be a Methodist. God has sent me here to serve Methodists and Anglicans and Catholics and Jews and Baptists and unbelievers and anyone else in the Regiment. I checked with Army Regulations, and I checked with God. I'm His representative here.

*****

Joy started to read the memoirs. She found a marked passage and read it. It was about how the Colonel met Lady Dalkeith, only she wasn't Lady Dalkeith then. She read it and she kept on reading.

"The devious, tricky man."

"The devious, tricky girl."

Then her face began to redden. She looked back to see if she hadn't turned over several pages at once. She read the passage again. And again. Right. That did it. She'd find Frank.

In her father's bed.

*****

She had a duty to check on the other nurses. Nurse Plummer was in her element, pampering her charges, to all intents and purposes acting like a nanny or a mother to several hundred young boys. She would have to make sure Nurse Plummer realised that not all of the boys would come back in one piece, that this wasn't a big play-time where everyone came in for tea when it was all over.

At the moment, Nurse Plummer was doing well, but she'd have to keep an eye on her when the casualties started to come in.

Nurse Stewart adored the attention. In a London hospital, she was just a short, dumpy, big-hearted nurse, one of many and always overlooked by men. Here she was treated like a lady. Men flirted with her, and she blossomed under the attention. She was sensible enough to know she'd be overlooked again when they returned to England, but she was determined to enjoy her moment.

She asked Emily about Sergeant Taylor, which was a puzzle.

"Why Sergeant Taylor?"

"Because he's kind and gentle and thoughtful."

Nurse Charrington's imagination hit a brick wall with that description. "Sergeant Taylor? Of the Training Platoon?"

"Yes. He's worried and we talk a lot. He misses his Doris."

"And you think you'll replace his Doris?"

"Don't be silly. No-one can do that. They were, well, it's like they're still together, only in different rooms."

"I see," Nurse Charrington said, although she didn't quite understand. "What are your plans?"

"Plans? Oh, I see. I think I'll start by making sure everyone is prepared for the heat and cold. Men can be so neglectful of taking precautions."

"That wasn't what I meant. I expect my nurses to know about nursing without my needing to instruct them."

"I know what you meant. What Sergeant Taylor and I get up to, if anything, is none of your concern." She sighed. "Not that we'll get up to anything. He has his Doris."

*****

The Officers' Mess was quiet, with only a few people present and most keeping conversations separate. As the ship drew closer to Persia, officers found there were more and more preparations that needed doing.

"Nurse Ward and Lieutenant Campbell?" Lady Dalkeith asked. "Do we need a word with them about arrangements when we reach Persia?"

Colonel Dalkeith considered the question. "I'd prefer them to make a decision without prompting. You really are the most terrible matchmaker."

"Really? I thought I was rather good at it."

"Now I know you're just trying to start an argument."

"Not in the slightest. You're just being over-sensitive." Lady Dalkeith sounded abrupt.

"I've been accused of many things but being sensitive is a new one."

"It's a long way down the list, I admit."

Some of the younger officers started to feel a bit awkward. The Colonel and Lady Dalkeith had been arguing more than normal recently, and this was getting personal.

Colonel Dalkeith put his napkin on the table. "I rather think, Maeve, that we should continue this discussion in privacy rather than in the Mess." He rose. "If you will excuse us, gentlemen. My wife and I have matters to discuss."

After they had left, the officers continued their conversations. The younger officers wondered how two people could argue so much and yet still remain apparently happily married. The older officers were not inclined to explain to the younger officers.

*****

Thomas cleared some space at the desk. He moved some papers, then started looking at them. Furley-Smith had written out a lot of notes on the situation in Persia. It was interesting, although there wasn't much a rifleman could do with the knowledge. Some information on the Cossacks and a note about how they probably had loyalties to Russia.

Notes on the Company Commanders, noting their strengths, weaknesses, and likely *modus operandi*.

Notes on the nurses' medical offices on the ship, with details on which doors were overlooked from where. His blood started to run cold when he saw timings noted for Nurse Charrington's office. There was no danger now that Furley-Smith was no longer around, but his fist was clenching nonetheless. He had an irrational desire to check that she was all right.

He calmed down. Nurse Charrington wouldn't appreciate being troubled. Certainly not by him and certainly not for such an irrational reason.

A thought entered his head. Like a worm, it stayed there. Furley-Smith left the whaling ship. The captain of that ship said he'd left outside port and swam to another ship.

What if he was lying?

What if Furley-Smith had bribed him to lie, to give him cover?

What if Furley-Smith had left much earlier, sneaked onto this ship and was hiding, lying in wait?

It was ridiculous. It was impossible. They'd searched the ship for stowaways. There was nowhere to hide for any length of time. There was the problem of food and drink.

He could be in disguise. No-one noticed stokers.

He would notice stokers, and Furley-Smith probably knew that. What about stewards?

Calm down. First thing to do was to look. He had the notes on what places overlooked Emily's office. Check those first.

*****

"Nurse Charrington, you've asked me before. My answer is the same. Alice and I are friends. Good friends. Now, can you please stop asking us the same question over and over."

Nurse Charrington sighed. It almost hurt to see how close Alice and Lieutenant Campbell had become.

Such things were a distraction. She couldn't afford them. Being around the Regiment was becoming increasingly painful. When she arrived in Persia, she could seek out a suitable replacement, then leave. She'd have her nursing and leave these constant reminders of having someone she might have cared for.

"My apologies. I just wish to ensure everything is ready for when we arrive in Persia. I think I can safely leave the welfare of Nurse Ward in your hands."

*****

Frank emerged from the Chaplain's office. He was thinking hard. He wasn't used to priests like that, but then this priest wasn't really a priest, and he was black. It was very complicated.

"Come on," said Joy, taking him by the hand. "I've been waiting for ages for you."

"Where we going?" Frank asked, being almost dragged along.

"They've lied to us and to think how much time we've wasted and keep up." Joy was pulling him forward.

Take control. That's what Sergeant Taylor would say. This was not doing his authority among the men any good. "No," he said, standing still. His arm was nearly jerked out of its socket, but he managed to pull Joy up short. "What is going on?"

"All this time, she's said we've had to wait and wait and wait. Wait for you to be Sergeant and for us to get married and for everything. And all the time, all the time, all the time."

"I don't understand. All the time, what?"

"*They* didn't wait. They, you know, the first day. Well, it was the second, sort of, and in her father's bed, and all this time. Well, they're at dinner, so the cabin's empty and *come on*."

"No."

"What do you mean, no? Don't you want to? We've been waiting so long."

"I mean no. Our first, it will be special. Not rushed, not thinking of anything else. Not because we getting back at someone else. What other people do, that not how we think. All that matter is what we want and that is for it to be right. You understand?"

"Frank, I love you so much. I want to make you happy. You're right, I suppose. Soon, please."

"Besides," said Frank. "Cabin not empty. You hear?"

They stood outside the cabin and Joy could hear someone inside. She remembered that she hadn't put the memoirs away. The Colonel and Lady Dalkeith would still be at dinner.

"Someone's going through the Colonel's things," Joy said. "We'll catch them, and the Colonel will be pleased with you catching these people red-handed. I'll open the door and you burst in."

*****

"Peter," said Windy, as they sat by Nurse Ward's office. "What are we going to do about Thomas and Nurse Charrington?"

"There's not much we can do. They're determined to be idiots. What can we do? Kidnap them and lock them in a room together until they get it right."

There was a long silence.

"Windy, that was a joke. It wouldn't work."

"It's got to be worth a try. Nurse Ward's office is always empty at night. We just need to make the door open the other way, lure them both inside, bar the door, and wait for results."

"Windy, even by your standards, that's a stupid idea."

"Why?"

"Because when they're locked in, they'll be trying to get out, not trying it on with each other."

"Is it worth a try?"

"They'll kill us."

"It's worth a try, then."

*****

"Why?" Lieutenant Hawkins asked. Frank stood at attention; his eyes fixed ahead. "Of all of you four disreputables, I thought that I could trust you to behave with a bit of sense. Why?"

"I heard noise in Colonel's cabin."

"You heard a noise in the Colonel's cabin. Are all the officers going to have to go around on tip toe?"

"I thought he being robbed."

"And you didn't stop to consider that the noise from the Colonel's cabin might have been from, oh, I don't know, the Colonel?"

"Colonel was at dinner."

"Self-evidently, he wasn't. He was, however, quite surprised. Didn't you think to knock?"

"It was important to catch thieves red-handed."

"There's only one door into the cabin. Where would the thieves go?"

"I not sure. There back room for Joy."

"Which is a back room with no exit. Is this your level of tactical expertise? The Colonel asked me to ensure that you received the appropriate consequence."

Here it comes, Frank thought. Busted from Corporal.

"I've looked through Army Regulations to find out exactly what is appropriate. Unsurprisingly, there's no mention of this situation. I discussed the matter with Sergeant Taylor. He agreed with me that he'd not come across a similar situation. Many times in which an officer or NCO came across a Rifleman, indulging. Junior officers have, on occasion, been so exposed. Colonels, however, well, that's a new one."

"I'm sorry, Sir."

"Oh, trust me, you will be. I'd thought of busting you back to Rifleman. The trouble is, who would we put in your place? Sergeant Taylor suggested promoting you to officer, as only an officer would be so, rash. I decided that this would be thoroughly inappropriate. I realised, and Sergeant Taylor agrees, that we have the perfect opportunity to make use of this previously unknown talent of yours."

Frank was puzzled. "Sir?"

"In due course, we will be arriving in Persia and settling into a base of operations. About ten minutes after we've done that, there will be locals who see a business opportunity. Traders, that sort of thing. They'll come flocking. Most of these will not be a problem."

Frank was getting a bad feeling about this.

Lieutenant Hawkins paused, then smiled. "It's an opportunity for you to display your talents. One of these establishment will be a brothel. We'll need to check to make sure that it's a clean establishment, run efficiently. Resolving disputes between the soldiers and the establishment. And, most importantly, we'll also need to recover soldiers from the establishment when they are required to be in the base. This last will be your duty. Normally, we cycle NCOs through this duty on a weekly basis, but since you've displayed such a talent, I've suggested, and Sergeant Taylor agrees with me, that you've earned a two-month stint. Good luck in explaining this duty to Miss Eliot."

*****

"Thomas, what are you playing at?" Windy asked. He'd seen Thomas prowling about the ship, looking into odd corners, quartering the decks, disturbing things, bothering the kitchen staff, and acting strangely. Even strange by Thomas' standards.

Thomas explained his theory. Windy considered this carefully.

"You're insane. It's been, what, three weeks since we left Cape Town? Where's he been hiding all that time without anyone noticing? What's he been eating and drinking? What's he been, there's just so much."

"What if he's been in disguise?"

"What as? One of Neptune's bears? Don't be ridiculous." Windy paused and put his hand to his chin. Thomas wondered briefly just how Windy managed to get such as close shave. He was still young, so he didn't need to shave much, but even so.

"Mind you," Windy continued. "No-one notices the stewards and that illness the officers got was suspiciously well-timed if he wanted to get settled in. If he could arrange that, then while everyone is rushing around dealing with it, he can stock up and hide. What's more, the food thefts wouldn't be noticed because the officers were eating less, so what he took would just look like normal consumption. And he'd know that he could stock up again while we were Crossing the Line. He may even have been disguised as a bear. The sailors were grumbling that a bear costume had gone missing. OK. He's been hidden for three weeks, so we're not going to find him easily. What we need to do is watch his prey. That's what big-game hunters do."

"Windy, what do you know about big-game hunting? You go hunting elephants in Whitechapel?"

"Why do you think they call it the Elephant and Castle? We got loads of elephants wandering the streets of London. That's why Alan Quartermain lives in London. Look, you'll be best at close protection. Peter and me can provide long-range cover and Frank can get his recruits to search the ship. They'll have better senses, what with growing up in a jungle. What you have to do is stick to Nurse Charrington like glue. You get on with that, and I'll speak to the others."

*****

Windy hurried to speak with Peter. "I've done it. I've found a way to get Thomas and Nurse Charrington back together. You see, I told him Furley-Smith might have stowed away and he needed to provide her with close protection."

"Windy, even by your standards," said Peter, exasperated.

"It worked, didn't it?"

*****

He didn't believe it, but it gave him an excuse to talk to Nurse Charrington. One last effort to find out if there was any chance of, well, he didn't know what, but he couldn't just give up. One last, final try.

She was eating in her office. Again. She looked up at him and sighed. "I trust this is a professional visit, not merely a social call. I have neither time nor inclination to waste on social matters."

She looks tired, Thomas thought. "It's a professional visit, Ma'am." He could observe the niceties of professional communication. "It concerns a possible threat to you. I have been instructed to provide close protection until the threat has been resolved."

"Really. Will pirates come swooping across the sea at night? Perhaps giant birds will swoop down and try to carry me off. Maybe the Regiment will mutiny and sail off into the sunset."

"If we sailed into the sunset, we'd run into Africa, Miss." He could see Nurse Charrington almost smile. "But seriously, Miss. It's possible Lieutenant Furley-Smith managed to stow away on board. Notes of his were found that suggested he planned to target you, Miss."

"Preposterous. If this a feeble attempt to spend time in my company, it is in extremely poor taste. Kindly leave and do not insult me with such a flimsy, transparent lie."

"No, Miss, I can't. In all probability, there is no threat. However, you are important to the Regiment. We can't take the chance. My duty is to ensure that you are protected."

"Why you? Why not any other rifleman? Anyone else."

"Because I'm big enough to deal with any threat, because I'm devious enough to outsmart any threat, and because I would lay down, lay down good odds that just my being here would scare any threat off. Besides, Lieutenant Furley-Smith views me as a primary target he wishes to harm. He'd target me ahead of you."

"I do not want you in the office. My work is confidential. I can't prevent you from standing guard outside, although it is a fool's errand. Outside. Kindly do not try to engage in any pleasantries. I will not welcome them."

As Thomas stepped outside, she shut the door firmly, almost with a slam. He wasn't sure, but he thought he could hear her crying. Maybe it was just his imagination, maybe it was just because that was how he felt.

*****

"I am not pleased, Joy. I am not pleased at all."

"No, Ma'am."

"I've granted you many privileges and I've allowed you certain freedoms because of your situation. I feel badly let down. I am very disappointed."

"Yes, Ma'am."

"Do you have anything to say for yourself?"

"Sorry, Ma'am."

"I'm extremely disappointed."

"Sorry, Ma'am."

"I only hope that you don't think that you can take liberties."

"Yes, Ma'am. I mean, no, Ma'am. Ma'am, it might help if Frank and I had a book we could read together and talk about. Maybe even argue over." Joy was annoyed, because when she was younger, Lady Dalkeith had done much worse if the Colonel's memoirs were right.

"That's an extraordinary suggestion."

She was committed now. "Ma'am, could we borrow Domestic Manners of the Americans? Colonel Dalkeith said that he enjoyed it."

"Did he really. I'm afraid it will be too advanced for Corporal Barry. It's quite unsuitable."

"Ma'am, I think he could manage it if we were reading it together. We might argue a bit, but you said that arguments tested a couple."

"I think you're getting ideas above your station, Joy."

Joy took a deep breath. She was scared, worried and nervous, all in one, but she couldn't back down now. "No, Ma'am. I'm going to be a Sergeant's wife. That means I have to act like one and that means being strong, because the other wives are going to depend on me. If I have to argue with the Colonel's Lady on their behalf, then that's what I've got to do."

"But you're not arguing on their behalf, are you."

"I need to be able to, Ma'am."

"Where on earth did you learn to be so stubborn?"

"You said I needed to grow a spine, Ma'am. I was kind of copying you, Ma'am."

"I see. Don't you think you're being very rude?"

Joy opened her mouth a couple of times. She was scared but she had to be a Sergeant's wife. She looked down at the ground. Then she remembered Lady Dalkeith saying the answer wasn't written on her shoes. She looked up and looked Lady Dalkeith in the eyes. If only her heart wasn't hammering so and if only she wasn't shaking so much. She had to stop being so scared. "Colonel Dalkeith explained. He said: 'I'm direct. You're blunt. He's rude.' Well, Ma'am, I'm just being direct."

She was going to die. Lady Dalkeith was just looking at her very coldly.

"I see. Well, you're not a Sergeant's wife yet, Joy. In addition, you have a lot to learn about being one. You will have to learn how to run a household. Move into Furley-Smith's old cabin. Start with that. There's not long till we reach Persia."

"Yes, Ma'am." Joy was a bit confused. "Does that mean?"

"It means that cabin will be where you stay until we reach Persia. Your own quarters. It might give Colonel Dalkeith some privacy."

"My own quarters, Ma'am?"

"I believe that's what I said. You've looked after a cabin under my supervision. It's time to see how you cope without someone constantly directing you."

"My own quarters, Ma'am? Yes, Ma'am. Ma'am, if Frank"

"If I learn that Corporal Barry has visited you inappropriately, then you will discover just how … direct I can be. You need to learn how to set a good example for the other wives. I shall also be checking on the cabin to make sure you keep it in the state it should be. You will continue to keep this cabin clean as well. You've become very lax in keeping the bed made."

*****

"What was that all about?" Colonel Dalkeith asked, returning and seeing Joy carrying her few belongings.

"Young Joy's growing up."

*****

Her own room. Her very own room, which she didn't have to share with anyone. Except Frank, of course. They could have some privacy. It would be a bit like being married. Frank wanted everything perfect, and this was close.

What if she messed it up? What if she wasn't, if Frank didn't like her when they were close? What if she let him down?

She was scared. That was silly. She loved Frank. But she was still scared, scared of letting him down.

She couldn't talk with him about this, or with any man. They wouldn't understand. She couldn't talk to the wives, because she had to be someone they could come to and see her as strong and knowing things.

She couldn't talk with Lady Dalkeith about it. She wouldn't understand. Perhaps worse, she might understand all too well, and then think that she wasn't old enough to have her own room. "You've shown that you're not ready. Maybe when you're older." She could just imagine her words.

Alice was still recovering. Nurse Charrington would know. It was a shame that she'd broken up with Thomas, but Nurse Charrington was still her friend.

She would understand and be able to help her.

*****

Damn. Peter was not happy. Frank and the recruits were searching the lifeboats. Damn. He was going to have to move things in a hurry. The ship had so many things that could be useful to the Regiment.

It's not theft if it's someone else's property, although the police hadn't seen it that way. If he didn't move things quickly, it would be found, and the Regiment wouldn't have it to use in Persia.

Still, at least he wouldn't be recognised if he wore the bear costume.

No, that was a Windy plan. People might notice a bear taking stuff out of a lifeboat. Just take the stuff and carry it, looking annoyed at being detailed off to do this. Prepare a reply in case anyone asked what he was doing. "Don't know, Sir. Sergeant told me to. He told me not to ask questions when I asked why."

If he was asked which Sergeant. "Sergeant Brown, Sir." None of the officers knew all the sergeants. By the time they realised there was no Sergeant Brown, he'd be long gone.

Where could he move the stuff to? Nurse Ward's office. No, that was busy during the day. While she'd be good about having it there, the stuff might not be safe from visitors. Some riflemen were very light-fingered, which was something the sergeants ought to put a stop to.

He'd store the stuff in Lieutenant Furley-Smith's old cabin. That was nice and empty.

*****

"Sit down, Alasdair. No need to worry. Just a little chat. I have to say, you've been very understanding with Nurse Ward. It's easy to locate you. You're either on duty or in her company."

"Is that a problem, Sir?"

"Not at all. Not while we're on the ship. Drink? It's the last of this Sicilian whisky."

"I'm afraid my father would have strong words if I were to drink whisky that wasn't from Scotland, Sir. When you say not while we're on this ship, Sir?"

"I understand Nurse Ward has been sleeping in your cabin."

"Sir, Nurse Ward has difficulty sleeping well if I am not around. You have my word there is nothing dishonourable between us."

"I believe you, Alasdair. If I didn't, we would be having a very different conversation. I wouldn't be offering you Sicilian whisky, for a start."

Lieutenant Campbell decided not to ask whether being offered Sicilian whisky was a good sign or a bad one. "I'm just keen to be useful, Sir."

"You've been very useful. The screw-guns. The rapport you've built with those working with you on them. The trust you've built up with Nurse Ward. All very positive. We're now getting close to Persia. The moment that we leave this ship, we will officially and formally be on a deployment status."

"I'm ready for that, Sir."

"That means I will expect and require all officers to set a good example. Don't you agree?"

"Absolutely, Sir."

"Officers will have their own quarters. Nothing fancy, all fairly basic, but they'll need a bit of privacy. Incidentally, have you decided on a batman?"

"Recruit Abe, Sir."

"Not Grant or Miller?"

"It's not possible to separate those two. Furthermore, they'll be key to the screw-guns. I don't want to distract them from that. Recruit Abe is keen, clean, and surprisingly bright. Mind you, he's also got it into his head that he could become an NCO."

"Alasdair, the Army has taken him on as a Recruit. That means the Army expects him to do any task he is suited for. If it turns out he's suited to be an NCO, then the Army will make him an NCO. That might seem unlikely, but if he can do it, then he'll do it. However, there's another matter. Nurse Ward and the issue of cohabitation. Dreadful word, but that is the word used in Regulations. Regulations are clear. Officers may share quarters with a lady if, and only if, that lady is their wife. I've been happy to turn a blind eye while on the ship. In Persia, it's another matter. You must set a good example to the men. Some of them have wives here, some have wives back in England. I suspect some have both. Some men will form attachments with local ladies who will not be allowed on the base outside of matrimony. Your cohabiting with Nurse Ward, however innocent or honourable it might be, will cease when we set foot on Persia."

"What if we're married, Sir? You said something about wives."

"Regulations permit officers to live with their wife. Curiously, they don't discuss the situation of an officer living with a husband. Given that Nurse Ward is, in fact, technically a Captain, an oversight. She technically outranks you, so her vowing to obey you would be an interesting puzzle in balancing the marriage ceremony with Army Regulations."

"That means I can continue to share a room with Nurse Ward if she consents to be my wife?"

"I can tell that you are an inexperienced officer, Alasdair, with your casual use of the word "if" there. Yes, if she consents, you will be doubly fortunate in acquiring both an estimable wife and superior quarters. That will be all."

*****

Joy looked around her new cabin. It was small. She could almost touch both sides of the room at the same time. The bed was high off the ground, with space under it for luggage. Not that she had much. There was a desk at the bottom of the bed and a small cabinet in the bottom of the desk.

She closed her eyes and tried to imagine being here with Frank. It was strange. She was excited by the prospect. She was excited, but she was also scared.

*****

Sergeant Taylor stopped Frank while the recruits were checking a lifeboat. "Corporal Barry. Exactly what are you doing?"

Frank explained. Sergeant Taylor did not look at all pleased.

"What have you done wrong?"

Frank thought desperately. He'd made sure the obvious targets were protected. He'd got a search party out to track things down. He'd got long cover on the targets. He hadn't disturbed people. But the way that Sergeant Taylor was looking told him that he'd forgotten something. If he didn't work it out, he'd never get to be sergeant. Not after messing up with the Colonel.

"Come on, Corporal. I'm waiting for your report."

Was it Frank's imagination? Had Sergeant Taylor put a slight emphasis on the last word?

"Report, Sergeant."

"Explain."

Frank thought furiously. "I started things without first reporting."

"And why is that a problem?"

"It could be that what we do clash with other plans."

"What else? Even more important."

NCOs know everything. "If I not report, higher people not have information."

"And? What if you're in the field?"

That was easy. "In field, may be casualties. If I not report, then become casualty, report never get through. Report first, so information known."

Sergeant Taylor's face relaxed. "Better late than never. Do you think this a fool's errand?"

Frank shrugged. "Not know. It not seem likely. If I him and get clear of ship, why would I come back? If he come back, he's after something."

"What would he be after? I'll speak with Lieutenant Hawkins. You continue with your disreputables. Your deployments are sound. You were an idiot for not reporting first. That's inexperience. Learn."

*****

The Chief Steward watched Joy take her belongings in the empty cabin. He wanted to get back at Corporal Barry but he was worried about comeback. The Corporal was a worry; the girl scared him. She had sounded serious.

Things had been going missing around the ship. That gave him an idea. If things are discovered in her cabin, then she would get into trouble. Plant a few, tell the Jimmy he'd seen her sneak things. Get her caught red-handed.

If he got caught, he could say he was delivering a sandwich, so he'd need to take one with him. He'd have to make sure she was out but that shouldn't be difficult. If she'd moved the things and nothing got found, he'd say it was just an honest mistake.

The question was, would that be enough of a distraction for the Lieutenant? He wished he'd never got caught up in this scheme, but he now just had to hope for the best.

*****

Nurse Charrington was busy. She told Joy to come back in the evening after dinner. She didn't tell Joy she'd have sandwiches here because Joy would tell her off and tell her to eat with everyone else and not spend all her time moping on her own.

She wasn't moping. She felt a bit lonely, but that was not a big thing. She had her work and she enjoyed it. That was more than most women could say.

Joy hadn't really said what she wanted to talk about, but got the impression it was more wanting to talk than anything being wrong.

She chided herself for thinking that Thomas was just outside and that it would be easy to open the door and talk with him. That would be a slippery slope. She couldn't permit that to happen. No-one can hurt you if you don't get close to anyone.

*****

Windy watched the people wandering past the offices and the cabins. If he was like the detectives, he'd be able to tell which of these people were acting suspiciously. What should he be looking for? Probably people that looked out of place.

"Or what should be in place, but isn't," said Peter. Windy hadn't heard him arrive, which was embarrassing as he was supposed to be keeping an eye out.

"How did you know what I was thinking?"

"You're predictable. Besides, I've read the same detective stuff you have, only it didn't take me as long to read them."

Windy looked at the pack Peter was carrying and sighed. "You know, property is theft is supposed to be a description, not an instruction."

"What's he doing here?" Peter asked, glancing towards the Chief Steward. The Chief Steward was walking to and fro along the deck, looking almost furtive.

*****

Just because he was on guard outside Emily's office didn't mean he had to stand at attention. That would look odd, for one thing. But standing around and chatting with Joy outside the office was nothing that anyone would remark on.

Joy was worried. She was worried Frank was putting things off. She asked if he was losing interest or scared or something.

"Don't use the word scared to him. He'll never admit to being scared of anything. And don't tell him I said this, but he's scared he's not good enough for you."

"That's silly. I love him to bits. Why does he think that?"

"Have you looked in a mirror recently?"

"Thomas, I'm a bit scared."

"What of? He loves you to bits. Honestly, am I going to have to drag you both to the altar?"

"It's not the getting married bit that's scary. Well, it is. It's everything. Being with someone. Being with someone. It's, well, what if, what if it all goes wrong?"

"For crying out loud," Thomas muttered to himself. He took a deep breath. "He loves you. You love him. Everything else is just details."

"It's still scary. Why did Nurse Charrington and you, you know?"

"Break up? I have no idea. She's said, well, different reasons. I don't understand. We've got nothing in common. Different parts of society. It would mean her giving up nursing. They're all just, well, it's obvious she simply doesn't want me and there's no kind way of saying that. I'd rather not talk about it."

"Give up nursing?"

"Hospitals don't accept married nurses. If a nurse marries, they have to give up their career."

"So? This isn't a hospital."

Thomas looked across the deck and shook his head sadly. "It doesn't matter anymore. Pity. I guess it's just as well I was stupid. It would just have made the breakup harder. Fate must be having a laugh at me right now. Guess I deserve it. Joy, if you don't mind, I'd like to be alone for a bit."

*****

Major Marshall and Colonel Dalkeith sat at a table in the Officers' Mess with a sheaf of papers between them.

"What do the numbers say?" Colonel Dalkeith asked.

Major Marshall shook his head sadly. "Same as usual. The funds we've been given for Regimental pay won't cover pay for the Regiment for the whole deployment. Usual explanation. Here we are. 'Funds have been adjusted to take account of expected levels of casualties. Pay to a soldier ceases upon their decease or invaliding out of the service.' The usual." Major Marshall braced himself for the next question.

"What level of casualties are they expecting?"

"Assuming that the casualties are evenly distributed through the ranks and over time, about 30 percent. They do say that any funds in excess of actual needs are to be returned. No mention of how any potential shortfall might be made up."

"As you say, Tristram, the usual. If I keep them alive, we end up not paying them. Any mention of restrictions on how to make up the shortfall?"

"The usual. Looting is strictly forbidden. No gifts to be accepted from local dignitaries. No extra-duty profiteering. And obviously, any shortfall in funding because we don't get enough boys butchered unnecessarily will be made up through the normal administrative formalities in the fullness of time."

"Assuming no casualties, when do we run out of money?"

"Nineteen months, eight days. It has also been assumed that the deployment will not be extended."

"Which it will be. I assume you checked that they supplied the amount supposedly supplied?"

"All accounted for, less the five percent Treasury handling fee."

"We're supposed to get recruits from the Persians. How are they being paid?"

"It has been assumed that the Persians will pay for them."

"Which they won't."

"Situation normal, Colonel. I hear there is horse racing in Persia. We could always put the funds on a horse. We've enough marksmen to take out the competition."

*****

Alasdair had spoken with Recruit Abe about being his batman in Persia. It took Abe a while to work out what would be involved, and he looked dismayed.

"I joined to fight, not to be a servant."

"As well as, not instead of."

"Will it make it easier for me to be a corporal?"

"Abe, the Army has taken you on as a Recruit. That means that if you have the talent and if there is a space, you'll do whatever job needs doing. That's the Regimental motto. We get the job done, whatever it takes."

"But will my being a man-bat make it easier?"

Alasdair thought about this. "It means I'll notice you more. If you do a good job, it'll help. If you don't, it means you won't get my approval."

"In that case I'll do it. What do I do?"

*****

"Alice, before we go to dinner, there's something we need to discuss."

"Alasdair, you sound so serious. I'm the serious one here."

"It's about when we get to Persia. Look, I'm not sure how to put this. It's nothing bad," he said quickly, see her starting to worry. "The thing is, this is going to sound strange, but you're my best friend."

"I thought a collie was supposed to be man's best friend. I'm not a man." Alice giggled nervously. She was confused by Alasdair at the moment.

"Please, this is important. The thing is, we've got a choice. When we get to Persia. It's complicated. Not complicated. Simple. But difficult. Only it's not difficult for me. It's easy for me, only what do you think?"

"Alasdair, I haven't got a clue what you're talking about."

"All you need to do is say either yes or no."

"Yes or no to what?"

"To the question."

"What question? You haven't asked me a question."

"Yes, I have."

"No, you haven't. Alasdair, I don't always understand you because I don't speak border collie, but I trust you. If you think it's a good idea, then I agree. Now, what have I agreed to?"

"It doesn't work like that. You've got to agree properly."

"Agree to what?"

"Will you marry me, you clot."

Alice was silent.

"Say something," Alasdair prompted.

"But Alasdair, we're friends. Friends, well, friends don't get married."

"Why not?"

"Because of, you know. Being intimate. That's kind of the point. I don't know if I can. It's not fair on you."

"Worst case, you can't. That means I get to spend the rest of my life with my best friend. That's the very worst case."

"What would your parents say?"

"Father would say something like: 'Does she know you're only a fourth son? There's no inheritance for you?' Mother would say: 'Is the poor girl insane? You're feckless, rash and have no sense.' My brothers would just ignore it, because what I do isn't important. What's important is whether you say yes or no."

"I don't know."

"Do you want to be with me?"

"Well, yes, but marriage is kind of a forever thing."

"That's true for every marriage. If you like, I'll make sure I'm house-trained."

"Can I think about it?"

*****

Sergeant Taylor reported to Lieutenant Hawkins, trying to keep a neutral voice over the prospect of Furley-Smith being on board.

"Why would he come on board? It doesn't make any sense."

"No, Sir."

"He'd be spotted quickly. It's not like there's anywhere to hide."

"No, Sir."

"He'd have no line of retreat if he was found."

"No, Sir."

"He'd be tried for desertion. Why would he come back?"

"It would have to be something he thought important, Sir."

"You think it's a possibility."

"I don't know, Sir. I don't think we've heard the last of him, Sir."

"I'm afraid you're right. If he's on the ship, he's going to want to get off it. Make sure that there are guards at the lifeboats. I'll have a word with Major Marshall."

"Very good, Sir. Not the Colonel?"

"The Major will advise the Colonel if required. At the moment, it's all supposition. The Major needs to be forewarned, though. He has access to the one thing that I can think of that might prompt Furley-Smith to take this insane risk, if, indeed, he is taking it."

"Which is, Sir?"

"Best kept unspoken, Sergeant."

*****

"You lucky devil." Thomas was jealous. "How did you swing that duty, Frank?"

"Looking after brothel not good duty. How do I explain it to Joy?"

"How do you explain what to me?" Joy asked, walking across.

Frank looked in panic towards Thomas. Thomas relented.

"It's his cooking skills. You're lucky, marrying a man who can cook. When we get to our base in Persia, the locals will set up trading establishments nearby. Frank impressed the officers with how he ran a clean kitchen, so he'll be responsible for keeping an eye on the soup kitchens."

"Soup kitchens," agreed Frank cautiously.

"Soup kitchens?" Joy enquired.

"That's right. Places that sell nourishing broth. Obviously, we need to be careful to make sure they're clean. Don't want soldiers catching any illness."

"I wouldn't have thought broth would be very popular. Not in the climate. Perhaps I should go along, ask some of the vendors for some recipes."

"Probably best not. They can get very protective over their recipes. Isn't that right, Frank."

Frank nodded vigorously.

"Just out of interest, Thomas," Joy asked. "How stupid do you think I am? Selling broth? I do know what a brothel is. And you, Francesco Barrilari, had better learn to be more honest with me over embarrassing things and not let Thomas try and mislead me. Soup kitchens, indeed."

"Sorry, Ma'am," said Thomas, almost automatically.

"I'll expect you to be on your best behaviour when policing them, Frank. You too, Thomas."

"Me?"

"Well obviously Frank will be the senior NCO on the duty, and who's he going to make sure is on duty with him?"

*****

The Chief Steward stood at the railing, looking out to sea, smoking a cigarette and thinking. It was quiet, almost deserted here, and getting dark. Things were getting out of hand. When the suggestion had been made, it had seemed like a game. It had seemed simple enough. He would hide the Lieutenant in his cabin, make sure that when they neared land, Major Marshall would be out of his cabin at the required time. For that, he'd get a thousand pounds.

Then things escalated. Just an extra thing. Take an impression of a key that Major Marshall kept on him. That had been difficult, but he'd managed it when the officers were sick. Then he had to get the engineers to turn that impression into a duplicate key and find answers to satisfy the curiosity of the engineers. Then there had been the problems with that Corporal making him look bad. He'd let standards slip in the galley because the Lieutenant was taking up so much of his time. The Corporal had shown him up, and the First Lieutenant had spoken to him about it.

Now he'd found out that the Lieutenant planned to steal the Regimental funds. The pay for the Regiment while it was on deployment. That was no longer a prank and bit of light thievery. This was deep stuff. If he was caught, he would be hanged.

Create distractions, make sure people are rushing around. He'd asked the Lieutenant about a bigger cut and the Lieutenant had laughed.

He did the sums. Eight hundred soldiers, £100 a year, two years. Plus NCOs and officers. Probably around £250,000. And the Lieutenant laughed at him asking for an increase.

He'd had enough. Although, in a strange way, he was reassured by the Lieutenant laughing at him. If he'd not intended to stick by the deal, he'd have agreed easily, knowing he'd not keep the deal anyway, so what did it matter. But he'd had enough. He couldn't take any more. He'd finish this cigarette and then go to the First Lieutenant, the Jimmy and tell all. He hadn't done anything very wrong yet.

The sea was flat, and yet the ship seemed to give a lurch. He staggered forward, almost tipping over the railing and into the sea, but luckily someone had grabbed him in time.

"Terribly sorry, old fellow," the person said, pushing him over the railing and into the sea. "Can't have you getting cold feet."

No alarm was raised, and the ship sailed on.

*****

"You two are idiots," said the Chaplain. Alice and Alasdair looked at each other. They weren't used to priests talking like that.

"It's just that we're friends," said Alice. "And there may be, problems with it being a proper marriage."

"That's commendable. You're taking marriage seriously. That means you're more fit to get married than most. Some get married because it's convenient for the business or are in debt or want to grab a title. Some people don't get a say in the matter. Do you think I chose my second, third, fourth, fifth and sixth wives? Of course not. My first wife chose them for me. To help her around the house."

"That doesn't sound terribly Christian," Alasdair said cautiously.

"Of course not. That was before I was a Christian."

"But we want a Christian marriage," said Alice.

"Precisely. You've just said it."

"Said what?"

"That you want to get married. You said you want a Christian marriage. Four questions. One. Alasdair, do you want to marry Alice?"

"Yes. I asked her because I like being with her, I like seeing her smile and she's the only girl who'll let me ruffle her hair."

"Two. Alice, do you want to marry Alasdair?"

"I don't know. I don't know if I can be a proper wife."

"That's not the question. Do you want to spend the rest of your life with him?"

She nodded. "But I don't know …"

"Three. Are there any reasons why you can't get married? Already married, one of you is the parent of the other, things like that. No? Good. Question four. Does God want you to get married? Because if He does, He'll sort out your problems, if you let Him. If He doesn't, He'll stop you."

"But we're, well, we're friends," Alice said.

The Chaplain looked up at the ceiling in exasperation. "Give me strength." He looked back down at Alasdair and Alice, leaning forward. "If you want to annoy Him, you'll keep on dithering about what's been obvious to literally everyone on the entire ship since we left Cape Town." He pointed at Alice. "You want to marry him." Then he pointed at Alasdair. "You want to marry her." He then pointed vaguely upwards. "He wants you two to get married and He'll sort the important stuff out. That's simple theology. You're both *silima*. Now, go away and come back when you've come to your senses."

*****

Outside, Alasdair turned to Alice. "You know, we'll never be able to tell our children how we decided to get married."

They'd taken five steps towards Alasdair's cabin, walking hand in hand, before Alice realised what he'd said. What was more, the thought of having children with Alasdair brought a smile to her face. He glanced at her, and frowned, puzzled.

"What's so funny?"

"I think I'd like my border collie to sleep on the bed tonight."

*****

There was a problem in the Officers' Mess. The Chief Steward hadn't arrived, and no-one could find him. The Leading Steward would normally take over, but he'd found and confiscated an illegally-held sauce bottle from a steward and was now indisposed. When the First Lieutenant of the ship found out, he would have a stern word with the Master-at-Arms over protocols during the rum ration issue. The rum ration had to be drunk at the time of issue under the watchful eye of the Master-at-Arms, but sailors always tried to store it.

Eventually, one of the stewards asked Frank to help out, and Abe went with him.

"If I'm going to be a man-bat, I'll need to know how to do this."

The stewards had a problem. They weren't running low on food, but they were running low on some specific foods and had an excess of some ingredients. Not all of what they had went together.

"What's this?" Frank asked.

"Cocoa. It's to make cocoa. The officers haven't drunk cocoa, just tea or coffee."

"Make thick sauce with it. What this?"

"It's sauce. It's in a sauce bottle," they said, warily.

Frank smelt the sauce. It smelt a bit like plums. "Use it with cocoa sauce. What this?"

"It's cheese."

"It got blue bits."

"It's supposed to be like that."

"Make another sauce. Use it with apricots. Make sure chicken well cooked. Put sausage with chicken."

Eventually, they were ready. Frank made sure the stewards served it carefully.

"Corporal Barry," said the Colonel. "Unusual to see you here."

"Chief Steward not here, Sir."

"And what are we eating today? We'll be safe? You're not going to try and poison us?"

"Sicilians use knife, Sir, not poison." A Sergeant always had to sound confident. "Is Persian recipe." If in doubt, spread the blame. "Rifleman O'Grady get recipe from Persian stokers."

"Yes, but what is it?"

"My mother always said ask what something is after eating, not before, Sir."

"That must make for an interesting restaurant experience. What is it?"

"Chicken and sausage, Sir. In brown sauce."

"Corporal," called one of the stewards. "This cheese sauce keeps going solid."

Frank returned to the kitchen and looked at the cheese. It was indeed solid. "Mix sauce from bottle into it."

"We did that, Corporal."

"Then cut into slices, serve like cake. Not so many apricots. Not many left. Apricots rare, expensive. Apricots not grow on trees."

Abe thought about saying something but remembered that NCOs were always right. White-man apricots probably didn't grow on trees. The stewards thought about saying something, but Corporal Barry looked frazzled. They decided contradicting a frazzled NCO with a reputation as a knife-fighter while he was holding a butcher's knife might not be a good career move.

The noise level from the Officers' Mess rose sharply. The cocoa sauce was proving popular. Frank ventured out.

"Tristram," said the Colonel. "Remember that trip out in '11? The Governor's daughter."

"Hard to forget that. First-class full of old fogeys and stuffed shirts."

"Then there was that fancy-dress party."

Frank noticed that Lady Dalkeith and Mrs Marshall were paying close attention to the story.

"There was that steward she took a shine to. Danced all night with him. Took him back to her room."

Major Marshall chuckled. "And then at breakfast, no more than half an hour after they had parted, he tried to speak to her."

"And she froze him absolutely stiff and said: 'In the circles in which I move,' she said."

"She said: 'In the circles in which I move, sleeping with a woman does not constitute an introduction.' Priceless."

*****

Thomas watched the deck, but nothing much seemed to be happening. Nurse Charrington stepped out of her office, and he stood up. She looked worried.

"Rifleman O'Grady. I'm sorry to disturb you. Have you seen Miss Eliot recently?"

"No. Why?"

"It's probably nothing. She wanted to speak to me about something. She's normally very dependable, but she hasn't turned up, nor has she sent word. I confess to being a bit concerned about her. However, it's probably nothing."

Thomas thought. Frank was busy in the Officers' Mess. Colonel and Lady Dalkeith would be there. There wasn't anything she'd said she'd be busy with.

"She's probably just fallen asleep. She's had an exciting few days."

"I can talk with her as easily in her cabin as here."

*****

Joy woke up on her bed. It was dark. She must have dozed off while reading the book Lady Dalkeith had loaned her. Lady Dalkeith might have enjoyed it, but it was, well, boring.

She must have been deeply asleep, because she only now just started to be aware that someone was sitting on the bed. She felt excited, thrilled, nervous – and a bit scared. "Frank?" she said, trying to stay calm while her heart started beating harder and faster.

"Not exactly," said Lieutenant Furley-Smith, placing a hand over her mouth to stop her screaming for help.

Joy tried to edge back from him and slid her hand under the pillow. She was scared and trying not to freeze up in terror.

"Looking for this?" He held up her knife and turned it over in his hand. "I remember you drawing a knife on me last time I tried to be friendly. Does your ugly Corporal know that you keep a knife under your pillow? I suppose he finds it exciting." He released his hold on her mouth slightly.

"What do you want?" she whispered.

"You know, I'm so close that I can taste success. But there's a problem. One that you can help me with." He rested the knife on her chest, the point towards her throat, and released her mouth fully.

"Why should I help you?" She stared at the point of the knife, then forced herself to look at him.

"I'm going to take you. Willingly or unwillingly, it's all the same to me. It's been a long time since I've been able to relieve the build-up of stress, so you're just what the doctor ordered. I've got what I came for and you'll be the cherry on the top. But I'm going to give you a choice. You see, I need to get to a boat and there are guards at the lifeboats. I need them out of the way to get a clear run. If that fat fool hadn't got cold feet, I'd be on my way by now. Here's your choice. After we've played, and by God, do I need the stress relief, you'll call the guards away from a boat. Do that, and you'll live. Refuse, or try to betray me, and you won't." He thought for a minute. "Who knows, after you've seen what playing with me is like, you might want to come with me, because I'll be rich beyond your wildest dreams."

"You'll never get away with it."

"Please, do you know how many times I've heard that? Help me and live, or die with honour. Actually, die dishonoured." He grabbed Joy's blouse while she tried to push him away when there was a knock at the door.

"Joy, is everything all right? You didn't come as you said you would."

"Tell her to go away. Tell her that you're busy with your Corporal. Tell her, or I'll ..." He paused. "That's O'Grady's girl. Tell her to go away, or I'll drag her in here and kill her and it will be your fault. Tell her." Furley-Smith hissed the words.

"I'm with Frank. Please go away."

*****

"She says that she's with Frank," Nurse Charrington said, uncertainly.

"She's lying. Frank's in the Officers' Mess. I know that for certain."

"Why is she lying?" Nurse Charrington wasn't sure what was going on, but this felt bad.

"Whatever it is," Thomas said grimly, "it's not good. Talk to her. I need to know where she is in the room."

Nurse Charrington was about to question Thomas, then realised that this looked like it might lie in his area of expertise rather than hers.

"Joy, this is urgent. It can't wait."

There was a pause. "Just go away. Please."

Thomas measured up the door. It opened inwards, so bursting in wouldn't be a problem. He had to angle it so that he ended up near Joy, so he'd be able to provide protection. He kept his eye on the door. "Again," he whispered to Emily.

"Joy, stop being so foolish."

"He's at the door! Run away," Joy shouted.

Thomas threw himself at the door, hitting it with his shoulder, and feeling a jar as the door slammed into someone. The person staggered to one side, stumbling and getting caught up in a pack on the floor. Joy was getting off the bed, her blouse in some disarray and trying to get to the desk. Thomas stood between the man and the bed.

"O'Grady. It's always you. Wherever I turn, it's always you and that infernal smile." Furley-Smith had a knife in one hand and was trying to pick up a heavy pack in the other while watching Thomas.

The momentum of the rush had thrown Thomas off-balance. Furley-Smith slashed downwards with his knife and Thomas felt something like a spider's thread touching the side of his face, and he heard someone scream. He recovered his balance and faced Furley-Smith. The knife Furley-Smith held seemed to have blood on it.

Thomas focused on the knife and on Furley-Smith's eyes. Like boxing, you got the first indication of an attack from the eyes. Furley-Smith kept glancing towards the door, desperation starting to show. Thomas had to cover both Joy and the door. That meant getting closer.

"Get someone, Emily. Guards at the boat. Quickly now."

It got Emily out of the way.

As she ran off, Furley-Smith saw his chance. There was no-one in the doorway. If he made it past O'Grady, he would be out of this trap. He tried to push past; Thomas moved to block him while Joy was fumbling at the desk. Furley-Smith raised the knife and stabbed at Thomas.

The stab grazed the inside of Thomas' arm, then hit the top of his chest, scoring a wound downwards, from which blood flowed freely. The knife got caught in his jacket and Thomas hit Furley-Smith, who staggered. Then there was a shattering explosion and the smell of cordite. Furley-Smith shrieked in pain, dropping his pack as a bullet grazed his shoulder.

Furley-Smith had his opening, though and made it out through the door. Two riflemen ran towards the cabin, Emily not far behind them. Furley-Smith took a despairing glance at the pack, realised he couldn't reach it, ran for the railing, and jumped over the side into the sea.

There was a splash, but by the time the riflemen reached the side, there was no sign of him.

"Thomas," said Nurse Charrington, "you're hurt." She sounded almost panicked.

"It's nothing," he said, then looked at the blood on his hand.

*****

He wasn't in his hammock. He was lying down, but he wasn't in his hammock. He was lying in a bed with bandages around his chest and arm. He could only see through one eye, and his arm hurt like hell.

"Let that be a lesson to you, Rifleman O'Grady," said Nurse Charrington.

"Last time I was told off for getting my first words wrong. Where am I?"

"Yes, you are starting to make a habit of waking up in a medical office. Please stop it. It's four nurses for the Regiment, not four nurses just for you."

Thomas smiled. This was like it had been between them before Cape Town. "What's the lesson I need to learn, Emily?"

"Nurse Charrington, if you please."

Just like that, the moment had gone, and the atmosphere was tense and frosty again. She removed the bandage on his chest, revealing a wound maybe ten inches long from the collarbone downwards. It wasn't a very deep wound, but it itched like the blazes.

Windy and Peter were shooed outside by Nurse Charrington. "Wait until I say you can come in. Sergeant Taylor, you may enter. I'm just changing Rifleman O'Grady's dressings. The lesson is this, Rifleman O'Grady. If you are going to stab someone, use an upward thrust. From that direction, the ribs leave the major organs unguarded, inviting serious wounds. The ribs form a barrier against a blow striking downwards from above. It delivers a wound that looks dramatic but is of no serious consequence. As for your eye, that's just swelling from a bruise. It'll come down soon enough."

"She's right," said Sergeant Taylor. "The way to a man's heart is through his stomach. What's true for a woman is also true for a Rifleman. Isn't that correct, Rifleman Miller?"

"Wouldn't know, Sergeant. I can't say I understand women."

"To judge by the number of love letters you got in Cape Town, I'd say you seem to understand them well enough, lad."

"Dally with them, Sergeant. Don't understand them."

"If you get to dally with them, then you understand them as much as you need to," said Peter.

"Rifleman Grant. Lady present," said Sergeant Taylor sharply. "Miss, when will Rifleman O'Grady be fit for duty?"

"I'll be keeping him under observation today. Make sure the wounds don't go bad. Light duties tomorrow. He should be back to normal after that."

"Very good. Only it seems to me, O'Grady, that you've shown that the Company is in sore need of bayonet practise."

Nurse Charrington coughed. "Sergeant Taylor, would you do me a service? Nurse Stewart was asking after Rifleman O'Grady. I'm rather busy. Perhaps you could update her on his progress."

When the others had left, Thomas looked at Nurse Charrington. "What was that all about? You're scheming something."

"I don't know what you're talking about, Rifleman O'Grady. It's important to update nurses on patient progress. That's basic protocol."

*****

There was another knock at the door to Nurse Charrington's medical office. It was Lieutenant Hawkins.

"I may as well just put the welcome mat out. Five minutes. No more."

"Keeping you updated, O'Grady. As far as we can tell, Furley-Smith made it off the ship, but he left the pack behind. There's a rowboat missing, so we assume he had it tied up alongside and made it to that. He's got two choices from here. He can try and reach Arabia, about 50 miles away, or he can try and reach India, about 150 miles away. Ma'am, what are your thoughts on Furley-Smith? As a nurse."

"He's deranged. Completely deranged. He's become obsessed with Rifleman O'Grady. He's used to getting his own way in everything, getting whatever or whoever he wants. Rifleman

O'Grady has been getting in his way. I rather fear his sense of entitlement will outweigh his sense of duty. I'm very much afraid that we've not heard the last of him."

*****

Frank knocked at the door.

"Goodness gracious, someone wishing to speak with Rifleman O'Grady. Now that's a surprise."

"I wish speak with Thomas alone, please. It personal. Matter of honour."

"I've got rounds to do. Rifleman O'Grady, you are to rest. You may sit up carefully. Do not engage in heavy exercise. Do not leave this cabin. Do not get into life-or-death duels above waterfalls, nor abduct a Sultan's harem to help serve broth in a soup kitchen. Do not attempt to swim to Arabia. Do not attempt to get into any scrapes. Is that clear?"

"Yes, Nurse Charrington. Ma'am, can I read the dictionary? I wish to find out if the word sarcasm has been expanded in meaning recently."

"You always have to have the last word, don't you, Rifleman O'Grady."

As Nurse Charrington closed the door, Thomas said: "Yes."

"You saved Joy from bad fate," said Frank. "You took wounds defending her."

"You're my buddy. She's your girl. What else would I do?"

"It more than that. It is debt I owe."

"We're buddies. No debt involved."

"It is family matter. You said we like brothers. We are brothers. You need help, Barrilari will stand with you."

Thomas thought Frank was taking this a bit seriously. It seemed to mean a lot to him. That said, he couldn't imagine a better friend to have on his side in a tight corner. He'd never had a brother before, so maybe this was what being part of a family was all about. "You're right. We're family."

*****

Alice and Alasdair walked to the Officers' Mess. Alice kept glancing up at Alasdair, seeing his smile and she felt happier than she'd ever been. She'd been scared and terrified ever since that night. Now everything was fine, and she'd found Alasdair.

There were only a few officers here for breakfast, but there was no way they'd be able to keep this a secret.

"I've, no, *we've* got an announcement," said Alasdair to the officers that were present. "I've asked Nurse Ward to consent to marrying me. She is obviously suffering from brain fever, because she has agreed."

"Congratulations," said Captain Filleul. "Who had the 19th?"

"That would be me," replied the Chaplain.

"Hang on," Alasdair said. "You're a Methodist. Methodists don't gamble."

"This wasn't gambling."

"Hang on, you pretty much told us God wanted us to get married," said Alasdair.

"Alasdair, obviously you should never gamble with someone who gets Divine advice," said Alice. She turned to the Chaplain. "Tell God He was right."

*****

"I don't know how to explain it more clearly, Rifleman O'Grady. I am not participating in any of your schemes. I do not care how you wish to dress it up. Deception remains deception and is not to be countenanced." Nurse Charrington was firm on this point. "I will be relieved when you are able to return to your duties, because you are a very troublesome patient."

"But it's to sort out the final puzzle to enable Frank and Joy to get married. Finding a Catholic priest."

"That's their problem. I rather think that disturbing someone's religious beliefs is not the wisest course of action you have undertaken."

"But I'm not. All I need is a letter in handwriting Frank doesn't recognise. He knows my handwriting."

"Are you suggesting that it is *not* deception to write a letter purporting to come from someone in the hierarchy of the Catholic Church answering a question that hasn't actually been posed to them."

"Exactly. It's the answer that would be given if the question had been asked. This wouldn't be deception. It would be anticipation." Thomas tried to sound convincing.

"I anticipate that it would not be perceived that way by Frank. He has made it clear that he wants a wedding according to Catholic rites. That is what he wants. I would suggest that if you value his friendship, that is what you should consider appropriate and not try to mislead him."

Thomas sighed. She was right, of course. It had been a good idea, getting a letter from the Catholic authorities saying that a marriage by a non-Catholic priest was acceptable where no Catholic priest was available. If Frank found out, he wouldn't see it as a good idea. He would see it as a betrayal.

What really hurt, though, was that Nurse Charrington would casually refer to Frank, Peter, Windy, and Joy, but she steadfastly referred to him as Rifleman O'Grady. He couldn't complain about the quality of nursing care he'd received, but, apart from one or two brief flashes, it had been very impersonal. He'd thought he'd noticed that she might care for him in the immediate aftermath of the fight with Furley-Smith, but it was apparent that had simply been wishful thinking on his part.

It was no good. He simply had to face up to the truth. He was not going to have a relationship with Emily. Nurse Charrington. It was folly to think otherwise. He had to accept that reality and live his life according to that essential fact.

The trouble was that the idea of dalliances had rather lost their attraction. When he looked back on those he had had, they hadn't given him the happiness he'd had with Emily, Nurse Charrington, on the voyage to Cape Town.

His friends wanted him to have a relationship. He could easily take the stance that as a Rifleman, he offered nothing to anyone, and a relationship was out of the question until he got promoted. Then all he needed to do was to refuse any promotion.

*****

She'd let herself slip. Seeing Thomas, Rifleman O'Grady, hurt and needing care had brought to the surface feelings that she had to bury. She'd started to relax in his company and that was wrong. She was a nurse, so she couldn't marry.

Thomas wasn't right for her. He was disruptive and distracting. He was from a different class and would return to it, whether he knew it or not. He could do so much better than her. He didn't understand her. She didn't understand him. It was impossible. Better a clean break than pretending it could be something and simply making matters worse in the long run.

If only Thomas would turn his attentions to someone else, then she could accept the situation. She would be unhappy for a time, but happiness was a luxury that she couldn't really afford.

It was a pity. Thomas had demonstrated with his defence of Joy that, beneath his charming, devious manner, he was dependable. He would make someone a fine, if frequently exasperating, husband. That someone could not be her.

*****

The Officers' Mess was crowded, although no officers were present. Lady Dalkeith stood at the front, looking over the wives, and Joy, who had been invited to attend this meeting. The invitation to the wives had made clear that attendance was mandatory. All of the 33 wives, with Joy apparently being regarded as a *de facto* wife, were present. Some looked as they knew what was coming, others seemed uncertain.

Lady Dalkeith glanced at her watch. "Good morning, Ladies. Thank you for attending. We are not far from arriving in Persia. It is the appropriate time that I indicate how you will be expected to behave, with specific reference to treatment of the local people, and also to the single men in the Regiment.

"Firstly, the local people. You will have servants to help you. Some of you might not be used to having servants. However one treats servants in England, certain standards apply here. A servant is an employee, not a friend. You may end up becoming friends, but first and foremost, they are an employee. You must ensure you are crystal clear about what standards you expect. Do not accept anything that does not meet those standards. If you decide all cutlery is to be cleaned before the day's work is finished, then even if you are tired and don't feel like checking, do not 'let it go, just this once', because just this once will become the new standard.

"Never, ever lie or deceive a local. They may like us or not, they may wish us here, or not. Whatever their opinion of us might be, the one thing that is essential is that they trust us to be fair. If your word is law, then the law has to be fair and just. Some of you will be familiar with what happens when the law is unjust. That will not happen here.

"In large part, your servant will be the conduit for communication with other local people, and will help you make purchases, and so on. They know the local language, so that is inevitable. In India, many wives never learned the local language, and they were at a major disadvantage. Servants took advantage of this ignorance. When I was first out in India, during discussions on payment, the servant told the vendor that I could afford to pay ten rupees for some trinket. I advised them both that while I might be able to afford that, I had no intention of paying more than two, for that is what I judged fair value to be. Learn the language and you are less likely to be taken advantage of. It is entirely up to you what language you speak with your servant. My custom is that I speak

English to them, and they speak their local language to me. Others have different views. Mrs Marshall, I know, takes the view that English is spoken when Major Marshall is present, and the local language when he is not. As I understand it, this enables the servant to advise her when her husband had returned home unexpectedly, without his realising she had been told. I understand for many years, he believed that she was psychically attuned to him and knew when he was in the house by the influence he had on the psychic aura.

"That leads me on to the issue of liaisons. Don't. Whether with a local or with a member of the Regiment or with a civilian visitor. Don't. You are very likely to get lonely when your husband is on deployment and there will be temptations. It's quite possible your husband might err and you think that what is sauce for the goose is sauce for the gander. Don't. Your husband needs absolute trust in you. When he is on deployment, if he has any worries or concerns about you, that is a part of his mind not focused on his job. That, in turn, means he is less likely to return. It also means that other Riflemen depending on him are placed in greater danger. Not all of our men will return. There will be tragic casualties. We must all do what we can to keep them to a minimum. However bored you get, it is better for you to be a bit bored than for several soldiers to be killed.

"A number of you have been learning, with varying degrees of success, how to handle firearms. Lessons in this will continue. It's unlikely that any of you will become marksmen, nor would you be expected to do so. The base will not be located in a dangerous part of the country. Indeed, you are likely to be safer than in some parts of London. That said, there are elements that wish us harm, and being able to defend oneself is a reassurance.

"Local customs. These are to be respected. You may disagree with some of them, but they are not to be made fun of. For example, a man here may, with perfect respectability, have three wives. In England, this might be seen as shocking. Even the French might regard going to a function with a wife and two mistresses as a little ostentatious. Here, the second and third wives are not mistresses but wives in their own right. Miss Eliot, could you please ensure that Rifleman Miller is made aware that he is not permitted to take three wives, or close approximations thereof, while in Persia.

"New recruits. The Regiment will acquire new recruits in Persia. These new recruits are members of the Regiment and are to be treated as such. They are not servants, exotic attractions, or whatever else. Don't take liberties with them and do not allow them to take liberties with you or anyone else.

"Cleanliness. This is vital and you must be unrelenting in striving for this. Clothes must be clean. Dirt can cause irritation on the skin, which can lead to wounds, which can, in this climate, fester. Dirt in a house attracts vermin and vermin here can be lethal. You must pay particular attention to bedding. All water is to be boiled before it is used. Food is to be thoroughly washed, and washed in boiled water. Remember that if it has unbroken peel or shell, then it may be safe to eat uncooked. Otherwise, it must be cooked thoroughly and in clean conditions. Everyone will, at some stage, suffer from food illness. It can be virulent, and dangerous. The nurses will look after you for the duration. When your husband is ill, the nurses will tell you what to do. Essentially, rest, try and stay clean, and drink plenty of fluid.

"There are many single men in the Regiment. Some of them may try to take liberties. Obviously, you will turn these down. They can lead to jealousy and your husband has to be able to trust you absolutely. On the ship, and in England, some held that it doesn't matter if no-one knows about it. Once we are in Persia, people will know. It is not possible to keep anything secret on deployment. This brings one to the issue of innocent sharing of interests in the absence of your husband. You and a single man may share a passion for golf. Simple rule of thumb. You must be seen to be behaving in a proper manner. If you are going off-base, take a chaperone with you.

"We are on deployment for two years. Those of a mathematical turn of mind will know that two years is longer than nine months. The nurses need to know at the first sign of such an event. Facilities here are not as luxurious as in England. Local doctors may be unreliable. The best course of action is for the Regiment to handle everything internally. That means we need to be prepared. That means we need as much warning as possible.

"Finally, new attachments to the Regiment. Some single men may form attachments with local ladies. Most of these will be a passing matter, ending when the Regiment moves on, or when the Rifleman tires of the lady. Unmarried ladies not employed by the Regiment are not permitted on the base without official invitations. Any temporary liaison will be conducted off the base. However, sometimes these attachments become serious, and the Rifleman may wish to marry a local lady. If permission is given by the Rifleman's officer and, ultimately, the Colonel, then they may be married. When that happens, the lady becomes a member of the Regiment, to be treated as such. They must learn to abide by the customs of the Regiment. They will be accorded the rights and responsibilities of a wife of the Regiment.

"That will be all."

*****

The ship was close to arriving in Persia. Joy wanted to speak with Nurse Charrington before they arrived but was finding it hard to find her. When she did find her, Nurse Charrington was busy, usually reading about the medical situation in Persia.

It was only by more or less forcing her way in that she got to speak with her. When she managed to do so, she found it hard to speak, she felt tongue-tied.

"What is it, Joy? I am very busy."

"I'm nervous and scared. Everything's just so much. Lady Dalkeith's giving me lots of responsibilities in Persia, because when I marry Frank, he'll be a Sergeant and I'll be the wife of the most senior NCO and I know she's doing it to make sure I'm busy, but it's scary. Then there's looking after a household. I've never done that. I don't know what to do." She paused. The next bit was really awkward. "And Frank. It'll be us. I've never been an us. I love him to bits, but I'm scared about personal things, and I'm scared he'll, well, I don't want to disappoint him, and I'm scared I will, and I'm scared it'll be all wrong, and sometimes I want him so much and sometimes I'm scared, and it would be so much easier just to not and hide away."

"Frank loves you. As for everything else, I don't know any of the answers to your questions. You really need to talk to someone who is married. It's not like I've ever been part of an us."

"But you and Thomas."

"Everyone keeps harping on about Rifleman O'Grady and myself. There is nothing between us. That is something that cannot happen. It's completely out of the question. There is no "us" for me. Not with Rifleman O'Grady, not with anyone."

"He doesn't know why. Why not, I mean. *I* don't know why not."

"It is, however, none of your business. I'll thank you not to talk about me behind my back. I've informed Rifleman O'Grady of the situation. That is an end to the matter."

"But he doesn't know why."

"That is a matter between him and me. If you want answers to your questions, I suggest that you speak to someone who has experience in the matter. I have no such experience. Now, kindly leave. I have a lot of work to do."

*****

"John, do you think that's a wise deployment?" Colonel Dalkeith asked. "Putting an ambitious Sicilian NCO in charge of looking after off-base brothels. With the devious O'Grady. I'm a little concerned that they might become quite adventurous in terms of determining how many brothels are under their control."

"I don't think that will be a problem, Sir."

"I admire your optimism. Why do you think it unlikely to be a problem?"

"The base is fifteen miles from the town. I doubt many soldiers will walk fifteen miles when what they need is just outside. That'll keep Barry and O'Grady busy close at hand, and not spreading their wings. Besides, O'Grady is so devious that whatever he gets up to will be something we haven't considered."

"I have to say, John, I don't find that last bit very reassuring."

*****

Lieutenant Hawkins told to the Training Platoon that they would be proceeding ahead of the Regiment to the site of the base to prepare the vicinity for the Regiment. "Once the Regiment arrives, we will no longer be the Training Platoon. We will be officially the Persian Company. We are very lucky, being the advance unit. We'll travel in luxury. A whole train ourselves. We won't be unloading the gear at the docks. We won't be unloading the gear from the train at our destination. We won't have the distraction of the ladies, who will be coming up with the Regiment. We'll even get to have a look around before the Regiment arrives. O'Grady, you look like you have a question."

"Yes, Sir. What's the catch?"

"And why, O'Grady, do you think there's a catch?"

"If there wasn't, one of the other companies would be doing it, Sir."

"How very cynical, O'Grady. Perhaps your mind will be put at rest by the fact that every man will be issued with 100 rounds. In the course of our strolls in the vicinity, we will check potential trouble spots and deal with them. We don't expect any trouble. It will be good experience for you to start live operations in a low-risk area. It is a low-risk area, but we have no intention of taking that for granted. Sergeant Taylor and myself will brief you in your squads on the train. Look on the bright side. There are 40 of us in a two-carriage train. The rest of the Regiment and associated personnel, nearly 1000 people, plus all the equipment, will be following in 20 carriages. One other thing, Lieutenant Campbell will be accompanying us. He will buy mules when we arrive. O'Grady, you claimed to be able to ride. You will assist Lieutenant Campbell. Everyone, gather your belongings and report on the main deck ready for disembarkation."

*****

The platoon formed up on the main deck as the ship docked. They arrived in the port in the cool of the evening. They were in full kit, helmets on the back of their packs, magazines across their chest. The platoon members felt very martial.

"Platoon, you have five minutes to say goodbye to loved ones. Rifleman Miller, I suspect for you that will be one minute per loved one. Reform ranks on the docks. Platoon, break ranks."

Joy hurried over to Frank and hugged him tightly. "Take care," she said. "Whatever you do, take care of yourself."

"Five days, then we're back together."

"I love you so much, Frank." Then she whispered something in his ear, and he looked both shocked and pleased.

"In five days," he said.

*****

Alice and Alasdair held hands awkwardly. Alice knew she had to be brave, and that Alasdair wouldn't want her to make a fuss. He ruffled her hair.

"Don't worry, I'll make sure I find a magic flying carpet for our new home."

She had to be brave and not show how scared she was.

*****

"Sergeant Taylor, I've a request," said Nurse Stewart. "Things are going to be very busy when we arrive. I would be grateful if you could make sure the men come to no harm, because having to deal with casualties will be very inconvenient. And, Sergeant Taylor, I want you to make sure that you come to no harm."

Sergeant Taylor was puzzled. He wasn't sure what she meant by that.

*****

Thomas saw Nurse Charrington standing to one side of the deck. She looked uncertain and worried.

"For God's sake, say goodbye to her," said Peter quietly. "Whatever you are to each other, you owe her a goodbye."

Thomas nodded and walked over. Nurse Charrington didn't come to him, but neither did she go away. When he reached her, he found he didn't know what to say.

"Rifleman O'Grady," she said, before also falling into silence.

"Nurse Charrington. Ma'am, are there any special requirements for the medical offices at the site? In the shade, in the sun?"

"Shade, please. Getting sun won't be a problem. Getting shade might be. Good water supply. That's essential."

"Very good, Ma'am." He tried to tell himself that the Regiment would be up in five days and that there was very little chance of anything happening.

"Don't frequent brothels until we've had chance to check their cleanliness."

"Of course, Ma'am."

"And Rifleman O'Grady," she said, and then paused.

Thomas drew himself straight. This was it. This was the moment it finally ended. He had to say this first. "Nurse Charrington, there's something I wish to discuss with you when you are settled into the base."

"And what might that be?"

Eyes focused on a point above the right shoulder, face expressionless, standing up straight, shoulders squared, hands down with thumbs along the seam of the trousers. "I want to tell you that I understand what I didn't after that fight in Cape Town. This, the reality of things, well, I understand now."

Seconds passed. Eventually, Nurse Charrington spoke. "We'll talk when I get to the base. Now, you must take care of your wounds. They're almost healed over, but they will itch, so don't scratch them. Keep your hat on to protect against the sun."

"And eat up my vegetables?"

There was the ghost of a smile on her face. "After you've washed them. And one last thing."

Seconds passed.

"What's the one last thing?" Thomas asked.

She looked at him, in full kit, rifle slung, full pack on his back, and the awareness that this wasn't a training exercise written on his face. "Be careful, Thomas," she said. On an impulse, she kissed his cheek, the merest touch before she turned and went back to her office.

*****

Peter and Windy stepped down onto the dockside straight away. Peter wanted to get off the ship quickly. He promptly found it difficult to walk on ground that didn't keep moving around.

"OK, we're off. I guess you've stuff you're trying to keep hidden." Windy kept between Peter and the ship, just to make it a bit harder for them to see him.

"No. Stuff to shift. Stalls. Come on." They walked briskly over to the stalls that were set up in a corner of the dock and were puzzled by the way the stall owners saw the uniforms and started covering up their wares. One wasn't quick enough, and Peter put a hand out to stop him covering it up. The owner's shoulders slumped, and he stood back.

Peter looked at the wares: metal pots and vases with intricate designs on. "These are really good. Pity we can't take much volume. Ask him how much for this cup, Windy."

"How? I don't speak Persian."

"Doesn't normally stop you. How are you going to collect a harem if you can't talk the language? OK, I'll give it a go. Mate, how much for this?" Peter pointed at the cup.

The stall owner shrugged.

"Fine. How mucho? Pounds? Readies?"

The stall-owner picked the cup up and held it out, reluctance in his face.

"He's giving it to you," Windy said, helpfully.

"Oh, I get it. It's the uniforms. He thinks we're taking it. Well, I'm not a thief."

"Peter, you are."

"I'm not. I don't steal from the working man. From the rich, or capitalists, sure, but they stole it with the sweat of our brow in the first place."

"There's not really a lot of point stealing from the poor. You're a right Robbing Hood you are."

"First Communist, he was. Robbed from the rich, redistributed wealth to the needy masses. Comrade Hood, until they ruined it by making him the Earl of Locksley and betrayed the revolution."

"Peter, you're digressing."

"How mucho? Pay?" Peter glanced around and took out a metal instrument from one of his pockets. "Micrometer screw-gauge for cup?" He then spent a couple of minutes demonstrating how the gauge worked, and the owner nodded suspiciously, warily. The exchange was made, and Peter and Windy returned to where the platoon was forming up.

"Bastards," Peter said.

"What?"

"Come on, it's obvious. Stall owners are used to soldiers just taking stuff. Bloody Persian soldiers. Thieves, every one of them."

Windy shook his head. *Peter* was complaining about soldiers who stole.

*****

The new recruits gathered around the Chaplain for a last-minute blessing. They were excited and keen. They were part of the platoon chosen to be the first to go into danger.

*****

The platoon formed up on the docks. Their packs were full and heavy, caps mostly on straight, rifles on their shoulders, helmets slung on their back packs. They were aware that this wasn't a training march, that they were heading into the unknown.

"Make sure you leave some girls unopened for us," called a rifleman from the ship. Chaff flowed between those going, and those staying.

"There's nice heavy lifting for you."

"Hear they've got a shortage of coffins where you're going."

A word from Sergeant Taylor and the platoon came to attention. Then a left turn and they marched off. They were only marching as far as the railway station and the real work wouldn't start until they got to their destination. Inevitably, they started to sing.

"They'll bury my body in an unmarked grave, who cares anyway?"

*****

"Well, Colonel, the die is cast. How many will there be left of them when we catch up?"

"That depends on whether or not they run into trouble, Tristram. Still, this is precisely what the platoon was set up for. Scouting out ahead to find out what the situation is. They go in blind so that we don't have to. This should be straightforward. We've been told there are no problems. It'll be good experience for them."

"And if there are problems?" Major Marshall asked.

"Then the Regiment will not walk blind into those problems."

The story continues in Book 3 of the Building Jerusalem series, Burning Gold. In this book, Thomas and his friends have to deal with the situations they find in Esfahan, Persia.

Coming soon in paperback, and currently available as an e-book.

Printed in Great Britain
by Amazon